New Literature and Philosophy of the Middle East

The Chaotic Imagination

Literatures and Cultures of the Islamic World

Edited by Hamid Dabashi

Hamid Dabashi is Hagop Kevorkian Professor of Iranian Studies and Comparative Literature at Columbia University. Hamid chaired the Department of Middle East and Asian Languages and Cultures from 2000 to 2005 and was a founding member of the Institute for Comparative Literature and Society. His most recent books include *Islamic Liberation Theology: Resisting the Empire; Makhmalbaf at Large: The Making of a Rebel Filmmaker; Iran: A People Interrupted;* and an edited volume, *Dreams of a Nation: On Palestinian Cinema.*

Released:

New Literature and Philosophy of the Middle East by Jason Bahbak Mohaghegh

Forthcoming:

Islam in the Eastern African Novel by Emad Mirmotahari
Urban Space in Contemporary Egyptian Literature by Mara Naaman

New Literature and Philosophy of the Middle East

The Chaotic Imagination

Jason Bahbak Mohaghegh

palgrave
macmillan

NEW LITERATURE AND PHILOSOPHY OF THE MIDDLE EAST
Copyright © Jason Bahbak Mohaghegh, 2010.

First published in 2010 by PALGRAVE MACMILLAN® in the United
States—a division of St. Martin's Press LLC, 175 Fifth Avenue, New York, NY
10010.

Where this book is distributed in the UK, Europe and the rest of the world, this
is by Palgrave Macmillan, a division of Macmillan Publishers Limited, registered
in England, company number 785998, of Houndmills, Basingstoke, Hampshire
RG21 6XS.

Palgrave Macmillan is the global academic imprint of the above companies and
has companies and representatives throughout the world.

Palgrave® and Macmillan® are registered trademarks in the United States, the
United Kingdom, Europe and other countries.

ISBN: 978-0-230-10812-7

Library of Congress Cataloging-in-Publication Data

Mohaghegh, Jason Bahbak, 1979–
    New literature and philosophy of the Middle East: the chaotic imagination /
Jason Bahbak Mohaghegh.
        p. cm.—(Literatures and cultures of the Islamic world)
        ISBN 978-0-230-10812-7 (hardback)
            1. Middle Eastern literature—History and criticism—Theory, etc. 2.
        Middle Eastern literature—20th century—History and criticism. 3.
        Philosophy, Modern. 4. Criticism—Middle East. I. Title.

        PJ307.M64 2010
        809'.8956—dc22   2010014343

A catalogue record of the book is available from the British Library.

Design by Scribe Inc.

First edition: November 2010

10 9 8 7 6 5 4 3 2 1

Printed in the United States of America.

For those who have threatened this before and those who will inflict this beyond . . .

Contents

Note from the Editor

The Islamic world is home to a vast body of literary production in multiple languages over the last 1,400 years. To be sure, long before the advent of Islam, multiple sites of significant literary and cultural productions existed from India to Iran to the Fertile Crescent to North Africa. After the advent of Islam in mid-seventh century CE, Arabic, Persian, Urdu, and Turkish in particular have produced some of the most glorious manifestations of world literature. From prose to poetry, modern to medieval, elitist to popular, oral to literary, these literatures are in much need of a wide range of renewed scholarly investigation and lucid presentation.

The purpose of this series is to take advantage of the most recent advances in literary studies, textual hermeneutics, critical theory, feminism, postcoloniality, and comparative literature to bring the spectrum of literatures and cultures of the Islamic world to a wider reception and appreciation. Usually the study of these literatures and cultures is divided between classical and modern periods. A central objective of this series is to cross over this artificial and inapplicable bifurcation and abandon the anxiety of periodization altogether. Much of what we understand today from this rich body of literary and cultural production is still under the influence of old-fashioned Orientalism or post-World War II area studies perspectives. Our hope is to bring together a body of scholarship that connects the vast arena of literary and cultural production in the Islamic world without the prejudices and drawback of outmoded perspectives. Toward this goal, we are committed to pathbreaking strategies of reading that collectively renew our awareness of the literary cosmopolitanism and cultural criticism in which these works of creative imagination were conceived in the first place.

Hamid Dabashi

Preface
(Of the Zero-World)

A chaotic text is an ever-present course of infliction. It is no longer possible to write (about) literature within any boundaries, whether national, disciplinary, or identitarian. If anything, evaluating literature within such constraints is the, by now, proverbial *death* of literature. The intent of this book, then, is that of tracing an emergent pathway of thought and expression making its way confidently from a once-colonized front (this is where the other postmodernism lives, the one that no one speaks of). We have heard what third-world authors have to say and have realized the extent of their capabilities, but this is the record of something else—the next menacing category: perhaps that of another zero-world. To this end, the work of figures born across such channels must be upheld as monstrously original, setting the stage for an innovative and incommensurate philosophical outlook. They are not derivative or imitative but fiercely positioned outside the constrictive boundaries of past modalities; that is, they speak of the unknown and the unforeseen, they write the unnamable, and they ultimately execute a vast becoming, always of devastating scale and proportion.

For this reason, the objective in placing these authors into immediate exchange with "Western" thought is not to incarcerate them within the confines of some centralized canon, but rather to allow for a toxic, abrasive confrontation that reveals the outstanding distance from such reigning conventions of knowing. If one is to actually read the text closely, then, and not reel at the surface-confluence of authors, one would note that almost every critical encounter between these two sides is a deeply antagonistic one in this analysis. For almost every continental circle resurrected, the "zero" authors are then set loose to unhinge and efface such world views, to leave each irrelevant in the final stride: every last one of them falls here, from the enlightenment to poststructuralism, from nihilism to existentialism, from phenomenology to ontology, from psychoanalysis to deconstruction; none of these prisons survive the diabolical movement of this ascendant pack and their counterparts. Every once-dominant thread is eluded, outdone, and surpassed, fully obsolesced in the wake of a rising, merciless literary province that preys upon the particular vulnerabilities of these former totalities. This is no prophetic glance; this is a violence happening. And so, if you were to tread beneath and inhabit the more sinister tensions of this text, you would perhaps discover that this whole enterprise is conjured as a form of epistemic warfare.

This notwithstanding, one realizes that such an initiative could work equally well, and perhaps even far more smoothly, if divorced entirely from Western zones. I have, at times, contemplated this conflictive-comparative methodology with the conclusion that the representation of the zero-world (and by extension my own engagement) as an independent sector of literary consciousness could easily extricate itself from any reference to the abandoned realms of Western thought. In order to sustain my interpretation of such pieces as embodying a true outsider perspective, one could return and excise every last echo of critical theory from the interior of the manuscript. With this tactic in mind, having already surveyed the entirety of the text, weighing the extent to which this removal is viable, one would find it in no way destabilizing to the overarching content of the work. Such excisions would only intensify concentration on the emergent categories at stake. Once again, the genesis of this project lay in an urgent desire to demonstrate the scathing farness of these apparitional voices, their singularity and stealth, their untamed techniques, to the extent of devising a decisively novel hermeneutic cosmology: that of a chaotic imagination. Hence, the primary thrust remains undeterred, the major components left intact and even enhanced, when coalesced without any relative correspondence to the history of Western thought. What would remain is an extremely intimate engagement with the thematic registers of the zero-world and its rare textual atmosphere, unfolding one domain after another within an expansive, volatile discourse of its own. This would no doubt require a remapping of the terrain of the project, but one undertaken without any loss of immediacy. And still, the intrusions remain, the faded Western walls restored here for a time, for, as was said, this is meant as an act of provocation; there is a fight that must still occur here. It follows, then, to stick to the originary purpose of a combative interface, as it keeps the project on its hidden guard.

The selection of the title was a convoluted process, one to which a great deal of attention was devoted, for a question arises: why are there no names? To this degree, the decision was calculated, not a random exclusion of the emergent authors who populate the oncoming chapters, no downplay of their influence. Instead, there is a perfectly strategic reason for not including these names, though referring explicitly to their inscriptions: that grand portions of the project are dedicated to depicting such texts as nameless artifacts, unsigned documents that illustrate a deliberate annihilation of the writing subject. In this anonymous territory of literary imagination—where identity disintegrates and all authors become shadowlike, where all voices become masks of an impersonal nightwalker consciousness—to cite such names at the outset would be to enter into a profound theoretical inconsistency with the internal argument. In essence, their enigmatic tonality, its madness and its fever, its hallucination and its amnesia, descends from the fact that they do not write as writers: they forget this designation with relentless precision (this is their own admission), erasing all self-awareness as a unitary, enclosed being, and instead becoming a faceless engraver, for this exhaustion is the very master code of their originality, the threshold of a previously untouched sphere. This conviction is forwarded continually, and so one would rather not sabotage such gestures with a naming act on the cover that then compromises the enlivening possibility of tracking nameless authors for miles within the book. With this established, I thought it most accurate to stay near to the ropes of their explicit conceptual elements—from burial to blindness, from annihilation to contagion, from the shadow to the inhuman, from desertion to deception—each its own particle of the emergent, chaotic experience.

With respect to the secondary literature, I have spent years pouring over these scholarly reflections and find every last one of them fundamentally problematic, most often insidiously or flagrantly Orientalist in nature. From the characterization of the zero-world author as a second-rate, second coming of Western modernism, from lavish psychoanalytic renderings to a host of gothic, surrealist, and absurdist associations, almost all of these strive to encapsulate this figure in some monumental archetype of nineteenth- and twentieth-century Western aesthetics. This contextualization, in my view, marks an artificial lineage without any lasting intellectual credibility, a reductionism that entraps the emergent in a constellation of supposed influences and therefore steals its potential to render a radical point of departure, a minor prism through which a previously imperceptible current might then insinuate itself. Stated concretely, none have afforded these ipso facto postcolonial authors the benefit of their ingenuity and versatility; none have dared to summon a hermeneutic framework tied to the specificity of their own distinctive maneuvers through language and consciousness. Instead, they superimpose a sequence of withered paradigms that would anaesthetize this obscurity and confusion that would conceal these criminal trespasses onto an elsewhere that literature has not yet openly acknowledged. Almost none has even attempted an intricate theoretical or philosophical unfolding, none has tried to read such borderline illegible narratives, none has even remotely suggested that such emergent textualities stand apart as a new beginning—an ominous, unexplored horizon of thought—thereby leaving a massive gap that this work launches a concerted effort to traverse.

For this reason, I believe that our responsibility to the emergent swarm is to unfreeze them from the sedentary, contrived historicity imposed by older trains of scholarship and to render in its place a challenging exposition of their accomplishment. These figures all claim to live apart from the rest, in houses of ruin that mirror their own estrangement from the rigidified cities and their decadent trances. I would like to honor that claim, then, by wrenching them away from the grasp of certain uninspired academic exercises that would betray such sovereign works as locatable mimicries. Once more, if you detect on my own side a similar willingness to throw such figures into the arena of Western commentaries, then remember that the imperative is not one of coercive unification but rather one of sending their work into jagged contrast and contestation with everything that has dared to exist before them. It is neither a futural vision that this manuscript offers nor a nostalgic retreat backward; instead, it serves an immediate transmission, at once a banned import and a tearing away from the arrested memory of the secondary scholarship and its oath to a languishing "West."

In the end, allowing this book a worldly breathing space has already won us an opening to inject something incendiary into the air—not to respect the paralyzing standard but to posit the unsafe thought. My allegiance, to be sure, is with the badlands of the "post"colonial site and its rogue arsenal, its displacement and delirious incantations, which is why we need to take chances here and offer new games to the forefront of our condition—one that allows us a fugitive, errant trajectory from tired social, political, and even cultural genealogies. Critique must be counterbalanced by reinvention, and so these voices signal the often-punishing avenues of a breakaway consciousness, each a formula of ecstatic desertion. We are compelled to trust in this foresight, to fulfill the instinct to risk with a work that experiments at the treacherous edges, and that might serve as a contagious reawakening of a gradually narcotized intellectual scene. There are countless individuals who seem to thirst for our provinces to open the floodgates to their emergent properties, the implicit secrecies of the outside. The desire is there, waiting for us to take a forceful stand and captivate, to smuggle these once subterranean, outcast visions into the heart of things and let them transform whatever lies around. My incisive influences have been architects of new corridors and chambers. I ask for nothing more than the right to do the same.

Despite the silence that has endured for years, there is now the strong belief that such words demand exposure, not simply because of the saturation of bloodless commentaries that have dominated the intellectual landscape for far too long, at once repetitive and suffocating, but because these pages carry an illumination toward which others will gravitate, though perhaps not knowing why. The anticipation of this potential event is answered by the arrival of a chaotic hour.

CHAPTER 1

Images of Chaos
An Introduction

It is my wish, when I have poured the . . . bitter wine of my life down the parched throat of my shadow, to say to him, "This is my life."
—Sadeq Hedayat, *The Blind Owl*

> A light in my hand
> a light across from me
> I go to the war of blackness.
> —Ahmad Shamlu, "In the Garden of the Mirror"

To decipher the chaotic imagination as the forerunner of an emergent literature is to enter into the most rare and secluded of expressive chambers, to draw consciousness itself downward and across the ropes of its own reinvention. It is to take the mind where it does not belong, where it has no rights, to the degree that thought and being are forced to take on a new relationality, a new stance upon the world, and, with it, an intention that never could have been anticipated. This project, then, marks the decisive hour when such artifacts of chaotic textuality find themselves exposed and released, raised from their underpasses and scattered across the terrain of literary experience, ready to carry out what must happen here.

Above all else, chaotic textuality must affirm conflict as an indispensable component of its endeavor; it must not only accept and brave the emergence of conflict but also actively pursue a new definition of creative violence. Indeed, it must even go so far as to strive toward the actualization of a will to *cruelty*; it must violate and overturn, tear and disfigure the cosmos of the text without judgment, without mercy, vowed only to the unrelenting and all-consuming practice of the brutal. In this way, one relinquishes the text and the world it embodies to a vast succession of agonies, turning the game of literary perception dark and catastrophic.

The question then poses itself, how exactly does chaotic textuality operate this will to cruelty—what are the tactics and strategies behind this process of hermeneutic carving? To answer, one might begin by introducing the concept of *fatality* to this discussion: in effect, what does it mean to engage with texts as if they were fatally oriented? First and foremost, such a suggestion would call for us to drastically readjust the very configuration of literary experience, its profile, and its drive, for here we would have to develop the taste for a certain annihilative immediacy. To envision and ultimately perform a fatal experience of the text, we would have to begin to play for lethal stakes, to recognize that the text is always already condemned, and ourselves alongside it—that it has no right to remain as it is, no right to permanence. We cannot allow the literary evocation to swear an allegiance with the totalitarian mythologies of being; rather, those who would initiate the chaotic event must become carriers of an infinite risk. They must throw the scales of textual unity into imbalance, into the endangerment of the uneven, an irrevocable wager whereby every utterance possesses within itself the possibility of its own undoing. As such, to summon the notion of fatality to the forefront of our literary imagination is to convert literature itself into a space of almost unbearable vulnerability—a valley of perpetual sabotage for which each idea, each inflection, and each interpretation draws the text imminently closer to the hour of a collapse. Here the text remains open and exposed at every turn, ominously porous and unguarded against scathing or transformative gestures, undertaking detriment and affliction of the harshest levels, even to the zero degree of its own desolation. In this way, chaos reminds us that literature remains a mortal transaction and that we should not deprive ourselves of the pleasure of watching texts die.

Advancing further, to orchestrate this injection of a fatal current into the chaotic imagination is to view the textual realm as a type of *threat*—the unremitting pronunciation of what warns away and what staggers the ground beneath. It threatens proximity with oblivion, contact with nothingness, by drawing the text ever nearer to a swift contortion of its meaning, its objective, and its place within the world. It is a destabilizing agent, one that throws the text into perplexity with itself and obscures its timeliness by forcing it to exist in an alternate temporality, always at the wrong time. Thus the chaotic engraves a new alertness into the air: that nothing is safe here—nothing immune—that no text is innocent, that all can be altered, or burned, and therefore, that nothing will remain untouched. It is this very inscription of fatality, this scarring reminder that the text proves endlessly susceptible—endlessly lain bare before the vision of its own end, damned almost—that sustains the limitlessness of our task. It reawakens us to the fact that thought itself is terminal and must remain so. Ideas are not meant to be haunted entities—they are meant to be hunted, leading us to always ask, in each new work we commandeer, what must fall here? For this reason, we must rid literature of its survival instinct.

To illustrate this point, the chaotic imagination must continually align itself with the tripartite conceptual matrix of fatality itself; that is, that it must maneuver toward conditions of *extremity, excess,* and *exhaustion.* Taking the first particle, then—that of "extremity"—the textual event must comprehend, as its imperative, the need to wrest consciousness toward an extreme manifestation of itself, toward the outer thresholds where its capacity for devastation looms and hovers, toward its multiple breaking points, where the victories and losses of the writing-act are at their most severe—a last boundary that marks not a limit but an edge. And so this movement toward extremity casts us into the next premise of fatality—that of "excess"—for it is here that the text begins to proliferate and entangle itself in overbearing and intricate new circuitries; it is here that the text becomes an effusion (and an unforming). Consequently, the interpretive moment must itself become a guarantor of this overkill, extracting and enhancing those elements of the text that convey the most jagged impact, lengthening its impulses to an untenable degree: the apotheosis of its hyper-presence. Where it locates speed in the text, it must accelerate it toward break-neck velocity; where it finds force, it must concentrate and harden such tones until they grow metallic and overwrought; where it uncovers desire, it must make language insatiate, the avatar of ecstasy; where it encounters rage, it must quicken the vitriol beyond reason, beyond the point of no return; and where it unearths complexity, it must escalate and interlace the pathways of the literary experience toward the rise of new labyrinthine constructions. Such is the abrasive potential of the chaotic: to restore the text to its fatal inclinations, to lure it into entropic quarters and turn it accursed, such that each gesture of expression, whether irradiated or obscure, culminates in a perishing—in an extinguishing—of the very possibility of the poetic expenditure: an ultimate exhaustion.

And still, what is left in the wake of this initiative to vanishing? What trails forward in the aftermath, if anything? Is there a trace beyond the smoke, beyond the ashes? Or is this damage a sign of the endgame of our trade—its pure finality? No, these are not nihilistic overtures, but they actually contain a veiled secrecy of affirmation.

Let us divert our attention back to the precise methods by which the chaotic imagination inhabits this new archetype of cruelty, beginning perhaps with the notion that such techniques of interpretation instantiate an unprecedented mode of *alchemy.* To speak of the chaotic text as alchemy, then, is to establish a regime of impurity, to irreparably alter the formula of existence, and to corrupt the order of things and become reborn in a polluted sensibility. Here language becomes an alloy (of the incommensurate): against the absolutism of essence, against the stranglehold of history. This alchemy negotiates itself as an amoral and treacherous venture—it eludes captivity not through desecration of the past, for the past was never sacred, but through colder schemes of erasure and eclipse, of blurring and contrivance. Thus our discourse here is not one of transgression or of the profane but rather one of sheer convolution. The only command, the only law before us, is that of recurring distortion. The chaotic text must fashion a generative prism, one of diluted substances and imperfections; it must tempt unnatural admixtures, fusing elements into contaminated alliance. We do not compare texts in order to synthesize them in some abstract, lifeless equilibrium—to sanitize or cleanse the surface; instead, we unload them toward corrosive depths, spheres of dissonance where they run their acids across one another, following asynchronous and lacerating lines, and forging unforeseen collusions. In this way, interpretation, like alchemy, must be traitorous. It must be conceived as an act of treason against the world, for to draw texts into a comparative encounter is nothing less than to set the stage for their radical betrayal. And we must betray literature; we must seek the triggers and the catalysts through which a text becomes a subterfuge—becomes the faintness of an amorphous zone—where articulations devour themselves, shatter, and regenerate in new, unacceptable maskings. To this end, the chaotic imagination must accentuate the pain of transfiguration—it must learn to play both in subtle malformations and in monstrous turnings, if only to reconvene us in a foreign atmosphere, a chamber where deception overrides truth, illusion supersedes authenticity, and where the dominion of reality has long since been overthrown. Stated otherwise, we must train ourselves to lie.

At this stage, we arrive at the nexus of another domain intrinsic to the chaotic imagination—one that steels itself for the chase: that of *piracy*. To apprehend the literary and philosophical task as an occasion of piracy is to consign it to a nomadic experience, a course of deviation and trespass for which all texts are wrenched from their point of origin, evicted, and turned toward the outside. This approach signals what is already dispossessed of itself, what is already foregone and abandoned, leaving the text wakeful of its own impending desertion: that it cannot stay where it is, that it is already invaded and unsettled, that it dwells nowhere and therefore must constantly tread elsewhere, beyond itself. As a cutthroat textuality—entirely deterritorialized, wrested from all delusions of context, from the confines of its presumed foundation—this pirated document now adheres only to a fugitive trajectory, a rationale of distance and almost imperceptible departure, of covert night-drifting. In this sense, the chaotic casts literature into indeterminate terrain—it executes the disconnect, the disembodiment, whereby all sensations of belonging are excised and for which a reflexive defiance of the borderlines alone remains. Against the frozen, static entrapment of identity and against the entrenchment of pseudodiscourses of locality, this piracy strikes at the walls of such enclosed concepts, traversing their systems of incarceration and thereafter leaving the text stranded, amid disturbed waters, in the existential no-man's-land. Beyond the one-dimensionality of the social, the hegemony of the political, and the codifications of the cultural, literature becomes a rogue world once more, for writing must always be in exile, irreversibly banished.

To this extent, chaotic interpretation itself fulfills the method of piracy, for it traffics the unspoken, it steals and scavenges, displaces and resituates the texts with which it plays. It is not a far transition from theory to theft or from the profession of the reader to the profession of the smuggler. Indeed, we must rob the text blind, for our counter-future lies in its destitution (the will to plunder). Literature must be restored to the hands of criminality.

Of the greatest consequence, yet another overarching function of the chaotic imagination is to make the text *inconsumable*, and we therein, as readers, must become architects of this inconsumability (the coarse and the disgraced). Without doubt, a mind-set like this must exalt the toxic—it must disclose the virulent strand that lies concealed in the recesses of the text, awaiting its chance to inflict, to spread its pestilence across the narrative. In this respect, the chaotic facilitates the oncoming of new plagues, unannounced convulsions, and nauseas; it is the source of vertigo, of disorientation and seizure, and of the aesthetic and existential fever that remains literature's singular power. Here language begins to choke—it motions toward incommunicability and silence, it becomes an outcast item, an unknown variable, irreducible and permanently alien, the emblem of an insidious dread (this cannot be taken in, beyond internalization). Still, when we speak of the trouble that chaos incites, the diametrical mischief it elicits, we must evade any pitfall of a metaphysical definition and instead perceive it viscerally. This marks the gateway to an unanticipated, though now extant, performativity of the literary and critical imagination; it allows us to extract the serrated facets of our interpretation and extend them immanently across the body of the text, poured like the waves of a cipher, a passcode or countercode that intercepts and then disrupts the transmission of the original meaning—an encryption impossible to unravel. The outlook suggested here, then—one of subordinating literary consciousness to the production of an inconsumable text—in some aspects mirrors the affect of a contagion, one whose inexorable spreading, whose seduction and havoc, elicits a textual frenzy, a paroxysm of heightened calibers—half riot, half trance but always inconsumable.

In the final scope, the coalescence of these disparate strands of thought—ranging from cruelty to fatality, from alchemy to piracy, and now even to the inner circles of the inconsumable—assumes its epilogue in the solidification of the textual encounter as a chaotic enterprise. The chaos that we undertake, therefore, is its own end—it exists for its own sake, as a tunnel into all-encompassing disarray, to an age of unrest and irresolution. Chaotic textuality must be designated neither as struggle nor as resistance, both of which parasitically fasten themselves to a dialectics of trauma and domination, but rather as a procession of indiscriminate battles, a war imaginary that throws dice at the subversive apex of literature's potential, to invoke and enforce a will to chaos. At once vivid and calamitous, the aim of the textual event must be to refine and sharpen the precision of an expressive mutiny, to make thought enigmatic and insurgent once again. And therein we must realize that we, too, have since become unsworn to guarding the world as it is—that we are engaged in a mercenary affair and must therefore leave literature at the doorstep of its own delirium.

Chaos-Becoming: The Existential Command

To write toward chaos, to think toward chaos, to will chaos as an irrevocable becoming: such is the imperative lain before this work, the farthest possibility to which this inquest will devote itself. The intent, therefore, is that of tracing the intricate ramifications of the idea of chaos for the experience of writing and thought, tracing its often-elusive movement through the trajectory of emergent literature and philosophy. Ultimately, these strands of conjecture will coincide toward a radical conclusion, an edge at which consciousness falls into alliance with its own anarchic potential, now structurally unsound, and where the writing-act itself becomes a vital exercise in the disquieting of worlds.

To achieve such a task, this work will first define the chaotic through a close comparative engagement with outsider commentaries on the subject, with the strongest focus given to such authors as Sadeq Hedayat (1903–51), Nima Yushij (1896–1960), Ahmad Shamlu (1925–2000), and Adonis (1930–), treading through and distilling the convoluted insights of such fronts so as to provide a necessary opening into further territories of perception. Herein a chain of paradoxes immediately arises: is existence itself intrinsically chaotic, or is it willed as a new becoming? Is chaos an affirmative or nihilistic experience of the world? Is chaos primarily creative or destructive? Is the expressive act, whether aesthetic or philosophical, somehow more intimately connected with a chaotic state? Is chaos a universalizing presence or is it a purely subjective phenomenon, or somehow beyond both definitions? Is it an illusion, or does it occur within the confines of the real? In light of such interplay, this work will advance a series of potential standpoints—positions that wade through this unlit topic and then bear further elaborate implications for the questions of being, reality, time, language, and the self. In the end, the dominant aim of this work is to offer an original approach to an unfolding phenomenon in contemporary thought—one that draws the unrest of knowledge and expression toward an unforeseen height, toward the disclosure of a chaos-consciousness.

Throughout our sustained involvement with the subject, there will be a necessity to extend the focus toward a select array of figures inspired by this premise of an emergent literature, gravitating around the masterworks that set apart. Indeed, these pieces, in close exchange with an extended intellectual backdrop, will set the outer boundary against which we will measure the still-surfacing textualities of the chaotic imagination, ever maneuvering our gaze between burial and blindness. For this reason, the greatest insistence will continually be placed on the accomplishments ascertained in such removed circles of contemporary writing, wherein the strident inroads shaped by the likes of Hedayat, Nima, Shamlu, and Adonis have offered an unrivaled evocation of the chaotic imaginary. And even more than this, it is perhaps in their writings alone that we begin to see the vast prophecies of postcoloniality and postmodernity realized, bordering finally on the location of an autonomous, yet formidable, vantage of consciousness.

This emergent textuality, though housed among an exclusive cadre of zero-world authors, its horizon fastened to the exteriority of Western thought, can also be seen as the culmination of a more global, long-held drive of the literary imagination. Hence, certain manifestations of continental philosophy will be enlisted here as well, taking into consideration the vast scholarship aimed toward this experiential elsewhere, across temporal and historical barriers, which together forge a multifaceted understanding of the theoretical plane. No doubt, to declare the world's disjointment is an old game, leading numerous figures to perceive their intellectual and poetic exertions as in partial alignment with the creative possibilities of chaos, and thereby confronting some appendage of this concept, either implicitly or explicitly, in the course of the writing-act. From Nietzsche's meditations on the abyss to Kafka's ominous descent into "not-night," from Bataille's search for the limit of inner experience to Michaux's broken experiments with hallucination, each author would, in some respect, enjoin a chaotic rapture. Nor does the interlacing exhaust itself here, for this signal toward a disordered region has undoubtedly worn myriad masks over time, manifesting and fading within countless spheres of speculation, infused and reinfused within several discourses. From Adorno's call for an irreconcilability of the dialectic to Benjamin's temporal arabesque, from Rilke's attachment to the open to the heteroglossic flux of the Bakhtininian carnivalesque, from the schizoid desire-production of Deleuzian nomadology to Foucault's micropolitics of resistance, from Blanchot's essential solitude to Beckett's enunciation of the unnamable, from Baudrillard's seductions of the hyperreal to Artaud's hysterical demand for the end of judgment, many have been tempted to the boundaries of this thematic outland. As gestures for articulating a position that might avoid the clutches of signification and control, each would attempt to negotiate a unique perspective on such malformed experiences of the world—one that would not prove escapist but rather salient in its undertones. The emergent text, then, is the smooth inflection of that imaginary for which these thinkers could only stir vague allusions, barely able to call it by its right name, though still competing for its vindication. They could not have known, perhaps, that the dislocated locale toward which their thoughts coasted lay too far off the map of their respective worlds and that the key beyond lay hidden somewhere in the blood of the ones they called the others.

And surely there are further indications and images to consider, including Schlegel's conception of chaos as what "consists not just in a comprehensive system but also in a feeling for the chaos outside that system," though he then warns that it "must still at bottom be simply necessary and rational; otherwise the whim becomes willful, becomes intolerant, and self-restriction turns into self-destruction."[1] Intriguingly, the progression of this work will stand in full opposition to such a viewpoint, drawn rather to the directives of self-annihilation and arationality as indispensable functions of the chaotic. Nor was Camus able to fulfill this command, striving to integrate its force throughout his own renderings of absurdity, yet always kept away by virtue of his admission that "I can refute everything in this world surrounding me that offends or enraptures me, except this chaos, this sovereign chance and this divine equivalence which springs from anarchy."[2] Here, however, the chaotic will be driven from the oppressive defeatism and futility expressed above by reinforcing its dissection from subjectivity, instead presenting the self to a conductive unreality and thus reflecting it beyond itself as the active presence of an inhuman turn. In addition, Michel Serres's *Genesis* is, in itself, at least partially dedicated to some anticipation of what he classifies as chaos, though the author then proceeds to frame it as a quasi-mystical force of an immemorial nature: "We must go back to the chaos of the ancient, to the opening, yawning wide . . . Time is a chaos, at first, it is first a disorder and a noise . . . not merely the primitive state, it accompanies my every step."[3] Here, however, the chaotic marks no resurrection of a primitive world but rather an extravagant departure from the history of being, an expressive wire being shaped as we speak.

Despite the wide spectrum of interpretations that seem to stand as precursor engagements, this project's execution of the chaotic occupies itself with the outskirts of such entrenched canons of knowing, monitoring that one crucial element still left unexplored: how consciousness itself might transform into chaos. No longer some external search, no longer mystically construed as the fixed property of some abstraction called "the world," no longer a source of nihilistic despair or idealistic redemption, here it is demanded that the chaotic be wrested out of the intrinsic capacity of thought itself. The poetic-philosophical mind then works ceaselessly for the realization of its own endemic din, and therein setting this project apart as what searches to test the waters of an apparently unfathomed wager: a *writing-toward-chaos*.

Such marks the summit at which the text attains its implosion-explosion: now contorted and multiplied, such that no condensation of a message is allowed, no protocol for understanding left standing, no dynamics of meaning-formation solidified, no acculturation of the reader embarked upon, no modality of analysis or criterion for judgment preserved, and no codification or decodification successful. Here all techniques of truth telling must unspeakably fail, ever refusing the closure of a whole, each new stirring just the prelude to a further inexhaustible obscurity. In effect, the ambition is to endorse the textual event as a vouching with chaos, its own raw self-reflexivity affording no ammunition for insight into its interiority, forever refracting itself, defying unity through storm, of the nowhere-everywhere, attesting to the fact that there can be no becoming while being still survives. It mobilizes the abrasion and demanifestation of all continuums, veering even at its most concentrated moments, extending no exemption from the reign of distortion, reaching not toward negation yet toward the transparently nebulous, a vision of darkened vantages, a traitor to all that is real.

From different angles of an emergent literary movement, this project dedicates itself to reconsidering such distinctive waves in contemporary thought, revealing with specificity how such decided evocations of chaos reflect a pivotal transition in the trajectory of knowledge and expression. Moreover, this often-tenuous motion to the hinterlands of critical and poetic consciousness brings into immediate relevance a further set of conceptual registers, incorporating themes as far-reaching as annihilation, rage, ecstasy, madness, deception, apocalypse, desertion, contagion, eternity, and the shadow. Beyond the restraints of truth or reality, beyond being itself, the literary impulse now enters into a far more unruly hour than ever before—one of opulent and indeterminate speculations—and confronts itself thereafter with a new imperative to restlessness.

By forging such a versatile constellation, pursuing theoretical axes across particular emergent strongholds, this work attempts to offer a unique approach to the orientations of textual experience. Furthermore, in traversing the uneven regions of the chaotic imagination, it seeks to unearth a potential manifestation of the writing-act as inherently antagonistic, a gateway into bewildered staring—one that commissions language as an instrument of tremor and upheaval, the perpetrator of an existential defacement. For it is amid such a procedure, one that carries the text to the razor's edge of its own expectant turmoil, that a perhaps unstipulated pathway unveils itself.

Chaotic Fatality: Toward the Annihilated

The event of *annihilation*: such marks the nefarious price of a chaotic imaginary, for to examine this potential, one must exceed the borders of subjectivity itself, pursuing an interval of intensity that surpasses and ransacks the unified—an intricate process of actualization, imposition, and misfortune. To follow this course would necessarily be to exile the author to the outworlds of epistemic, ontological, and phenomenological definition beyond the deterrence of power, the dominant ideologies of history, and the conspiracies of identity. With the mandates of singularity disbanded and all structures of totality drawn toward abolition, a virulent brand of hermeneutics begins to surface, one that sustains textual experience as a prism of subversion, innovation, and becoming. Such marks the collision moment in which literature and philosophy attain their own chaotic extremity amid the evacuation of all that is.

A colossal facet of this inspection resides within the annihilative principle forwarded here as a hardened instinct for ruin, one culminating in the fusion of appearance and disappearance, tragedy and delirium, creation and destruction. For it is amid such an unsteady condition of the writing-act, where nothingness and excess tangle, where finality is brought into full proximity with consciousness, that the literary world overthrows itself. Indeed, the poetics of annihilation serves as a prelude to the poetics of chaos by depleting the constraints of being, an occasion of imminent sacrifice suspended somewhere between rage and sublimity. For it is in this manner that the disciplinary technologies of thought begin to erode, disallowing any epistemological certainty or submission to routinized instrumentality. The emergent text now bars itself from the symbolic orders of the mind—no descent into self-regulation, no self-automated models of signification, no faith in causation, and, more than anything, no search for rapid closure. For it is through the materialization of such an annihilative event—itself a ferocious convolution of mortality and power—that the textual encounter might evade its own entrapment, capsizing its self-imposed captivity so as to trespass through the entryway of a chaos-becoming.

Having arranged this backdrop, it will eventually become clearer as to how the literary-poetic mosaics of an emergent work assert themselves with maximum relevance in tracking the chaotic imaginary, since such writers insist time and again upon the thematics of self-extrication, a process undertaken with unbridled stylistic and conceptual precision. In this vein, they proceed toward the threshold of textual annihilation by commissioning the writing-act as an imperative to solitude, a radical drawing away toward the most volatile provinces of consciousness. Neither a delusion of transcendence nor a desire for diversion, this withdrawal instead marks the highest instant of the trial:

an existential compression that sharpens the hunger for the chaotic through self-containment and self-annihilation, proving that

> there is no agreement for me with the sky or earth
> Since for me there is no awakening
> I am not myself.[4]

For it is here, within the chasms of subjectivity's complete disassociation from the world, that desertion is first experienced and endured, the spirit of finitude brought clashing fiercely against a now undefended consciousness. Beyond all temporal and spatial parameters, having strained beyond the protectorates of man and history, it is here that the authorial "I" begins to feel the breath of the void, exposed to a self-enveloping inquisition, staring at the possibility of its own impermanence. This is how the writing-act unpacks itself without origin, with one declaring that

> Though banished,
> I love all those who banished me
> who crowned my brow with chains
> and waited to betray me,[5]

and then another referencing the same image of a barren expanse in the statement that "I was born without roots, upon salt-ridden earth, in a desert more removed than the dust-covered memories of the last row of palm trees, on the edge of the last dry river."[6] In similar stride, one commences *The Blind Owl* within a state of perishing and deterioration, surrounded only by four broken walls, positioned "beyond the edge of the city in a quiet region completely isolated and around which lie ruins,"[7] as an exaltation of abandonment turning toward annihilation, for emergent literature remains an insinuation that cannot be traced backward—one that owes nothing to what came before.

As already shown, it is at the compact nexus of this incursion that the authorial "I" must seal a covenant with its own end—that it must risk the paled grasp of nothingness if ever it is to eliminate its bonds. Here the once-insurmountable crease between subjectivity and existence, the structures of the inner and the outer, finds itself razed as once-subtle provocations of the trial now morph into incendiary cataclysms of awareness. The architect of this mal-attesting writing-act, a consciousness once held hostage, now forfeits the deprivation and enslavement of subjectivity and motions gradually toward an incurable, engulfing pattern. It is in this sense that one advances into the world-afflicting cruelty of the following verse, wrenching existence toward closeness, disentanglement, and excoriation: "Above the narrow passing, the pulverized, desolate, drunk wind reels downward. The entire earth is desolated by it."[8] Nor are the others here strangers to the mercurial chambers of annihilation, consecrating their own alliance with this prechaotic instant through an endless self-extinguishing, challenging being's pretense to immutability by splitting the order of things apart. The technique, however, differs slightly across practitioners: whereas one might elicit annihilation by carving inward and then assuming a combative stance vis-à-vis the self, another invokes a less overt departure—a subsidence won only after the overexpenditure of thought. In this latter streak of imagination, literary subjectivity is first ejected toward the heights of its power and seduction, a dynamic effusion of consciousness, ever quickening its velocity, only then to exhaust its force and vanish as if exorcised into breathlessness. To this degree, the former's rhetoric of adversariality and self-conquest is supplemented by the second's more cloaked manipulation of transience and disintegration, though both eventually converge toward the same destination of a squandered literary soul. Following this, a pivotal excerpt from the conclusion of *The Blind Owl* undrapes the elegant way in which the author takes his narrator toward the experiential ridge and then toward overflowing: "My whole body was filled with burning heat and I felt that I was suffocating. It seemed to me in my feverish condition that everything had expanded and had lost all distinctness of outline."[9] The ceiling of thought's detention raises here.

In that, annihilation epitomizes an instance of vicious travel, of variance and vanquishing, so must it wrench itself forward as an abrasion of the totality of consciousness. The velocity of this textual disaster is often driven onward by a thought-scarring affect, such that Hedayat's own first line in *The Blind Owl* states that "there are sores in life which slowly erode the mind in solitude like a canker,"[10] while Shamlu writes that "my honor lies in the eternity of my pain."[11] Beyond this, Shamlu composes an explicit testament to the inescapability of annihilation in another renowned work titled "Nocturnal":

> At night
> when anguish coalesces in the cold of the garden
> I listen for the death coughs of my decaying chained hands,
> their moan and their rattle.[12]

The significance of this acceptance of cruelty within the confines of the literary space is undeniable: that subjectivity is overcome through persistent injury, through a chronic wearing-down. And yet the will to annihilation sketched here does not in any way represent a death wish, for it is neither a diminishing nor a negation but rather raises the stakes of existential experience by transmitting the authorial self beyond its own limits and toward its chaotic possibility. In its worst throes, the annihilative event remains affirmative, as the arrival of an ascendant instinct, which is why the tone of such emergent writers appears ecstatic even from within the straits of decimation. Rather than arrest the narrative, it unlocks it to an impassioned rise and fall, a drowning in-between lyricism and dissolution—the simultaneous exertion of finality and the infinite.

The postulate of an advancing rank of creativity borne by annihilation, one of self-targeting war, carries with it a hostile assertion against subjectivity and world that enjoins the irrevocable blurring of possibility and impossibility. Nor is this axiom entirely foreign to the trajectories of modern philosophy but rather bears a corresponding resonance for certain radical modifications of consciousness. Hence, one might try to track the echoes of this existential thematics onto the continental front as well, drawing motifs of destruction together so as to establish the arena for a postontological exodus: from Kierkegaard's proclamation that "I die death itself"[13] to Bataille's claim that "he who does not 'die' from being merely a man will never be other than a man";[14] from the Nietzschean calling for an experience of the end wherein "from love of life, one should desire a different death: free, conscious, without accident, without ambush"[15] to Cioran's prospect of a futurity that would "let all form become formless, and chaos swallow the structure of the world in a gigantic maelstrom, that would let be tremendous commotion and noise, terror, and explosion, and then let be eternal silence and total forgetfulness";[16] and finally, to Deleuze and Guattari's meditation on a life overrun by "desiring machines for whom the self and the non-self, outside and inside, no longer have any meaning whatsoever."[17] Thus it would definitely seem as if this clandestine tendency has come to assume a prevalent philosophical status, such that one could even turn to Benjamin's own defense of the "destructive character" that "knows only one watchword: make room; only one activity: clearing way . . . For destroying rejuvenates in clearing away the traces of our own age; it cheers because everything cleared away means to the destroyer a complete reduction, indeed eradication, of his own condition."[18] And still, despite such persuasions, these statements remain a far cry from what is undertaken in this project, for such thinkers remain hostage to the restricted framework of death, unable to supplant this now scorched definition with the fiendish innovations of an annihilative technique. Moreover, it is the emergent literature and its league of zero-world authors who take up the burden of then negotiating the aftermath (the postapocalyptic gulf), for it is what arises from this inquisition—what survives the test of annihilation and what witnesses its own waste—that will then fulfill the near unbearable criterion of chaos: to supply an "I" without subjectivity, to exercise a literary body no longer starved for self-referentiality, to compose an affective universe without recourse to the myth of origin, and to express a singular voice without access to a name.

While continental treatments of destruction uphold death as a complete emancipation from the coercive grip of mortality, some pure transgression of the end's checkpoint, the chaotic imaginary enables annihilation to impart itself as a recurring landmine of consciousness. Thereafter, textuality itself becomes an unbound isle, as nothing lasts to rule its atmosphere save a reign of shadow figures. Strangely, Nietzsche's own prismatic world view implies this potential revaluation, one for which all articulations incite a tightrope walk across the abyss. Beyond even the aphoristic simplicity of the statement that "whoever must be a creator always annihilates," there ensues a further exploration of this precept in the agitated wanderings of his antiprophet, the one who is found pacing in search of a "free death."[19] This lethal spiraling is not an isolated venture but rather takes on an all-pervasive influence in every textual stage, from the assertion of "those who sacrifice themselves for the earth . . . so that the overman may live some day" to those whose demise is "a spur and a promise to the survivors"; these are pronouncements overrun with the concept of "going under" and guided by a demented laughter, itself the most rampant and unremitting emblem of annihilation, one that "was no human laughter; and now a thirst gnaws at me, a longing that never grows still . . . my longing for this laughter."[20] And then, slowly, as the second of annihilation escalates, the work growing at once more forbidding and yet self-assured, more intoxicated and yet closer to the edge of its own undoing, Nietzsche summons this laughter once again as the corridor to an eternal contestation. Thus "The Drunken Song" pounds itself out across the damaged world of the text, each free rhythm a proliferation of chaotic conversions, one that draws into effectuation the extinction of the author's own identity alongside that of the last man, a midnight slot straddling the threshold of an unknown daybreak, a surpassing borne by the incantation that "what has become perfect, all that is ripe wants to die," leaving a textual plane forever stranded in "the drunken happiness of dying at midnight."[21] Not just one slides under here, beneath and across the dregs of finitude, for must not others be brought down as well?

Such is the deep and unmistakable association between the writing-act and the conceptual terrain of fatality, the accession of a self-striking, leaving texts that are in fact somatic transcriptions of revulsion and misuse. And this, in turn, all rests on the near-catastrophic redefinition of literary consciousness via its newfound intimacy with perishing, bringing no disenchantment or loss but an ecstatic mode that frees language to the untold. It is when the writing-act becomes complicit in the betrayal of the author, carving against the presumed authority of its own storyteller by bringing consciousness closer to neglect and sleep, that this very annihilative task allows language to supersede its last remaining obstacle. Accordingly, a once-unrecognized omen becomes the now concentrated look of the emergent circle, the foresight of one becoming the incision of the other: to will chaos toward an inhuman juncture.

Chaotic Shadowing: The Poetics of Rage

To speak of *rage* is to speak of excess and then of the impending shadow (the blackout period). Amid the text's commingling with the annihilative moment, a common intuition seems to arise between the emergent authors as to the rightful status of rage as the next phase in the realization of a chaotic imaginary. To accomplish this, though, the author must now adhere to an unprecedented strategy, one that predicates itself upon the manipulation of consciousness toward fury, an experiment won through overacceleration (to make severe). In this way, the literary event compels itself to build continually, to strain itself through recurrence and magnification, leading language to the crossroads of its own angered dispersal. As a performativity of ignition and collapse, this new movement constitutes itself upon the need to take words into breakdown, such that all modes of expression thereafter become techniques of disclosure and inundation.

This orchestration of literary rage brings to light a strange immediacy with the violence of language itself, particularly by facilitating an irreparable confrontation with the regimes of its structure, transplanting expression with wrath. Here consciousness transitions to an immanent disposition, only then to fold from this imperious scale, embarking upon strategies that expand the annihilation of language and narrative to an unsafe register. This, in turn, marks the inclination of the emergent authors to revert to an all-encircling narrative, not simply allowing but in fact encouraging the text to take on a monolithic preeminence, to exert its dominant trance above all others, and ultimately to become existence itself. Thus one can observe the monstrous consciousness of Hedayat's narrator in *The Blind Owl*, a nonfigure that then comes to occupy an immoderate textual supremacy, perceiving everything as a mutated reflection of itself—every other, and with it, every object, event, or image, is synthesized back into the empire of the narrator's own account, leaving no space unscathed: "All of these grimacing faces existed inside me and formed part of me: horrible, criminal, ludicrous masks which changed at a single movement of my fingertip . . . I saw all of them within me. They were reflected in me as in a mirror; the forms of all of them existed inside me but none of them belonged to me."[22] The authorial voice therefore augments, in horizontal overlappings, a devouring consciousness that inevitably expels itself, a knotted logic of spreading and dissolution that no ordered narrative will be able to last.

As an unstoppable will to possession, an existential black hole, it is this very onset of rage that ensures the opening of textual experience to a strange vulnerability. One can conceive of this proposition as an increasingly troubled accumulation of the text, a temporary heightening of the stakes of the writing-act and enjoinment of its unquestioned rule, letting it loose to pervade all facets until overrun by its own immensity. Once again, extremity becomes fatality. And in doing so—in entitling the text to exploit its own environment, in unleashing it to take and to spill across all quadrants with an almost vampiric drive, to traverse each layer in craving—literary consciousness effectively inverts the insularity to which it had previously fastened itself. This marks a crucial maneuver of the rising chaotic imagination, for it is such a distended complexion, obsessively amplified to the extent that no occurrence can stand beyond the text's grasp that makes writing forfeit the interiority-exteriority divide upon which it was originally based. Although this trespass will later transform itself into a chaotic suffusion, for now, it is sufficient to witness how this proliferation of the literary mode has set the stage for a condition of serial infiltration. For sure, it is at this median stage of the text's scattered grasping that an anarchic infinity is increasingly won, without the barricade of metaphysics or the idealism of subjective experience, unbolting the word from its prior internment and casting it toward an irradiated multiplicity, such that perception itself becomes a source of inconstant shots. It is amid this tremendous incorporation of the world—confiscating everything it envisions—that the text gradually floods itself, handed over to a deluge of the most agitated proportions, shouldering existence, and therein overwhelmed beyond belief.

The invidious potentials of rage underlying such chaotic writing assume their most graphic impact here, amid a torrential enhancement and disintegration, a submergence in the armageddon of being. And it is specifically at this crossroads—having examined the deterioration of textual form through a quickening, having sketched its meridians of catastrophe—that one can begin to translate an unrivaled subversion of metaphysics. Building upon this point, there is no doubt that the paths demarcated toward this chaotic implementation, though striving to surmount metaphysics in one turbulent gesture, take consciousness right into the very heart of its syllogisms, driven by the contention that it must endure what it would strive to overcome and eventually obliterate. Literary consciousness, at this elevation of rage, is therefore unabashedly steeped in metaphysical impasses, drenched in hyperpresencing, the infinite absorption of the continuum of textual experience, often with the authorial "I" assuming itself the sole incarnation of this new cosmos. Nevertheless, this state of accumulation proves unsustainable in the final scope and is therefore evacuated soon enough, the expenditure of its conquest now drained of the ability to prolong itself, reaching the evaporation of its downpour.

Following this premise into the work of emergent authors, each page carries consciousness toward a grueling immanence, inducing a concurrent extension and degeneration, its tortured projection as "the one" and "the many," and therein recounting its experience as a fusion of both thirst and decay: "I had become like a madman and I derived an exquisite pleasure from the pain I felt . . . I had become a god. I was greater than God, and I felt within me the eternal, infinite flux . . . The sun was setting."[23] As is evident in this excerpt, literary consciousness here arrives at the distressed site of a metamorphosis— the authorial "I" now having granted itself the accursed right of totalization and yet thereafter compelled to answer for its own supremacy. In positing this unconventional stance—one that stalks the notion of being toward its own detrimental apex, one that tempts and then torments its reign—the work can subsequently tread into Hedayat's next realization: that the real is nothing but the author's own misshapen hallucination, unhinged by the confession that "it has all been myself, all along," and then afterward begging for an end to subjectivity and existence in his call to "surrender myself to the sleep of oblivion."[24] Such marks the irrefutable turn from rage toward formlessness.

And still, the ambiguity hovers, for what remains in the aftermath of rage and annihilation and what is inspired from the trenches of such formlessness? The resolution to this inquiry lies in the formulation of a *shadow-becoming*, for the chaotic imaginary can be charted through the sinuous hallways and interstices of the darkness that then gathers around the text. As language reclines into an indistinct procession of words, exposing the most immaterial vicinities of textual experience, the shadow-becoming ordains itself beyond the rift of being and nonbeing—an anonymous defender of both transience and the eternal, its own alien inexorability undermines the continuity of time, space, and man.

It is here that one encounters Hedayat's own manic insistence upon the shadow from the outset of his work, reiterating over and again the urgency with which he seeks to inhabit the sphere of this unknown image: "If I have now made up my mind to write it is only in order to reveal myself to my shadow."[25] Nor is it incidental that Nietzsche also makes use of the shadow as a guarantor of the overman, first noting, in *The Gay Science*, "how his shadow stands even now behind everyone"; then later carried through to the poetic refrain "now light, now shadows, all a game";[26] then to Zarathustra's injunction that "you shall go as a shadow of that which must come";[27] and then, lastly, writing in *Ecce Homo*, "I will complete it: for a shadow came to me—the most silent, the lightest of all things came to me! The beauty of the superman came to me as a shadow: what are the gods to me now!"[28] As this coalition of excerpts makes apparent, it is the circuitous operation of the shadow-becoming, taking place across an ever-changing, nonsequential narrative pathway, which binds together the currents of annihilation, rage, and chaos. For it is the shadow's impermanence alone that can elicit the transfiguration toward an emergent literature of the inhuman.

The exodus from rage to the domain of the shadow-becoming marks not the extinction of thought through negation but rather an effusion of thought through convolution (there is no deflection of fume) Here consciousness stands in the service of the unclear—it no longer upholds an equivalence of form or content but rather wavers at every point, questioning the textual case while then morphing into the impossibility and unreadability of its own answer. The authors of the emergent quarters call upon writing to occupy this cryptic inclination, that of the shadow-becoming, to ruthlessly acquire its touch, allowing it to sweep across the textual landscape and cloud over the lasting illuminations of meaning:

> A concealed shadow
> materializes from a path.
> This shadow, on its path
> extends no look to the other shadows upon the shore . . .
> There, amidst the most afar of far-off shadows,
> it selects its place
> and sits watching the path, in concealment.[29]

Thus the shadow coats itself across the literary world, exemplifying an undefeated symbol of what will not bow before the myth of being, an aerial paragon in the face of which all truth formations become obsolete and all attempts at explanation drastically fail.

In the final casting, it is through this shadow-becoming, through the endangerment borne by its silence, that the chaotic imagination initiates its greatest offensive. As an undying textual dusk takes over, each literary occasion finds itself already cloaked in its own debris, already shaded by its own ephemerality and surrendered to a tilted destiny. Hence, it is in no way irrelevant that Hedayat's own masterwork consummates itself at this extraordinary point, at the axis of being's eclipse, at the dead end of vision, with the shadow now dwelling at the forefront as the progenitor of all desire, sensation, and contemplation: "The only thing that makes me write is the need, the over-mastering need, at this moment more urgent than ever it was in the past, to create a channel between my thoughts and my unsubstantial self, my shadow."[30] And still, the shadow's terror is never that of paralysis but that of unbearable speed and transversal, of the disorientation and imbalance that allows the emergent consciousness to breathe. Such is the exposure described by the author toward the conclusion, one that leaves his silhouette susceptible to the slightest exhale and to the harshness of ever-widening distance: "The moment that I made a move, he slipped out through the doorway . . . I went back to my room and opened the window . . . He was running with all his might and in the end he disappeared into the mist."[31] This shadow-becoming, then, as a near-fanatic diffusion of secrecy, demands that each textual state encounter a downfall at its own hands (as a prerequisite of the next), always leaving behind a traceless string of casualties and transfigurations. Beyond the twilight of the idols, beneath the oncoming daybreak, each hour finds itself stranded in an evening of interminable incoherence and extinguishing—the spell of an everlasting, textual midnight. And what persists of consciousness in the wake of this covert affair is altogether another thing: the continued invocation of the "I," though now jarred of its former subservience, no longer chained to its past taxonomies but prey to overreacting reflections. Now left open to illegibility—stripped of the perilous force of centrality and the delusion of intention, relegated to a concrete rule of the instinct, bound by nothing, owing nothing, fearing nothing, beyond the need for being—the literary experience becomes one of pure blindness.

Chaotic Deception: The Ascendance of the Imaginary

The ascendant *imaginary* can be described as the entry point into that nonstate for which the knowing subject becomes a distant concern, possibility mutates toward the limitless, and chaos is experienced as a *deception* of the premier degree. Along these lines, this project will evaluate this unreality as a motioning to chaotic discord—one that summons phantasmic lawlessness against the restrictive epistemologies of truth, wrenching itself against all technologies of regulation and control. In this mask, the chaotic comes to articulate itself as an impulse of perpetual conjuration, unraveling orthodoxy into sacrilege, elevating convulsive discontinuity above systematicity and the insistent quest for order, cohesion, and mastery. It carries the will to "execute fantasia," where one remains loyal to an inexistent yet transpiring event, stretching across sectors, mechanisms, and morphologies that carve into the authoritarian injunctions of being-in-the-world, leaving its prescriptions dismantled from every side as one seeks a noble dishonesty.

Beyond the unconscious, beyond the dream, this imaginary precipitates a new hallucinatory aspect, a seditious vehicle through which consciousness itself becomes a self-enacted mirage. As the suffocated prism of reality passes into blurring, the imaginary materializes as an accessory of the purely untamed, setting its insurgency against unity and totality, superseding the constrictive impositions of power and truth and the hierarchies of knowledge they inevitably sustain, so as to submerge existence in a reckless derangement of its components. No amnesty or enlightenment, only rhapsodic uproar: a volition too fast for breath, one through which disintegration and madness relentlessly enmesh, through which a certain rebellion becomes instinctive and a certain refraction becomes inevitable. This is how the first pretense is embodied and breaks through, inviting the chaotic to flood itself across the spectrum of experience.

Thus to position oneself aside the fugitive potential of the chaotic imagination is to surrender the text to a certain sorcery, a rare instinct for the creative trick, and thereby charging this emergent literature to craft the underhanded schemes of a textual unreality. We are not above treating literature neither as espionage nor even as bribery. And so this is no longer the passive witness to an overconstructed world, no longer Beckett's penetrating minimalism of the absurd, nor Nietzsche's own Dionysian assault against the "surface-depth" binary, nor even Adorno's resounding notice that "fantasy alone . . . can establish that relation between objects which is the irrevocable source of all judgment: should fantasy be driven out, judgment too, the real act of knowledge, is exorcised."[32] Fantasy, absurdism, and even intoxication have become obsolete currencies here, for the chaotic must be perpetrated and delivered by fluent hands: this is not a province of distant speculation but one of acute deceit. Nor are we still talking of some secluded night reverie, an uncaptured sphere for which all ontological and phenomenological axioms invariably efface themselves beneath the shroud of a poetic dreamscape: "The night dream does not belong to us. It is not our possession. With regard to us, it is an abductor, the most disconcerting of abductors: it abducts our being from us. Nights, night have no history. They are not linked to one another . . . The night has no future . . . To go and be absent from the house of beings who are absent, such is precisely absolute flight, the resignation from all the forces of the being, the dispersion of all the beings of our being. Thus we sink into the absolute dream."[33] No, the emergent authors are convinced that the night belongs to them; that they are the abductors, turning the absolute dream into the chaotic imaginary; and that the rising tide of their vision will cast unspeakable impact upon existence. For it is precisely this dominion of a now manifest unreality—one for which the mania of untruth rebels endlessly against the grip of authenticity—that aspires to Baudrillard's own enigmatic assertion that "the perfect crime would be the elimination of the real world."[34] With that said, it is exclusively the task of the chaotic imagination to make this happen, since the emergent writers alone—as master thieves of consciousness—embody the perfect agents for just such a criminal enterprise.

Once more, such impressions converge at an unpopulated zone of conjecture, sealing a new conviction for this emergent literary enterprise: that visceral deception must constitute the challenge of the writing-act. From the belief in the text as a mimetic transposition of the ideal to the reflexive treatment of the word as a thing-in-itself, language has almost always oriented itself toward a supplication of the real, each statement consisting of a sanctuary from what consciousness must never concede, suppressing with every means at its disposal that one pronouncement that threatens to bring it crashing down: that all is subsumed in the reign of illusion. The chaotic imagination, however, orchestrates the converse: it works in smokescreens, disassembles the unity of the real, unfazed before the arrival of a writhing, hyperfictive age.

Unmistakably, the suggestion of the world as unreal has found its way into an array of critical inquiries, all of which condemn the self-prostituting discourse of the "true life" rather than inhabiting its diversion, only now and then experimenting with simulation (to show things as they are not) and dissimulation (to camouflage the way things are). This notwithstanding, the aspiration here will defect from such negational reactions, instead deciding to enter into a cunning trade, the lucid interchange of untruths, matching artifice for artifice. Beyond the reverse mourning of the real and the authority of authenticity that it implicitly resuscitates, and equally beyond the immobilizing search for the promise of a surrogate metareality, this project administrates its own format of the imaginary. This is how the enforcement of a chaos-becoming will relay itself elsewhere, beyond all standing designs, and therein yielding to immediacy with a new gamesmanship: that of complete existential distortion.

Thus textuality calls itself toward the approaching base of a staged imaginary—an invented nexus of language beyond the hindrances of essence, beyond the shredded lungs of actuality, beyond the unconfessed legends of being, now searing forward as an open volatility of the lived dreamscape. As the advent of a transparent, exhilarated nonstate, the unreal launches itself through a shape-shifting cauldron, one of surging evocations—a paroxysm of thought and image for which all textual perception descends toward the unknowable. This is what is called for in order to uphold the word itself as an unarrested illusion, to traverse the margins of subjectivity and objectivity and dispossess all utterances of their self-endowed hegemony, to supersede dialectics and metaphor and to therein submit representation to the most ultrapaced disruptions (as a tirade of the incomprehensible and the unsaid). A pure asymmetricality of literary consciousness follows now, one for which all expression is a mere concoction of paradoxes with no valid recourse, no return across the tightrope into the reasoned, and no way out from the play of fabrications.

It is here that the emergent authors carefully interject their apprehension of the last stage of the chaotic, reviving the now annihilated consciousness as an intermediary between the will to aesthetic creation and the inescapable unreality of the emergent world. Nor does annihilation evacuate the writing-act of a personal voice, for it is within this ragged aftermath that the "I" not only persists but also arcs itself outward with ferocious rapidity, assimilating all it contacts into a crucible of curved mirrorings. This self is no longer what it once was—no longer an edifice of stasis, no longer convinced of its own entitlement to a reality principle. Rather, what emerges now in the service of the chaotic is a phantom "I," a spectral outcast of consciousness, with scarecrow limbs, an irradiated storytelling of the inexistent one (itself a seamless apparition). Herein lies the importance of Hedayat's following commentary: "I even deny the existence of the humans on earth. Do the living really even have an existence? Are they more than the construct of the imagination? Or are they merely a handful of shadows, the result of dreadful nightmares, or the frightening dream of an opium addict? An illusion to begin with, on earth we were nothing more than a deceit; even now we are but a collection of absurd, superstitious ideas."[35] And Adonis, showing the same sensitivity to this transformative course, wages his own larceny against the real, forsaking it to an apocryphal counterprayer:

> I want to pray on my knees
> to owls with splintered wings,
> to embers,
> to the winds,
> to slaughterhouses and a thousand drunkards,
> to stars hidden at the sky's center,
> to death by pestilence.[36]

In this light, literary consciousness must now resuscitate itself as an insurrection against the caging of the real, defending itself against the latter's leaden compartments by generating new, subterranean deceptions of its own, allowing for a derelict perception to transpire, and therein fueling the possibility for a chaotic typology of thought.

There is no one formula for such an illusory revolution of consciousness, only a series of different tactics that convert the once-unitary subject into an oblique network. Such emergent textualities access the imaginary across profuse and disparate fronts, each possessed of their own unique maneuverings, two of which include the shadow (already discussed) and the mirror image, which, in turn, reveal separate methodologies of blurring and fragmentation. As a parallel, Deleuze and Guattari themselves approximate such an effort toward existential multiplicity in their own schizoid view of nomadological thought, stating at the outset that they write only in order "to make ourselves unrecognizable in turn. To render imperceptible, not ourselves, but what makes us act, feel, and think . . . To reach, not the point where one no longer says I, but the point where it is no longer of any importance whether one says I. We are no longer ourselves. Each will know his own. We have been aided, inspired, multiplied."[37] It is exactly such a procedure that Hedayat recalls from abstraction and sets into a palpable aesthetic-existential operation, and thus to read *The Blind Owl* is to observe the skeletal transfiguration of a conceivably human form into a shadow collectivity. And yet, amazingly, from the very first dealings of the narrative, this intention is disclosed, foretelling the inevitable hazing of self and world ("I must make myself known to him").[38] The entire design of consciousness, its penalties and reverberations, proceeds from this original sentiment such that, by the nonconclusion of the text, Hedayat has so interwoven his own literary consciousness with the fine unrealities of the shadow that the two become interchangeable emissaries of the chaotic. He writes further, "In this room which was steadily shrinking and growing dark like the grave, night had surrounded me with its fearful shadows . . . The shadow that I cast upon the wall was much denser and more distinct than my real body. My shadow had become more real than myself."[39] As this obsidian mass, itself a mystified reciprocity of lapse and resurgence, slowly hands the text over to an emergent terrain, so does the authorial perspective steadily reconstitute itself as an envoy of the chaotic unreal. As the peripheries of the authentic world gradually shred themselves, the shadow materializes as a guard of resistant impossibility, unwinding its caustic intimations against all machineries of the regimented mind, therein conveying textual experience toward a hallucinogenic nightfall.

In the eventual recognition of the necessity for a mode of literary consciousness that might effectively bridge the frontiers of the chaotic and the imaginary, the emergent author conscripts yet another entity, an equally ethereal, yet villainous, alternate: the shattered mirror image. Hence, alongside the unclear contours of the shadow, the emergent literature poses its exception to the real through spasmatic cycles of fragmentation, consistently summoning the imagery of fractured reflections to illustrate its bond with the phantasmatic. This is the poetic appetite of the one who "herald[s] a day that never came,"[40] for it is just such an untempered distribution of thought that provides the emergent figure the medium for an intersection between chaos and unreality (world omission). Having escalated consciousness toward an elaborate refraction, the poet then subsumes the entire world in quarreling, such that this episode in fact overturns psychoanalytic schemas of the double by altogether erasing the boundary between interiority and exteriority and consciousness and the unconscious (only mislaid surfaces). Yet another example of this textual cleaving-consolidation reveals itself in one of Shamlu's most serpentine pieces, entitled "The Banquet," wherein he writes,

> And, now, the absolute right of the world
> is nothing more than these two blood-leaking, downtrod-
>   den eyes . . .
> in this head
> looming behind the glass and the stone
> watching you.[41]

Always circumventing itself, evasive and amorphous, Shamlu's splintered mirror imaging selects as its method not the obscure blindings of the shadow but rather the ravenous hyperinsinuation of visions, such that even the reader—the one being watched and now coerced to recirculate his gaze—is made an accomplice to the ever-twisting web of the text. Here the once-airtight continuum of reality, its primordial claims and tyrannies of the One, is rationed to the several-all-at-once, leaving in its wake an irrecoverable breach, a recursive circularity through which the world itself is transferred to sporadic, snaking affects. In summation, it might be argued that such zero-world authors have innovated a new perspective on the (ir)responsibility of literature to the production of emergent illusion, one for which all paralyzing hermeneutic classifications immediately consign themselves to futility, for which the authority of discursive frameworks cave in, their absolutism overrun by the fragility of shadows and mirror shards.

In this way, the chaotic imaginary seethes beyond nihilism, beyond the last edge of disbelief, as the forerunner of a mounting age of entrancement. Nevertheless, even in its surpassing it excises for itself the strength of the abyss, steals from it the inveterate lesson of irreconcilability, ransoms techniques of erasure to carry toward the chaotic aftermath, such that the journey across empty space incites a revised denotation of the eternal. As occurred before, Hedayat surfaces here in the active orchestration of nihilism as a passage into chronic chaos, such that his own text is pervaded by an aimless deprivation, a nonsphere without genesis or end, where synthesis and comprehensibility become luxuries no longer afforded to consciousness. It is in this respect that the blind owl eloquently negotiates the textual chasm sought after here, across disparate, yet intertwined, fronts, always raving against the icons of redemption, always imposing mist before the sight of meaning, never mournful but rather condoning the vanished horizon. Thus the chaotic imaginary relegates literary experience to a purgatorial strandedness, with no promise of deliverance, no serenity of closure, denied all expectation, now wholly subdued by the asphyxiation of the all-perishing text. And it is the blind owl that makes this event profound, raising despair to the level of a law so as to purge it beyond exhaustion, each narrative pace drawn ever forward by a surreptitious anticipation of oblivion. Nowhere is this more ingeniously construed than in the successive attention to decapitation, the consecutive beheadings that signal, in turn, an onslaught against ordered thought, invoking the triviality of a world that does not bend to reason, perception ruled only by the maniacal craft of words: "I have seen so many contradictory things and have heard so many words of different sorts, my eyes have seen so much of the worn-out surface of various objects-the thin, tough rind behind which the spirit is hidden-that now I believe nothing."[42] Consciousness no longer guarantees anything, now wrung beyond recognition, a looking glass built only to show visitations of chaotic instability.

To accentuate the intricacies of this condition even further, one can then relocate the gaze to the emergent author's faultless skill in the use of darkness, night, and opium haze, all configured as mediums of brutal confusion, of arcane galleries and cisterns, an era of the uneven. Here all beings deteriorate, since conveyed to a menacing reign of impersonal hosts, a legion of the unformed and the annihilated, ever verging on the precipice of a world fading. And then still, somehow, the chaotic bends the abyss against itself and into a poetics of metal, wresting agony and impermanence beyond negation, beyond absence, and recommissioning them as sentinels of rage and becoming, intonations of a slanted soundscape—"a laugh so deep that it was impossible to guess from what remote recess of the body it proceeded."[43] No longer a symptom of decline or resignation, immobility or indecision, the advent of the text's unreality unlocks a new sensibility—one of disturbance over doubt, anticipatory risk over randomness, swathing everything it touches in an unsecured elation, where even the end turns restive and unstrung, where thought itself tears across the borders of time and space, and where laughter brings dread and dread brings laughter. A sudden motion across the lairs of nihilism and outward to a backbreaking region of cruelty and desire, where the mind disowns itself and futility enhances velocity and where the cold air of the nothing preserves a climate of perpetual aggravation. The abandonment, then the return: the chaosing of old worlds now turned strangers to themselves.

The imaginary described here is thoroughly nontranscendent in its ambitions, for it marks a concerted methodology of confrontation and provocation, of increasing closeness to an existence-turned-illusion that patrols textuality into irrepressible seizure. Beyond idealism, never allowed the frailty of distance or futurity, the chaotic imagination holds the reins of being's contravention, rending it apart, honoring and electrifying the loss through further adulteration: a new wakefulness, unanchored and abrupt in its striations, attentive yet saturated with expert nonactuality. And it is now—without the pretense of legitimacy, without recollection of rationality or functionality—that language foregoes its claim to interlocute the absolute, turns against its former role as a conveyor of the supposed nature of things and strikes a fresh pact with the emergent lie. As a consequence, the writing-act starts to gesture toward its own insurmountable unreality, its perfect imperfection, beyond the entombed dualism of the known and the hidden, beyond the passivity of the narcotized mind, toward an unseen terrain of friction, runaway and unslaked.

Taking such inquiries to a warranted extreme, the imaginary begins to evince a radical alteration in the writing-act itself, one that abuses language, as a punishment unfailing, and that devalues the sanctity of the word and takes it under siege. It is not enough to expose language—to call out the farce of communication and the insupportability of objective knowledge, to reveal the signifier and the signified as equally contrived, loosely arranged, self-referential phenomena—and thereby to derail expression at its base. No, an emergent literature must go farther: it must generate novel lines of incommunicability; it must compose territories of the incalculable, drafting contrivance after contrivance; and it then must seek to impose these original ranks of illusory consciousness forward in an arduous textual event. At this point, expression must grow irrevocably chaotic, raiding itself, privileging its own transparent chimera, as a tongue that detours and stabs, spreading its irrelevance in waves of ceaseless treachery. It takes on an assassin's temper, turning allegory into knife, each inflection a rant uncontained, each verse an evisceration of iron and upheaval. Language is thereafter left open to execution; for once in the hands of chaos, it arms itself, it scathes and punctures, enhancing its potential for the destruction of essence, turning imagination into infliction. It grants itself the right to devour, to consume, and to expend indiscriminately, becoming a force of rarefied movement, of hazard and immolation, such that each articulation stays invasive, not simply as a haunting but as an incessant perforation of the surrounding world. And so the literary instinct is overtaken by a straight compulsion: to pierce and chain its reader, to whip itself against exteriority and make thought predatory, to sentence desire to blaze and serration, and to seek venues of slander and effectuate actions of the inconsumable.

In conclusion, the relation between literature, subjectivity, and chaos, though often striking a treacherous bond, must be reflected upon further through a sojourn into the thematics of annihilation, rage, and deception. From there it must endeavor to draw more widespread implications for the basis of consciousness itself. This notwithstanding, it bears recitation that such trespasses, while not exclusive to a singular tradition or style, include and encompass only a select domain of contemporary thought, once again prompting us to envisage a still emergent movement stationed outside the well-guarded temples of the center. Indeed, to write *on* chaos, to write *as* chaos, and then to write chaos itself: each of these embody eluding yet undeniable possibilities in the exploration of literature's outer potential, thresholds of dissension ever realigning to dare textual experience forward, and thus calling upon the writing-act to affirm its long-held right over the wager that is the chaotic imagination.

TACTIC 1

Desertion (Chaotic Movement)

I. Exhaustion
(disentanglement, compulsion, the edge)

II. Evacuation
(solitude, the nowhere, the vagrant)

III. Rage
(innocence, forgetting, coldness)

IV. Return
(betrayal, the nightwalker, the unearthly)

In addressing the opaque future of such works, and in sketching a concrete outlook for this craft, one must also allow for the rise of a new interpretive prism—an alertness that searches after the chaotic currents at play within the writing act and beyond. To this extent, the textual encounter must adjoin itself to a certain tactical criteria leading toward nothing less than the betrayal of thought itself: (1) it must lure consciousness into desertion; (2) it must perceive textual artifacts as forces of immanent contagion; (3) it must identify the text as a carrier of the shadow-becoming; and (4) it must conceive the setting of the inhuman. Such is the torn strategy, the unsolicited method by which a chaotic imaginary is uncovered and set loose upon existence as well as its course of navigation (one piece of its mapping reflected in the chart). Thus each conceptual arcade outlined in this sector will be echoed by equivalent excerpts below, exhibiting the correspondence between such critical arsenals and their creative employment in the wake of an emergent literary realm.

The chaotic imagination, inasmuch as it disarms past conventions of narrative, communication, and representation, must begin from a deserter position that tacitly expresses the unearthly. By concentrating on the two distinct, yet interwoven, dimensions intrinsic to this desertion experience—the evacuation and the return—one advances a vision of the emergent chaos-consciousness as a drastic redefinition of subjectivity itself—one that reorients being toward unforeseen and mercurial trajectories and thus toward an existential outside. Specifically, the intent here is to demonstrate the complex ways in which desertion reconstitutes itself as a vagrant compendium—a knot of expression beyond the dialectical entrapments of power and resistance, universality and individualism, and self and other (to seek illegitimate virtuosities). Rather, the inhuman terrain under consideration here would present itself as a discursive nowhere—a fractal exteriority that alters and generates vivid, intensified hierarchies of instinct, desire, and knowing. In the end, this encounter will culminate with a speculation on the far-reaching significance of the deserter's second arrival—one that takes the chaotic imagination toward an energetic, tangential reengagement with the world and which therein steers the often treacherous border between cruelty and affirmation, the catastrophic and the creative.[1]

I. Exhaustion
(Disentanglement, Compulsion, the Edge)

The first intimation one encounters in the attempt to decode the customs of the deserter is that of a figure slung toward *exhaustion*: one since drained of that conviction that would seek to uphold the mythologies of the real, now vacated of that breath that still seeks inclusion in the damaged allegory of man. This crucial deprivation—this outcry of the worn and discontented—leaves the planes of thought and experience barren, subjectivity now unhinged from itself, from its surroundings, and from the countless machinations that enforce the spell between self and world. In this respect, exhaustion marks a certain zero degree of consciousness, its descent and its lowness, its degraded floor: a broken threshold whereby the once-insidious bond between interiority and exteriority now finds itself forever overturned. It is here that being begins to fast, where starvation and estrangement are torn to the brink of extremity, a site of famine and disaster:

> I am a worn face
> I am a ship run aground upon the shore.
> From this ship stranded upon the shore,
> I scream.
> Abandoned in my torment and cast aside
> upon the ghastly road of this desolate coast,
> the water at a distance.[2]

And still, this is no purification ritual but rather a process of relentless *disentanglement*, the chords of subjectivity undone—extraction after extraction—the strings of ideologies unraveled until drawn to inevitable departure. Across this uneven atmosphere, one becomes unsworn to world, allegiances now extinguished, for in this intricate relation between excision and exodus lies the labyrinthine rationale of discontemporaneity and its many rungs of nonbelonging.

Nevertheless, in trailing this aberrant narrative backward, returning so as to unearth its occluded beginnings, the question poses itself: what specific existential impulse enjoins one toward desertion (precursor to the chaotic imagination)? And why wager with the distance?

Here one confronts the distinctive corridor of *compulsion*, prism of travel, reenchantment, and rupture, for here the deserter sights an elusive strand—some radical, extraneous potential, a previously unseen current that then initiates a rotation away, and lures it apart from the rest toward the slow pulse of an undisclosed terrain. This is the genesis of its automation across, as the will grows saturated, hovering between its old cosmology and the cryptographies of an untouched arena. This is the radius of its temptation, its astonishment, one that transports a distracted, thirsting consciousness beyond the smokescreens of the real:

> In my unbalanced ship,
> In my aimless and inane words,
> there is a fever beyond the threshold.[3]

As a consequence, this compulsive imagination understands the boundary between the real and the desert as an *edge*: the sharpened precipice that is blindness, an infinity matrix in whose immanent vertigo thought falls (through the beastliness of the open). Such is its proficiency, its transformative component and brutality principle, verged on flight toward the alternate: that there is no turning back or away from beyond the edge, since it is irreversibility itself.

One talks differently here, beneath a horizon doomed: where the mistaken etch their bad ink upon the mouth, where those of sloth now conceive a new idolatry—a worship of noise and portals—and where speech clasps itself to negligence (so as to speak the unbelieving).

II. Evacuation
(Solitude, the Nowhere, the Vagrant)

At this stage in the deserter's story, consciousness is tested with the imperative to *evacuation*—to surrender to that fugitive trajectory, that errant detour through which one is wrenched somewhere unspeakable, a shadow-scape of existential experience. This evacuation is at once an abandonment and a concerted motion elsewhere—a stirring toward the displaced vicinity, the chasm wherein nothing can dwell for long, not even the nothing, where entrance is already the call to ejection, where the law of impermanence rules alone. In this sense, desertion embodies a forsaken movement, an enigmatic traversal for which all occurrences chase themselves and become emulations of a striated passage. Here one attests to the misadventurism of the wanderer (to know no peace) and to an era of rogue thought:

> In this infinite fever,
> a scream rises from within me.
> In the time of death, with death,
> Where there is nothing but horror and danger,
> Nonsense and superficiality and disquiet . . .[4]

Now cut from the cloth of an exilic epoch, the deserter calls itself to heightened *solitude*—a refuge distempered, ungoverned—as the regime of disavowal gives way to grave, immense vulnerability before presence and absence (where thought broods). There are waves in this seclusion, waves that radiate disorientation, and under whose pull consciousness braves an indefinite exposure, undefended before the extreme polarities of void and excess. More precisely, this solitude entails the rare simultaneity of a spectral episode, wavering between influx and disintegration, between the stark materiality and immateriality of isolation, over and again, a ruinous procedure whereby the deserter mind is made to synchronize the internalization of waste and unrest and to ravage itself therein, always risking extinction. Stated otherwise, evacuation takes place on amorphous dust, giving rise to a solitude that is mania itself: a solitude of fever and velocity, of backbreaking oscillation, where the surface of perception becomes antagonized, dissonant, and an emblem of abrasion. Such is the chaotic interlude that the deserter must undertake—its jagged intercourse, its nocturnal frenzy and war.

Similarly, the infusion of this solitary air, its plague and its disquiet, will become the prelude to a new spatiality, that of *the nowhere*—the nowhere that consigns all that passes to suspension, to the sightlessness of being's final sundown. In effect, the nowhere is space-in-convolution, a temporary atrophic lair and pale geography of susceptibility (where thought scours). No doubt, strange intensities illuminate this arid expanse—vanguard of the unknown, interlacing at will, concocting new grades of desire—toward the creation of a perforated affective landscape: its horror and its silence, its awe and its devastation, and its evading delirium. And still, this nowhere does not bring entrenchment, it is not a phenomenon of the arrested nor the grasp of the sequestered; rather it agitates, it aligns consciousness with a deviant course, accelerates its nomadic inclinations and its longing to stray. This turns the deserter into one who intentionally sets out to become lost, who trails the unruly, each thought a deliberate stride toward the drift. Such is the clandestine trade in operation here, one of pure submergence—into raptness, into the volatile—where the senses hang and drown in the ether of a formless interval:

> It is night,
> and with this night the earth resembles a cadaver in its
> tomb
> And in fear I tell myself: What if the flood spreads
> everywhere?
> What if the rain never ceases,
> until the world finds itself sunken in the water
> like a small boat?[5]

Ultimately, having tread the nowhere, the deserter imagination takes upon itself the mask of *the vagrant*, for the supreme solitude traced here is not the same as being alone with oneself; rather, it is to be without recourse even to oneself—the self that personified the dejected transmission of the real's master code. We speak, then, of a dire mood within which one is made aware of a dim, faceless shade (the advent of a phantom consciousness). Hence, it is to be subjectively nonsituated, the imbalance of growing close to an alienated semblance, transferred to that chamber—to that maleficent vice through which the self is leveled, even the echo razed, the "I" now ominously becoming "something." And this something is always vicious and indefinite. This is what it entails to invoke a thoroughly extrinsic modality or to become the emissary of a self-eclipsing realm beyond the confinement of essence, beyond the debris of identity, now anonymous, impersonal, caught in the ontological vagueness of a permanent self-expulsion. And here, even the name slips into illegibility, where language drags forward only the inexpressible resonance of survival. This is not the howl of animality but the incomprehensible scream of the inhuman, its foreign yet unbearable tongue, its trespassing accent, as the vagrant becomes the outside itself.

III. Rage
(Innocence, Forgetting, Coldness)

What reigns in the aftermath of the evacuated; what tremor or evocation nears in the subsequent gap? In response to such an inquiry, one uncovers the central component of the desertion experience—*rage*—for nothing less than its severity will suffice to carry out this wayward pathway to its fulfillment. Hence, one studies how it thrives, how it preys, and the occupations of its all-devouring status, only to detect a counterintuitive schematic at work beneath the ground: that it succeeds, that it throws itself forward by virtue of its innocence, its forgetting, and its coldness:

> A night of profound darkening . . .
> The prophecy of a storm, a downpour
> and I am drenched in fear.[6]

Rage proceeds as a state of *innocence*, already acquitted of its ways, with no answer offered—not in the sense of having been absolved of past but of being untied ahead of itself, a forward-moving clearance, license to unstoppable pressure; that is, that whatever happens here must happen, dissolved of accountability and thus capable of anything, to become an agent of sheer delivery, to trouble and commit at will, obedient only to the laws of speed and power, to perpetrate collapsibility. There is no judgment in rage, no inquisition, no anchor to its perfect rhythm, just a nemesis relationality to all that is. This is what allows the steady escalation, its quickening, and its capacity for storm—no future, just the uncontained whisperings of a perilous present.

Along these lines, rage also emanates an amnesic influence, wresting consciousness toward a strategic lapse, an essential forfeiture: stated concretely, the annihilation of future by innocence must be fortified by a synchronized annihilation of past by *forgetting*. One forgets as one destroys, one consummates desertion through transience: such is the blackout period of rage, its supraconscious phase (to spare no chronicle). And in this assault against the tyranny of memory, now immune to the inheritance of time, the drive to mourning also fades from sight. Thus one contemplates the end of the remnant, the murder of the witness, so as to disown the engravings of testimony. This rising imaginary marks a force untied from history, palpable yet traceless, impact without imprint, leaving nothing in its wake but the outcome of a transfigured constellation. For this is how rage remains a generalized reflex, without a unified object or reason, undifferentiated and all enveloping, an unreadable blur and inundation (of the substratum):

> With their forgetting
> I purchase forgetfulness.
> From their sweet words,
> I derive pain.
> And from within my pain blood overflows!
> How can I turn water dry?[7]

In the final scope, rage divulges an outstanding *coldness*. As the scales of experience are increasingly angered, consciousness develops into an incendiary substance—its concentration, its manifesting, its hypercirculation—to the extent of an awful calming, the cataclysmic sway of its stillness. Such marks the crossroads at which fury ices itself, crystallized into a now remote, severed ecstasy. But what this coldness implies about the deserter is even far more telling: that the secret at the heart of this one is that *it does not need to exist*. Authenticity is now obsolete, the detritus of the introspective self left irrelevant and faithless (to go unrescued). Such is the key to its intimidation: having relinquished the pathologies of being, the deserter instead becomes an agile, mean-streaked event—an interception of hazards. The deserter becomes the weapon of immediacy, the unstable formula of infliction—conviction wrought impassively, without trembling, just the free terror of neutrality. For to convey that frozen rage that serves as the forerunner of a deserter metamorphosis, one speaks only in fatalistic incantations (to become the appointed)—beyond indifference, beyond idleness, this winter of effacement, this withdrawn, ungrieving curve is what grants the deserter its ragged immortality.

IV. Return
(Betrayal, the Nightwalker, the Unearthly)

At this point, one transposes the critical stare to the negotiation of the deserter's *return*, following the arc of its necessity, for it is here that consciousness finds itself strapped with a new injunction: to take the real hostage, to steal back once more and ransack, with cunning and sinister intent, to overthrow the city and leave it disgraced. Thus the deserter restores itself to its earlier homeland through the invisible option of a marauder, coming full circle, though with different eyes, subsumed in a ring of sedition. This figure now reappears as a rage simulacrum bound neither to duplicate nor even negate the real yet to insert itself as a distortion-machine. The return, as such, is in actuality an infiltration, a raid of menacing proportions for which, from this instant forward, nothing will remain as it was:

> In this night of terrorizing darkness,
> who knows what will come of us once the dawn arrives?
> Will the daylight cast the menacing face of the storm
> towards extinguishing?[8]

To allow for the depths of a deserted imagination is not merely to accept the death of man but to affirm one's function in the ongoing pursuit of the *betrayal* of man. In fact, to elicit this exotic-endotic shift requires a subordination of consciousness to treason, to proceed from a careful impulse to criminality, and to inhabit the guise of a saboteur and a vandal, the carrier of immanent deface-ment. Such is the basic calculation of betrayal: to be outside while still within, to maintain the sensation of banishment while trafficking in vitriol, and to become the intimate punishing thread—the new malice—though the gaze remains afar.

From this traitorous plot, one can develop a further suggestion: that of equating the deserter with *the nightwalker*, a figure more aerial than solid, more illusory than true: the one of hideous legend. Desertion itself is parallel to wad-ing through a circumstance of chronic insomnia, a symptom closer to trance than to waking, the desecrated vigil of the sleepless—of the languid pacing—defection from the others' ceremony of collective oblivion, as if one were the last to roam the earth. The nightwalker, one since temporally disintoxicated, becomes a secret accomplice to the dark, existing at a vacant and aimless hour, puncturing the haze of empty streets (where thought prowls). As a result, this consciousness must always relegate itself to an intruder typology where every-thing is held suspect and is, by extension, adversarial, its every gesture consti-tuted as a smooth interference—the forbidden alertness of one who holds the passkey, who harbors the buried riddles of the real, and who maneuvers in ways that are covert, fluid, versatile. The idea itself becomes incisive here, amid its weariness, everything now the insinuation of a slight havoc:

> It is not without reason, not in vain, that yellow has turned
>   red
> It is not without reason, not in vain, that the redness has
>   thrown its color across the wall . . .
> The day of the guest-slaughtering guesthouse is pitch-black
> all souls entangled in disarray
> some people asleep
> some people coarse and ill-mannered
> some people of simplicity.[9]

In this regard, amid the hardened bond it strikes with the outside, and now the subtlety of its invasion, amid the proliferation of its indeterminate violence, the deserter can be said to have trained itself toward *the unearthly*. This lethal contact, though, is not the sign of disengagement but reengagement from the combative angle of an unrelated tribe, a pack now led by its fine hostility—what strives for the defeat of being, to evict the strongholds of man and earth. Thus the unearthly is nothing less than rampant deterritorialization and, eventually, the execution of the real, the visitation of a once-accursed past now becoming the dangerous moment—its untold threat and its unwanted burning.

A line drawn in-between, signifying the great existential separation at stake, and the impending collision it warrants, this emergent literature brought ever forward by its one singular need: to overrun the hiding places, the thrones of false subjectivities, and impostor empires of being. And so the chaotic imagination reels toward a conclusive juncture: to speak in the assassin's idiom, to stain the real with the facticity of its imminent death, as a creature at once lawless and tainted, unborn to all that stands.

CHAPTER 2

First Annihilation
Fall of Being, Burial of the Real

> I no longer have any ambition or any desire to get my own [life] back. Whatever was human in me I have lost, I have allowed to get lost. In life a man must either become angelic or human or animal. I have become none of these things.
> —Sadeq Hedayat, "Buried Alive: The Jottings of a Madman"

The first annihilation is an advancement toward the eclipse of being, an involuntary torrent and perishing that gels exultation, despair, and frenzied ruination from within (soul-destitution). It is the eleventh hour of man and the last stand with metaphysics fused into a singular experience of erosion—one that drives thought to fragmentation, rampage, and eviction—that unbraces it beyond the borderlines of consciousness and toward the martial throes of dissolution. It erupts, subdues, impoverishes, and overindulges with manic strides, played out at hyper speed, ultrapaced, to the extent that the self becomes an accelerated paragon of disintegration. This is its reckoning, one that wrests existence into the transient rhythms of the extreme and the sublimity of ultimate collapse, one that summons, tempts, and shatters toward the trial of desire's end (becoming-devastation).

This section marks a concerted attempt to intertwine certain currents of emergent literature with contemporary philosophy, drawing more edged experimentations in writing and thought from both provinces of expression into a volatile thematics of annihilation. Through this comparative analysis, a sustained theoretical commentary will arise—one that culminates in a new definition of the relationship between existential experience and the concept of finality, as the prelude to a chaotic turn, and that therefore possesses vast implications for further discourses of being, reality, consciousness, desire, and will. As such, this inquiry will challenge itself to uncover the potential for an alternative, and perhaps unprecedented, perspective on the overcoming of sub-jectivity—one that aligns creation and destruction toward the event of a chaotic imagination and therefore coalesces the following principles at its forefront: the overturning of nihilism and death; the annihilation of the self and the other; the abandonment of the real; the poetics of nonbeing; the affirmation of ecstasy, risk, and desecration; and annihilation as infinite time-space, apocalypse, and return. Specifically, a principal concentration will be given to Sadeq Hedayat's "Buried Alive," a text of unsurpassed magnitude for the prospect of such literary fields that will then be set against the looming edifice of "Western" thought and its suppositions of death in modernity. In this way, one will come to understand what it means to write beyond the death drive: to speak of a textual realm that is buried alive.

Punishment: Vengeance, Indeterminacy, Unknown Agony

There are two men (if one can even call them such anymore): one hanging from a cross, soon to be burned, and the other standing in the center of a decrepit room, enveloped in a lethal gas, gradually choking his way to oblivion. And both laughing wildly. What does one make of this, if anything?

This might be the daring price of consciousness: what must inexorably graze itself? Annihilation brings to attainment a new philosophy of this crossing: one for which the most incendiary conclusion is prolonged and for which the trag-edy of the "what if" subsides into irrelevance, as one becomes a practitioner of mistrust. When one poses the question, must not all things at last be taken by death? One assigns an inevitability toward which the thread of existence continually unravels, though never contemplating the potential to trouble, manipulate, or transfigure the destination. For beyond the overwrought fact that one must die, a surpassing attention must be given to the question of *how* one dies and on whose terms and, even further, to what else is taken down alongside oneself (some things die in order to kill). The design here, then, is to locate a consciousness aligned with such second variables, guiding itself toward an end beyond the operation of the ordinary—an explosive finality that will designate annihilation as the moment of division from the real while at the same time confining it to burial. If most die common deaths, then this crea-ture will do anything but, making the harsh exodus toward the nondomain of the postsubjective unreal. Of the greatest weight here, however, is to delineate how the annihilative subject at once constitutes itself as a becoming-outside-the-world and a becoming-against-the-world, though neither is commensurate with a transcendental or dialectical positing, but rather emerges as the necessary, ultimate outcome of a becoming-outside-the-real. Though driven by the ethos of the fight—one that leads consciousness toward an unmediated confrontation with its own mortality—it is not bound by it but stands as the exhaustion of ontological totality from within itself, now beyond the stringent unity of the "is." Thus the writing of "Buried Alive," quoted at the opening of this venture, itself ever on the verge of a chaotic extreme, will be enlisted alongside several theoretical trends within this work, across all contextual borders, in order to reveal the process by which such a proposition might become an acute possibility—that annihilation could be the currency of an unfathomed incident.[1]

With this opening in place, one positioned at the edge of being itself, it becomes clear as to how such a possibility is immediately deterred by the constraints of "the real." The preservation of its apparatus of power, meaning, knowledge, and order is predicated, in major part, upon a constant distancing of the experience of death from the operation of subjectivity, making it remote, external to consciousness, and deferred to a foreign horizon. In order to sustain compliance to the palpitations of the system, such a matrix must somehow relegate the end to a concealed state, casting it into absentia, disavowing its place within the discursive and symbolic order. And still, fatality remains an unstable substance; it spills over, beyond the tablets of epistemological definition (as the uncontainable), and it is precisely in that overabundance—that impassable dross left over—that the antecedent to a chaotic becoming can perhaps begin to disclose itself.

In recognition of this resistant threat, the self-appointed "real" must act upon death in a way that weakens its position of influence vis-à-vis subjectivity, making it relatively harmless. At the outset, this occurs through a virtual excising of death from the activity of life, cutting the inherent relation between the two spheres, disrupting their interconnectedness and placing in its wake a widescale inability of the individual to fathom its own mortality. In large part, one sees this devolution in the treatment of death as a consequence of the Enlightenment's assimilation of myth—a prior mode of historical consciousness that acknowledged the inseparability of life and death though always casting it in a shower of metaphysical significations. But amid the dialectical transfiguration of the world into an epoch of instrumentalized reason, this disenchanted subjectivity is robbed even of the right to the delusion of meaning in death, and so is left alienated from its own terminality. Whereas earlier theological narratives were able to disperse the fear of death by coating it in an idealized metaphysical purpose, modernity must sever the bond between subjectivity and its own successive demise, making it vulnerable to a new language of the everyday in which finality is perpetually detained and postponed. This is how the experiential thrust of death is relegated to disbelief, as certified by several attentive critics: from Adorno's observation that "in the socialized society, in the inescapably dense web of immanence, death is felt exclusively as external and strange,"[2] to Heidegger's note that "one says that death certainly comes, but not right away.

With this 'but' . . . the they denies that death is certain,"[3] to Freud's insight that "we displayed an unmistakable tendency to 'shelve' death, to eliminate it from life."[4]What remains, then, is a pretense-sentiment of timelessness, a false immortality through which the subject's relation to death becomes one of a passive spectator, abandoned to schism and irreconcilability. Such is the allegory of the human, one for which only disappearance remains.

From here death falls under the watchful eye of power, becoming its chosen instrument of punishment, using its volatility to quell, its estrangement to isolate, its discolorations to prosecute, an insidious technique of confinement. Such is the wisdom of the mock execution, wherein, after a series of unfulfilled stagings, the victim usually begs for death, preferring the assurance of an end to an indefinitely suspended terminality. Judgment is now everywhere, witness to the strategic use of finality to achieve a self-regulating, self-monitoring subjectivity, itself a guarantor of allegiance to the collective trance. It targets consciousness with arresting despair and impermanence, trying to extract a desire for reabsorption, confirmation, and vicious self-dejection, exerting its gestures of negation and reclaiming from all sides. The emergent author, however, defects at this same moment, taking no solace in the old internment, superseding the coldness of death for the fever-dream of annihilation. Along such lines, Hedayat describes how, one night, he finds himself sitting in an alleyway, watching as people walk by, unable to invest himself in any of their stirrings or to feel any sort of communion with his concocted surroundings: "A drunken woman staggered past me. In the dim uncertain light of a gas lamp I saw a man and woman talking as they passed . . . On the benches in the streets wretched people without any homes were sleeping."[5] Here the crowds become nothing more than scattered images, aimless passings that plague him in their frivolous discontinuity, adhering to a protocol of surrender. And it is key to observe that it is exactly at this instant, when discursive production begins to lose its hold, that the real enhances its onslaught against the protagonist's consciousness. Everywhere he goes, he hears the pulsating sounds of the clock assaulting him, striving to bring him back toward the monotony of the social body, to condition him once more to fall in line, and to submit to the hypnotic intonations of the temporal order: "Tick tock—the clock keeps on and on with the same noise against my ear. I want to pick it up and throw it out of the window—this fearsome sound that beats the passing of time into my head with a hammer!"[6] Never knowing anything but what he was told to be, and in the absence of any alternative experiential frame of reference, the real is able to retaliate, infesting his thoughts at every turn, hurling him toward a breakdown.

The Vagrants: Dislocation from the Real

Annihilation is to select an alternate conduit, one of dislocated turns and ever-transpiring extrications, wrenched away from the terror-bound abstraction of death and now skating the fringes of a more metallic sojourn. This interim oblivion, this ecstatic outsider configuration, rebels against all sectors of the known world (until there is nowhere left to go), lapsed into a phase of nihilistic stalling, for this is its preemptive simulation of nothingness, striving to overcome finality as mind-body are sacrificed at the altar of deprivation. But this holds true only for the time being, for the annihilated will return from the recesses of this retraction from the world, this time combative and this time with eyes set for an affective clash.

And yet some subjects survive the reprisal, slowly ranging their way toward the annihilation of subjectivity altogether, becoming vagrants of consciousness. What facilitates this preliminary break remains equivocal, though it is not of the nature of an "encounter"—in effect, a presyntactic, prelogical moment of openness in which something occurs beyond the mandates of a despotic world. In this case, rather than produce a heightened mode of intersubjectivity, enriching the exchange of self and other, it is in fact oriented toward a withdrawal of relationality on any level. It is the experience of a defection from one's own being-in-the-world, a tearing away from all that one once knew, such that Hedayat writes, "These thoughts, these sensations, are the result of the whole cycle of my life, of my way of life, of the ideas I inherited, and what I have seen, heard, felt, and thought about. And it is all these things which have created the irrelevant and useless creature I am now."[7] It is a release from the past, from that forced inheritance, through which subjectivity was initially constituted, beginning a tradition whereby he would always be nothing more than a drone recipient of reality's surreptitious discourse.

To abandon the bondage of the One, consciousness must now entertain a falling from mastery into vulnerability and ambiguity. This gravitation is the necessary step of temporary nihilism; it is the recognition of aimlessness and, with it, the absurd futility of a search for transcendental meaning. Nevertheless, at first, this resignation is anything but emancipatory, yet instead it freezes subjectivity in unconcern, petrifying being as all movement comes to appear inane. This is why Hedayat begins the tale in a condition of existential immobility, asserting, "I feel bored, weary, tired out—I can rake up no energy or enthusiasm for anything . . . I want to smoke a cigarette, but I don't feel like it . . . I saw how very weak and thin I've become. It was even an effort to walk."[8] Anything but an instant of utopian revelation, this revocation of belief bears with it a pronouncement of the meaninglessness of existence without any claim to deliverance, leaving only the listlessness of a life without purpose or function, enticed only by the suggestion of "go[ing] away . . . a long way away . . . to escape myself."[9] But in fact, this turn toward incapacitation, toward the unmoving, marks a vital wrenching away from the assurance of clarity offered by the world and into the obscurity of an unreality rotating along the axis of nothingness, a vision of nonvision whereby one "can see straight through my dark, mean, useless life from one end to the other."[10] Radical disconnect and disaffection come to reign as subjectivity relinquishes its own claim to supremacy, becoming derelict or an alleyway consciousness. And from here, by obviating a destructive eventuality of the most hideous register, the genocide of self, annihilation makes irrelevant the threshold dividing being and nonbeing—this is why it occupies such a dominant role in the chaotic interstices. Annihilation demands infinite nonconcealment of subjectivity's own liability before nothingness, wringing the end into full transparency and exposure, though as a means of gradual entitlement to the seizures and saturations of the instant.

To track this further, the transition toward nihilism begins a descent into the abyss of nonmeaning in which the will to truth is gradually exorcised from subjectivity, halting it in that downcast space where we are no longer allowed to know anything. Thus one witnesses an increasing hostility in both narratives to all artifacts of the absolute, not simply as a turning away from sources of discursive production but also as a divisive countervailing of their indoctrinating assertions. With regard to Hedayat, this subversive charge against truth takes the form of a disavowal of self—the self that was nothing more than the fabrication of reality's order, evident in such statements as "I was born by mistake"[11] and the following admission that "for some days now I had been trying to tell my fortune with cards. Somehow I had found faith in these superstitions . . . I could not do anything else. I wanted to gamble with my own future."[12] Prepared to relinquish his own drive for systematic coherency to the rampant instability of chance, wagering his life on a card game (or a dice throw), he is slowly summoning or acquiring a taste for the unknown. Such an excerpt illuminates the fact that Hedayat is now approaching that disjunctive ontological expanse where infinite risk is preeminent and the assurance of conviction finds itself susceptible to constant vitiation (groundlessness): "I had never taken life seriously. The world, people—I had always seen it as a silly game, a disgrace, an inane and pointless affair."[13] Thus nihilism is inhaled as a temporary antidote to the spells of the real.

Without doubt, an annihilative consciousness wages its own offensive against truth, but on more numerous fronts, converting every corner of human reality into a battlefield, each instant signaling the tremor of an apocalyptic reckoning with illusion. For this reason, it also comes into head-on collision with the symbolic order of things, arriving at the recognition of truth as untruth, now unmasked as a masquerade of metaphors. Having apprehended this simulacrum of existence, the annihilated then sets out to interrupt its transmission—through heresy and renunciation—severing its once-blind adherence to standard conventions of knowing. It places postsubjective reflection above history; it maneuvers against the law, exposing its prescriptions as an obstacle, its drive for equalization and synthesis an affront to the prospect of a new sight for deception. Even metaphysics is disputed, scratched, and dislodged; here, shedding itself of once-imposed suffocating totalities, and with it, the text now carries the message of an erratic thrust: a singular act of desanctification, not by drawing the text's inner heterodoxy into a sphere of unregulated free play but by uplifting chaotic experience above all acts of interpretation, leaving a dangerous hermeneutic formula.

Such a writing-act risks condemnations of derangement and apostasy, disrupting translatability by casting language to the crossroads of an annihilative culmination, spending itself on a postrepresentational anarchy. A bad literary practice starts here: one of transparent imposture, agitating the word away from its tyrannical hold, decoding the signification barrage that inundates textuality from its first hours. Meaning dissipates as the chain of discursive production and consumption comes undone, ending the agreement between the sign and signifier, the sign and signified, and the knowing subject and its supposed objective world. What remains in its place is a thing that shakes uncontrollably, vibrating amid the antiprogrammatic bareness of thought—a territory opened to chaotic infinity. Thus one notes that the emergent author is constantly declaring that "perhaps I'm talking nonsense,"[14] parallel to speaking in tongues, for in both cases, there is an effort to go beyond the frontiers of intelligibility, weaving a cord that might destabilize the operation of meaning altogether, and with it a conspiracy to break the deal between subjectivity and the real. It is the overthrow of reality's will to truth, but it cannot stop there.

Annihilation of the Other: The Disavowal of Intersubjectivity

It was already done long before the incursion. As stated, to annihilate the other is to allow consciousness to exist in the aftermath of all things, allowing it to transport itself and to hover beyond the extinction point of being. Here there remains no forced ties; the annihilated no longer owes the other anything and thereby evades the inevitable regression into a power relationship. Besides, if the other embodies nothing more than a suspect derivation of the real, one who wants to bring the now solitary subject crashing back into its dismal sphere of social regimentation—either through temptation or punishment, the embrace or the choke hold—then the only tenable encounter lies within a fight for survival against the other. Here justice becomes necessary cruelty. The other must be existentially contested, if not eviscerated, not as individuals who themselves are incognizant of their own enslavement—for they are not the architects of hegemony but the servants to a system they no longer even see—but instead through an eradication of the specimen of otherness and interconnection. Disentanglement cannot come from a dialogue that fosters complacency but from a screaming match that highlights the cataclysmic discord between the annihilative will and the presumed inescapability of a being-in-the-world that nullifies its trajectory. The encounter must be one of warfare, a street fight declared by a becoming-outside-the-other now propelled forward into a becoming-against-the-other, whose collision heralds the requiem for all claims to ontological substance. As others have noted, destruction clears a path for the expectation of the future, here designated as an aftermath, one materialized in a present for which the other must come under the blade—the abolition of subjectivity and intersubjectivity together, prelude to the emergent. Philosophy must begin again, this time as a discipline of assassination.

With the descent into the condensed meaninglessness of nihilistic torment, and this then affirmatively transfigured into an eradication of the subject's will to truth, the notion of intersubjectivity needs to be drastically reconfigured as well. This prechaotic sector must elicit a new experience with the other that will carry both toward the vertex of annihilation. Hence, one discovers that from the onset of Hedayat's narrative, there lies an overriding distrust of the possibility of alliance with those around him, though at first the language remains in passive voice, as if this withdrawal was inflicted upon him, as in the following excerpt: "I passed by crowds and crowded places. In the middle of the ceaseless traffic and the noises of horseshoes, carts, motor horns, and the continual tumult and scuffle, I was completely alone. I felt I had been turned out of the society of men in disgrace."[15] Indeed, at this stage, the author is yet to realize that it is his own annihilative consciousness that has enjoined this solitude, something within him that, while in no sense commissioning a zone of autonomous interiority, at the same time is no longer constrained by exteriority. Thus in his inability to define this seclusion in the limited terms that he has been afforded as the remnant of a constituted subjectivity, he is compelled to ascribe it to some failure enacted upon him. This passive attribution continues in the following metaphor, in which he writes, "In the middle of so many millions of people it was as though I was sitting in a wrecked boat, lost in the middle of the sea."[16] Again, the author assumes no accountability whatsoever, portraying his escape from the hegemony of the real as one of a helpless creature subordinated to the cruelty of fate, leading him where it will, not knowing that he is leading himself where he must go and where his own will has brought him. The sensation of loss is also crucial, since this mutation into what will later be an antagonistic, ahistorical postsubjectivity first necessitates a forfeiture of what was and what is (thought without mourning). And it is here that the gradual insertion of a will to solitude, as an active, incisive tactic to place oneself at the outskirts of reality, and ultimately to dispel universality itself, begins to manifest: "Looking out of my sixth floor window I saw people walking about in the street below; their black shadows and the passing cars appeared small. I gave my bare body up to the cold and it made me writhe."[17] Though it carries him toward a merciless agony, throwing him into pain-racked shivers, it is he who has given himself up to this state of affliction. No longer the deviant cast out from civilization into the wasteland, he is now the one who has elected himself into the wasteland, no longer a convict but a deserter. It is in this defection that Hedayat rejects the positing of a self-discovery in the other, riled against Merlau-Ponty's premise that "by myself I cannot be free, nor can I be a consciousness or a man; and that other whom I first saw as my rival is my rival only because he is myself."[18] Instead, the emergent author develops a sensitivity to the other's devious invitations, for otherness is but another appendage to an oppressive world, carrying its ontological chains everywhere with it. A postsubjective rupture, then, cannot occur by a resubjection of oneself to a relationship with the other—what is nothing more than a loosely veiled missionary of reality's discourse. If anything, resistance emanates from a willingness to see oneself not only as different from the other but also in opposition to what it represents behind the fraudulence of that vampiric call for consonance. The altruistic handshake is in fact a stranglehold—the economy of hospitality a grip of living death, the narcotization of subjectivity itself—which occurs coterminous with the birth of subjectivity. And it is in this vein that Hedayat refutes all hope of communicability with the crowds, writing, "There are sentiments, there are things, which it is impossible to explain to another person, which can't be said."[19] In another place, in contemplation of his own imminent self-destruction, he begins to conjecture as to the response of those who might find his body but then turns against this pondering and asks, "What does it matter that other people are upset, weep, or don't weep?"[20] Those tears, the tears of humanity, in itself a term that is little more than a euphemism for a collection of disembodied prey, fail to move him, for he knows where they come from—a reality that is anything but real. And so he takes dynamic steps to bring into unfamiliarity everything that he once held dear, traversing to the heart of subjectivity's investment in the world, and by denouncing its blood-hold over him, implodes the entire web of power-basing affiliations that revolve around this centralizing entity: "I took out the pictures of my relatives and looked at them. I imagined each one as I had seen them. I liked them, and I did not like them. I wanted to see them, and I did not want to . . . I tore up the pictures. No, I felt no attachment."[21] As is shown here, every tie must be made perishable—its insincerity divulged and left mutilated—if this annihilative consciousness is to elude the ring of casualties. Moreover, the wavering tone—vacillating between like and dislike, desire and repulsion, and coalescing remarkably in the nonpathos of indifference—is the key component in this shearing of intersubjectivity. Hatred, anger, and resentment, as dialectical negations of love for the other, would have flung him back into a bond—a negative reactivity; but indifference, and indifference alone, can remove the weight from his shoulders. He has now kindled a becoming-outside-the-other, which is the only way that he can remain unscathed when he later becomes a becoming-against-the-other, taking on a frozen, effective temperament. Once crucified at their hands, the annihilated was taught to suspect the other—to spite even its shadow—and broke loose from the paranoiac requisitions of society, culture, and humanity. Now he has learned to deduce the others again, to read through the covert reasoning, having no use for what they offer. Thus this transitional interiority, one that will eventually dismantle itself, serves as a corridor toward the restive extraterritorialization of consciousness—an in-between process in the overcoming of context (surging into wayward straits).

Nevertheless, Hedayat will take a further step toward a nonintersubjective mode of affinity, but one of a different kind: an alliance that will hasten the ultimate nonstate of annihilation toward which the narrative must jaggedly progress. His new companions are the dead—his surrogate others the corpses he beholds with an almost sensual astonishment—for they are the reflection of that darkening toward which he shall inescapably will himself, an association illustrated in the following passage: "Involuntarily, I went into the cemetery . . . A deep silence ruled over the place. I walked slowly, staring at the gravestones, the crosses they'd put over them . . . I read the names of those who had been buried. I felt sorry I wasn't there instead of them . . . I felt jealous of the dead whose bodies had dissolved under the earth . . . I did not feel the cold. It was as though the dead were nearer to me than the living. I understood their language better."[22] As a consequence, it becomes obvious as to how the annihilated here becomes a pathological antisurvivor, soothed by the graves (this most barren settlement). No, the annihilative consciousness of this project inhabits a far different position, for it is most alone when in the company of man, shuddering throughout that realm of the real that epitomizes the more grotesque death, and it is most predisposed to the tombs, for it envisions itself already among them—already beyond subjectivity and the dependency it engenders, since expelled into soullessness. One separates, supersedes, and enacts discontemporaneity and nonalignment; one takes to quintessential wandering, a radical departure from self-iconization and toward a new contempt. This is no reversal, for to go back to the zero degree of subjectivity is untenable; rather, being must revolve around the pivot point of inconstancy by virtue of its avaricious desire for nonbeing until losing itself beyond the mechanistic disenchantment of this dualism, supplanting it with an intimate, ungoverned will to distraction.

This brings one back to the initial matter concerning the annulment of intersubjectivity, for to allow consciousness' disclosure to the world (as an ordercentric space) would be to endanger the freedom that is afforded it by the existential outside to which it has conferred itself. Furthermore, although under a different motive and to a different end, it is in this sense that the becoming-outside-the-other, and even the later version of the becoming-against-the-other, converges with that "deliberate bracketing" of the phenomenological outlook in which "pure" consciousness is attained once the world is excluded: "We have excluded the whole world with all physical things, living beings, and humans, ourselves included."[23] The similarities between annihilation and this phenomenological reduction are striking yet ultimately nonanalogous, since the former, in its foresight, has cautiously inserted a supraontological security clause of sorts: to dispossess the "I" of its unqualified mastery, instead evoking the image of a spilling over, beyond the containment of being. This is no retreat into elite interiority, no resignation or elevation allowed, and thus rests apart from Kierkegaard's genius who does not "define himself teleologically in relation to any other person, as if there were anyone who stood in need of him . . . [but] consists in his relating himself immanently to himself . . . [as] the unity of modest resignation in the world and proud elevation above the world."[24] Annihilative consciousness, rather, marks an immense distinction: it foregoes this self-encompassed seclusion and draws an axiomatic line between solitude and a forward-bending multiplicity—a lone projection that then becomes the swarm of all possible ideas. Strangely, this fluctuation is not a testimony to some original insularity that then usurps the totality of being but rather that sends itself to the aftermath of being, already envisioned beyond the instant of annihilation (consolidated eternity). This depiction corresponds to another corollary—that of a consciousness sought after by self-adulterating singularities, though here divorced from idealized categories of transcendence. Hence, the destruction of intersubjectivity alone can defend the annihilated from entrapment in the totality of the real, encompassing both everything and nothing, and presence and absence, in one stride, running in a place where time is evacuated. Time therefore only exists in dialogue with the other and must be unmade, circumscribed within the boundless enclosure of a chaotic imagination that has long since broken from a broken world.

Lived Aesthetics: The Spectacle of Creation and Destruction

Some have said that we write in order not to die and that consciousness invariably flees the night in which a solitary "someone" approaches. But what about a subject who writes precisely so as to die, though to die a different death? Others have said that art is unstained by the blood of history. But what about a mode of artistic creation that is covered in blood, one that deliberately bleeds itself and draws blood in turn? This is the type of aesthetic at stake in the annihilative episode (no work is guiltless).[25]

One comes upon the first axiom of an emergent literature: that the text gains infinite power only as it kills its own pages. With this strain in mind, Hedayat construes the work of art as a locale of noxious contradictions, galvanizing paradox within paradox, thereby providing an appropriate medium of expression for annihilation's antagonistic stance against the world. In this respect, the narratives invoked here contravene a major aspect of other aesthetic theories, able to advance in hostile patterns against the real without operating in any existential relationality (even negative relationality) to its target.[26] No, this long-sought condition can only be attained through fanatic extraneity, a rabid desynchronization of being and chaotic becoming, to the extent that the two spheres fall away and into mutual irrelevance, having nothing to do with one another. There is no longer anything to say between them—no justifiable common ground, only the estrangement of necessary enmity. This precept is to be found in Hedayat's story, as the moment of artistic creation becomes a channel for disidentification, an exorcism that at once provides comfort, remission, and an arsenal in the times of greatest adversity, but that most of all sets the stage for a lasting evacuation of consciousness from reality's totalitarian seal: "Now that I have written these things down, I feel a bit quieter. It has consoled me. It is as though a heavy load had been taken off my shoulders. How good it would be if one could write everything."[27] Moreover, at one point he mentions, "I stopped and stared at canvases in shop windows and regretted not having become a painter. It was the only work I liked and enjoyed."[28] Unlike the case of other aesthetic theories, there is an exigency for the emergent authors in positing the work as an independent space—an impersonal breathing ground removed from the asphyxiation of the world—and yet realizing that this is won only by converting subjectivity itself into a complete exteriority (the desert).

Even further, what some fail to anticipate in their endeavor to make of the aesthetic a quasi autonomous, but nonetheless historically relevant, sphere is the prospect of writing aesthetic criticism as an aesthetic process that mobilizes an outsider becoming. This brings textuality in closest opposition to the straitjacketed parameters of the real while still housed in an undesignated beyond. The prior impression frames the relationship of the critic to the work of art as one of mere articulation, extracting the social-truth content from the indescribable element of the aesthetic imagination and using it to make vitreous the dialectical monstrosity of Enlightenment modernity that ideology otherwise conceals. And yet implicit to Hedayat's "Buried Alive" is a thoroughly novel conception of the critic as one who no longer participates at the registers of witnessing and subsequent communication but as one who becomes evenly proficient in discharging the radical capacity of art to divest power of its covers from an outer vantage. Nowhere is this more visible than in the author's recollection of a concert in which he was moved by a certain sensorial collaboration between his own consciousness and a singer's voice. His immediate reaction was to lament the artist's finitude, dispirited at the recognition of his evanescence over time: "I thought to myself 'This man should never die.' I couldn't believe it possible that one day this voice would sing no more."[29] Nevertheless, it is precisely the transience that augments its experiential magnetism, such that, if anything, an understanding of its necessary decay should not deter the object but should encourage it even further—that is, if consciousness spins the pleasure-pain ratio beyond the fear of imminent loss. Despite Hedayat's initial reservations in this direction, he will nonetheless invest himself in the slipping intonations of the music, and, in turn, wagering on his ability to endure its unavoidable diminishment, inundating himself in the moment without mourning: "The high notes and the low notes, the mistakes and wailing that came from those strings made me feel as though the bow was sliding back and forth over the marrow of my bones; every atom of my being was permeated with their playing; vibrating, I was borne up in the power of the music."[30] But aesthetic internalization does not exhaust the far-reaching implications of this quote, for several other things are at play here that will at once acknowledge, and then overturn, the complicity with languishing. In the first place, the way in which the protagonist is so fantastically overtaken, allowing the resonances to invade him from all angles, demonstrates a revocation of the idea of aesthetic disinterestedness. The experience of art here is not simply a sanctuary from the blind drive of humanity but in fact administers a rearrangement or demolition of subjectivity itself. This is why, in light of a realization of transience that brings into relief the connection between art and death, and between generation and decomposition, a sudden sensuality arises in the concert hall: "In the darkness . . . her eyes had the look of intoxication. I was in a very strange mood as well, a state of exotic sadness impossible to describe . . . We pressed each other close . . . I played with her hands, and she clung tightly to me. Now it's as though I dreamt it."[31] The work of art has broached the author's consciousness, compelling him to imitate, and then supplement, it in his own creative fashion—to pose a renovated, visceral equivalent in the domain of being now locking arms with nonbeing: one sensory effect inciting another through carnal intimacy, yet ever tied still to the unreal (recollected here as a dreamscape). If the aesthetic has penetrated his consciousness, imparting its sublimity through the endorsement of its own tapering, then Hedayat will scream his own half-sorrowful, half-exalted nonstate back to it through a physical incarnation. There is one major distinction at work here: that annihilation is not the death drive, not hidden in the layers of an infernal unconscious, but rather standing beyond the universal, structural registers of the psyche, leaving a state of exception without precedent or determinism—just a fatal gradient tied to the chaotic imaginary. And in taking this (il)logic to its extreme allocation, it becomes apparent how being might reach its most epic or tragic form in the duration of its demise, which is why one wills oneself toward the annihilative precipice—it is then that subjectivity might attain an irradiated height (amid the exiting): the orientation of a lived aesthetic, turning finality into infinite performativity.

In building on this newfound circularity of the artist and spectator-turned-artist, one must pay attention to the intricate way in which Hedayat writes of this particular experience as a collusion of multiple sectors of consciousness. For, indeed, his storytelling is in itself a complicated aesthetic interface. The author's words are never more poetic than when he writes on artistry itself, not out of some vulgar romanticism but because anything less would epitomize a treachery. He seizes upon the text as a platform for another text—never of lesser, but of rivaling, proportions, triggering a series of unstrung aesthetic detonations. Adamantly denying the subservience of the critic to the work of art, and alongside it the necessity of writing on art in a tone marked by sobriety, Hedayat evinces a staunch insistence on the imperative to write on art artistically, and then to perform it as existential innovation (supramimetic). He will not consign himself to the inertia of the audience but will take on the burden of participation and errant reinvention, matching musical genius with literary genius and not the cold solemnity of philosophical abstraction (which remains embedded in the schism of style and content).[32] This is something that the annihilative critic explicitly professes and embodies: refusing to forego an interloping presence in the act of interpretation—to hide the "I" behind the curtains of a feigned objectivity of observation—but rather becoming a physical enhancement of the work. And this is what is perhaps most unique about an emergent author's treatment of the aesthetic beyond the implicit servility of the countersigning reader: that he valiantly risks involvement, falling into collaboration with the insurgent impact of the artwork by immortalizing it through a second annihilative work. This, in turn, gives rise to a measureless stream of potentially similar and dissimilar reactions that, in each gesticulation, resuscitate the hazard. The cyclicality is then perpetuated, the critic ensuring the endurance and distortion of the artistic experience through undeterred reinvocations, though always in a fresh and mutating medium, of what was itself a transformative occasion of the work. If the work is met by a critical text that is in itself an aesthetic invasion, then the process simply goes on without conclusion, inspiring new responses and new perspectives, denying transience in the interminability of transient visions and therein giving way to a paradoxical rise and fall that commingles evanescence and the promise of forever in a ceaseless exercise of the transitory. And what is accomplished by this reciprocity, this circular exchange between the premier work and the critic-now-turned-artist? A continual concentration and dispersal, intersection and alteration, of creative vitalities in discontinuity; in brief, the eternal return of the aesthetic imagination.

Annihilative criticism is therefore a necromancic function, reanimating the departed piece. Such is the expressive trajectory developed thus far: an outcry that would make the passage of time at once emphatically accelerated and yet impenetrable to closure, legislating an emergency intrusion that then forecasts outbreak. This breach, without acquiescence, creates an insurmountable stronghold, durable against the machinations of the center, by refueling the ambiguity of the creative turn, unsettling and propagating its tension, force, confusion, disturbance, and demonic incoherence. In this way, annihilation turns criticism itself into an irregular and nonderivative reservoir of aesthetic production, again producing a forward trail that staves off inscription into history and in fact corroding the historical through an elusive storytelling. To achieve this, the aesthetic takes on an annihilative immediacy, as one becomes a rundown author to every text one encounters, promoting outrageous applications, at once trampling and episodic, each line viewed through the prism of resurrection and finale. This is the nexus of its fascination and its seductive pursuit: an enforcement whereby the critical moment becomes an execution. Its ferocity melds persecutor and persecuted and brings the reader in-between the friction, concussion, and vivification of sides (between author and critic). The reader partakes of the critical-creative violence, a third party made to stand by, amid this procession-unto-arson, silenced by shock, not knowing where to stand, deserted by both fronts, violated by both fronts, and watching what seems like a concert of dispersed utterances. If the poetic normally remains bound to oracles, omens, and allusions, then annihilation excuses this poverty, for it brings poetics before the eyes—in front of being, in the now—as an abhorrent image of exhaustion and fury, forcing it to look at it head-on as an impending present. And with this change in design, the chaotic is no longer some mystical terrain or transcendent site removed from the obscene theater of the real—it looms within it at its core as a now diffused potential. The figure of annihilation, standing at the edge of self-slaughter, overlooking the spellbound hordes, is activated sublimity itself, having adapted the ephemerality of the aesthetic into a sustained postontological modality about to elicit its own unraveling. Thus the textual execution, in its epic calamity, becomes an archetype for the push and pull of an untamed existence (uncaring presence). Ever-beckoning desolation, the author, critic, and reader become that loss of the world for which no one weeps.

Beyond the Occult: The Last Outpost of the Real

Emergent literatures are often associated with the occult, its supernatural wrongs and murderous dissensions, and its ascriptions of recondite, sinister, and otherwise paranormal endowments. Nevertheless, such arcane insinuations circumscribe a lighter terror than the parameters of annihilation allow, for the latter derails understanding, clasped between amazement and the unbearable, within a new asymmetricality and quasi-epileptic distaste. A different tactic takes hold here.

Within the confines of this analysis, it is also of pressing importance to observe the way in which emergent texts that have historically been labeled "occult" in fact hold this characterization in somewhat negative standing vis-à-vis the transition into an annihilative consciousness. If one takes the image of a crossroads, one that is positioned at a median place between the subjectivity of the real and that of the chaotic unreal, then the occult is stationed here as an off-route recoil back into the real. Herein lies the opposition between the annihilative event and the occult, the former as a projection into the possibility or impossibility of the chaotic endeavor and the latter as a negational reaction that, in spite of its calculated eccentricity, always perceives itself as tied to the world. Its protests of distance are in fact never autonomous from the inner workings of the real, and so it works in agreement as one of its most outward-reaching limbs. But the argument becomes more complex than a mere dismissal of the occult as the disguised functionary of a rigid social order since it sets the stage for a crucial excursion. Undoubtedly, just as it was necessary for consciousness to endure the nihilistic impulse only then to overcome it, so must consciousness crash itself into the unsteady terrain of the occult in order to then go beyond it, impervious to its blockade. It is the farthest one can go while still within the real—the last outpost before the backwoods of annihilation—and so one must pass through it to get to where one is going (the nowhere, the bad country, the becoming-outside-the-real).

Even though it has no static pedagogy, supplanting normalized idioms with a precarious language of meaningless and disaffected signifiers, the occult soon divulges itself as a manifestation of the social apparatus. Its magic is formalistic: it sets apart its own private space of the sacred, its own system of authentic rites. This brings to mind Mauss's general theory of magic, which finds that, while "it is private, secret, mysterious, and approaches the limit of a prohibited rite,"[33] in the final analysis, "the idea of the sacred is a social idea, that is, it is a product of collective activities . . . [and] we were forced to conclude, therefore, that magical practices . . . are social practices."[34] And so in order to promote its own irregularity, the occult needs to cement a certain idea of original truth against which it then proceeds to strike its head in nonsensical striations; if it will constitute itself as the abnormal, then it must first solidify an already sedimentary conception of absolute normality. It finds itself increasingly caught in the entrapment of dialectics—the extraordinary needing the ordinary, the supernatural needing the natural—setting a dependency that stifles the being-nonbeing divide rather than disencumbering it. In the hyperneurotic obsession with its own departure from the social world, the occult must always hearken back to attesting how it deviates from that world, and, in the process, it establishes the social as the centralized referent against which it defines its every move, bestowing on it an almost magnetic ability to pull things back into itself. The occult, therefore, in no way disbands the positivist infatuation with the circumscription of pure boundaries, nor with the demarcation of what is real, but in fact tacitly condones it through transgression. By existing at the limit, it produces the limit; by pushing social understanding to the so-called periphery, it verifies a point of conceptual origin from which existence must presumably begin and to which it must always compare itself. By claiming to oppose the calculus of representation, it takes the latter at its own word, giving it a foundational credence it has not earned and legitimating its unchallenged reign. This is why it is stressed here that a becoming-against-the-world can only come to fruition once it has already established itself as a becoming-outside-the-world, crystallizing its sovereignty at the edge of annihilation. The occult, on the other hand, presumes to go against, while not yet beyond; as a result, it is caught in its own inadequacy, unifying rather than sabotaging. This reveals that metaphysics and the occult are not so different after all but comprise two sides of the same hegemony. Both carve out their own space of the sacred, if even a diabolical sacred; both are inventions that dispel the absurdism of mortality by providing a delusion of depth, a pseudosomething underlying the surface, in order to neutralize the incarnations of the chaotic. Both provide the real with its rationale by contesting it; both promote the communal dormancy, obedience, and experiential stagnation of man. Like all narratives of resistance, such liminal spheres are conspirators in the authentication of the real's totality, straying no further than the outer bolts of the cell.

And yet the occult is a necessary stage in the disorienting climb toward annihilative consciousness—the last checkpoint along the way in subjectivity's strife with its being-in-the-world and the watchtower before the borderlands. It is undeniable, that there lies a congruity between the coagulation of a becoming-outside-the-real and the discharge of an occultish experience, for again, the latter—as the self-asserted limit of reality, its inverted mirroring—must be tread over in order for there to be a traversal of reality itself. This is why Hedayat, in his violence against subjectivity's crosscurrents, goes through a crucial period of haunting, drawn under by a torrent of nightmarish images:

> Last night I could not get to sleep . . . Disconnected thoughts and disturbing scenes passed scenes passed in front of my eyes . . . It was a nightmare—I was neither awake nor asleep, but I saw these things . . . I saw a package of paper open itself in the air. Sheet after sheet peeled itself off. A group of soldiers passed by, but I couldn't see their faces. It was a dark, worrying, spine-chilling night, full of terrible, angry forms . . . a circle of fire like an enormous whirling Catherine wheel, a corpse floating in the river, eyes watching me from all sides . . . An old man with a bloody face was tied to a pillar. He was looking at me laughing; his teeth flashed. A bat with cold wings flew into my face. I was walking along a dark rope. Under it lay a whirlpool . . . A hand placed itself on my shoulder, a freezing cold hand squeezed my throat. My heart seemed to stop beating. Moanings, strange and evil, rose from the depths of the nocturnal darkness, faces, one side of them blank and in shadow, kept appearing and disappearing.[35]

In consideration of this selection, one exemplifying an occultish interlace, it is astounding to track how nearly every hallucination he sketches can be construed as emblematic of an unfeeling clash with the symbolic order of the real. The hidden gaze of power is embodied by the faceless soldiers and the eyes watching from all sides—the old man's laugh its mode of regulation and judgment, the hand on his throat the obvious coercion of consciousness via the threat of death's indeterminacy. Against these ghastly forms, however, are emblems of potential liberation: the corpse floating in the river is the fatality of his old identity, the one he has willed to a dismissal, braced then by the stopping of his heart, for the being-in-the-world must shut down before arriving at the hyperontological (yet soon to be supraontological) plane of a becoming-outside-the-world. Finally, the description of a rope crossing is reminiscent of a slanted movement between annihilation and the chaotic unreal.

To reiterate, the occult lies at the second banks of reality's matrix, and it is only after having been stranded at the rim of this vortex that the leap into the annihilative chasm becomes a possibility, and with it, the frenetic spiral into the chaotic imaginary. Nevertheless, it warrants stating once more that the annihilative subject cannot remain at the register of the occult but must make a passage beyond it (the countermiraculous). Aside from the dialectical endangerment previously noted, there is a further defect associated with occultism in that it debilitates thought by clouding the lines between the conditional and the unconditional.[36] This being said, if subjectivity were to stay within the terrain of the occult, then it would degenerate into an ontological hiding place—a hollow refuge in the darkness quarantined from the pain of finality that in fact is only another recess of reality's self-replicating device. And this is its downfall, for though it is true that the occult resides just before the outskirts of the world, it is nonetheless a part of it, whereas annihilation must rest on the other side of its sealed doors. Annihilation is a phantasmagoric article without surrealist layers, disengaged from all fixations with "what is not," commissioning an unsolvable thought that turns fear into horror and horror into an unspeakable ecstatic vice.

The Instinct Uncaged: Impulse to Ruin

The instinct is an undecided transaction: sacrifice without the sacred, acceleration without paradigm, desire without anticipation, rampage without goal (in the service of annihilation). This is by no means to be mistaken for the hyperbolic attestations of free will or pure intentionality since it is a ravenous craving that forces subjectivity into the throes of struggle with past (what it was) and present (what it is but can be no more) for the sake of unearthing a space for the recklessness of chaotic antifuturity (what it could be once it no longer "is," though annihilating itself before assuming a state of being). What needs to be made clear, however, is that this incident is not geared toward a restitution but rather calls for the unanticipated creation of instinct out of the absence that pervades subjectivity's false origins. The instinct does not exist prior to the myth of subjectivity or even coterminous with its inauguration but rather arises only in that instant when consciousness somehow decides to break from the legacy of its incarceration in the real, orienting itself toward annihilation via a relinquishing of its own lineage. Thus the instinct is an unfounded thing—a tension of the inexistent, a force of exile, forgetting, and rage. It is neither recovered nor discovered but actively innovated as a countervailance to the cramped stratifications of the "historical"—the antidote to the enslaved "soul"—but only once the former has already perpetrated its misdeed (the rough erasure).

In this sense, the conceptual introduction of the instinct obliges one to forge a new viewpoint with regard to its function, one that in fact disclaims all functionality and that therein might overturn its traditional conflation with the "I" by revealing their heated oppositionality amid the vulturish event of annihilation. But beforehand, in recounting what has led philosophical study to its deflated point—now overrun with the defeatism of the death of the subject—we recognize this blank interval as the requisite manifestation of a certain ethical impasse. The axes of meaning, power, and order had joined to condemn subjectivity to a self-perpetuating bleakness—the seamlessness of the real—thus leaving it with no way out but to elevate itself to the level of truth, for if existence was to be a cemetery, then it would turn inward, finding a sanctum in itself. Yet when this interiority became more than just a flight response, when the self ceased its status as an escape from the profanity of the world and steadily took on a totalitarian property beyond all expectation, when man not only took himself as the measure of all things but then tried to make the everything fall in line with his command, philosophy rushed to the forefront to unmake what it had become, burning down its own edifice. In the wake of a self that would ascend to supremacy upon the carcass of the other, exporting its lust for conquest via the alleyways of the subject-object hierarchy, the proclamation of a death may have seemed the only right thing. But in time, this denial has left the still lingering vestiges of consciousness with nowhere to roam—sedentary, comatose, curbing both thought and action, turning reflection and experience into a whisper, making one scared to take a stand, to say anything for fear that every utterance may be a violation in itself. To save itself from being implicated in the gruesome obscenity of "modernity," thought has slipped into the existential numbness of postmodernity, intentionality rightfully dismissed but now left stranded between the unjust monumentalism of sublation and the equally unjust inheritance of an enervated subject who no longer knows who it is and no longer tries to sense it for fear that the very effort will make of it an aberrance of being. But maybe the repose has gone on for too long. The real, for its purpose, would keep one just barely breathing, leaving one in that purgatorial space where the everyday becomes only a vegetative simulacrum of life—and theory, in spite of itself, has followed suit in the ruse, more than ready to relegate itself to a disconsolate resignation to the way things are. Indeed, postmodernity has ushered in a new reign of the nihilistic, and like all forms of nihilism, it must be overcome, but this time in an unforeseen way through the formlessness of the unreal instinct. And so aware of yet shifting eyes from this prior atrophy, recalling yet refusing the exigency of that remission of subjectivity, that ontological emergency that facilitated the reprieve of all talk of an outside, perhaps it is time to bring instinctuality out of absentia—to revive it, to call it back from its caesura and breathe life into it once more; to spell the end of subjectivity all over again (but this time assuring a worthy aftermath).

From the onset of its fabrication, subjectivity exists without access to an instinctive arsenal, helplessly cast to the conditioned whims of a communal charade of the real. Under the auspices of its being-in-the-world, consciousness is taught to crave the constancy hypothesis, dispatching itself always toward the reduction of excitation to a minimum and bringing it into an indefinite form of stasis. This is why Hedayat remembers his past as one of imprisonment, conjuring the simulacrum of a caged animal: "Those who were awake in their cages kept walking back and forth like this, just like this. At that time also I had become like those animals . . . I felt within myself that I was like them. This listless walking about, circling around myself."[37] Caught behind the bars, pacing without aim, the world at large becomes the cage, interring consciousness. But something draws him forward, neither a preceding sensibility nor something springing from the automations of subjectivity, but pulling him beyond the nihilistic admission of his own existential indenture and into the irreconcilable pressurings of an annihilative instinct (a compression before the bursting). The view that resistance be posited as the constant and active production of meaninglessness as an achievement in and of itself, something that treads the limit between complete abdication to nihilism and the resuscitation of restrictive polarities of sense and nonsense, is insufficient in fulfilling the project enlisted here. Instead, the undoing of subjectivity requires an overcoming of both nihilistic resentment and humanist idealism, and the median space in-between, consciousness brought into a state where values forfeit their credibility and meaning itself falls under the sway of transvaluation, giving rise to the seismic experience of the "everything-all-at-once" (immanent annihilation).

It is never so easy, though, for one must suffer immensely before being able to activate this rash, indiscriminate engagement, akin to a ravishment, a raid from within. This is why the creation of the instinct is no graceful appropriation but one that relentlessly harasses subjectivity, contriving cruelty, turning desire against itself, leaving interiority to violate itself over and again.[38] All emergent authors strongly coincide on this point: that one must languish before unspeakable agony in order to locate such an impulse; that the page must be brought to wailing, arousal, and denial; and that it must suffer something of drastic straits and intent on existential decimation. Caught within a brutalizing yet elegant back-and-forth between the ignition of desire and its immediate suppression, flailing between anticipation and abandonment to emptiness, consciousness finds itself gradually wearing down, falling apart piece by piece, unable to keep pace with the quaking of this instinctive demand. An accursed and predatory invitation, simultaneously persuading subjectivity (quickening its operation) while undressing its defenses, the emergent text vindicates the expedition toward annihilation via an all-consuming sentiment of affliction—a "going under"—leaving the "I" exposed before molestations of raptorial nature (self-ejection).

Accordingly, the emergent author goes through a comparable experience in which he at once seizes upon this instinct and then finds that it has eluded him, leaving him arrested between the extremes of ecstasy and torture, and as such, travels with breakneck speed (within the course of two paragraphs) from the dens of existential rapture to those of existential misery. At first he chronicles the following experience: "I became submerged in my thoughts. I chased after them as though I had taken wing and careened through space. I had become light and nimble in a way impossible to describe . . . In this state simple, empty thoughts which come to one take on a fantastic and magical form . . . Space swells. The passing of time is unperceived."[39] If anything, this bears a likeness to that condition of vertigo, which, alongside annihilation's own dual inclination, its concurrent amplification and reduction, brings at once a sensation of falling and also the longing to jump. For immediately following this enchantment comes an acute sense of anguish that corrodes the prior euphoric state and supplants it with the sharpest sense of disintegration: "My senses rolled like waves above my body, but I was conscious of being awake . . . My legs had gone cold and numb, my body motionless . . . An endless grief and sorrow overtook me . . . It was very difficult and painful. I felt cold. For more than half an hour I trembled violently . . . Then came the fever—a burning fever with the sweat pouring off my body. My heart stopped beating. I could not breathe."[40] Forced to endure each brink of the existential spectrum, thrown down from self-mastery to the base, to lowliness, in the unruly trek toward a becoming-outside-the-real, the annihilative subject is left unguarded against the most profound ontological trial: grappling with self-discrimination. This is greatness without the masquerade of invincibility: to be drenched in the most piercing hurt, a slicing inward, yet taken over by an aching for more still. And because thus far he has only been a subject who has rejected the real, tossing himself below into the lairs of nihilistic despair without having clawed his way out—abiding the destructive phase of his metathesis (the slashing against all sanctity) and not yet the creative (the forging of the chaotic unreal)—he is unaware as to why he is plagued by distress and, what is more, cannot ascertain the catalytic source that assails his consciousness from within its own borders. This is its sinking ordeal, a serial wretchedness that appears as the devious plot of some external force: "Some blind and terrible power rides on our heads. There are some people whose fate is governed by an evil star under which they get crushed and want to get crushed."[41] But then one sees a new angle to this fatalism, a more intimate gash whereby "fate may rule, but it is I who have made my fate, and now I can't get away from it. I can't escape from myself."[42] It is no autonomous destiny that has brought this crisis to pass, but something far closer and more powerful in its precision, consigning all thoughts of choice to futility, consigning thought *itself* to futility—a devouring from the inside.

Nor should the mistake be made to conflate this instinct with a kind of asceticism, for it does not make one see—disclosing some instant of spontaneous revelation whereby truth passes illuminated before the eyes—but rather casts one toward blindness and chaotic obscurity. The way in which this is accomplished is through nothing less than an entropy of being, an outcome served best by the exploits of annihilation, itself a decisive overthrow of both the real and the nihilistic drives that have governed subjectivity until this juncture. The annihilative principle will amputate the past from being, abusing it so as to disabuse it of its partitioning from nonbeing, razing the deceit it has inflicted so as to clear the ground for an event that must be carried through by willed fatality alone. This is the intricacy of the second mirror stage, the first bringing a disenfranchisement, the second opening up the possibility for an instinctive ascertainment. Herein lies the significance of Hedayat's unfamiliarity with his own reflection: "I went and stood in front of the picture on the wall and looked at it. I don't know what thoughts were passing through my head, but the picture seemed like a stranger to me. I said to myself, 'What has this man got to do with me?' But I recognized the face. I had seen it a lot."[43] Hence, as one stares into the mirror, subjectivity is splintered once more (to seek what is blown apart). With the being-in-the-world now turned foreigner to a consciousness on the verge of its becoming-outside-the-world, the face envisages its own contortion, presenting itself as unwavering metonymy and giving itself over to a uniquely estranged countenance. One is veiled from oneself—screened, parted, giving way to an incompatible profession, a split decree and impulsive counterenunciation that then abridges itself in the emanation of a chaotic tone. Beyond the totalitarian unity of consciousness, this monologue of conflicting echoes sets its task, now armed to bring fury to a world since depleted.

When this newly generated annihilative consciousness does make its return to the world, this time to take it beneath, it does so amid the burden and adversity integral to the instinct's unstoppable self-testing. This marks the irruption of the annihilative laugh as a force extracted from the exertions of vulnerability, wrought from within trembling, though now a refined avalanche that can use the atrocity of the world to install its own grave repercussion, having borne something far more damaging in its injunctions than the real. It is the expenditure of a consciousness negotiating its way across a rhapsody, commanding without destination, which is why Hedayat cannot conceive a way to describe it but as to say that "from all the pores of my body this pleasant warmth seeped out."[44] The eroticism is unequivocal, the tone winding into a torrid outpouring—a sudden and abrupt escalation—where everything is subordinated to compulsion, to the insatiate rushing of heat. This is why one finds Hedayat bursting into bizarre fits of laughter toward the end of his story, a trend of effusion that will resurface as the herald of the chaotic in *The Blind Owl*, remarking here, "I don't know whether I have bewitched everybody or have become bewitched myself, but one thought is driving me mad and I can't contain my laughter. Every now and then laugher catches at the bottom of my throat."[45] And this laugh, as the elegy of subjectivity, does possess the ability to shake power at its roots, as it is not from the self-indulgent amusement of cynicism and ideology; nor is it a sign of the damned, the co-opted, nor the complicit but rather a recalibration of the disrespecting, the unkind, and the disreputable. There are more scathing laughters still, and annihilation, in its enigmatic diagnosis, graphs the wild palpitations of such a sound, one that nails the impossible into a new sovereignty.[46] It is a connective punishment, strung across the scaffold, that initiates the most provocative tirade against identity, sharing a covenant with hallucination and fantasia to maim the past, undermining the dogmatism of the "I" with an auditory overdose that cannot be owned by structure or words nor held hostage by idioms or referents—a rebellion against meaning altogether. No longer the silent laugh of the philosopher, this sonic annihilation shelters a volcanic upheaval: it is the savage allure of illusion, wracked with dissonance, shrill-pitched, carrying the blaring resonance of its sedition into the future of the now (instantaneous eternity), and vindicating the instinct by resounding its fluctuations as a chaotic return.

Existential Warfare: Becoming-Outside-the-Real, Becoming-Inhuman

One is dealing with what is not even human anymore; too subtle, vast, and apparitional; no longer able to walk in straight lines for all paths have been scorched; no longer delineated by any exteriority termed the real nor any interiority termed the self, now freed to a phantom drive that wants nothing aside from war. Furthermore, the assailment of this becoming-outside-the-real would also stand beyond the narrow judgment of a moral dialect of good and evil, foregoing its rigid dualism and making the heedless voyage toward a fuller deployment of the creative-destructive body. If power is amorphous, shape-shifting, and stabbing from every bend, then the annihilated must withstand it through a consciousness beyond binaries—an impassioned existential hardship beyond ethical orientations, now plunged amid the jarring intimations of chaos. This fight turns everything into the adversary, though never dialectically, yet in fact by overcoming the dialectic through emergent dislocations. If there is to be a lethal synthesis in every historical act, then this vying with the real will culminate in a synthetic wrenching toward the ahistoricality of the chaotic unreal, which then turns back upon the dialectic behind it only to eradicate it and leave behind an uncongealed nonstate. Stated another way, the point is not to steal back from the real the object of its original theft—that is, to recapture being—but rather to defect to the extent that the revoked object grows obsolete—as the loss becomes archaic—and thereby robbing the real of the satisfaction of its initial robbery.

Contemporary thought has, for the most part, elided this strategy, ever in the task of fleeing from what poses the greatest danger, unready to bank on its own ability to survive, which, in the maximum scope, serves as testimony to its continued subordination to these very perils and its continued investment in a discourse of false heroic engagement for which finality still remains unaddressed. And even more so, this somewhat frail regression into a rhetoric of the "trenches" only reinforces the supposed actuality of the "within," its severe fixation with the negotiation of some agency belying its own continued dependency on what has conceived the contract, never asking how these walls around consciousness could be stripped of such entitlement—for to talk of negation is to pay homage to a center already unacknowledged by the inhuman. Thus the compromised theorist spends time ridiculously jumping back and forth across lines drawn in the sand, back and forth like a child at play (though without the innocence), as if transgression and liminality were the exclusive tactical possibilities. Conversely, annihilative consciousness walks across the line without even a split second of pause, for it does not perceive the limits of the real and thus will not waste its time contemplating its own traversal. It does not aspire to transgression but *is* the outside now wrought inward, its pack of infinitesimal incisions. The most uncompromising danger seethes here, not in the artificial crossing of artificial borders but in the forgetting—in the amnesic ability to lose sight of the borders, insurgency no longer a decision or determination but the reflex of a becoming inhuman.

Annihilation, in this formless casting, accepts with fluidity the invitation to leave all things unresolved, fighting thought's potential one-dimensionality and leaving the question mark to cast its wraith-like silhouette upon consciousness. Thus Hedayat, striking against directionality, writes, "I no longer want to forgive, or be forgiven, to go to the left, or to go to the right. I want to close my eyes to the future and forget the past."[47] This sensibility articulates itself in elliptical movements of temptation, combustion, and ransack; it spirals, this war-drunkenness, against the dominion of subjectivity and ontology, against man, and even against life and death. It is a training ground for impiety, and once there—beyond the dueling and yet mutually fortifying constraints of virtue and depravity—there can be no turning back, no slipping back through the trial of instinct, the outpost of the occult, the meaninglessness of the nihilistic, and into the jailhouse of the symbolic order. Whatever has been relinquished along the way is now irrecoverable, showing the irreversibility of the outside; one can no longer be named, no longer be imprinted or cornered, having disarmed meaning through the active conversion of disbelief into anger and war hungering. This is how annihilation instructs one to become content among the wreckage and debris of one's own inhumanity, having shed oneself of the famine of collectivity, and in the process instigating a chaos-consciousness that intuitively seeks ruination; there is no gap—no impasse—between self and world, only a barter of ashes. The emergent figure holds the humanist signs of good and evil under duress, the dichotomy mangled by the fatal convolution of an explosive, undifferentiated episode whereby the becoming-inhuman necessitates a becoming-outside and against-the-world—the trademark of pure combat.

Such terminologies owe nothing to the other (save the end of all things) without responsibility or commitment, justice or vengeance, to mobilize a foreign territory of speculation—one that suppresses and retaliates from the void. The annihilated leaves all tainted, circumventing the empathic and loosening the tribulation, with both coldness and lust, the will to condemnation exclusive to a postuniversal consciousness. For that reason, the emergent author must play his role in the annihilative drama, and the people must play theirs, secured to the violence perpetrated all around, never as victim, with no compensation extended, no redress solicited, but because the instinct has demanded it. Here one acts upon everything but speaks only to oneself, and always the final words—barely audible, self-sufficient, in the esoteric idiom of cruelty, at once ingrained and indifferent toward the injury. To ingest and spit back the logic of penalty: annihilation is thus an unrelenting desire for lesion, a will to scarring beyond the metaphysics of good and evil and beyond the dismal perpetuation of man—a technique of warfare both against itself and against the world. And what trails here? The impetus to slander, endanger, and sting; to draft a missive to the other now grueling to hear; to electrify an animosity intent, a chiasmatic turning beyond alterity, beyond the colonizing iteration of egalitarian mythologies and toward a menacing era of intermissions. Here we are accountable to atrocity alone. Here we seek proximity, but that of a mercenary typology, as thought becomes the duty of a contract killer.

Final Simulation: Annihilation Contra Death

Annihilation transpires within the fading of organs (where physiology wanes, where mind wanes), and in this way, does not set out to conquer death but rather to consummate a life that never was, though happening now, as an inexistent becoming. The law strapped to the shoulders of subjectivity tells it to coil around itself, to recede into its own aridness, taught to drown within the quicksand of the real and thus forego the trespass into the shadowlands. Annihilative consciousness avoids this, though, linking itself to an alternative starvation, and does so through an unbound engagement with finality, counseling with abrasion. It brings the frontier of its own mortality into close view, heeding its call and calling back to it, in turn, the two summoning each other in an exchange of defiant outcries. The annihilated will endure what the world has made intolerable.

Among the most crucial elements of this chaotic motion is the entanglement with impermanence, a vile affirmation that paves the road for annihilation's onset. There is an extensive philosophical tradition that advocates the necessity of a one-on-one showdown with death as the basis of some conglomeration of self-consciousness. One might turn to Hegel's proposition that "the life of Spirit is not that which is frightened of death, and spares itself destruction, but that life which assumes death and lives with it . . . [for] Spirit attains its truth only by finding itself in absolute dismemberment"[48] or to Schopenhauer's claim that "the terrors of death offer considerable resistance; they stand like a sentinel at the gate leading out of this world."[49] One might turn to Kierkegaard's commentary that "the certainty is the unchanging, and the uncertainty is the brief statement: It is possible"[50] or to Freud's warning that "if you would endure life, be prepared for death."[51] One might turn to Bataille's fact that "it is easy to understand that consciousness of death is essentially self-consciousness—but that, reciprocally, consciousness of self required that of death"[52] or to Gadamer's equation "that it is unable to achieve true-being-for-self without overcoming its attachment to life, i.e. without annihilation of itself as mere 'life.'"[53] One might turn to Nancy's statement of a "negation without remainder . . . no self to make sense of it. Pure event. Disaster"[54] or to Žižek's assessment that "there is no solution, no escape from it; the thing to do is not to 'overcome,' to 'abolish' it, but to come to terms with it, to learn to recognize it in its terrifying dimension."[55] Here we will move onward, though, implementing a certain alternative fatal arrangement as the precursor to something else.

This leaves a horrendous counterpart to the dying: across the dual axes of certainty and uncertainty, annihilation spares nothing and pardons nothing, which is actualized in Hedayat's comment that "only people who have washed their hands of life and are fed up with everything can make really great achievements."[56] Such is the junction between exhaustion and invincibility, at once indefinite and plausible, a fine line that will be seen once more in this project (we keep score here). This warns of a despoiled complexity, for the overarching thesis here is that death's complexion is not something to be abolished or internalized but rather supplanted and handed over to the wirings of an unframed annihilative event—one of consent without capitulation, an emergent fatality substituting the codified prototype handed down from centers of phenomenological, psychoanalytic, and metaphysical authority. Under this revamped understanding, the experience of terminality—its dread and its despair—would render a gateway to the overcoming of an entrenched death drive. It is a caustic transpiration that does not flatten or obfuscate the kinship with extinction, one for which there is no longer any recourse to the blindfolds of the real nor to the presupposed immortality of the "I"—for the occlusion has since been removed—but rather transports the experiential topography of death elsewhere. Within this new mapping, the annihilative event, hailing ruination, is itself an aggressive extension toward finality that disassembles death, leaving a mode of incandescence—an intensity that outlasts the end.

Beyond this, annihilation is not invested in the question or mission of authenticity but in fact tranquilizes this quotient through an evolving reformulation: one that undermines temporality by bringing past, present, and future into a discontinuous anatomy. The pedestals of time-space are now slung across indescribable strata—left vague, transfigured, and disfigured—anchored to no utopian horizon, with no redemptive way out, just a petition to mystification (to blaspheme even the ground). For what about a consciousness that wants nothing from life as it is, neither from history's salvation nor from the bankrupt promise of a lost state of being who no longer craves the dues it is supposedly owed—one for whom life can no longer offer it anything it would want? This is the fatigue threshold across which the emergent imagination plays its game, leaving death for an untold substitute: annihilation as a massacre without single objective, the havoc of a cancellation that seeks neither retribution nor revolution to enforce its maniacal becomings but simply undertakes its duties of immolation.

To restate this pivotal position, annihilation is not death but rather the dying that converts death into vitality and into delirium and apocalyptic presence. Accordingly, within the emergent textuality elaborated upon thus far, the confrontation with the prohibitions of death unfolds across four distinct stages, though none of these occur either as linear or prescriptive instances, yet they catch themselves in a convoluted back-and-forth: *the alleviation, the imperative, the rehearsal,* and *the application.* The first concrete step, the alleviation of fear, is embodied by the gradual immunization of subjectivity against its own anxious hold, untying any preordained aversion to what always approaches (the nothingness). Where both the socialized subject and the nihilist fail, annihilative consciousness succeeds, for it feels a rising, incorruptible exertion toward the expiring (not as an absolute state, yet as the portal to a chaotic nonstate). For this reason, annihilation is more farsighted than a radical negativity, and rather navigates the subtle transition seen in the eyes of the one now buried alive, from the contemplation that "perhaps I shall never wake up again" to the more emphatic "other people are afraid of death, I am afraid of my own importunate clinging life."[57] In this instant, horror finds itself replaced not by acquiescence but by recognition and, later, even desire, for it is in this passage that consciousness invigorates, pursues, and even escalates finality toward an irretrievable imperative (the second stage). Thus the narrative undergoes an increasing shift, from accord to urgency, convening the literary act around an endemic annihilation instinct (this is its pedal). From within the bowels of language itself, the emergent author makes a harsh insistence, deploying an integral, unfaltering "must," as in Hedayat's repetition of the phrase "I must go."[58] No longer allowed to inhabit the margins, he charges himself with the burden of throwing consciousness into the middle of the foray, embarking upon a self-mutilating pattern that will undo ontology altogether, wrenching it toward complete disgrace. And still, the imperative preserves obscurity above all else, for here the clarity of the event is thwarted over and again, untouched by explanation, unbending before representation, unvanquished by the regimentation of epistemological matrices and the gradations of judgment they necessarily presume. As annihilation scrapes itself against all taxonomies of the "is," it dethrones those delusions of meaning, logic, and knowledge that deter the expensive illusions sought after here.

Next, there is a disclosure toward the third stage of the rehearsal, for which consciousness must continually replicate the image of imminent annihilation by incarnating its worst thought. This simulation causes perception to leap, occupying that thin drift between annihilation and the annihilated, dying and death, and then caving the interval that separates them. Thus, it has already happened—its effectuation and its aftershock one and the same. All writing here becomes an ominous scene of foreshadowing, signaling a basic display that one knows must happen, each line a reflection of fatal discipline. These rehearsals are often explicit, as in the example of Hedayat's narrator who walks before the mirror in his apartment, contorts the expression of his face, and mimes what he envisions his appearance will look like when they find him lifeless in his room the next day: "I half closed my eyes, opened my mouth a little, and held my head on one side as though I was dead. Then I said to myself: 'Tomorrow morning I shall look just like that.'"[59] Hence, he compresses present and future into a strange posturing of the death countenance, already projecting himself into the anticipated role of a corpse, as some preemptive appeal to the violence that will be enlisted soon enough. This consciousness portrays now what it will enact then and must thereafter reproduce as an eternal continuum, all so that when the time comes, there will be no hesitation, no regret, no second-guessing of himself—this is its own existential training. But there is yet another advantageous element to this occasion—namely that, above all else, Hedayat's earlier statement that "whatever writings and papers I had I destroyed all of it"[60] disproves the inevitability of a dying-for-the-other. For by ridding himself of his journals, "the jottings of a madman," he shows his abiding madness and inhumanity, that is, that the task was not done for them but, in fact, against them (or rather against the enervated world they collectively represent). With no need for them to know, he shows that the other has disappeared from the equation altogether, even in the sense of self-as-other since the text is lost even to himself, extricated from his control. He is no longer even the witness to his own annihilation but an apprentice to its disappearance.

All this leads into a postulate of tracelessness and irrelevance, an impersonal quarter of experience. Nevertheless, the preparation of the rehearsal extends even further, and what is perhaps most remarkable about the ensuing line of Hedayat's story is that it devotes itself to laying a highly methodical groundwork for the moment of application (articulating its pathways until it becomes instinctive). It is a detailed process, as the author describes the exact steps in which he readies the cyanide poison in order to facilitate the eventual downfall: "Twenty grams kills instantly or within two minutes. To keep it from spoiling

I had wrapped it up in a piece of silver foil, covered it with a layer of wax, put in a glass jar, and shut the lid firmly."[61] What is extraordinary here is that he lists these arrangements with a steadied tone, almost reflexively, drained of any concern whatsoever and, what is more, carries out these sequential acts with an industrious attention to the minutiae of its effects. It seems calculated, deliberate, well thought-out and orchestrated with startling precision, and fundamentally wakeful of what will happen as an outcome, for there is no subjectivity at stake any longer, only a sharpened chaotic instinct. It is not at all a suicidal temperament, itself the hostile symptom of a being-in-the-world, since the emergent author has thoroughly acquitted itself of such melancholic drops. One must discriminate an antipsychology: this is no distortion or displacement of trauma but rather the supreme eradication of all repressive models, as the annihilative modality administers its dominance over the ego (this excavation knows no surface-depth). A new architectonics of desiccation rises before consciousness as it awaits an almost inconceivable proposal, searching toward an event irreducible to either accident or control (this is a new fanaticism). For through the stage of application, which is far more than some offhand reading through the lines, subjectivity has perished already, has seen itself evaporate into nothingness up close, and has conceived of it in the nearest standing as a forerunner of chaotic experience. Death might be impossible, as some have said, but annihilation is all too possible, for the incomprehensible work of annihilation materializes what death denies: a tactile alertness of fatality without detention by mastery or passivity (instead, a third strategy), such that Hedayat attests that he must be "counted among the dead already."[62] And of course this untimely immediacy with the end is fully earned, having been attained long before the affair itself comes to pass, generated by a will that is neither haphazard nor causal, leading Hedayat to declare that "you can't just die for the asking."[63] This is why, by the time annihilation comes, though the world will be cleft in half by it, the act is almost a formality to the one who wastes away (what is this composure?). From here on, his vanishing belongs to him alone; they cannot take it from him, though they will try, and he will go to awful lengths to prove it.

Annihilation elucidates something: the unconstrained induction of an outsider existence, an experience of ultimate exilic presence (to be given over to what is neither here nor there). If the concern of "why" is not yet satisfied—why consciousness must undertake annihilation, or why it constitutes something far richer than the category of death—then one must first confront this figure's disinterest with the importance of a motive (here, there is only the doing, the wonderment of action). There is another answer though: annihilation emits a counterintuitive demonstration of life force closer to the notion of monstrous vitalism or of the undead—not to that life that could have been (though not allowed to be) yet to that inexistent thread that thrives outside and against being and is therefore willed in each moment through the ceremonies of annihilative experience. Herein lies the strength of the emergent text: to become an encoding for the chaotic imagination, ever raking the columns of the real—the one for which the author ultimately gives itself as an offering. And this is what such writers imply when they tell of an undying loyalty through death: that in their self-squandering, they have sworn an oath to a certain now, an immediate potentiality of life represented in their own drowning, one that they will not lower themselves to break even at the maximal cost. They will give more than the others and they will keep their word better, always to the forsaken, to the accumulation of a reckoning with no impending world (only a carving).

Execution: Becoming-against-the-World

There are those who eye the gallows in unique anticipation (the quickening). The matter of annihilation evokes that most rare constellation: insurgency without the hazard of dialectics, action without the foul rasp of ideology, an outside without transgression, excess without a subsequent haunting, entrusted to no cause yet still capable of the ultimate flooding. One can inspect the description of the execution scene in "Buried Alive," reminiscent of a nonatrophic climax in which the spectacle shows itself as an adamant unreality and sustains itself therein: "No I am neither living nor asleep. I don't like anything. I don't hate anything. I've gotten to know death, I've gotten really used to his company . . . I don't envy the dead anymore. I must be considered belonging to their world. I am with them. I am buried alive."[64] Yet it is crucial to remember that this compacted instant is less about the reconstitution of consciousness, since that has already happened, and more about the decisive fulfillment of the transition from a becoming-outside-the-world to a becoming-against-the-world. Here the other is made to feel implicated in the arrival of a decomposing real, compelled to partake of its ambitious fusion of infinity and desolation. For Hedayat, this occurs with full-blown translucence, turning the text into a staging ground—standing in the middle of the public square to be whipped, amputated, decapitated, and burned before the onlookers, having tempted this advent at every turn. And it is just this horrid physicality of it all—the total desecration of the body, already torched—that is symbolic of something more insidious—a lone neurosis that has crept its way into the mind of the real and is in turn conveyed onto the crowds through the mechanisms of ritual: that they are not certain they can actually kill him. But the grating carnivalesque of the execution only provides annihilative consciousness with an opportunity to play upon that distress, icing up the pain and channeling it elsewhere, orchestrating the battery of the spirit to the favor of the chaotic. The execution is inconclusive; it only seems a last stand, as the ones who carry it out (the readers) distrust their own inquisition—for what if there is even the slightest chance that annihilation does mark a beginning? Some among them know the risk here: that this killing could follow them, visited still by aftershocks that would catapult the soul into such a gruesome revulsion of itself, stalked by the exceptional image of a crime now etched forever on the slender frame of a man suicided—his downcast eyes the reminder of an infraction that will not go away. But this one wagers even more when his blood is shed, since he is anything but a messianic figure, seeking no transcendence, no innocence, no authenticity; his rotations murmur of an accursed identity. What does one make of those eyes of his: not a trace of sorrow but glowing with outlandish delight as if he senses what happens next—the aftermath that the others will never comprehend, until too late—a seer of the emergent that holds them already? No, his longing comes from somewhere else: the desire for an apotheosis beyond metaphysics, sprawling forward from that dim-lit region of annihilation where one can be god-like without deification— toward disproportionate searing.

In the case of Hedayat, there is, at first glance, no tangible public space in which the execution occurs, for presumably he withers in his apartment, enfolded and alone in his demise and writing only a foreboding last line about the aftermath: "These notes were found with a pack of cards in the drawer of his table. He himself had fallen back on the bed. He had forgotten to breathe."[65] But it is not as harmless as it may seem, for the execution as an exterior event has indeed taken place, just without one's knowing it, and not as a sullen wallowing over the wrongs inflicted and incurred, yet as an untempered rage issued forth against those it contacts, drawing it into collusion. This is not constrained to the use of the word "found," which implies that someone has come across his corpse on the bed and is made to confront it, for that is only a microcosm of the larger arena in which the annihilative narrative plays itself out. Rather, the text itself embodies the event of a public execution—one that serves simultaneously as requiem to the world at large and, what is more, one to which we, as readers, bear witness in each thickening second. In the sudden shift from first to third person, one comes to inhabit the finishing site, or rather recognize that one has dwelled there all along, held fast within a text that is more a tomb and torture chamber than anything—watching him expire, doing nothing, becoming something not even worthy of his other, yet condemned nonetheless to the obsidian void alongside him. He will not let one sit by as he is converted into the epitome of a captive, for, though within a small dwelling, our author is never under confinement. No, he is never so defenseless as one would like to think, foregone but able to turn his banishment against the reader. Here the state of emergency marks an excess of the invalid, whereby reality is invited to gnaw at itself, sovereignty loses its grip, the rule of law forfeits its relevance to both authenticity and intelligibility, and the victim becomes a detached concept in the wake of the one who self-annihilates before any bastion of authority can determine whether its killing will be worth anything (and whether it even took place). This is a functional criminal indulgence—one that no reality composition could have prophesized; this chaotic forfeiture deflects classification, remaining outside all significatory jurisdictions (the poor design). And it is amid this leaning of the scales toward annihilation that any discourse of entitlement dissipates; it does not ask whether consciousness has the right to confiscate the entire edifice of the real, as the world finds itself startled and alarmed by an exception that deactivates all rules, ill-equipped to handle what is happening right before it—or not happening—and yet ever beyond its grasp.

Here one becomes an intensity without plateau. But one must press further to perceive what is in actual operation beneath the obvious repercussions of annihilation, which is to say, its ethereal negotiation of nonactuality. Power has always had its death cadres, and with them a homicidal-genocidal lineage, such that the hands of history will never wash themselves clean of the stains. But the event of annihilation is unlike the mass slayings of those nameless souls who fall before the firing squad and fade into the recesses of anonymity. There is something more at work here, something visceral that compels power to invoke its most vicious side in turn, culminating in a spectacle of carnal proportions. A muscular precinct is discovered, one in which a radical morphology of subversion begins to evolve beyond the political, an insurrectionary front that attacks the sphere of power from a realm already far within and outside it. It is the onslaught of defacement at its heightened pulse, a defacement that serves no greater purpose than the administration of an annihilative nodule.[66] Indeed, the emergent author builds a rift into authorial consciousness—half-butcher, half-calligrapher, though both hysterical, and in full nearness to the extravagance of the chaotic imagination; all dimensions are brought to the inner circle of power's depravity, entrapped by a writer who has severed the jugular vein of reality and left one standing with dagger in hand, making one answer, though unheard of to oneself.

Hence, as the annihilated is led to the pyre, the crowds must lash out against him; they must learn to hate him, for cannot allow themselves to admit what they already know—that the flames call to them as well. Still, there are some who cry for him, but they, too, are misled, prompted by a want to outline and delimit the dementia of the blaze. And he smiles back at all of them, for he thrives both off that voyeuristic anger that protests too much and off that sympathy that is itself an insincere self-protection—a collector of curses and tears. Those who shriek their wrath are wrestling with a hate for their own mortality, raving against the loss they, too, must accept, just as those who moan their pity engage in a preemptive depression toward their own oncoming death, while also catering to a self-aggrandizing condescension toward the "victim" (mercy as an imperial sadism). They think they are presiding over a spiritual catastrophe, having no idea that it is actually warfare, an existential war in which they will become casualties over and again. For if the supreme weapon of culture is to make death turn against death, and shrouding it therein, then annihilation impairs this attempt by making it encircle, irradiating its glare. This rogue act of sacrilege encroaches upon their denial, the monadic obliviousness of the public space, yelling its thin secrets into the night air. And after they are told, after having watched being writhe before them in one massive eruption, things can no longer just snap back into place; the murder of one must obtain the lapse of all subjectivity, rousing the lethal conflagration of the "I." Annihilation is that unsheathing of the postsacred sacrifice—the obliteration that cuts itself into the mind, piercing the constancy of the legions, exuding their trauma as its becoming, and leaving, in the meanwhile, a singed imprint that can never be allayed, never deciphered in full (extemporaneous waves).

Yet one must risk greatly in order to engrave this ambiguated occasion into consciousness, hastening a becoming that at this point comes to resemble survival in some remote features and in its most lunatic capacity.[67] This is not the martyr's naïve elegy to self-sacrifice—the sigh amid the impaling—nor is it a crude will to death framing resistance as a suicidal drive. It is not that it knows it cannot beat power at its own game, and so simply chooses to end the diversion, but something far more mercurial. In the armageddon that ensues from this one parodic travesty, being reveals its nefarious origins, yet this time thieved of its bond with essence. Symbols are unslaked, yet as reflections without a real, expressions without a redispensation of truth telling, a range of images and impressions without referent or potential for representation; with this admission, existence turns to annihilative illusion once more. These unreal encryptions inadvertently betray the treachery that has made subjectivity play out its own delusion for so long—too long—all the while inattentive to its harms, for in the textual execution, the author hovers midway between the brazen conceit of power and the callous stupor of the crowds that look on. The immediacy of his scandal shreds the identitarian emblems of the community of believers, showing their emptiness, proliferating a discontent with what they have been told by scattering their myths to the wind. His impiety is a heteronomic slap to the face of metaphysics and man tumbling from the domes of a chaotic vanguard. The agent of an unswerving agonism, he devours the certainty of their customs with the bite of the anarchic, embedding doubt in the texture of social consciousness by placing himself under erasure. Within immersion, amid the unchecked volatility of the fire that engulfs him, the annihilated challenges the presumed immutability of all structures, invalidating all devotion to the determinism of the one.

The one commissioned to perform the specific action—the hangman—is almost extraneous in the development of annihilative consciousness, for one is no longer fooled by the real's ability to disguise itself through diffusion. This is no longer the vague biopolitical relation between the state and the body, for here the executioner is not the one who commits the killing but the manager that stands behind him in the shades, clutching itself against intimations of order as if to a screen, thinking it has won, though not realizing that its adversary is itself an immortal product, a shadow-becoming.[68] The way this concealment is undone is through a cryptic binding together of agents, a terror apparatus integrating all into a dissonant yet singular instrument, joining them in an intercourse of incineration (this is a dire holocaust against thought itself). As the gray of smoke, the onyx of night, and the red of blood and fire blend together in a whirlwind confederation of tones, the experience of textual annihilation brings the geometry of being down upon the readers' shoulders. And yet again, there is a determination here to rob the event of a dialectical treatment, for the execution is a stage on which everyone must play a part, and never a safe one, wound together in a multifarious gathering of "those who will go wrong." Just as this exploration shows how annihilation is not the antithesis of life, never a calculus of negation, so is it never the sphere of something so weak as a synthesis but, rather, an interactive theatricality. It is a tripartite drama, a tragicomedy revolving around the respective roles of power, the annihilated, and the crowds: power kills, the annihilated (as a becoming-outside/against-the-world) defies that death through a new tactic of the dying, and the crowds patrol, repulsed and attracted at the same time. The author aligns himself in nonanalogical relation to those who behold him, remaining at once pervasive and tangential, the experience as a whole inciting an unindividuated convergence. As he burns, his ashes are sent out to the crowds as a hologramic missive, a captivating premonition demanding observance in the now, performatively simulating the process of their own doom and their own cremation (paying for their attendance). His drop into the caverns of nonbeing becomes theirs—his steel coffin their fortune, the martial rhythm of his descent setting the pace for their own enkindling. He makes of himself an example—and they, the heirs of this example—through which the crowds see their own faint subsidence mirrored back to them, internalizing his pangs, suffering with him through the death throes. And yet *he* does not suffer. No, he laughs.

No cries of repentance, no hope for the paradisiac, no upward glance to the heavens—just a single, ungrieving laugh. This is unfathomable to the real, for the impassioned laugh accentuates, punctuates, and inflects that incommunicability that cannot be legislated—giving rise to a postpaleonymic phenomenon that vacates the utterance as all vocabularies are obsolesced by the event. It disallows coercion into a phenomenological frigidity by instilling itself in a type of continuation without susceptibility to subjective memory, and thus it cannot be discursively or institutionally memorialized as an objectivity either, leaving only the irrelevance of translation and the schisms of interpretation. In its refusal of codification, it flips the social on its side, fraying an already rotted fabric. As for the scene in its entirety, its affective power lies not just within the brutal visuality of it all but also in the antipsychic invasion that takes place, as the susurrations of the dying compress claustrophobically around the collective consciousness, grabbing it by the throat, constricting and squeezing the air out of it. Annihilation disturbs the equilibrium by making it harmonic in its dissension, concordantly discordant in multidirectional pathways of violence, the paradox being that the annihilated wills an onslaught against the other in the onslaught against itself, turning the hunter into the hunted. The event is therefore highly localized and omnipresent, acute and enveloping, an infiltration of bad omens and bad tidings. The execution intertwines the persecuted, persecutor, and spectator in an anatomy of cruelty and then circulates the outrage in a sequence of turbulent pulsations, bringing together the general and the particular in a paroxysm of raw energies—gyrating, spasmatic, unsavable. By extension, the episteme dismantles itself in the wake of an alternate universe of sensation—one born in fumes, one that teases and provokes an existential shock totally unreadable, beyond time, space, and knowledge (the imperceptible). And this is where the other becomes a variable again, not out of some innate sense of responsibility or commitment but out of a drastically antagonistic (nonnegational) antiintersubjectivity in which the annihilated fades—not for the other but against the other and, what is more, in order to make the other fade alongside it (the all-target). This is a covert luring, a doubling request to kill and be killed: the annihilated wants them in the dense haze of struggle, without focus, without premise or barriers. And that they would grant him this shows that they had no idea what they were getting into, nor what they were giving up, for this would entice them into a nonsynchronous synergy, one that rivets together those who make it happen, those who let it happen, and the one who hangs in the balance while pouring the elixir of imbalance down their throats.

There are so many emergent narratives for which figures are seen staring off into the distance in the end, thus prompting one to wonder at the target of their looking outward. Of course, the first reaction would be that it is the ascertaining of a certain metaphysical contentment, but in consideration of the speculations advanced here, this would prove intolerable. Instead, this afar stare shows that consciousness, amid the nonabstracted moment of annihilation, in the breathlessness immediacy of that ignition, on its way out, has finally met the gaze of reality, that gaze that typically camouflages itself behind a thousand veils. But no longer, for the annihilated casts its vision beyond the smoke screen of the everyday, extracting power from its safe haven, and looking through its facade. As the enemy's features become detectable once more, the annihilated stands across, beyond, and within it, reciprocating blackness for blackness, watchful, unflinching, a staring match for the ages: chaotic malformation *contra* the real itself (desire enflamed).

Such is the oblation of the last exhale, its glaring intoxication in the trenches of finality's highest and lowest hour, as the shade sets in from all sides. And all the while, man sits and watches the contest of wills, unable to believe what passes before him. The quenching—and then it is over for all involved (endlessly over).

The Annihilative Return: Eternal Threat

This is a persuasive trade of eclipse and resurgence—annihilation as accomplice to an everlasting sentence. If ever there were a way to cheat death, then it may rest here in this particular delivery—this eternal deterioration. Whereas the crowd offers the illusion of immortality, annihilation yields an immortal illusion; in this respect, existence is no longer a one-time affair but a chronic reenvisioning and repetition-compulsion. Such is the paradoxical guise of chaotic inevitability: a disclosure that spans beyond the fragility of being, projecting itself as an enduring nonfuture. Yet it does not escort a repetition of the same, for here annihilative consciousness always recovers itself in altered form, the nonequivalence of formlessness, borne across an arc leading to chaos alone: from the inception of a being-in-the-world (the real) that then became a weak version of a becoming-against-the-world (nihilism), then transfigured into a becoming-outside-the-world (the instinct), then returning as a fiercer version of the becoming-against-the-world (annihilation), and eventually, once on the other side of finality, surfacing as a becoming chaos. In the same sense, the return of the aftermath is somehow divergent from the past, protracting contrariety; it is annihilative consciousness that wills the friction, disallowing the passage of a homogenized impression from one age to the other. It is the prismatic unloading of an imagined, enacted world, circulating myriad stakes, supplanting the timid concession of the "it has been so" for the disjointed valor of the "many things will become so." Undoubtedly, this is no longer the cry of the helpless nihilist who throws clenched fists up at the overdetermined tyranny of the world—filled with resentment, filled with crude fatalism—but rather the elated laugh of willed fatality. This is what can be inferred from the acclamation of a zero-world philosophy: no apathetic consent to what presumably must be, but rather allegiance to a destiny that one has issued forth oneself, written not in the stars but against the stars, chiseled in the coarse continuum of the real by one's own hands (though with no self remaining to account).

Proceeding further, the emergent text becomes even more immoderate in its goals, for it chases after something superior to a haunting. Indeed, to render being slain at the altar of possibility is to ask for more than ghostliness: it is to ask for spectral warfare. Here apparitionality fractures into a cloud of emergent potentials—never as a unitary force of "what has passed" but as an aerial multiplicity of "what never goes away"—animating in different venues, possessing new and manifold war spirits that carry on their own experiential transitions, through their own vaporous arsenals, as bastard legacies of the becoming. The eternal, activated by the annihilative moment, rejuvenates its aggravated mist, reappearing at times, yet against time, in unexpected intervals to enliven an otherwise disenchanted world. Since it stirs in the creases beyond being and nonbeing, this annihilative enterprise can revive itself over and again, shattering the idols of the epoch, exposing their bankruptcy—a reminder of an inhuman vendetta (though with no memory), ravaging an already ravaged world.

For sure, the emergent authors implement what has been theorized here, assuming the price of becoming instantiations of a lived aesthetic, scoring images of the meridian. For Hedayat, there is no better testament to his partaking of this ever-projecting, annihilative energy than in the reference to a scorpion enveloped in a ring of flames, and so choosing to bring its own hyper-circular life to a close with the puncture of a single strike: "A hundred times these thoughts have come into my head. There's nothing new about them. I have heard if they put a circle of fire around a scorpion, it stings itself. Isn't there a ring of fire around me?"[69] One perceives a new volition, then—one of custody over the ring formation, over the sting that must descend, over the striking. Nor will those who watch even avow the "happening" of his termination, warping the records, the likeness of this scare. While death in the streets of the everyday is easy enough to contain, this other annihilation remains labyrinthine, a disaster hovering over the province of the real. It will not lend itself to closure, asserting its force in a nonsphere invulnerable to ontological justification, estranged to thought, disturbing the mind as a ragged finality without end. It subsists beyond actuality, beyond authenticity, but still working its spell; and it is just this that the real fears most. For this reason, power must scamper to erase the memory of such a figure from the archives as soon as the deed is done, after the last stand, but to no avail, for even the next second is already too late—the acrid wound this figure has left on the world cannot be healed. Power will attempt to impose an elision, but it cannot persist, for the scourge has already been put into motion. They cannot deter the contagion from resuscitating itself; they cannot wipe the slate clean of its blood. Annihilation leaves a disorganized silence that can never be drowned out, privileged to forever, replaying itself indefinitely in the mind of man, always once more. This is why it will come back, but each time unlike the last, knifing through in those rare interstices when the world lets down its guard, too sure of its borrowed claims to reality and forever (expert fault). It is then that it arrives once more, a clear intimidation, proving that everything is impermanent, that all is mortal, that, in the end, all must perish—it is simply a question of how and on what terms. The interminable infliction: its chaotic echo lingers on in the wake of annihilation, pounding out the convulsions of a still ascendant threat.

TACTIC 2

Contagion (Chaotic Transmission)

I. Contamination
(collusion, infiltration, the outside)

II. Impurity
(suspicion, imperfection, the fractured)

III. Mutation
(proliferation, alliance, impermanence)

IV. The Unnatural
(violation, state of exception,
state of emergency)

V. Convulsion
(movement, frenzy, oblivion)

VI. Dehumanization
(vulnerability, risk,
the accident)

VII. Seduction
(desire, torment,
immediacy/infinity)

VIII. Excess
(intensity, speed, consumption)

IX. Contagion-Body
(materiality, immersion)
(delirium)

X. Contagion-Time
(inevitability, indeterminacy)
(recurrence)

XI. Contagion-Space
(entrapment,
deterritorialization)
(the cellular)

XII. Secrecy
(covering, imperceptibility, the infinitesimal)

XIII. Sabotage
(affliction, insurgency, endurance)

Here an emergent textuality reassigns itself, shifting its interpretive vista from desertion to contagion. As a salient alternative to the systematic production of discourse, the chaotic imagination proposes its theory of contagion as an epistemic countercurrent, one for which the thinking act itself becomes a contaminant, an afflicted state or deviant stroke. In this respect, the phenomenon of contagion would strategically deprive knowledge of both its totalitarian and essentialist impulses, forcing consciousness itself to undergo a misguided reconfiguration, now an insubordinate space of violation and mutation. The chaotic devotes its concentration to elaborating upon this notion as a particular narrative of sabotage, one that seizes upon the intrinsic violence of knowing, not in order to suppress it but only so as to reanimate its radical potential for initiating new slits of creative cruelty. In contradistinction to the hegemonic traps of the conventional power-knowledge relation, the understanding of knowledge-as-contagion would render all epistemological codes dynamic, multiple, and ultimately formless, that is, as a fever or delirium without constraint or hierarchy and without a centralized truth principle (only a limitless will to expansion and infliction). This possibility, in turn— one through which all impressions are left virulent and amorphous—would mark an extreme breaking point whereby knowledge itself is cast toward the inconsumable (i.e., an irreconcilable collapse of consciousness). A more acute definition of "the inconsumable" is pursued here as well, the vast implications of its theoretical foundation explored via further commentaries on secrecy and deception, so as to demarcate the criterion by which the regime of meaning and reason might descend into infinite convulsion.

Beyond this point, the chaotic endeavors to demonstrate how this conceptual prism of contagion, at once acerbic and transformative, might escape abstraction and become a tactical manifestation. To achieve this, a contaminating consciousness would be one left immanently vulnerable to risk and aberration, a zone of impurity and disorientation whose basic intent would be to restore the dangerous exchange between knowledge and chaos (i.e., the jagged turning point at which knowledge becomes unknowable). Along these lines, each cognitive episode would become an event of unnatural transmission, each text a carrier of the pandemic capacity of language—one that would subvert and metamorphose perception toward asynchronous trajectories, toward fracture and disquiet. In this sense, to modulate our conceptions of institutionalized and instrumentalized knowledge toward the will of permanent contagion would be to reinstantiate thought as an affirmative scourge of the mind, a deleterious challenge to the one-dimensionality of the real—one that is found marring absolutism by freeing thought to the paroxysms of experimentalism and originality, thus disclosing it to its own anarchic toxicity.

And so, once again, this project will trace a myriad of domains innate to the operation of the textual contagion, at once tracking its vulgarity and its sophistication, its indiscriminate transmission in a time unseen, its sudden rhythm, its precision, its aesthetics of relentlessness, its immortality and its undoing, its quickening and its oblivion, and its vampiric induction and exhaustion, all of which together arrange the backdrop for an insatiate, chaotic becoming.

I. Contamination
(Collusion, Infiltration, the Outside)

I had become like a screech-owl, but my cries caught in my throat and I spat them out in the form of clots of blood. Perhaps screech-owls are subject to a disease which makes them think as I think.

—Sadeq Hedayat, *The Blind Owl*

To speak of the contagion is, first and foremost, to wrest existence into unremitting *contamination*, an unstable province for which thoughts continually assemble and disassemble themselves, breaking and bleeding into one another to yield as yet unfamiliar admixtures. Only one occupation matters here: to damage and adulterate, in verminal collections, to become of the diseased. For contamination to occur, however, there must first arise a state of extreme openness, one for which the borders gradually erode—and therein configuring the stage for a polluted interface—an unanticipated entanglement of alien strands. The advent of this contaminated condition takes place either through an episode of *collusion* synthesizing two known elements into an unknown hybrid and foul composite, or through the *infiltration* of a foreign agent, releasing an outside toxin that casts all it touches into disarray and metamorphosis. These tactics signal distinctive axes—those of a maligned sentience—the former based on an almost alchemical process of commingling and fusion, generating new intensities by synchronizing preexistent, though previously distant, archetypes, and the latter based on the origination of a purely extraneous current, turning the entire edifice of thought elsewhere by streaking an outcast thread across its surface. And it is the arrival of this outcast presence, this shade of abrasion, that perhaps allows us to fathom *the outside* of thought itself.

II. Impurity
(Suspicion, Imperfection, the Fractured)

Whoever saw me yesterday saw a wasted, sickly young man. Today he would see a bent old man with white hair, burnt-out eyes . . . I am afraid to look out of the window of my room or to look at myself in the mirror for everywhere I see my own shadow multiplied indefinitely.

—Sadeq Hedayat, *The Blind Owl*

In order to grasp the affirmative consequences of such a conversion of knowledge into contagion, we must first reorient our conception of the knowing-act toward *impurity*, that is, that thought is always already tainted—a defilement, the functionary of a corrupted outlook. And still this indecency, this abandonment of the myth of the pristine and of the spotless, casts the contagion beyond the dialectics of the sacred and the profane, beyond the asphyxiated dualism of law and transgression, instead drawing it toward lower and more hazardous destinies, toward a state of reflexive, all-enveloping *suspicion*. To allude to the suspect is to invite incompletion—to gather the defect, the evisceration of the sacrosanct, the retraction of its engraved boundaries, the overthrow of its absolutism—a fate that belongs to this alone, for the contagion above all else entitles itself to activate a state of *imperfection*. In this sense, desanctification does not constitute a choice of the contaminated mind; rather, it is involuntary defacement and this is the instantaneous paragon of its becoming—to embody the rancid interruption of worlds, to instigate the smear and the side-disjuncture through which existence is left irrevocably stranded in fault (the exact distaste). Hence, we can begin to understand how the genesis of the contagion also renders the formula for a *fractured* world, the totality undone, by leaving all facets intrinsically disconnected and therefore incomplete, each venture relegated to an unfinished and unrealized attempt, without closure or reduction, satiation or synthesis, yet perpetually straying beyond itself in a ritual of desertions and defections.

III. Mutation
(Proliferation, Alliance, Impermanence)

> But when I looked into the mirror a moment ago I did not recognize myself. No, the old 'I' has died and rotted away, but no barrier, no gulf, exists between it and the new one.
>
> —Sadeq Hedayat, *The Blind Owl*

In light of the processes of desecration and imperfection through which the contagion automatically contests a totalitarian definition of existence, itself a requiem of the universal, we can proceed to isolate its overriding intent as one of *mutation*. In contrast to the worn spells of being, the will to mutation asserts itself as an aberrant scheme, one that realigns consciousness toward a volatile and erratic plane—a minefield of deviant possibilities. Against such a variable backdrop—one of diverse trials—things are seen to exist only to be altered and reinvented, dynamically unsettled and transfigured, decodified and commissioned toward redesigned purposes. In this respect, mutation is also a will to *proliferation*, for it consigns knowledge to an at-once smooth and jagged interplay—a rise and fall through which consciousness itself becomes nothing more than a versatile game of collapse and revival, dissolution and regeneration. From this platform, then, we can advance toward a theory of the contagion as a constant wave of *alliance*, multitudes of disturbance, each singular rank splintering into new and undiscovered rows, fulfilling itself only in the wake of an amorphous turn toward some other disparate modality. Thus the contagion maneuvers as a succession of fragmented chains, acausal and alogical interlacings, assemblages in defiance of rationality and essence, relinquishing unity for divergence (where thought is measured by viscosity). Here multiplicity becomes the prism through which knowledge is consigned to *impermanence*, a transitory yet resilient status wherein each strain is compelled to extend itself, shatter, and shapeshift elsewhere toward some alternate contortion, thereby upholding the cycle through which a mutated world thrives and circulates itself.

IV. The Unnatural
(Violation, State of Exception, State of Emergency)

The reason for this incomprehension is that mankind has not yet discovered a cure for this disease.

—Sadeq Hedayat, *The Blind Owl*

From here one perceives the contagion as an experience of *the unnatural*, the ill conceived, the source of a punishing, unslaked experimentalism—one that treads the ridge between lunacy and dread, interest and mutilation. In this sense, the contagion carries within itself a twofold event, possessed of double, entwined dimensions: on the one side, it is the *violation* of "what is," marking a radical erasure of the original regime of being, its irreparable effacement, and yet on the other side, it clears a pathway for a *state of exception* to occasion itself, the dawning of an anomalous breed in the aftermath. This state of exception, in turn, imparts the unnatural by manifesting a single gesture that interminably upsets the balance, wrenching the order of things toward the uneven, a lone challenge that attests to the fact that all discourses can be eluded and punctured, all imprisoning narratives and confining epistemologies unbraced, all meaning formations undermined and refashioned. Thus the state of exception marks the introduction of a rare substance, an apostate hour of consciousness whereby a self-enclosed sequence of thought is faced with the precise variable that evades and supersedes it—an unmediated confrontation with what cannot be owned by its injunctions, incapable of assimilation or integration into the general mechanism. Rather, it menaces the apparatus altogether, overloading the device to the point of malfunction; in doing so, the contagion threatens the collapse of the center not from a peripheral vantage but from an undetectable, unmapped nowhere now working its way inward—it stains the delusion of thought's authenticity with some elite wrong turn, dismembering all remnants of a truth principle and leaving only the exempted to reign in the wake of its decline. This collision between the rule and its inorganic, dislocated exception, however, plunges the experience of the unnatural to even stranger depths, for it is amid the heightened indecision, which then begins to pulsate, that knowledge now enters into the *state of emergency*—a circumstance of sheer irresolution, where untamed sensations of ambiguity and groundlessness give rise to an empire of urgent disputes, an existential dizziness of the most scathing registers.

V. Convulsion
(Movement, Frenzy, Oblivion)

> In spite of fever and giddiness I experienced a peculiar animation and restlessness
> which were stronger than any thought I might have had.
> —Sadeq Hedayat, *The Blind Owl*

The state of emergency, no doubt, elicits a drastic refraction in the security of knowledge, one that turns consciousness itself into a type of *convulsion*. For to view thought as a paroxysmal event—a tremulous vein unstrung from its surrounding world—is to emphasize the correlation between the contagion and *movement*. The contagion, above all else, is a phenomenon of motion, a slithering device that affords consciousness its itinerant possibility; it remains unbound and ever writhing, traversing the walls of its current locatedness, surpassing the normalizing positions of its own historicity so as to bear itself forward as an impetus of passage and wandering. Nevertheless, this turbulent disposition—one that stirs and unravels, that supplants regulation with dissonance and reification with tension—produces the next stage of the convulsion: the onset of *frenzy*. In this particular casting, it refers to a rampant decontextualization of the mind—its gradual insomnia—such that perception becomes a syndrome of the nerves, where things remain as just shaking "things," deprived of representation. Reality now escapes the mimetic imposition and instead surrenders itself to the dominion of an irreconcilable spasm, an uncontrolled seizure that blurs the skin of the real and relays the continuum of thought toward panic and toward the suffusion of an internal riot. And still, it is the affective result of this tripartite coalition of convulsion, movement, and frenzy that proves the most intriguing for our analysis of the textual contagion; that is, that it engenders an indefinite phase of subjective *oblivion*. Here we see the underlying freneticism of a postepistemological event—one that commissions itself toward revolutionary unknowing—that brings alongside itself an ominous descent of subjectivity into trance and forgetting (apotheosis of the obliterated mind). This crucial eradication of the self-reflecting one, this withdrawal of the once-unassailable token of being, shows an alarming line of inquiry—one that tapers, grinds, and tightens the focus.

VI. Dehumanization
(Vulnerability, Risk, the Accident)

My lips were closed, yet I was afraid of my voice . . . I had become like the flies . . . [that] fling themselves recklessly against door and walls until they fall dead around the floor.

—Sadeq Hedayat, *The Blind Owl*

Without fail, the contagion relies upon its unique ability to extract *dehumanization* from the recesses of the human—to bring it into stark contact with the still unearthed power of the thing and thus with the crossroads of extinction. It achieves this primarily by virtue of standing man before his most nightmarish realization—what terrorizes the very skeleton of consciousness—namely, that the objective world, and even more arbitrarily, the arrival of a reckless and base artifact at any given moment, can lay waste to the self-designated supremacy of the human. Despite its protestations of dominance, despite its impostor construction of the subject-object divide and its phantom ethics of agency, the human is reminded that nothing is sovereign or autonomous here, that everything can be overtaken and faded, that things are not as polarized as it maintains, and that there are no binaries; rather, things are inexpressibly close and can draw ever nearer by the second. It is amid this corrosive recognition that being remains completely unguarded—that the once-dominant position occupied by the subject in its own ontological taxonomy now lies defeated and overrun; that the borderlines between self and world, interiority and exteriority, remain incessantly susceptible to invasion and perforation; and that consciousness forfeits its insularity and enjoins a new, excruciating *vulnerability*. Hence, to make consciousness run like a contagion is to make it an inhuman affair, and what is more to subordinate the once-knowing subject to a condition of unspeakable endangerment for which the survival-instinct is irredeemably suspended (*risk*). Herein lies the significance of the death of man—not merely as a declaration or prophetic vision yet as a recurring practice, for it is in the evacuation of the human (and its oppressive archaeologies of naming) that unspoken traces begin to galvanize themselves, tempting existence toward a chaotic temperament. The desolating potential of the contagion rests in its equalizing role—that it levels being entirely, unfolding it across a horizontal rather than vertical axis, never stratifying or compartmentalizing its targets but filtering all through an illicit serum. All are casualties here, for the contagion supplicates the same at every doorstep, and what it does not receive willingly, it takes, impoverishing and dispensing of its own volition, thus isolating the fine shift from dereliction to theft. Most importantly, though, is that this aspect restores existence to disastrous fluctuations, thus leading us here to enlist a conceptual notion of *the accident*—in its catastrophic determinations and summonings—to the forefront of experience.

VII. Seduction
(Desire, Torment, Immediacy/Infinity)

That magnetic mirror drew my entire being toward it with inconceivable force.
—Sadeq Hedayat, *The Blind Owl*

Having outlined this rotation toward vulnerability, risk, and accident, it warrants a brief note to demonstrate how the contagion in fact uncovers a new standard of *seduction* as well—one that holds consciousness hostage in an attraction-repulsion ratio. Any wager is also possessed of a certain magnetism—an allure and captivation that signals the perilous undertaking, the arousal of the sickened—where all knowing becomes a grotesque mesmerism and a gaze toward stigma and wreckage. In this shape, the contagion not only inhabits the stance of a dice throw but also confers consciousness to the most harrowing levels of *desire* by placing existence itself in the scales (to fly away, beyond the crash). Thus the penalties are elevated to incomparable heights, as desire begins to play for mortal stakes, casting the venture into a *tormenting* seduction with chance. It reawakens consciousness to the fact that being has a price and, even more than this, appropriates the fatal circuit in order to rewire the affective matrix of experience: the sheer severity of the thinking act, one that now drifts across the plateaus of its own imminent ruin, enables desire to haze the division between once-binary oppositions. It is amid the outbreak of the contagion, and the extravagance it confers, that one witnesses the intersection of exhilaration and loss, enchantment and horror, and rapture and distress (the jurisdiction of the spine). For this reason, the contagion not only accentuates but also lures knowledge to the ledge of a strained *immediacy* with experience, such that the conventional dualism between mind and sensation, and eventually mind and body, extinguishes itself once and for all. The contagion trails across contradiction, tying and untying a multifarious array of experiential cords—from despair, resignation, indifference, chill, and silence to ecstasy, hysteria, madness, and rage. What arises in its place, then, is a sleek reciprocity, thought and experience embedded in an almost liquid transaction—a limitless commerce that coalesces and frays the pathways of pain and pleasure, creation and destruction (to make unwell). Indeed, the infection works all ways and across all terrain, spiraling toward countless junctures, for the immediacy of the contagion is also its entrance point to a recontrived *infinite*.

VIII. Excess
(Intensity, Speed, Consumption)

I felt that they enabled me to see with my own eyes all the weird shapes, all the comical, horrible, unbelievable which lurked in the recesses of my mind . . . At all events I now knew what possibilities existed within me, I appreciated my own capabilities.

—Sadeq Hedayat, *The Blind Owl*

Trekking onward, it is in light of the contagion's astounding wrath, its innumerable propulsions and muscularity, that one must construe it as a vitalistic procedure—for its intent, though violent and even lethal, sweeps beyond all nihilistic overtones, striving neither for a negation nor absencing of the world but rather for an escalation toward hyperpresence, toward measureless, electrocuted indications of *excess*. It seeks a maximum reaction in every particularity, to incite, flay, and exasperate the encounter. It engages the spectrum of experience toward cataclysmic outpourings, taking each instance to an incendiary degree, even to the threshold of its eruption or combustion. In this regard, the contagion's only code, its only imperative, is that of *intensity*: to thrust experience to the breaking point of its excitation (to vie for its impossibility). Furthermore, its unfailing weapon in attaining and actualizing this technique of intensity is that of *speed*, and also its slowness and its waiting as indispensable components of its speed, for in the selective variations of its velocity, we are able to excavate the cornerstone of the contagion's strength: its inexorability. As something unarrested, beyond deterrence, it accelerates and decelerates in accordance with its own relentless necessity, each application an overture to the rapidity of a compulsive will, and the merciless poetics of its speed in turn illuminating yet a further conceptual realm: that of *consumption*. That the contagion feeds, that it searches after still-unscratched hosts, that it improves its scope in increasingly faster and more ghastly paces, is an obvious feature of its choreography; but that it spreads and devours without judgment, that it uplifts and then drains the utility of each entity it crosses without judgment, brings us to another untold nexus.

IX. Contagion-Body
(Materiality, Immersion, Delirium)

I was dominated by my body, by each atom of my material being, and they shouted aloud their song of victory. Doomed, helpless in this boundless sea, I bowed my head in surrender.

—Sadeq Hedayat, *The Blind Owl*

Building upon this notion, it is critical to return to the issue of *the body* and its inescapable relation to the rise of a textual contagion, for it casts into question the very conflict that has always persisted between abstraction and nonabstraction. Stated otherwise, the contagion is a profoundly *material* event; its athleticism is unmistakable, for it persists by virtue of imposing itself as a palpable, visceral phenomenon, one that is distinctly performative in its willingness to execute and enact its texture at every turn (a thought-becoming-fangs). And still, the contagion is also a deeply abstract event in that it remains incomprehensible; it is all saturating and yet completely illegible; it effectuates itself as a concentrated, tangible endeavor, rendering its incisions in tactile ways, and yet resists being deciphered. Beyond this unreadability of the contagious moment, though, there resides a supermasochistic enterprise—one that imposes unheard pressures upon the grain of consciousness, draped as a talisman of vicious corporeal effusions toward the construction of a body that damns itself, a mind that damns itself, that incurs the full cost of becoming (*immersion*). All the physical outlets preside here, the entire sensual arc evinced in the wake of the contagion's uncompromising rise: trembling, fever, nausea, disorientation, intoxication, expulsion, purging, hallucination, and disintegration. Such is the intimacy of the contagion: to make consciousness concrete once more, to draw it into undefended exposure with agony—with its entrails—even to contemplate its own disappearance into nothingness—into the necrotic void—in the realization that this ailment somehow enhances the mind-body expanse. To be poisoned is not simply to die but also to withstand change, to undergo everything, to inhale everything, and to abide what passes. Such is the careening task of the contagion: to train and exercise feeling to the outer edges of its own laceration toward the inscription of an undesignated hurt, the entrenchment of what has since grown wound-addicted. And this proceeds until the last straits of *delirium*, one that leads into fatigue, for all expenditures must fulfill themselves in an inconclusive tiring, a torching effect derived not from atrophy but from irradiation, overabuse, and overextension.

X. Contagion-Time
(Inevitability, Indeterminacy, Recurrence)

> All the thoughts which are bubbling in my brain at this moment belong to this passing instant and know nothing of hours, minutes, and dates. An incident of yesterday may for me be less significant, less recent, than something that happened a thousand years ago.
>
> —Sadeq Hedayat, *The Blind Owl*

The contagion is an abductor of real *time* that thieves the regimentation of the clock's chronology and instead implicates the meanwhile in the throes of an irretrievable brutality. The contagion involves existence in a convoluted, malevolent temporality—one of kindred metastatic assignments, one that martyrs both past and present and converts the future into a courier of its devastation. This is why the awareness of the contagion always comes too late, past the point of no return, for it enlists a conception of future that extricates temporality from its linear incarcerations and instead projects it into runaway trajectories. Thus it remains amenable to the most remote temporal arrangements, able to steal and condense time to the unbearably short-lived (hastening the sense of its duration) or to attenuate time to the unbearably prolonged (the stretching of a period into an eternity). In the one case, one begs for more time, and, in the other, one simply begs for no more. To achieve this end, the contagion-in-time must skillfully negotiate the paradox of *inevitability* and *indeterminacy*; it must espouse the conviction that "this will happen," while at the same time leaving the particular evocation of "this" suspended and indistinct. And yet it is this vast certainty and uncertainty, this maladjusted imagination—at once transient, episodic, and unavoidable—that ensures the possibility of the contagion's *recurrence*, for it must persist, without question, as a maloccasioned ring. This tide of indeterminate inevitability—as something that must come back, though not necessarily in the same guise or with the same reverberations—commands itself to transpire in incalculable visitations, sealing a deranged circularity. Nor does this culminate in a tyranny of the same, for the return here is not a guarantor of the recurrence of the contagion's form but rather vouches the return of its formlessness; it is a repetition, a maniacal repetition in fact, but only as a resuscitation of the impulse to distortion, never what it used to be, never uttering the same incantation twice.

XI. Contagion-Space
(Entrapment, Deterritorialization, the Cellular)

The world seemed to me like a forlorn, empty house and my heart was filled with trepidation, as though I were now obliged to go barefoot and explore every room in that house. I would pass through room after room.

—Sadeq Hedayat, *The Blind Owl*

Parallel to the stolen time in which this pestilence devises and accomplishes itself, the contagion's sharpened adaptation of *space* proves equally instrumental to its interlocking objectives. As a result, to be watchful of its particular angulations—its intermittent invasions, its floodings, its spreadings—is to recognize the atmospheric contours within which it dwells and propagates itself as a jaw. First among these, however, is its ability to acculturate any spatial outpost into a zone of playful *entrapment*, an aisle of immanently extended snares and triggers, at once an ambush and an architectonics of downfall. And with this, consciousness becomes a crippled dome—half-sanatorium, half-womb—that englobes itself without atonement. Pertaining to this entrapment, the contagion's manipulation of space here relies on a largely phantasmal experience, one that convenes its surrounding reality through elusive organizations of its own unreality, countering actuality with artifice, simulation, and illusory wrackings—an existential version of smoke and mirrors. Moreover, the contagion induces a far-reaching *deterritorialization*, removing the supposed perimeter through which it is contained, and thereby annulling the dichotomy of the center and the margin (to become unquarantined). That it tears and punctures these constraints is not incidental since the contagion charges itself to remain ever oriented toward the meso-outside, always trespassing beyond itself through affixation (to attack other articles)—for as much as we gauge the contagion by its intrusion, its eventual chiseling away at the host's interiority, it is by nature an extrinsic phenomenon; like all sublime sources of evil, it motions outwards (by going through). In this way, the spatiality of the contagion is in fact best depicted as a slick "across," a transitional soil always conducting itself somewhere other than where it stands—an envoy transferred between lapses—and thereby revealing why it proves so adept at agitating rigid notions of territoriality. Finally, beyond even the paradoxical functions, or rather dysfunctions, of entrapment and deterritorialization—an event that at once compresses and liberates the area it circumscribes—resides the image of its *cellularity*. To track the flashes of its cellular outlines is to apprehend its hyperaccess, its proficiency in aggravating and transfiguring spaces from one configuration to another, as if sliding between overlapping chambers: from the prison to the labyrinth, from the alley to the underground, from the dead end to the edge, from the arena to the abyss, and then to the desert. The contagion weaves itself into all spheres, with each of these ennobling flagrantly different passions: the prison, where things cave in toward decadence; the labyrinth, where things chase restively for a way out; the alley, where things hover amid sinister intentions; the underpass, where things haunt the surface from below; the dead end, where things surrender, detained before futility; the edge, where the air thins and the body sways toward the fall; the arena, where things fight desperate for their lives; the abyss, where things cry out for banished redemptions; and the desert, where things roam aimless, victims of the sands. Indeed, all of these spatial intimations abide by the schismatic topography of the contagion, each cell adhering to the lawlessness of its acidic cosmology.

XII. Secrecy
(Covering, Imperceptibility, the Infinitesimal)

A little further away under an archway a strange old man is sitting . . . it seems to me that this man's face has figured in most of my nightmares. What crass, obstinate ideas have grown up, weed-like, inside that shaven greenish skull under its embroidered turban, behind that low forehead?

—Sadeq Hedayat, *The Blind Owl*

Yet another important trait of the contagion, one that holds inestimable repercussions for the construction of knowledge, is its mastery of *secrecy*—that it camouflages and masks itself, preferring to remain hidden and esoteric, self-eclipsing, and yet all encompassing in its influence. This basic *covering*, in turn—one that preserves its obscurity, leaving it anonymous, shrouded, unnamable—while still granting it an immanent range, striking at everything from unpronounced domains, from shadow sites and blind spots, is what lies at the heart of the contagion's capacity to prevail (to swathe all opposition). This is its adulation of *imperceptibility*, as a covert practitioner of stillness and of cloaking, able to navigate between invisibility and exposure, therein resurrecting the occluded vow between thought and criminality. To be exact, the contagion is always a subterranean incident, an underground, insidious misgiving that trades in deceptions and false signs, that preys and stalks in subtlety, following the world closely while itself remaining an unseen, faceless imprint. To know, then, means to know one has been bitten. It is this imperceptibility alone that assures the contagion its near-impenetrable persistence and its faint thickening, for it confers an attribute of *the infinitesimal*, at once enigmatic and slight, as the thought venom transmits its impact in discreet particles and molecularized ignitions, as an unrest borne by minutiae and the ceaseless intrusions of the minor. Herein lies its great intricacy and precision, its microduress and horrendous minimalism, amid the complex foldings of an invidious arsenal. Thus the question poses itself, what would happen were consciousness to advance in infestations and swarms, in the surreptitious, viral procession of arteries?

XIII. Sabotage
(Affliction, Insurgency, Endurance)

I have not the least desire to save my carcass, and in any case it would be quite impossible for me to deny the crime, even supposing that I could remove the bloodstains. But before I fall into their hands I shall swallow a glass from the bottle of [poisoned] wine, my heirloom, which I keep on the top shelf.

—Sadeq Hedayat, *The Blind Owl*

In conclusion, if it is such that the discourses of knowing have consistently forwarded a sanitized image of themselves as enlightening and humanistic, then perhaps one must digress toward the darkened vicinity of a menacing counterpart in order to unveil a strategy of epistemic convalescence, even at the expense of a becoming-inconsumable—in effect, to hand oneself over to *sabotage* (to inject the insoluble rivulet). Nevertheless, to entertain this posture is to open the passage to an epoch of *affliction*, to subvert reality by razing the barriers through which it encases its own will to atrocity, to allow the craft of violence to change hands from coercion to engulfing, and thereby to embark upon a seamless vivisection of existence itself. Consciousness would become traitorous to the known world, each articulation a display of *insurgency* and an inflection of treachery against all things. Thus an age of contagion is an age of betrayal (thought-as-extortion). The contagion betrays even itself; in fact, it can only meet its demise at its own hands, since the antidote to its fury lies in its own vitriol—a second immortality captured from the coatings of its own miasma (pharmaconic trouble). Just as it turns systems upon themselves, making the host body capsize its own constitution, hijacking the operational logic of an entity's own core so as to invert its preservation instinct, so does it similarly submerge its own being, turning upon itself in a sorcery of desiccations.

And still, it is from within this self-annihilating spectacle, amid its half-euphoric, half-warped oscillations, at once shackled and slaughtered, that we might begin to excise a rare immunity (postmedicinal), thus lending us the final virtue to which we ascribe the contagion's ascent: what lies beyond *endurance*.

CHAPTER 3

Second Annihilation
Betrayal, Fracture, and the Poetic Edge

And these ones
having stared into the face of peril
are defenders of fire
the living, marching alongside death
ahead of death
forever living even after having crossed beyond death
and forever hearing the name
with which they existed . . .
They stand face-to-face with the thunder
illuminate the house
and perish.

—Ahmad Shamlu, "Requiem"

In watching this emergent literature closely, one discovers that there are still other sides to venture, other tactics of navigation and infliction that might coalesce into a chaotic imaginary. Thus it reenters the domain of this textual perishing, once again to stage a night raid of being, with new weaponries at hand yet driven by the same recurring desire: to execute a stance beyond the forbidden—to give consciousness over to its own relentless abrasion—to a reckoning at the poetic edge. So now it devises another covert annihilation, one that lashes against the chaining, against the machinations—one that persists as a scar upon the pale body of the real (ever unhealing). Without a messianic stride toward the universal or the redemptive, without the far-reaching delusions of the martyr's yielding to death, without even an echo of salvation afforded, this consciousness inhabits the spirit of concentrated warfare in its most bare form. Here is where it burns, surrender long since having become an impossibility, as a pulsation like no other—one that breathes the cadence, performs the experience of the end, and therein overturns the mythic walls of the real for the transparent phantasms of the unreal.

This chapter attempts to portray a second phase of the annihilative episode as an image of treacherous extremity—a breaking of world—uncovering the conditions under which consciousness could arrive at a sabotaging outlook—one beyond constraint—by reconceptualizing the encounter as "betrayal." By aligning the selected writings of the contemporary poet Ahmad Shamlu with frequent digressions and alternative philosophical renderings, this dimension of the project will bring various articulations into conjunction so as to cultivate a necessary connection between chaotic terminality and the experience of a second annihilation. By drawing focus to such literary and existential innovations, as forerunners of this emergent textuality, a menacing poetics of rage and creation will be brought forward, lending concrete texture to the event of second annihilation and its impending relevance. In this line, the precepts of annihilation yet again converge to incite a transformation beyond the laws of being, enabling a limitless chaotic experience that incorporates the following conceptual planes: solitude, nihilism, instinct, fracturing, transmission (laughter, silence, the scream), catastrophe, the trial, the second mirror stage, and the execution.

Betrayal: The Nihilistic Overture

> Timelessly-spacelessly
> in estrangement
> in an age not yet having fulfilled itself—
> Such was I born amidst the woods of creatures and stone . . .
> My first journey was a return from the hope-eroding visions
> of sand and
> thorn . . .
> I realized there were no tidings
> For a mirage lay in between.
>
> —Ahmad Shamlu, "The Beginning"

Nihilism here is no longer the sensation of man betrayed by the world but rather the world betrayed by an emergent consciousness—an existence forsaken and then the darkening. This circle's standoff plays itself out along the following lines: that they will bring the nothing to life, and that they alone will break the void upon the real by discerning their own alternate composition from the rest, motivated by this one recognition: that though *in* the real, they are not *of* it and never have been.

An emergent voice stands beyond alienation, resistance, and otherness; instead, it represents a sentry of nonrelational becomings, wrongfully entrapped in an improper here and now but retaining its inexplicable separatism, its abjection, staying close to the discomfort of being held in foreign lands. This consciousness must inhabit a cooler posture: to understand its presence in the real as that of an imported fixture, its situation that of a malcontented visitor, not merely to have come from elsewhere but to have been made otherwise, covered in the unpleasure of a basic incompatibility, with no prospect of belonging.

In charting annihilation's return, one must begin at the axis of a cataclysmic loss, for it is at that moment when consciousness first evacuates itself of all it once held sacred, abandoning the delusions to which it had fastened itself so desperately and therein awakening to the new untruth—that a radical break in the continuum of thought appears. It is within this originary rift, thrusting assurances of "what is" into crisis, unveiling the deception of the real in all its grotesque concealment of its own illegitimacy, that the annihilative impulse makes itself visible as an instrument of treason, released into a world that cannot bear its presence. By penetrating into the formative instant of this affair, it becomes apparent as to how this ethos inaugurates itself alongside a sudden vacancy of meaning, yet one arising only out of a strong prior investment in its mirage of possibility and then making the explosive transition into disbelief. Thus what will soon regenerate itself as the experience of the abyss cannot spring from a hollow nihilism, doubt contrived as a shielding against engagement, converting nothingness into an escapist space through which subjectivity ventures to dodge the trappings of the real. Rather, annihilation occurs in the aftermath of what would have first risked fiercely with meaning, having tied itself to the latter with intrepid proximity, having shared an unparalleled intimacy with its customs and only then striving to go beyond and toward infinite illusion. After all, one first learns the tricks of unreality from the real, its own cunning apparitionality rendering a map to be used later.

This emergent class of the nihilistic must pay careful attention to the paces between the recognition that *it never was* and the growing, perilous distance that such awareness brings. It must remain invariably focused upon where it treads for fear of losing balance and of being detected, no manufactured militancy able to supplant the necessary stealth of an outsider consciousness. As such, one registers this departure from the real not as one of triumphant rejection but as a harrowing elusion—an out-of-sight tearing away—turning one's back upon what one once held close in realization that it was always an unsuited, out-of-place exchange. Herein rests the opposition of annihilation to transcendent desire, demanding that consciousness first ascend the twisted staircase of the real to stand upon its most elevated platform, overlooking its elegant schemes, before then summoning the courage to step over, spiraling toward the climes of the chaotic (only to return later as an aberration to the real). The emergent consciousness, therefore, was not born of this apparatus but records its implication as one of enslavement—that it was shackled to reality's metaphysical smokescreen, involved in fraudulent allegiances. Yet this is no victimization path, for though once stationed in the heart of the absolute, subjected to the intoxicating hymns of its truth telling, this one now finds itself prepared to forsake that solace to come out of hiding and lay itself bare before the gathering darkness. It is only after having crawled out from within the trenches of man that the dawning of an emergent singularity can take place and can recall its own long-shielded inhuman capacity, the vanishing of one a gateway into the hyperpresence of the other, and therein actualizing a labored existential crossing. This nihilistic overture, at once an entirely self-contained contest and yet also an archetypal embodiment (of the quitting of being), by wrenching consciousness into direct confrontation with the imperfection and impermanence of existence, heralds the first intersection of thought with annihilation's potential for a world betrayal.

In having amputated its already invalid covenant with being, since forgetting how to kneel, this prechaotic consciousness gradually deletes the personal stake in finality, giving way to a disemboweled antiuniverse. And it is from within this transition toward the disintegration of identity that the architectonics of the real begin to disassemble as well, their structures dissolving into immateriality as perception comes to mistrust itself. Herein Shamlu recounts the tale of his own initial fall from an empyreal faith, knowing that the march toward the abyss persists as a tragedy that must be played out from start to finish, act by act, skipping no lines in the implicit awareness that all shortcuts but deter him from the fatality he is to accept inward (and eventually impose outward with traitorous consequences). Throughout the intricate composition of "The First I Saw in the World," there is an almost tightly wound sequentiality at work, charting the precision with which all ontological convictions disband in the wake of another evolving mood. This displays the poet's own determination to prove that the onset of annihilative consciousness cannot be rushed, nor hastened through expectation, but rather that it be performed with vigilance, training itself to automatic deviation. And so the piece begins with a frail overtone of assurance in life "as it is," showing that he had tread the uneven pathways of the real, convinced that they would lead somewhere, before he dared to stray:

> The first I saw in the world
> I howled in ecstasy:
> It is I, ah
> that ultimate miracle
> upon the small planet of green and water.[1]

Yet with such a declaration behind him, in having approached the meridians of an immaculate belief, casting an awed gaze at his surroundings, he now prepares himself for the drop from purity. His eyes since adjusted, he begins to see through to being's translucent quarters and the uninspired indecency of all so-called illuminations therein, realizing that what he had known before was nothing more than a narcotizing effect, a false elation injected by the real:

> Once I had existed for some time in the world
> I pulsated within myself from wonderment:
> to be the inheritor of that unthinkable insignificance
> which with my eyes and ears I saw and heard.[2]

From here the third verse trails even further, relaying consciousness to a degraded status:

> After a while of looking upon my surroundings
> in disbelief a cry broke from my throat:
> look how terrorizingly the razor rests at my head
> in the grasp of that to which I had tied everlasting faith.[3]

And finally, the fourth stanza concludes this ever-collapsing pattern with the ominous image of a blood-stained axe, reflecting at once the annihilative event and the impending warfare with the real—both requisites of the bleeding chaotic imaginary—relinquishing all ties to the gradations of reprisal:

> And now that I abandon this small place of weakness
> there is within me nothing save a sigh of regret:
> an axe drowning in blood
> upon the pedestal of belief without assurance and
> a blood-covered rivulet streaming down from the heights
>   of faith.[4]

Now altered, this one thieves himself of the anesthetizing comfort that had accompanied such truth hallucinations, conveying himself to a sudden recession of belief in this last stand with being, and therein compelled toward an inhospitable voice, a postlinguistic hiss, which hurls thought into the hypertrophic gulf below (beyond even nonbeing). Though once detained in the entanglements of its web, riveted to the fraud of essence, he has now broken loose from the prison house of the real, refusing to accept a life sentence as consciousness suspends itself in midair like the escaping poetic sigh, fading into absentia, self-exiled into the shaded vicinities of the unknowable.

As despair seeps in from every angle of this nihilistic interlude, identity forsakes itself to the radical decomposition of the "I," detracting from the search inward while simultaneously transferring itself to the discontinuity of a prechaotic drought. Thus in Shamlu's pronouncement that "the distance was teaching no hope,"[5] one negotiates the internalization of an exteriorized nothing and thereby surpasses the prophecy of the world's midnight—that "in the age of the night of the world, the abyss of the world must be experienced and endured."[6] Here the emergent consciousness must not only endure but also become the infliction of this night. Once again, *to become the infliction of this night*, or as Nima asks carefully,

> In such a darkened night
> who would trample unconscious upon these clamoring
> skulls? Who would tear into the silence of this fatal
> night
> wherein at every instant an exile weaves a new spell?[7]

To deliver the attrition event, to give thought over to the free-rein sensation of disarray, linking spheres in a disorienting nonstate—this is to be demanded by the arriving poetic imaginary. Beyond the gravitational pull of judgment, now emitting unfocused strains, each a flood and an indeterminacy, the abyss now reveals itself as a negative simulacrum of what will later manifest as the chaotic edge.

This preliminary phase is not purely self-actualizing, not occurring in a domain of isolation, but rather emanates from an immediate encounter of vulnerability before the real. The nihilistic therefore occasions consciousness to grasp the lack that defined its past, casting a defenseless light upon the dynamics of its entrenchment within the surrounding world. As a crucial digression, though, a third possibility has been elided in the articulation of this conceptual paradigm, one that diametrically contradicts the wrackings of annihilation: namely, a state stranded somewhere between the two poles of submission and elusion, enslavement and escape. In this median position, consciousness would presumably recognize both the inescapability of the nothing and the smothering hold of the real, but while unprepared to regress back into inauthenticity, at the same time would not orient its being-in-the-world toward a chaotic reconfiguration. What would result, instead, is a despicable ceremony of existential self-flagellation—a purgatorial subjectivity left perpetually gnawing at itself, writhing in uncertainty, recoiling from the world, and cannibalizing itself with every breath. A rather grating example of this arrested half-way state discloses itself in the work of Nader Naderpour, Shamlu's poetic nemesis, who ultimately gave in to bemoaning his own immobility—nowhere more evident than in his work entitled "Distorted Mirror":

> Mine is that of an overturned candle
> which from warring with the night is drenched in blood
> from head to foot . . .
> My being is empty of that old fire,
> my blue smoke is scattered in the eye of space,
> my song sleeps in the ashes of old age.[8]

Though a slight transition from the older, undifferentiated world does take place, the poetic imagination cannot advance beyond a pathological wailing, raising disillusionment to the level of orthodoxy, in turn resembling the nihilistic affect that must precede the onset of annihilation but cannot be allowed to survive it.

It is through downfall that an evacuation of the nihilistic strand takes place, confers thought beyond the insidious drive to totality and toward inconstant adulterations of the aesthetic and the technological. It attends to a grand-scale stratagem approximating neither the egomaniacal rampage of later existentialism nor the resignation of a being-in-the-world, but rather charging itself to detonate the ontological debate altogether, becoming an incommensurate force rather than a derivative property. Without definition, and unsusceptible to the temptations of either a dialectical or transcendental position, it stands itself against existence from every front as an apocalyptic collision of intensities without unified purpose, and equally without a centralized self to administer the clash. Since exploded into a suprasubjective site that rejects the terms of being in their entirety, annihilation signs no peace treaty of synthesis with the real, wanting no part of its game, and so attacks it with all the fury it can summon from a place already beyond its fictive origins—from the hyperfictive outside.

This prechaotic nihilism, subsumed within nothing, too unstable for a singular articulation, hands itself to the nonregime of illusion, viewing things across the ceilings of distortion. But how does one initiate a war of illusion contra delusion? To begin with, consciousness must enlist a veering against the world-as-real through a familiarity with its modalities, in particular the imperial violence it enlists against subjectivity through domination over the precept of "what is." From within the brutal open-endedness of the imaginary, it rips the mask from the world, staring into the face of its most obtrusive breach: that it will command devotion by any means necessary, dispersing only sullen, inflexible entrancements. In response to this, the emergent consciousness distinguishes its own characterization of power—one ruled by the impulse to overturn the extant and to issue pathways of dissidence and insatiation. Thus

it tramples, as a posttwilight restlessness, across the trembling and the decadence, materializing obscurity and therein proliferating a host of convoluted
insights. As a strategy of sporadic diversion, it shakes man to the marrow of his
already-vacuous identity, while also serving as an invective against the tyranny
of a chimerical world-historical process, one grounded in the rusted premises of
linearity and rationality but with decimating backlashes nonetheless.

With this same uncompromising intonation, Shamlu does not hesitate in
drawing the conclusion of disenchantment, documenting the real's surrounding barbarism as a "cavern of hope and disappointment . . . all around which
each cliff was silence and submission."[9] And so once more, in the "Anthem of
the Supreme Wish," the poetic figure walks amid the ruins of time, crouch-
ing upon the ground and lifting a handful of dust into the air, letting it pour
back to the earth in an hourglass fashion and shaking at the wrong that calls
itself the real. For the poet, the "substantial world" chokes consciousness in its
unfounded claim to depth, making it lose itself in the ethereality of its black
fog, converting man into a death-bringer, the relinquishment of passion for
which he writes that

> it would not take years to learn
> that each ruin embodies the absence of Man
> for Man's presence lies in resurrection and regeneration
> Like a gash
> a lifelong
> bleeding
> like a gash
> a lifelong
> hurt pulsating
> eyes opening to the earth in a cry
> and in wrath vanishing
> such was the great absence
> such was the tale of desecration.[10]

It is from this nexus, though, after having soaked itself in the evening of nihilistic torment, that annihilation surfaces to sculpt and graph its tremors upon a
world now turned unreal, disallowing the survival of the "I" and therein bid-
ding irresolution to reign.

And now in sight, one observes the tinted frontier of an emergent literature, its frigid, addictive glow, that of the night-as-day and day-as-night (textual
equinox). Such is the upheaval of nihilism as a new functionary of the chaotic,
surmounting the drive to mastery through devastation, facilitating the alliance
of annihilation (as the eviction of ontology) and the unreal (as the eviction

of phenomenology) in one strike. As the experience of the approaching will to misconception coincides with the disappearance of an objective world, the chaotic's attack on actuality leaves behind its ill-born excess, its friction without representation, the severe antagonism of forces without design, as an unclear aesthetic event comes to legislate the hazing of vision. What remains, then, is a poetics of synthetic gravity wherein thought skulks and shields itself, a devious orbit beyond the quiet surveillance of the real, at times torn by a melancholic south wind, at times shivered with existential holes and perishable forms, yet always walking beneath the mantle of imperceptibility.

Toward Solitude: Singularity, the Desert, and the Edge

Overcoming necessitates an unmitigated dissociation from everything, turning cold to the world and therein leaving consciousness in an irreconcilable state, hostage to incommensurability. For it is from this vantage of nonproximity and imagination wrenched away from the trappings of equivalence that a narrative of impending disquiet looms, now set to unnerve the order of things.

There are those who live under bridges; but to announce the fabrication of the real, to strip it of the silken robes in which it cloaks its havoc of the same and show its tattered rags, to speak its untruth with no assurance of a surrogate truth, the prechaotic mind must pay dearly. There is an alertness to this penalty, as the poetic figure proves acceptant of the retribution that will be carried out upon him, heralding his own imminent clash with a world that will not tolerate such insurgency, knowing that they come for him:

> Their eyes affection and hate,
> their teeth
> in a smile of determination
> are the hanging curved daggers of the moon
> in the bandit night.[11]

Still, he will not go away, thriving off his discord with the pseudoconsonance of the real, every word he writes disturbing the fluid transmission of its lie— though itself a lie—and growing stronger for it. In fact, here consciousness is serially approaching an annihilative terrain wherein wounds will bring the sharpest exultation, and the final wound will designate its freedom from the real (and from itself). He therefore writes to the assemblies that gradually set their sights upon his destruction, a wary smile cast upon his face, deriding their intentions that are all too legible to him:

The dagger of this evil would not have cut me
If there had been any trace of virtue in your hearts
Your caress would not carry the stain of my blood
If it was not covered in resentment
If not then why when we kiss does my mouth bleed,
If not then why does your laughter make tears fall from my
    eyes?[12]

He is somehow apprised of the modulations they have in store, sensitive to the plagues that infest the history of being, and now turned against him with vicious capacity. But he will bear it and, what is more, will own the wreckage accomplished against him, facilitating a great theft through the unfailing articulation of his own loss, with the event of annihilation depriving the real of the satisfaction. Throughout the course of such texts, the emergent author reiterates this sentiment of besetting, leaving vague warnings to himself: that the world will not allow for the existence of a rogue imagination, one that it cannot hold, cannot subordinate to its hierarchies of knowledge, and one that will not confess its predetermined influence. It will have its vengeance, of this much he is certain, in one way or another, and all the while calling it justice and so he foreshadows the onslaught over and again. He leaves premonitions strewn across the page, as if to remind the guardians of the real that he has already seen their arrival. In defense of its own impostor status, its pristine front, the real must set its complex techniques of regimentation against the runaway desire of the "I" under annihilation, endeavoring to reintegrate consciousness within the dungeons of its mediocrity (upholding the walls). And yet despite the assaults waged, the derangement of the chaotic begins to wear away at that aura of authenticity through which all edifices of truth console themselves, bringing it crashing down into the nonrevelation that it was never anything to begin with. One must extend beyond, and be hated for it (to be held forever guilty).

The outcome of this offensive by the real, with consciousness under siege from every corner, is a drawing back of oneself outside oneself: the beginning of a will to solitude. Solitude here, then, is not a movement toward interiority, nor even toward pure exteriority, but rather into the compression of the nowhere or edge (outpost of a chaotic imaginary). This extradition is not a sign of weakness, nor even a defensive maneuver, but rather a moment of rigid fortification, for this temporary defection from the real endows consciousness with the necessary time to refine its hunger for the end—there is no solace in that space beyond the company of man, no hint of serenity, no province of the dreamscape, only a merciless preparation for what is to come. An attack persists there—across the isolation, across the entrails—far more scathing than anything the watchmen of the real could devise, one that is unrelenting, wrought from the inside out—by oneself, upon oneself—until all is destitute. Although the chaotic will eventually blur the lines of interiority and exteriority altogether, it first requires an extraction, far from the other and without recourse to self. It must embrace this interim detachment, not under the false auspices of an esoteric knowing, not as an ascetic withdrawal, but as an invaluable element of sedition. This is its ruthless organization—that of a disobedient, inborn musculature transcribing segmentation and panic (the mutiny of the chosen). And it is here, beyond the grasp of subjectivity and intersubjectivity, that the fabric of annihilation will begin to unstitch its animosity so that the "I" may one day return to the world, this time able to fight back, phantom *contra* phantom.

It is through a will to solitude that consciousness comes to address itself to a deserter's fate and with it to the unbound possibility of annihilation, instigating a command to demise and therein accentuating an already explicit transience. With this tactic in place, Shamlu is, time and again, found trekking this solitary tale, winding beyond the narrow, dismal straits of the past to find himself on the outer banks of an unfamiliar shore, often standing at the equator of his own desolation. In a piece titled "Anthem for the One Who Left and the One Who Stayed Behind," he paints the image of an excursion to the sea with his father; having forestalled their connection to the real, they come upon its arid yet labyrinthine sands, inundated by the alienation of a wasteland:

> Upon the low breakwater,
> saturated with the salt of the sea and the blackness of the
>   night,
> we stood once more.
> Submerged . . . with tongues ensnared,
> taking sanctuary in ourselves,
> in fear of ourselves,
> exhausted,
> breathless at those left behind,
> in the salt-lipped darkness of the beach,
> we hearkened to the successive syllables of the waves.[13]

To become "breathless" here is a sign of the exhausted, the one of the most arduous voyage, demanding every last shred of energy, draining life-force with every step toward the farthest. To act as the one with "tongue ensnared" is because words have long since become obsolete conveyors of the becoming, ravaged of their proficiency in predicting or protecting, but even more so because where he now treads there is no one left to whom he might speak, including even the ghost of his father that accompanies him yet resides away and in a nonrelational pose. Moving onward, Shamlu tells of how a forbidding boat then appears from out of the ocean's mist, "gliding along as would a coffin borne upon a thousand hands," and at its helm a solitary rower who wears the reaper's face:

> At this moment my gaze pierced the torn and warped
>   darkness,
> and rested upon his countenance.
> His eye-sockets were vacant of sphere and expression,
> and drops of blood poured from his dark, empty sockets
>   upon his bony cheek,
> and so were the pores and nails of the crow perched upon
>   the shoulder of the sailor.[14]

This overseer is nothing short of a death apotheosis, and so one observes the poetic imagination forging an immediate interplay between the will to solitude, the experience of desertion, and, ultimately, the projection toward annihilation—the beginning and the end lain bare upon the ghoulish coastline. And then, without warning, the narrative is interrupted by the calm injunction of the oarsman—"only one, he who is most tired"—a horrid mandate at the sound of which Shamlu's father falls back, receding from the night, turning inward in a desperate need to find protection:

> And thus was he engaged with himself,
> shrinking,
> shrinking from within,
> a bowel, a bowel immersed within oneself.
> Like a well dug that is dug in one, that one might get into
>   oneself, going in search of oneself
> and it is precisely here that the tragedy begins.
> To enter into oneself, and to wander into the dominion of
>   the dark,
> and joy, alas, alas, alas, is itself another pain in another
>   domain,
> in-between the two poles of idiocy and vulgarity.[15]

But the messenger of the dark repeats the command, and the poet steps forward, beyond the relics of his past, beyond the margins of permanence, beyond the limitations of the known and into a vessel that sits like an open tomb before him, nodding gently toward this fatal embarkation, in certification of the union that they will share time and again, foreshadowing an annihilation that cannot be stopped, that must not be stopped:

> And of the two of us
> it was I who crossed over the agitated waters of the sea,
> not he,
> as an anchorless boat,
> conscious of its own eternal homelessness . . .
> And hence could I feel the weariness of my rage
> burdened upon the lean bones of my fragile shoulders.[16]

And so the emergent body finds itself thrown toward the dying that is solitude, the solitude that is dying, tracking a straight line into the fading infinite, yet for this offering now equipped with an immunity that will serve consciousness well in its ensuing raid upon the real.

To reinforce this occurrence, it is obvious as to how the formulation of the deserter becomes more complicated under the circumstance of physical coercion, such that Shamlu establishes himself as the poetic vanguard of the torture chamber while retaining his posture of disconnect. With material incarceration and disciplinary procedures directed against him with merciless consistency, consciousness here would have to enforce the will to solitude from within its own burial, reconfiguring its orchestration and performance from within the asphyxiating enclosure of an eroded prison cell. In effect, how does one assert distance, betraying existence when one's own body is continually harassed by the real? A particle of this near-impossible answer resides in "The Reward," whereupon Shamlu highlights the dramatic distinction between himself and the rest with whom he shares his immediate space, both the guards and the convict element, noting his own trespasses as discontemporaneous with theirs, a different rank of criminality, writing,

> But I have killed no one upon a dark and stormy night
> But I have not tied a path to that of the usurer
> But I at midnight have not jumped from rooftop to
>   rooftop.[17]

At once beyond the real, while ever held fast within it, consciousness must somehow maneuver beyond the frontiers of its confinement while being encircled by a thousand locks and pressures such that, even as they strike at it, it is never "really there," unbending amid the interrogations, the threats, the brandings that stand as inscriptions upon its flesh. And yet it is present, engaged within its dissimilarity, witnessing at a different register, withstanding the impositions upon it while at the same time refusing concordance, a paradoxical fusion of implication and divestment, a dispossession from within deprivation carried forward by the almost chant-like recurrence of the phrase "But I." He feels it, he senses the torture and endures its pain without dilution, though it does not happen to him; it happens to the stranger he was once supposed to be. Notwithstanding this fierce expression of distance, consciousness not only disjoints itself but also appropriates the damaged state, exploiting the lacerating affects of the persecuted, revoking the binary of the ontological and the physical by striking a simultaneity of the beyond and the within. This provides the tedious duality of mind and body with its highest exception: the image of a scar-torn poet pacing in a cage while also existing outside it, skirting the delicate edges of a will to annihilation that does not transcend yet reconjectures the terms of its reality. Here the once-steady binary of thought and experience diffuses into a single creative and destructive outpouring, now commissioning desire to hasten the arrival of the end, turning even the harshest inflictions of pain into a chaotic ransom.

And so the will to solitude bends itself to a self-banishing principle, a smooth itinerancy for which thought lends itself over to rampant decontextualization. Similarly, annihilation finds itself closely intertwined with a process of ceaseless supraontological motion, constantly on the move, evading dormancy, eluding the one-dimensional positings of both being and nonbeing, partaking of an exilic consciousness. This is the wanderer's victory, for here the inability to remain stationary, turning invariably unstill, finds itself coupled with the experience of seclusion in which the invincibility of the real, the immutability of its presumed oneness, is first challenged, a now restive undertone sealing its preliminary bond with the chaotic. Certainly Shamlu exacts the same inference from his own contact with annihilation—that one assures a becoming-alone through the nomadic rhythm—revealed by the fact that he must leave the side of his patriarch upon the sterile beaches of the real and join the oarsman upon the riotous waves, discharged to roam in agitated strides without destination or course. In this facet, annihilation bears partial similarity to Adorno's own dislike of the systematic, of that semblance of the aggregate that led him to say that "the whole is always the untrue" and that "the best mode of conduct, in the face of all this, still seems to be an uncommitted, suspended one . . . It is a part of morality not to be at home in one's home."[18] Still, the annihilated then takes this gesture toward critical unrest a step further, allowing the uncommitted to become an unending expenditure of its own, subjectivity bringing itself to unrivaled heights just so as to then plunge itself downward once more in an act of euphoric self-slaying. Yet to attain such a strange, hostile affair, wherein the illicit subversion of the world and self-slaughter are wrapped together in one extraordinary moment of violence, requires a consciousness that, as Bataille says, would "never stop taking risks—[for] this is the condition for the intoxication of the heart. Which indeed is a confrontation with the sickening depths in things. To risk is to touch life's limit, go as far as you can, live on the edge of gaping nothingness!"[19] And even Heidegger invokes the terminology of a "venture" that "includes flinging into danger" and halts only amid its release into the Open: "Drawing as so drawn, they fuse with the boundless, the infinite. They do not dissolve into void nothingness, but they redeem themselves into the whole of the Open."[20] Annihilation is the entryway into this "open," though here it forms no totality (it becomes the irreparable, it becomes misrecognition). And yet, the fact that all three continental figures refer to this method as that of a "moral" process remains implausible, as the emergent authors realize that it is altogether unlikely that annihilation makes possible the genesis of a new compound of the ethical, if even an ethics beyond ethics—it follows the standard of lawlessness alone, an honor borne by cruelty.

Once more, this subsidence from the empire of the real does not mark a regression into a transcendent state, for solitude here is in fact constitutive of an all-saturating edge that later envelops the real in aggravated inflections from beyond its mythic contours. The transcendental drive, however, in being met with silence from the skies, fashions its own sanctuary through the channels of hyperindividuation, dismissing all that rests outside its own barriers, though culminating in a slave morality that lacks even the strength to pay the genocidal price of the return. With disdain for itself and the world, hiding from what it discards, it convinces itself of the profundity of its inaction, glorifying the void. Yet whereas the transcendental outlook endows the impassive glance with a mystical suggestion, the annihilative impulse struggles throughout, not guarding itself—but disclosing itself—in iridescence and incomprehensible transparency. In fact, it is the real that perpetrates the recession, spreading its truth allusions so as to negate an engagement with the intrigue of a chaotic imaginary—a constrictive disavowal imparted by idealisms, epistemologies, and dialectics. Such formulaic articulations ward off the more dangerous abstractions of the emergent consciousness, its afflictions and digressions, afraid to push the fragility of these essentialisms into contestation with a self-confessed, improvised unreality. Whereas desertion condones its own self-accomplished fantasia, implementing an allegorical casting, the real decries its primeval impossibility, enveloping itself in reproductions of order. Its mechanistic vices fear the approach of an annihilative age and fear the hands that bring fatality to its doorstep. Moreover, the exclusionary nature of transcendence in fact assists the real by converting subjectivity into a haven—a remote expanse wherein the mind can indulge a vulgar, dejected masochism, disfiguring the experience of the "alone" into a prostrated operation before some delusional essence. Left to a subterranean malaise, the transcendent engraves its own weakness into thought, deforming what was already a deformity, making the self a supplicant of its own alienation—a metaphysical beggar.

Annihilation, though, as a surging through countersubjective routes, prohibits the mutation of consciousness into a metaphysical category, searching out no "way" from within the unfathomed but rather crashing recklessly through its winding back alleys and passages, assuming the status of a dynamic action while inattentive to the questions of consequence and meaning (the incendiary performativity of the outcast). Nor does the eventual return from solitude entail a journey to retaliation, nor even a revisiting of the site of the first thought encroachment, as some frantic reversal toward the inaugural wound of being. No, this siren's call toward the supposed depths of subjectivity fails to enchant the way it had before, now falling on deaf ears amid the rise of annihilative desire, now too far from its echoes, since guided to a point where truth is the sovereign of decay and wherein one must massacre oneself in order to breathe.

Trial by Fire: Inquisitions of the Instinct

Annihilation calls out the inception of the coarsest trial, sharpening the new chaotic imagination gained in desertion. The circuitry of coherence, itself an artificial totality, is therefore left disrupted, centers dissolved into oblivion, as consciousness gradually accepts the test of finality (and therein threatens itself). Nevertheless, the trial does not bring absence; it is excess itself, such that this rending of bonds does not leave a lack in its wake but rather a blood surplus, a supraontological accumulation whereby chaotic possibility begins to exceed the boundaries of its former world. A notorious ultimatum resides here, one of a knowledge-becoming-fire, seared throughout, the limits of being and nonbeing no longer able to contain the impassioned contortions of this emergent consciousness, overflowing into a space where living and dying coincide as indistinct forces, blazing toward the inner circle of annihilation.

Here the articulation of loss palpitates, achieving a certain decline and yet securing an obscure vindication in its entombing, consuming itself only so as to aspire toward an unseen, voluminous presence. It is therein that Shamlu once wrote the following as a chronicle of his own unsubdued existence:

> To be carried forth upon the dark spear,
> like the exposed genesis of a wound.
> To embark upon the unparalleled voyage of possibility
> throughout in chains
> to burn away upon one's flame
> down to the last remaining ember,
> upon the fire of a sanctity

discovered by the slaves
in the dust of the way.[21]

As an indefinite procedure, one of hardships self-scathing, annihilation, above all, features its daring to enter the most unruly territory conceivable—that topography of the chaotic wherein one must yield consciousness to the sting of eternity. And with it, any endeavor to register the intricacies of such an experience dissipates into irrelevance, for it persists beyond language, born into a sphere where words come upon a pathological overturn, and all that can be heard is the self-automating process of a hearing. This is its audition, with thought untied across asymmetrical checkpoints, and thus opposing itself to the internal unity of being (the investigation, the inspection, the case). Rather, the emergent consciousness must sever the wires of that connection, exposing it as a counterfeit accomplice, and in its place extending itself toward the harshest irregularity of the tribunal.

Tracking this same chaotic line of dispute, Shamlu speaks of a battle-worn confederation in "The Banquet," conjuring a parallel imagery of the annihilative trial in his enunciation that

We are neither deceased
cast away upon the distant shelves
nor living
in the chests.
The bloody doorway
and the blood-spattered carpet alone
stand witness that
barefoot
we have walked upon a trail of swords.[22]

In this episode and particularly in the reference to an incandescent spattering, one notes an adjoining of the spheres of becoming and decimation (here characterized by the vision of the bleeding body). And undoubtedly, it is at this crossroads between annihilation and overproduction, riddled with torrential allegories of gushing and effusion, that one brings about an impossible extrication (intemperance, drowning). This is a metamorphosis without limit, as the raw impact of the trial stays the same, maintaining itself as a fanatical, defenseless simultaneity of tarnishing and acquisition. Though Freud's label of "the oceanic" approaches this inquest, as "a sensation of eternity, a feeling as of something limitless, unbounded,"[23] it is Nietzsche who asserts the all-importance of the trial in the following passage: "One has to test oneself to see that one is destined for independence and command—and do it at the right time. One should not dodge one's tests, though they may be the most dangerous game one could play and are tests that are taken in the end before no witness or judge but ourselves."[24] This is how the abyss becomes a vise, leading Bataille to speak of entrance "into a dead end. There all possibilities are exhausted; the 'possible' slips away and the impossible prevails. To face the impossible—exorbitant, indubitable . . . Forgetting of everything."[25] A counterintuitive conclusion dawns: such travails bear consciousness toward a subtle destination, as the merciless thirst to commit sacrilege after sacrilege against oneself—all ontological inferences mutilated—leaves a new coating of power. And so annihilation, as an infatuation with the rough intersections of nothingness and excess, becomes an affirmative position vis-à-vis consciousness—its fresh asset—just as it ventures to rake it of its supremacy.

This median moment in the formation of the annihilative instinct is accompanied by a tragic and ecstatic experience, an affective disparity through which consciousness introduces itself to an unsound continuum—one that dilates between unfair modes of intuition, absorption, and meditation. Thus the emergent movement understands the fascinating necessity of suffering, even to the point of self-eradication, all of the same contention that pain itself must become a generative entity. Even textuality is impacted here, irrevocably turned upon itself, leaving a sordid corrugation of words, of inscrutable ideas and offending expressions. Nowhere does this adjustment of the writing-act attain a more decisive role than in the poetic signals of these contemporary verses, wherein language becomes the handle to a calculated unreason and wherein the author must surpass a mass of self-instilled misfortunes, returning from the recesses where distress becomes reclaimed exhilaration. As Shamlu declares, they are those

> who have withstood the night
> unarmed
> awaiting the daybreak
> and returning with
> a noble virginity
> secured
> from the whore-houses of barter.[26]

And yet it is in this slicing away from the sophisticated tricks of the real that a particular morphology becomes evident and, with it, the new instinct—this assuming that it is not restored, for it never was in the first place, but rather that it comes into being at the precise moment when consciousness elicits its own desecration and comes out smiling from the affair, coaxing further deface-ment. For it is then alone, amid the delirium of ruination, that the profile of existential experience grows misshapen, thrust into an unaccustomed possession—that of a rapturous torment, a tormented rapture, as the energy of its annihilation instinct makes itself known, spanning paradise and agony, all subsumed in that one perfect sway, the undulation of the trial.

Still, the idea of instinct, being that it occupies a leading position in the course of this project, warrants further inquiry: here it is given over to an annihilative shape that might coincide with the idea of "the will" while eluding the trappings of its past constructions, disallowing the totalitarian regression that has plagued the concept throughout the philosophical tradition. For the instinct, as it is articulated within annihilation, partakes of a strange concurrence of control and volatility—its velocity, its razor precision, its immediate trigger—ranging far from the deterioration of the pure mind. This is no longer Heidegger's "command of self-assertive production" that has brought the epoch toward "the single endless winter,"[27] but something closer to Nietzsche's description of "a thought [that] flashes up like lightning, with necessity, unfalteringly formed—I have never had any choice. An ecstasy whose tremendous tension sometimes discharges itself in a flood of tears, while one's steps now involuntarily rush along, now involuntarily lag; a complete being outside of oneself with the distinct consciousness of a multitude of subtle shudders."[28] The instinct here precipitates a negligent response, entirely beyond subjectivity's grasp, for just as the "I" must go beyond the real, so must the instinct go beyond the "I" as one evolves a further innocence. One is therefore never fully in charge of the command, itself an impassioned device—suggestive and erratic, seething somewhere between sovereignty and detention—though this is no inherent power (it is concocted power). The instinct is never commensurate with self-mastery, unavailable to domestication by a subject-object relation, though somehow ordaining the present's transvaluation of itself, as a subversive transfusion. As Deleuze writes, "Destruction becomes active, aggression profoundly linked to affirmation. Critique is destruction as joy, the aggression of the creator. The creator of values cannot be distinguished from a destroyer, from a criminal or from a critic."[29] Assuredly, it is through this criminal coexistence of the destructive and the creative, the tragic and the ecstatic, that one inadvertently unlocks the core of an annihilation instinct: the defeat of the moment in the name of a chaotic surfacing.

The instinct is anathema to the barricades of a neutralized consciousness, just as freedom itself is an abomination here, but rather coils around as an involuntary reflex, the uninvited exertion. At once a reservoir and inculcation, it collaborates with unnoticed detriments, until cementing its own durable enclave; it is what implants itself and pulverizes thought, as an impassable captivation. It is a pendulous volition, this ungoverned conquest, both fast and slow—an erosion practice that entitles itself to sketch the variances of mind (especially at the instant of its undoing). One looks, then, to Shamlu's remark that "from the beginning I felt as if I was being stalked by Satan,"[30] and then elsewhere, he qualifies that

> neither God nor Satan but an idol composed your destiny
> an idol whom others worshipped
> an idol whom the other ones worshipped.[31]

Behind such words, one asks, is the instinct a new idolatry? Is this what Bataille means in his own echoing sentiment that "my destiny was such that IN SPITE OF MYSELF I slowly sketch erosion and ruin. Could I have avoided it? Everything in me wanted it that way"?[32] Here the poetic imagination recognizes the evil of this fatalistic current, though unable to name the entity that impels one against oneself and, by extension, against the real, first ascribing it to the predeterminations of a demonic design but then later to something beyond the known (and beyond oneself): "another idol." The acute formlessness of the instinct, perpetually emergent, claiming no source and therein beyond all phenomenological validity, remains clandestine in its ability to spur one toward the fatal cut, obliging consciousness to act toward annihilation while at the same time evading seizure, always on the verge of breaking back into disarray if one comes too close. And so by embodying the most unpredictable impulse, an insurgent drive even in the hands of what would wield it, it stands as the forerunner of the chaotic. Never in collusion with the real or with power, the annihilation instinct is instead always a will to the power of the unreal, fighting the prevalent and hence forcing consciousness to extinguish its own right to "be" in the service of inauthenticity and nonactuality. It registers the instance when subjectivity first plays host to the priority of its own corrosion, reeling against itself, and all the while substantiating Shamlu's enflamed standard—"I was . . . and I became"[33]—one that circulates an inhuman allocation through clever, rancorous transitions. And so it is at this curvature alone, amid a trial marked by the ellipsis—when consciousness approaches its eleventh hour—that annihilation, chaos, and the instinct are consolidated into a swarm, an accursed triumvirate. But by then it is too late and also too soon.

Fractured Thought: The Second Mirror Stage

Here one confronts the mirror again, the endlessness of a clash from within, until the shattering (no "within" left). Consciousness traverses itself from inside its own blockade, not as a nullification but as a radical dispersal of its singularity, advancing into an almost ritualistic procedure of fragmentation. As a manic procession of forgetting and diffusion, annihilation escalates the stakes of experience to an incinerating extent, igniting all that once held together, exaggerating the "I" to an epic stance before rending it into a chaotic pack. Now dispossessed of any delusion of constancy, this splintering consciousness finds itself dismembered at the apex of the unformed, revolving around the axis of its own infinite fracturing until thought partitions viciously into a stream of adversarial components.

While carving into itself, annihilative consciousness is driven into tension, unbowing before being, though shuddering before the becoming. It is pushed to a place where desertion again becomes inevitable, for if it is to succumb to the everyday procedures of the real, then it must abdicate its reciprocity with the new instinct. But if it wishes to cross the restrictive borders of the "objective world," then a killing must occur. What this latter variable entails, then, is the ceding to a second mirror stage, one in which, as has been traced already, the subjectivity of a being-in-the-world stands face-to-face with the option of its becoming-outside-the-world, and then recongregating as a nondialectical, warlike becoming-against-the-world that will result in the overtaking of the real. Now the first mirror stage, as it is codified within psychoanalytic theory, claims that the original constitution of subjectivity necessitates an act of violent fragmentation, the crystallization of a lack, one through which it begins to perceive itself within the context of a world (and yet somehow kept apart from it). This in turn facilitates an alienation from the real and, with it, an assimilation into the repressive operation of a symbolic order, trading unity for prohibition (irrevocable self-separation). Nevertheless, if that now estranged compartment of the self is to resurface, as an attempt to regain the experience of "the Real," then it can do so only as an instrument of the death wish, appearing as a malformed double whose monstrosity must always decide itself in an inversion of ego preservation. Yet the event of annihilation cancels this premise, for the Freudian conjecture that "having been an assurance of immortality, it [the double] becomes the uncanny harbinger of death"[34] loses its place to another immortality wrought through the annihilation of the mirror. This reversal is clear in the writings of the emergent author, one whose accentuation of the force of supraontological doubling is not simply upheld as an aesthetic strategy but also as an existential imperative, one that unhinges psychoanalysis through misconstrued morphologies of convulsion, terror, and density. In studying such rotations more closely, one comes upon the realization that this is anything but a collapse into a dejected death wish, since it does not arise from some drastic attempt to reinscribe the original world of the Real, but rather generates a self-devouring existential condition whereby the authorial imagination forfeits itself to the synergy of an eruptive unreality. This is no resurrection of consciousness in pure and cohesive form, no hegemony of the knowing subject, but an eradication of the last traces of identity and the unconscious—the interlacing with the mirror provides a more hazardous exploration of the fatal potential, turning oblivion toward sensual contortions. In strong pursuit of this counterlegacy, Shamlu salvages the project of the double and harnesses it toward a suffocating, gaunt, and yet emancipatory conclusion that "the one whose hand would visit destruction against me is myself!"[35] Subjectivity withering from within, met by a vanquishing at the hands of none other than itself, all of this a preface for the advent of its multiplicity, to become the clans, vehicles of a rising chaos-consciousness.

The way this multitude is won is through the ragged disintoxication of a second mirror stage. The psychoanalytic schematic does not anticipate this possibility: a doubling in which there is no intention of recovery, no expedition to the zero degree of subjectivity, not even a whisper of the primordial, but still one that can elicit a surpassing of the subject-object divide, leaving a totally unrelated creature in its wake. But Shamlu can fathom it and, even more, will perform it in his own indulgence of the replica, handed over to the predatory throes of a self-interrogation. To accomplish this, one must first situate a poetic hatred against memory, against all archives of that manufactured subjectivity of the real, all remnants of what could not divulge existence to illusion. Consciousness must loathe all traces, even that of the witness (manifest in itself), ascribing to the perception that "he is most intolerant of himself" and that he

> goes to bed
> as do the vagrant prostitutes revolted at their own bodies,
> feeling ourselves damned and ravished by sorrow.[36]

Self-maiming, inciting riots against the presumed consistency of being, the "I" begins to disingrain itself from its past, now released into a self-brutalizing schism, challenging that part of itself that was never its own to begin with, inviting it to a contest of terrorizing proportions—a vortex of threat and masochistic excitation:

> I am Morning,
> Wounded ultimately
> From having risen to wage war with myself,
> as there are no wars more exhausting than this.
> For before you stirrup your war-horse
> you know
> that the immense shadow of the vulture with its spread-out
>   wings
> has enveloped the battlefield.
> And fate has buried you as a blood-stained melted thing.

And there is no way out
from defeat and death.[37]

In rebellion against its visors, subjectivity stares across the unraveling of what once presumed to be—an overhaul now endemic, with quickened strides—bent toward fragmentation. Yet as the verse tells, there is no way out, for this disintegrated path is the only way to where the will to annihilation must take him, even to the frontiers of a maximum pain, such that he continues on later pages:

It is the time when I spit out the entirety of my hatred in
    an endless uproar
I am the first and last Morning
I am Abel standing on the platform of contempt
I am the honor of the universe, having lashed myself
Such that the black fire of my agony
leaves Hell, in its poverty, shamed.[38]

Here the ordeal hits its most electrifying point, for amid this bisection there occurs both a showdown and a forewarning of what comes soon outside of the abyss, back in the heart of the real, once consciousness reconvenes itself against an already dismantled world. It is in this instant of division alone that the becoming-outside-the-world wrestles with a new horizon—the hardened prospect of its becoming-against-itself, a conflict weighing with exacting urgency—and therefore leading Shamlu to say of himself that

never did one so devastatingly rise up
to slay oneself
as I conducted the act of living.[39]

The physicality of this invasion is then accompanied by a rhetorical offensive in which the poetic consciousness, under the pen name "Morning," outlasts an avalanche of indictments at its own hands, refracting the self into diverging roles—one fragment as prosecutor, the other as judge, the third as an accused, and the text itself as executioner—beginning with the following pronouncement and reply:

I find against you, Morning
that in every gathering you sat alone!
I sat alone?
No
For I sat only disconnected from I and we.[40]

The notion of the trial becomes literal, or rather existence itself now turns perversely emblematic, as the poet comes before the hallucinatory court of his interiority, itself now the outside where space goes nowhere, standing across the shards of identity and giving an account of the next prosecution:

> I find against you, Morning
> that you sat in such ruin!
> Ruin?
> I sat in ruin?
> Yes,
> And with an outlook of hope gazed at my own victory . . .
>   [but] my sky
> yes
> with harsh shortsightedness was captured.[41]

As a keen fixation, one circling purposefully around an already decentered "I," this uneven monologue does not actually seek testimony but rather the purging of testimony through an excruciating carnivalesque of the forgotten. With no acquittal, and no pretense to innocence, this expedition drenches the scales of being in the dementia of a supraontological inquisition—until consciousness exhausts itself, shedding enslavement through adversity, tiring out of its own indefensibility. Beyond the suspect magnetism of the real through which consciousness grows addicted, indebted to its own self-negating encapsulation, there is a definitive breach where no side is left standing, thereby clearing an expanse for the chaotic imaginary. Hence, one can interpret the emergent authors as cautiously rescinding protection over their own subjectivity, waiving the drive for self-preservation and instead delivering themselves over to a compulsive violation, grasping toward fatality until annihilative desire alone courses through their veins, so as to make of themselves a more savage weapon: a true blade against the world. While he repeats this transfer over and again throughout his work, Shamlu might be said to dispense the most obvious martial shock in his "Anthem to the Man Who Killed Himself," writing,

> I gave him no water
> I said no prayer,
> I plunged a dagger into his throat
> And in a long gasp
> I killed him
> He had my name
> And no one was as close to me
> He made me a stranger to you
> He died

died
died
and now . . .
This is I.[42]

And yet this "I" is no subject, no human, no being: it is the broken one who now looks to break existence.

Whereas the first mirror stage ripped subjectivity apart so as to render it frail, exposed before the constraints of a symbolic order, the second mirror stage allows for a different momentum to proceed from the scattered ashes of annihilation. This version will not bring the "I" back, for that is impossible, nor above, for that is an offbeat hymn of the ascetic ideal, but will bring it outward and against, wrested toward that unstable terrain of the chaotic wherein events bear dreadful progeny. That way, when these slivers of chaotic force reenter the domain of the real, they will not suffer from that prior vulnerability (unified interiority) but will integrate their aggression intact, endowed with a foreign immortalization. The fragile thing that it used to exploit—that pathology of the victim it both assembled and injured—is since gone, put out of its misery, and in its place now stands a soulless, tribal intensity, one that has learned to strike as a collection of particles and in hordes, one that carries the acrid taste for illusory war. This is where all emergent authors join the storm, crafting effective delineations of an inhuman facade that is not somehow dialectically occupied with the real and also the most proficient in discerning the inevitability of a second mirror stage, foretelling its approach with distinctive theoretical complexity. There are no testaments here, only tortured maxims—axial fractures that set the elements of consciousness against one another, giving way to countless textual scenes wherein being must watch itself dive under, leaving body and soul scorched. Although, afterward, these figures will gradually call for something beyond such polarities—striving for an undifferentiated nonstate that marks the conquest of dualism—here they must facilitate a rabid disconcertion of consciousness by sectioning it into dissonant compositions as a preemptive orientation toward chaotic infinity. Amid suspicions of an infernal influence, these chaotic literatures are riddled with self-targeting distrust, as if some unanticipated turmoil lingers in each sentence and as if each line carries within itself another more unsightly likeness. As an event that punctures the continuity of the "I"—the one becoming many, the human becoming inhuman, molecularizing it from the vantage of chronic altercation—the serrated nature of the second mirror stage initiates its disruptive exchange. And still later in the chase, this imperative for the shaving apart of consciousness reinvigorates itself, though now through a repetitive confrontation with the shadow-becoming, a silhouette of the forthcoming, the exalted imminent, and therein a spectral reminder of the need to forget the real. Though one writes at horrendous, desperate pace, the emergent consciousness cannot seem to shake its blindfold, cannot outrun this jagged figment—one that strains and abuses the relics of being, one that clouds existence with tentative dematerializations, one that unshoulders experience to cellularity, to aerial strife.

Nor is there completion, for with every step back in the real, the fracturing must be enacted over and again, demanding an unrelenting, self-combative stance that would prevent the "I" from reestablishing its orthodoxy. Across such a zone of cracked forms, consciousness itself drawn into crevices, the real forfeits its most understated technique of subjugation (division), no longer able to cleave what has already taken itself to the rim of the mirror's wrath, and ruptured therein. Its vengeance would only restore the chaotic to its own rhythm—gaping, unbraced—for one cannot kill what already stands beyond death itself; one cannot cut what is nothing more than an infinite array of incisions.

Emergent Poetics: The Scream, the Laugh

What is the poetic imaginary that can encompass an annihilative drive and that can speak to the nowhere provinces where consciousness resurfaces from the underside of its self-reflexive battling to announce its war on the real (stirring slowly from externality to immanence)? In having cast the idiom of the crowds aside, no longer allowing language's conspiracy with being, subjectivity, and truth, the chaotic returns with an innovated mode of expression—the unheard—slithering past the fringes of intelligibility. Yet the question remains as to what this emergent cry sounds like and how this chaotic voice avows its own call to arms, thus giving rise to the defiant textuality of the scream and the laugh.

In one respect, words must here transfigure into screams. This is its endorsement and revulsion of world—its endurance, its agony. This scream evinces an ecstatic condemnation—an amalgam of exhilaration, desire, and rage—such as when Shamlu writes that "there was no greater wish left to me / than to stand from within the furor of a lost scream,"[43] a craving then elsewhere transferred to injunction: "I must let a scream burst forth from the depths of my being."[44] And it is this extraordinary convergence that one sees in another piece, wherein the poet screeches to those around him that

> the garden of decadence is a treasured legacy!
> The garden of decadence.
> The garden of decadence.
> The garden of decadence . . .[45]

The juxtaposition is therefore sketched—that if the real preserves its reign through droning, the recitation of a muted complicity, then so must the chaotic howl into the calm, interposing the toxic utterance. This distinction between the drone and the scream is also a paragon of the struggle between the being-in-the-world and the becoming-outside-the-world and against-the-world, the subject-formation of the first mirror stage and the subject-fracturing of the second—the complacent and the annihilative, the slave and the warrior:

> You must remain silent
> if your message is nothing
> save deceptions
> Yet if you have the chance to wail
> in freedom
> then resound the message
> and brace it with your life.[46]

Through this poetics of the scream, itself an alliance of excess and nothingness, one perforates the hypnotic whirring of empty space, devising a blaring expressive modality that overthrows the dominion of man and God:

> A No, just one No
> was sufficient
> to seal my fate.
> I screamed No
> I refused to sink down . . .
> I was not a groveling slave
> and my path to the heavens
> was not that of submission and subservience.
> I deserved a God of another kind,
> one worthy of a creature
> who does not lower itself
> for the unavailing scraps.
> And a God of another kind
> I created.[47]

Standing beyond metaphysics, a nemesis to all idols, the sound of annihilation supplants the sacred word, a lone scream sufficient to fulfill the contention that all divinities must die.[48] Nor does this scream fall susceptible to a dialectical logic, for the "no" here is not at all a mere negation but more the approximation of a ravenous turn (across the swamplands of thought).[49] As the crossing of the last threshold, annihilation transports consciousness into a rogue architectonics, where the discourse of the limit becomes irrelevant, where transgression grows obsolete, where this fugitive cry can now expel itself in seamless, indiscriminate throes. There is a different air here beyond the straits of being: here the desert is a crucible through which the scream transmits its vitality encryption, reviving the atmosphere:

> To exist within a scream . . .
> The insurgent soaring of a fountain that cannot elude the
>   world
> and is merely straining for deliverance.
> And the glory of perishing within the fountain of a scream
> as the earth wrenches you toward itself ferociously to
>   acquire richness.[50]

As the conduit of enigmatic articulations, permitting no phenomenological remainder, adherent to no taxonomy of sense and nonsense, the emergent scream wrests itself forward in spasmatic outbreaks against the real. It is the sound of fatality itself—its almost imperceptible pitch—for it is within this concentrated upsurge, its secrecy imposed upon the world, that the poetic imaginary saves itself for the chaotic. It ricochets toward something far beyond the criterion of understanding, having already "extracted the last word from the tongue,"[51] and for which the only feature left to distinguish such ciphers is this spreading violence of the scream:

> I am not a tale for you to tell
> I am not a melody for you to sing
> I am not a voice for you to hear
> Nor anything for you to see
> Nor anything for you to know
> I am a shared pain
> Scream me![52]

So it is the scream that brings to the forefront the fundamental contrast between a chaotic consciousness, ever under annihilation, and the stillness of man, ever retreating from impermanence: the scream that is at once terror, omen, warning, and delirium.

Along corresponding lines, the chaotic can take on another expressive profile, one just as piercing—also an infiltration developing from that same recess of the throat in which annihilation thrives: the laugh. Here one immediately looks to the orchestration of laughter as the explicit solicitation of chaotic creativity—one that is beyond irony and beyond parody, for it is mercenary illusion that speaks here.

To begin, though, it is critical to discriminate between three typologies of the laugh, the first of which is the vacant, complacent laugh of the crowds, itself a mere vitality simulation that estranges consciousness from itself—this laughter is nothing short of a cover, a pseudohumanity concealing the long-past death of man. According to Adorno and Horkheimer, this is the triumphant clatter of instrumental reason, a stark triviality born from the fact that "there is laughter because there is nothing left to laugh at."[53] The second laugh belongs to power itself, the custodians of the iron cage whose every statement guards over a decrepit will to truth—a grating sound that stands like a sentinel at the faded altars of normality, reason, and knowledge. It mocks what does not surrender to its self-professed authority, scorns the omission, striving to incapacitate those vigilante strands that the disciples of the real cannot contain. This is the laugh of judgment (antisolidarity). The emergent authors closely experience this tone and its disastrous implications: the way it stalks, penetrates, and holds down, following them throughout, such that almost every engagement with the real is wracked by this sadistic resonance, as if fated to hear its bleak reverberation wherever they tread, beaten by its rattle. And still, the will to annihilation will laugh back, and harder—that of the last laugh, in the most lethal sense.

Power's laugh cannot go unchecked, yet it must be met by something that excels beyond all narrative regimes: the laughter that is a spell, an incantation. So is born the chaotic laugh as what steals itself back from the edge to shake the foundation of the real's monotonality, a bond between sorcery and sound, bringing impiety to a world that takes itself far too seriously, initiating a dangerous auditory dance. Having entered into the arena with its own mirror image, and therein issuing from its capacity to straddle the provinces beyond being and nonbeing, consciousness steers itself toward an amorphous laughter—half grave, half frivolous—which will hang as a talisman from the neck of the real. What surfaces thereafter is a prismatic infusion that impairs the self-assigned sanctity of the world, scrounging auras in the name of illusion, flashing throughout its coercive matrices so as to level the temples and bastions that uphold its disenchanted rule. At once outlandish and scathing, diffusing unabashed disrespect of the everything, this emergent laugh constitutes itself as a curse, light and yet virulent. Its insignificance prostrates existence itself, a vile incident fusing wonderment, distortion, and hurt, ejecting itself beyond the strangulations of identity and toward an unidentified fatality. As the spectacle of emergent poetics illustrates, the laugh of a chaotic becoming is heavily interconnected with annihilation—with its strange magic, being that it originates from an experience of incredible pain, lying somewhere beyond life and death and thus touching upon the very impasse of an infinite terminality. Casting thought, desire, and language across the margins of a recurring end, annihilation confers consciousness into instant conjuration, a passage toward the extreme unreal from within which an inexistent laughter then irradiates. With that said, here there is an innate association of joy to doom—the laugh to ecstatic fatality, dementia to knowing—one cannot say which because it is both, for the two are already one, caught in the same malediction.

This chaotic laugh is an absurd severity—the most acidic deception, the game of illusion made concrete and perilous. It is frenzied, orgiastic, a trickery held poised under the grip of annihilation, and it flies shamelessly in the face of morality and metaphysics, bad conscience and ressentiment, rationality and the ascetic ideal. As an unadorned act of heresy, inadvertently profane, it is the elegy of both reality and nihilism, the apotheosis of a poetics of the lie that turns nothingness into an awaiting consciousness. Nor is the annihilated unaware of what it does and its repercussions: it knows it will be punished for this, for this alien accent and misinflection, and still, it stays rapt such that, with an almost sublime curiosity, it searches after its ordeals. But what is one after in this unquenchable focus on the arrival? Perhaps one wants to know for sure, to press them to the outer banks of their atrocity; perhaps one wants to know how far they will go, how far their own cruelty spans, to what degree they are prepared to excoriate the one who traffics such laughter. Thus this annihilative dialect is an invitation to power to show itself, to provoke and tempt its craving for retribution, though itself standing in place all the while, teeth flashing in anticipation, whispering "come and take what can never be yours."

But it is not over yet—not even close. There is one more plateau left to transverse—that of the worst test, for it demands that consciousness sustain laughter in the moment of finality's crisis, annihilation before the real (to become the obliterated). Can it still laugh then, when they come for it? Here is Shamlu's own response to that inquiry, an excerpt from his "Hour of Execution":

> In the lock the key turned . . .
> A smile trembled on his lips
> Like the image of water dancing on the ceiling
> from the reflection of the shining sun
> In the lock the key turned . . .[54]

There is no incensement or grieving, no profession of epic heroism, no somber expression of a sacrifice set to uphold its tragic destiny—just the reflection of a solitary laugh, in all its perfect obscenity, and an existence betrayed.

The Torture Chamber: Immediacy, Inversion, Immortal Mortality

> How it burns, the bitterness of this confession, that a man
> hostile and enraged
> behind the stone walls of beating legends,
> pained and feverish, has collapsed.
> A man who at night, every night, amidst the jagged stones,
> shaved flowers
> And now
> throws his prized sledgehammer to the wayside.
>
> —Shamlu, "Behind the Wall"

One enters the torture chamber, sphere of a second dissolving, beneath the immediacy of the next existential fall out. This time, the annihilated will not do the deed itself, though it alone has set the stage for what is to happen; it must now deflect the act to the enemy, to make the real perform the remission. In doing so, it becomes the exception that proves the vulgarity of the rule, enticing the world toward a kill, a collision that it entertains no hope of winning, one that ends with an end, and a return. Yet the overriding intent here is more opaque than an imposition of guilt, for there is yet another reason to hand over the active role: to leave power's hands stained with the barbaric disturbance of annihilation—to force it to speak untruth in the cacophony of its opponent's last gasp. Nor is it an attempt to unmask the executioner, nor to awaken the entranced minions whose unreflective subjectivities serve the real. No, this violence is a revelation and this exhale proves something: that none of it belongs to them anymore.

Above all else, the inexorable scene of annihilation to which the emergent authors fasten themselves, evidenced in almost every passage, invests the maximum honor in dying well and, moreover, assigns an almost rhapsodic esteem to the possibility of a willed fatality that then extends itself indefinitely. Infiltrating the space of the pyre, this all-consuming instant unsheathes itself against the columns of an ordered world, deshrouding its faint occlusions and making it partake in an exodus beyond the constrictive regions of being. Thus consciousness undertakes its second annihilation—its incarnations of chaotic warfare poised not to lay waste to the real but rather to lure it outside and to the site of blindness. With nothing spared, the chaotic channels its immoderate influence across the burial rooms of the known, rousing a transvaluation of thought and experience that might extract a new acumen from the dying world. Once again, Shamlu provides an outline of such happenings, nowhere more evident than in the following stanza from his "Requiem":

They said:
We do not want, we do not want to die.
And it was, one might say, a sort of chant
Like horses galloping down a winding and treacherous
    mountain pass
down to the plain,
men with drawn swords upon their backs.
And as long as they stood with themselves
they held nothing in their palms
but wind,
Nothing but wind and their own blood,
For they did not want,
did not want,
did not want,
to die.[55]

In an almost counterintuitive turn, this steadfast refrain—chanting "we do not want to die"—serves, in fact, as a clenching of the annihilative moment to the real. It should not be read as a plea for life—as if turning into supplicants before the scaffolds of power—but as a rally cry to the commandeering of the world as an instrument of the chaotic. To have implored and to have requested mercy would have compromised the event with acquiescence, whereas the defiant axiom of "we do not want to die" instead clasps fatality to itself and its nemesis so as to taint the latter with its impurity. To stain it with even the slightest chaotic intimation is to open it to the other's immanent possibility. Such an inference is justified in consideration of Shamlu's "Of My Death I Spoke," wherein he writes,

A while after the green tumult of another spring
was heard in the passage of weeks
with aged snow
Of my death
I spoke,[56]

and in his "Nocturne 9" that

Death I have seen
in a saddened stare, death I held within my hands
Death I lived
with a saddened melody
saddened
and in a life hard long and hard tired.[57]

By replaying the annihilative episode in the core of the real—a waning for which all instinct hunts itself into combustion—the chaotic pounds and confers itself against what it surrounds and surveys. And all it requires is one becoming-outside-the-world, one body, one consciousness, to accept the heat-stroking cost: with all the consuls of the real—essence, meaning, structure, order—now surrendered to this evanescing nexus, the annihilated exposes the ruse, initiating an inversion of amazing proportions. It spills its fatal tonic across the feigned boundaries between them, diluting the sides, until all are taken down and transformed.

Consciousness and finality here coincide in emulation of the chaotic, such that the event of annihilation must not be viewed as a typical sacrifice; it is in fact the defeat of the sacred, and it must therefore be distinguished from either a metaphysical or ideological logic that always carries with it a sanctifying, cleansing function. Instead, although this occurrence follows no uniform rationale, the emergent literatures together give rise to a rare genre that might be called a suprasubjective epic, forging an existential armageddon that nonetheless remains nonidealized (the executed abstraction). While conveyed in cryptic evocations, annihilation stays firmly grounded in a performative aspect, etched across the torso of those involved in the drama. Hence, if the real solidifies its advantage through a constant extortion of subjectivity, then the revocation of this systematic disillusionment must also occur through a tangible overthrow—the cancellation of being itself, a price satisfied by the oblation of that very subjectivity to the stone-grip of the annihilated. This is a challenge for which there is no otherwise, using the execution as a destabilizing sacraphobic imprint, turning the firing squad against itself and thereby revoking the essence of man.[58] This is no theological quest, no transubstantiation of sacrifice into some ethereal, yet all-encompassing, ideal type of being, but rather a recognition of the primacy of the unreal. To distill this tirade, there is no more immediate manifestation of the chaotic than in the temptation to the end of all things—an enforcement in the highest and lowest sense, one that streaks itself across the world without deference to it and one that entertains itself with collapsibility.

This is an indispensable principle: the second annihilation must instantiate the inconsumable and then escort this experience of the inconsumable into the veins of the real. This alone opens the floodgates to a moment of great trespass, betraying the captivity of the knowing subject and its simulations of authenticity. Thus chaotic sublimity owes its advent to the commotion of the second annihilation—its desolate gaze—the first time having called for survival and the second for the suspension of survival. It takes place without prophetic vision, not for the sake of anything—neither for the world nor for the crowds that stand by and watch silently, neither indebted to some totalizing assertion of enlightenment nor to the perseverance of a universal relationality. Nothing is extricated from the annihilative occasion save a decisive, chaotic outcome of disaster. With the conceptual basis of mission and duty disbanded, annihilation bears no resemblance to a being-toward-death for which finality is dealt with only as a remote temporal speculation in the service of an equally remote historical destiny. Conversely, it serves the acute unreality of existence above all else, and does so in instantaneous proximity (causation is eliminated)—here the "I" commences its passage, not entertained by distant possibilities and inaccessible horizons but grounded in a lived coalescence of intensities (beyond the encasement of all timescapes).

Once again, the emergent principle of annihilation proves contrary, in several ways, to prior philosophical positions dealing with death, as has been shown at varying levels throughout this work, since most withhold from demarcating the intricate correlation between the former and chaotic experience. On one side, there is no ethical dying-for-the-other for an annihilative consciousness; it has undergone the internal self-othering of the second mirror stage, a fracturing and banishment of the interiority-exteriority schism that then released it from the dictates of being, with no dichotomy (there is only force to speak of here). On the other side, there is no temporal lapse, no futural displacement, for here the ending happens, activated in an eternally reinvented now, assuming its place as the ultimate reflection of consciousness' creative strength. What if the last hour were always, instead, this unmastered second, the death-right resting in the hands of desire at this very instant? Herein stands the process of annihilation at its peak—beyond the real, beyond good and evil, beyond the search for the other, and beyond the helplessness of a far-off "futurity."[59] And so death is defeated, dragged down by the emergent trajectories of annihilation.

Chaos is not to be subordinated to the equally passive sanctuary concepts of accident, randomness, and even chance. For annihilation, in its graphic burden, in its countervalor, does not allow thought to conceal itself in the asylum of indeterminacy; rather, it assures chance, while itself not guided by chance, nor does it waive its own morphology of immanence under the auspices of an externalized faith in the "universal." Though it gives unrest, the delivery of the chaotic remains an inevitability that cannot be prolonged or disclaimed; it is an unmatched compulsion, as noted in the frequent emphasis of the word "must" by those experimenting with its emergent poetics. Here one might take Hedayat's image of a cadaver pressed upon his chest at the close of *The Blind Owl*; whether as a symbol of his past, that thing called man now slain at his hands, or of his future—what he knows he will become (the unknowable). In either case, he stands in the present with a corpse behind him and a corpse in front, facing, on either side, the remnant of a deathly existence in the real and the murky warnings of a will to annihilation, a midway space that commands fatality both backward and forward. This is the source of an abrupt declaration, one that provides another literary-existential equivalent in the fusion of the aesthetic imagination and the experience of terminality, always as what must happen "now" and at the unwavering insistence of the instinct (its metallic intuition). The emergent consciousness therefore continues along a path as much condemned as liberated, as much a ghost as living, feeling itself gone and providing the manifest example of what wills itself toward immersion, fluctuation, and fever.

On other levels, the second annihilation can be seen as an original revolutionary momentum, one that remains unsworn: to what has come before, to what prevails now, and to the prospect of an evolution. Since the argument here does not elide the question of the political, but rather attempts to enhance it, this analysis should in turn have answered the question as to how this extermination axiom can at once avoid a dialectical negation and yet launch its visceral affront to the real. Without utopian concerns for the human condition, already in itself beyond the straits of man, such that Shamlu would sever all thoughts of solidarity with the masses in his admission of distaste for having become "a plaything in the hands and tongues of people,"[60] a chaos-consciousness takes on no messianic pretensions. Through synthetic closeness (though always of distance), the second annihilation simultaneously attacks three ranks of the real: that of the wardens of the atrocity (power), that of the legions of complicity (the conformant crowd), and that of the annihilated itself (the entropic "I"). This notwithstanding, the assault is motivated by a paradox of cohesion within disarrangement, nondifferentiation within chaos, such that this catastrophic encounter catches all in the same experiential lattice—the coagulation of a disharmonic chorus, one that will concurrently brave several cadences. As a convoluted ambush, a rogue style of combat that nevertheless remains transparent in its orchestration, annihilative warfare lays bare the foul insecurities of the real by drawing the latter into the very treachery it undertakes and therein takes the conflict lines across one another. This mode of anarchic insurrection, then, is neither a salvation nor a countering of the specificity of what is in place—it rather constitutes an untiring suspension of the possibility that anything "is," ripping the very ground away from underneath the citadel of being. And it is within the scraping of the names of those who, as Shamlu writes, "smell your heart . . . and flog love at the roadblock . . . [who] feed the fire with the kindling of song and poetry . . . [who] knock upon the door at night to kill the light . . . stationed at the crossroads with blood-covered clubs and scythes . . . and resect smiles from lips and songs from mouths,"[61] that an unrestrained deconsolidation of the political issues forth. This anticipates an extravagant switch, one of quasi-millenarial transpositions, wherein everything is cast into the air of reversibility. From beneath the assassin's axe, annihilative consciousness inflicts its casualty upon multiple registers, the identities of each part of the machinery effaced by a now anonymous event, all who spectate driven toward the center of an act that will decenter everything. As the supraontological violation compounds its presence outward until all is subsumed within its rings, the death droves turned back upon their own source, the very edifice of perception is embraced in a kinship of the gallows—and from within that inverted bondage, the myth of man begins to submerge, falter, and disband.

Annihilation is not the pure end, but rather the breaking point, for by erasing the borderline between the "outside" and the "within," annihilation unveils the real as what had never fully won the world, branding errant impressions upon its back in unslaked fashion. With no calming, loyal only to its velocities, this occasion leaves in its wake an ambiguous legacy: the tremulous following of a chaotic nonstate. Herein lies the significance of Shamlu's statement that "my heaven is the jungle of hemlock / my martyrdom has no end,"[62] underscoring the merger of infinity with decimation, timelessness with transience, and refinement with brutality. Thus the field of time must be purged for an oncoming that seeks no permanent status, leaving an immortal replication of mortal experience (the poetics of the once bitten).[63] As has been made apparent, the emergent authors conscript themselves as envoys of this eternal simulation of the breaking, wherein existence is made unbearable to itself and culminates in the forewarnings of a now interloping consciousness (the one who has since come back).

And yet two problematic concerns arise from such articulations, both of which can be defused upon closer examination: (1) that while such figures thoroughly reject any suggestion of logic or sequentiality—discarding the notion of a rational or teleological progression of experience—they then go on to speak of an endless repetition that, in its outer resonance, seemingly betrays the lawlessness of the chaotic outlook and (2) that these writers remain infatuated with some image of a privileged aftermath when their conceptual arrangements should dictate that past, present, and future always already be contained or embodied in a chaotic immediacy. From there one accuses, for in either case, are such orientations not comprised by a submissive intermission of the active instinct—an inferior resurrection of faith in something other—or is it even a manifestation of that insidious sense of expectancy that lies at the heart of metaphysical pathologies? To reinforce this criticism, one might concentrate upon the fact that such zero-world voices speak constantly of a posttwilight event, while Shamlu names his poetic identity "Morning," playing upon the symbolics of the cosmological revolution to foreshadow some impending transfiguration. In this vein, the emergent consciousness frequently establishes itself as an oracle to some nearing faction—the unwanted species, those who will appropriate the reins of untruth and depose the epoch, the thinkers of the great distraction—at once an advent and a reckoning. Somewhat comparably, Shamlu's eminent piece "With Eyes," from within its own anguish and its futility, also encourages a seemingly progressive shift that might be mistaken for a saving way, potentially implying that there is in fact a true direction to be pursued and, with it, an absolute horizon to be won:

> If only I could weep the blood of my veins
> drop
> by drop
> by drop
> until they believed me.
> If only I could
> —just one moment if only I could—
> lift this dejected people upon my shoulders
> . . . so that they could see with their own eyes
> where their sun lies . . . and would believe me.[64]

And still, such a bitter enunciation of the "if only," with the poetic imagination now even thrusting itself into the role of an unacknowledged leader, would appear fully out of place in light of the nihilistic-ecstatic devouring that Shamlu has elected in former instances. It is at this nexus, then, that the emergent writers must be divorced from such false meditations on the question of the future, since it is precisely their confidence in chaotic cyclicality that will release them from the iron discourses of transcendence, redemption, and change. The emergent, as an entwining of temporal and existential threads, does not afford a universal mutation of existence toward a higher plane—no escape, no rescue—but only repossesses the same infinitizing conflict of being, contra the chaotic, that has been waged throughout, sustaining into timelessness that vivified tension through which an incision is made into the tenacity of "what is." There is no camouflage of this thought and no final resolution—it is no longer the "war for a cause" but the "war as the cause," replaying the crucifixion of the "I" with varying textures of scandal and hysteria. And herein lies the promise of its eternality: that there will be more to take up arms against the real, more to ally themselves with illusion against the oppression of actuality and knowing, more to wrench subjectivity into the frenzied underpass of chaotic desire (to become unmade). This is why annihilation is also an instinctive return and a contaminated synergy, for it perpetuates the inscription of the process in its entirety—from the nihilistic interlude to the will to solitude, from the fractured subject to the trial by fire, from the poetic scream-laugh to the execution—all draped together in the peaceless words and actions of this consciousness, occurrences printed across existence by an aristocracy of the injured. As a consequence, the annihilative consciousness of the present is already the materialization of its fulfillment, collapsed into a spiral, a lunatic whip that flashes from one enemy temporality to another, a rage-propulsion against existence that takes the shape of an affirmative circularity. Thus Shamlu questions, "How impure would I be if I did not make of my faith a mountain, / an everlasting memory upon the plane of this transient earth?"[65] Although never reactive in its maneuvers, the chaotic wrests itself forward as a discontemporaneous contender, the categorical use of the word "upon" demonstrating a certain essential intimacy with that same caged world across which consciousness directs its rampage. There must be perfect nearness in chaotic warfare; thus a reality formation desperate for exemption must be ever challenged by self-resuscitating impermanence, ensuring its restoration just as it tears away at itself—a becoming born of carnage—and yet recovering itself over and again, matching brutality for brutality, conserving its angered ethos. It is in this way that annihilation punctures time.

One arrives at a theoretical-experiential clearance: that annihilation is no longer what is yet to happen (futurity), but rather an escalating line across what could happen (potentiality), what will happen (eventuality), what must happen (prophecy), what has already happened (fatality), and what will happen again (eternity). Being and nonbeing are undone simultaneously before the experience of a second annihilation, such that it at once scours *the emergent* and *the aftermath*. It matters less that death incur the exit of being than that one mark this as an entryway of its own, that the last rites of subjectivity be delegated toward a chaotic initiation, not with the decadence of a search for authenticity yet with the elation of an existence taking leave of itself. From this, a new poetic deliberation rises, one that winds expression into raving, madness into declaration, and where the intoxication of illusion is maintained fast and in full view of an instinctive aesthetic. And so on the other side of the earth, we again come upon the emergent author's own battle with the torture chamber, where raw physicality walks hand-in-hand with thought, scarred everywhere and in-between, watching as the real sets loose its regiments of order upon the one who "broke the winter,"[66] ensuring that "each dawn is punctured by the chorus of twelve bullets."[67] Demanding compliance or mutilation, power's watchmen would work upon this lone frame over and again from within its own graveyard of the damned, plundering body and soul until there was "a scream and nothing more."[68] But here is the secrecy revealed: that he wanted it. Each blow to the face, each broken bottle cutting its way gradually down his back, each lingering scent of a burn from where they had put out their cigarettes on his flesh, each companion that fell beneath the awful efficiency of the guillotine, proved his point all the more: that he could still conjure the exhilaration of the unreal from within the lairs of the most hellish suffering. This is no one's martyr. If one stares more closely, beyond the bleeding torso, beyond the convulsive breathing of a beaten body that one is so tempted to romanticize, one sees something else, something so much harder to take because it roams beyond the outskirts of comprehension—beyond Man and God, beyond consciousness itself—not an icon, not an archetype but an intensity that died for the dying alone, not for us or even for itself, but because it had to—because the instinct asks for perishing and because there was no other way to chaos but through the corridors of annihilation.

TACTIC 3

Shadow-Becoming
(Chaotic Appearance)

I. Eclipse
(potential,
conquest)

II. Blurring
(obscurity, distortion)

III. Seclusion
(the formless, the
unformed)

IV. Infliction
(survival, induction, catastrophe)

I. The Banished

Time: Eternity
(circularity)
(midnight)

Space: Excursion
(distance, forestalling)
(the desert, the
elsewhere, the farthest)

Sensation: Waste
(deprivation)
(imbalance)

Expression: Entrancement
(the chant, the echo)

Postidentity: Abandonment
(the disowned, the accursed)

Tactic: Fascination
(madness, effusion, radiation)
(the spectacle)

II. The Imprisoned

Time: Standstill
(slowness)
(daybreak)

Space: Enclosure
(confinement,
proximity)
(the cell, the torture-
chamber, the
subterranean)

Sensation: Pain
(abrasion)
(restlessness)

Expression: Malice
(the outcry, the scream)

Postidentity: Mania
(the condemned, the infuriated)

Tactic: Captivation
(estrangement, anger, impulse)
(the encryption)

III. The Concealed

Time: Dementia	Space: Immanence	Sensation: Immateriality
(the mal-occasioned)	(disappearance, involution)	(despair)
(dusk)	(the alley, the labyrinth, the lattice)	(extinguishing)

Expression: Undertone
(the whisper, silence)

Postidentity: Invisibility
(the unwanted, the unseen)

Tactic: Insinuation
(invasion, reflection, reversal)
(the mirror)

As one endeavors to speculate upon the unfolding fate of this emergent pact, its awaiting heights and abysses, one is compelled to acknowledge the gaining position of the shadow. For this shadow-becoming, as a wayfare strand of consciousness, one that amends the contours of subjectivity, that invites it across untried domains, has in turn conceived the passage for a new literary-existential paragon.

To ascertain such recent shifts, this piece will concentrate on three distinct, yet interwoven, postidentities, each adhering to a different condition of this shadow writing: that of the banished, the imprisoned, and the concealed. Accordingly, this tripartite legion of authors allows us to advance a prediction, perhaps for the first time, of a reclusive textuality—one that skates plateaus of disarray. In following this avant-garde tide, a series of thematic elements will be raised and applied as an ardent philosophical-poetic gesture: one of valor, depravity, and martial scale. For this convergence, presumably, will reveal the ways in which such ascending circles of thought have innovated a dynamic though hazardous prospect, one that patrols an unfit liminality.

One begins, then, from the involved conceptual registers that motivate the shadow's imagination, as reflected in the preliminary mapping above, itself an overview, network, and collection of decoded ideas.[1]

Eclipse: Blurring, Seclusion, Infliction

> There is no door, there is no road, there is no night, there is
> no moon, neither day nor sun,
> We
> are standing outside of time
> With an embittered knife in our side
> No one speaks with anyone
> For the quiet speaks with a thousand tongues.
> —Ahmad Shamlu, "Nocturnal"

There is something that binds the shadows—a consistency of drives, an oath of unsworn, shattered axioms. From within their respective travesties, they attempt to supersede the determinism of being-foregone, no longer of the omitted and the missing, but rather consenting to the outer reaches into which they are coerced, grappling in equal strides with their revulsion and their delirium, their oppression and their boundlessness, so as to arrange a new hierarchy of writing.

Across the last rows of the intangible, there is a sensation that *eclipses*: this signifies a rare transposition, the darkening that carries its own impossible illumination, one that draws a thick curtain over the real, that coats the mythologies of the enlightened and leaves the watcher's gaze transfixed, riveted to the anxious slit between not-day and not-night.

The power of the eclipse rests in its *chaos potential*, for it is this dire image that halts the pulse of all who stand witness, that temporarily disallows all thought of return, where nothing can be resumed until the veil is lifted, and where to look too close is to burn one's eyes. Thus it is an ominous declaration to the real, that it remains on borrowed time, and that the incipient wave it embodies, its rancor and its disturbance, cannot be deterred. The shadow is therefore at once a foreshadowing and an effectuation, always magnified by the fact that its influx already seals its fulfillment, reminding the onlooker that it was over long before this, before it even started, all players locked into a steel ring of inevitability. Here the warning is already the requiem, the threat already the realization—an impending disquiet already the full accumulation of the storm. The eclipse descends, devastates, and withdraws all in the same breath, a split-second gesture enough to guarantee the collapse of a world.

And what lies at the heart of this momentary yet irrevocable breach? Nothing less than the fatal *conquest* of the human itself: for humanity died a long time ago, though trailing beyond its own obsolescence, clinging now only as an unwelcome residuum, the replication of a forsaken possibility. Unable to mouth the words that it has lost, it continues a sick and desperate endgame, scrounging to prolong the last trivial moves, though defeat was imminent far before this point. The shadow arrives, then, as the ringleader of an existential ailment, one born of irreparable cuts and wrong turns, to accept the assassin's role and break the tired dominion of man, for only a bloodless entity can overthrow a bloodless reign. This suprahuman hour is itself an epochal transference, a localized apocalypse, not the end of *all* time but the end of *this* time, charged to vacate the throne, to discard the altars and their overhanging idols, in search of a single clearance. And still, this is not meant to rescue anyone, for even the hostages of man will meet the same perishing—no, there is no amnesty extended here, only the shadow outlives this, and even then.

Advancing further into the eclipse, a question arises: if the shadow is at once the endangerment and extinction of the real, its complete betrayal, its electrocution and dispersal, then how does one begin to track its unrighteous pattern? In answer, one must devise a new epistemology, an antiepistemology of *blurring*, one that is persistently unknowing itself, one that is premised on the convoluted interplay between simulation and dissimulation, between the lie and the hidden; for if the shadow itself maneuvers across countenances, at once a blank slate and an impostor, at once possessed of accurate and amorphous contours, stranding itself between opacity and translucence, awakening and sleep, then one must tread toward that strange impasse where materiality and immateriality collaborate to begin a new trade—to ravage the base of vision.

Above all else, it is this recurrent technique of self-blurring that in turn allows the shadow to become a prosthetic for both *obscurity* and *distortion*, to scar existence with indecision and convert the real into a vessel for its pandemoniac stillness. Though both comprise essential schemes, rendering avenues by which the shadow then manufactures itself as an incomprehensible event, once again the lean yet crucial difference between obscurity and distortion rests across the distinct, recoiling axes of dissimulation and simulation. In the first instance, the shadow strives to shroud intent, to screen itself and thereby remain an undetectable presence—without origin or destination, past or future, wading in anonymity—in the dim-lit recess of what leaves only an illegible signature. In this way, it becomes an indecipherable constellation—its vanquishing and intensity cast beneath an extended layer, revealing no remnant of an interiority through the smokescreen, no soul through the haze. And yet one senses that it carries a strict design—that it wants something, seeks for something—though the imperative complicates itself through unremitting camouflage, its "truth" vanishing behind protective curvatures. On the other side, the shadow can also safeguard its enigmatic status by wresting itself into multiple, inauthentic projections—a contortionist frame, proliferating not merely a disguise but an alien semblance that then divulges the misimpression; a decoy-presence set in motion to mislead sight—it pretends to show itself, though it offers only an errant disclosure, an alternate transvisual flare set to generate strategic misinterpretations, to distract and throw understanding off course. In the wake of this diversion, one believes that one sees, but in actuality is met only by a meticulously constructed phantom-subject, a postidentitarian sorcery, the hollow simulacrum of what is already behind the real, capitalizing on its temporary fixation, its perplexity and interruption, in order to steal its way through. Such is the shadow's elemental alignment with illusion, exploiting its black magic so as to gain uninvited entrance, to infiltrate and disgrace what rules (though never as itself).

This notwithstanding, even when brought face-to-face with the shadow—with its endless processions of blurring, its pathways of obscurity and distortion—one cannot interrogate its genealogy, for one cannot puncture its extreme *seclusion*. One speaks of it as a solitary intimation because it confesses no history, no record of its evolution—and itself maintains no edifice of memory, no awareness beyond the constant resonance of its mission, of what it must do here and now, as if all has been eradicated save the lone obligation that brings it to the doorstep of the real. One can infer its disconnect from the existence it pervades, damages, and abandons, its unconditional aversion to universality, and yet therein uncovering an almost indescribable dualism, an ill-founded schism encompassed by the shadow's possibility: that of *the formless* and *the unformed*. More specifically, the shadow, at times, seems to manifest a potent implication in the real, as if it once belonged among their strata—its agility in stabbing through these elaborate spheres demonstrates an ingrained familiarity with their methods, their lust and their shame, the expertise of an insider-turned-traitor, and thus immune to resubjection. It circulates through the maze of the real as if it had long since imprinted itself with the map, had internalized the winding landscape of its corridors, which again leaves it suspect to an unanticipated accusation: that the shadow was once part of this, once embedded in its ways, and then later strayed, escaping toward formlessness. To this end, the shadow here embodies the aftermath of the disembodiment of the real, an omen of its next incarnation, once drawn outside itself. It is the smoke that remains once the walls erode, the oblivion that settles beyond the point of irreversibility. Nevertheless, there are countless junctures at which the shadow illustrates no recognition of its target, appearing excessively detached, as if born across discontinuous outworlds—a pure foreigner to the real and therefore reminiscent of the unformed. This insurmountable disconnect leads one to a countersuggestion: that the shadow elicits obliteration against an irrelevant world. It is hard to tell what configuration is more disconcerting: the one who knows the enemy-object too well, trained in its divergent meanings, and hence becomes a studied, intimate practitioner of harm, or the one who has never traveled within its circuitries, who approaches from wild, extraneous territories, with slanted thirsts and moods—the first a gateway to treason, to the vengeance of "the once was," and the second to indifference, to the merciless arms of "the never-was."

In any case, the unassuming impact of the shadow resides in its elite ability to accommodate both encounters, to synchronize the formless and the unformed as conspiring experiences of solitude, to strike as the native and the intruder, at once the punishing backlash and the unforeseen plague.

In the final estimation, one must recall the smooth functionality that allows the shadow to instill itself as a source of chronic discord: namely, that it constitutes a will to *infliction*. The implication of this statement is clear: that it does not shudder, doubt, or hesitate to envelop whatever enters its line of sight, and that it perceives itself as an enforcement, of ruthless inundation and engulfing—the jagged onset of a devastated moment. Thus all shadow-becomings, from whatever disparate vantage, uphold the same criterion, the same critical protocol: that they render themselves as concurrent modalities of *survival*, *induction*, and *catastrophe*.

Here is where the analysis divides, where one is required to follow three separate trajectories, each corresponding to a singular voice of this emergent shadow consciousness: (1) that of the banished; (2) that of the imprisoned; and (3) that of the concealed. By drafting the myriad stories of this triumvirate, unearthing their grave aspirations and their routes of deception and sabotage, this project stalks the fractured destiny of a new poetics, a previously unattainable performativity of the word wherein the writing act becomes nothing more than a vague outline, and the text, a delineation of creative atrocity.

Shadow Space: Excursion, Enclosure, Immanence

> Here there are four prisons
> In each prison several tunnels,
> In each tunnel several quarters,
> In each quarter several men in chains.
>
> —Ahmad Shamlu, "The Reward"

To translate such fugitive arcs, one must first confront the respective spaces in which these poetic imaginaries cultivate themselves, for each stays close to a chosen prism, an uneven angulation of subversive instinct. These are all geographies of limitless violence, sites of alignment and misalignment through which consciousness initiates its languid rituals of the tormented, for they emanate from fanatical circumstances of suffering, sentences given down by a homicidal reality principle.

The spatial experience of the banished is one of *excursion*: to be flung toward that radical exteriority of the outcast, the voided name, province of the barren, of the sands and of the carrion, where one is buried alive, and yet moves still, aimless and starved. Thus the shadow-author is drawn into an exodus without exit, one of infinite *distance*, surrounded by debris and ruin, taunted by an atrophic horizon, where thought becomes an exercise in scavenging and *forestalling*, left to wander across serrated, abstract lines of dust (insane animation). One asks, what is envied here, amid the exogenic peril, the shock of this antidwelling? And so this shadow poetics must consign itself to the following precincts: *the desert, the elsewhere*, and *the farthest*.

Conversely, the spatial experience of the imprisoned is one of raw *enclosure*, the radical interiority that demands endurance, medium of hardness and compression, of thrashing and defiance, of the paralyzed chest , grounded and locked down. This is its metallic cosmos, its unbending atmospheric challenge, a culture of aggression and breaking, of the chisel and the bars, of what strikes, what pounds, where thought is consumed by awful solidity, met each evening by the visitation of the guards and the dialectics of the firing squad. Here the shadow-author is drawn into unspeakable immediacy, encased in stone and rusted iron, where the cage alone holds sway—arrogant in its immersion, its dampness, and its asphyxiating *proximity*—and where the body subsides to *confinement*, wracked by the ever-present rattle of chains and the turning of keys. Our kind is often slain here, and slain here often (stoic deflection). And so this shadow poetics must consign itself to the following precincts: *the cell, the torture-chamber*, and *the subterranean*.

Finally, one ventures across the spatial experience of the concealed as that of *immanence*, a radical elusivity for which one is damned to circulate both everywhere and nowhere, a zone of insubstantial hovering, of subtle *disappearance* and atomized emergence. Such is the ethereal environment of the caught-in-between, subsumed in the aerial drift of the one who is no one, now no more than an obsidian passenger, casualty of the wind, snaking through the perforated tissue that martyrs thought itself. Beyond this, both its agony and its cunning lie in its uncontrollable *involution*: that it is poured through all events, fused into every admixture, grasped in an alchemical hell devoid of even the most miniscule autonomy; it lurks across everything, this fiend race, enslaved to reckless inclusion, spun from one web to another (incommensurate coagulation). And so this shadow poetics must consign itself to the following precincts: *the alley, the labyrinth*, and *the lattice*.

And yet none will be subjugated or undone by these tainted settings. Soon enough, they will turn them against themselves, and against the world beyond them.

Shadow-Time: Eternity, Standstill, Dementia

> But I . . . in the aerial core of my own dreams,
> nothing is heard but the cold echo of the bitter song of
> these desert weeds that grow, and rot, and wither, and fall.
> If only I did not have these shackles, perhaps then Morning,
> could have passed over the remote and sliding memory of
> the cold and lowly dirt of this level . . .
> This is the crime!
> This is the crime!
>
> —Ahmad Shamlu, "Nocturnal"

Of equal, if not surpassing, brutality, one turns to the shadow's experience of time—its disabling miracle—for how do the seconds elapse when banished, imprisoned, or concealed? The clock rotates differently here, amid indefinite pulsations.

Starting again from the aged roads of the banished, one notes that this elected state delivers the lesion of one time frame alone: that of *the eternal*. Here eternity reveals its sinister underside, as an energy of improper resurrection and sadistic *circularity*, exercising its necromancic craft across the field of being, for in this poetic timescape, nothing is extended the luxury of death, its finality and closure, but rather is draped in a more menacing process: that of interminable dying (where all lasts too long). Things restore themselves in horrid cycles, though without self-recollection, as if chased by the same amnesic nightmare, over and again, and always forgetting the way out. Time thereafter becomes the exhibition for a corrupted immortality, for the gaunt perversion of forever, brandishing its profane repetition-compulsion by resetting all events to their zero calibration, reeling in synthetic, ceaseless reproductions of the present. Hence this shadow-rank responds to only one temporal thematic: that of permanent *midnight*.

Within the context of the imprisoned, however, time inhabits a different molding: that of *the standstill*. This is not eternity but rather perfected *slowness*, a timescape of severity and barricades, where all become relics of mechanistic decay, where they wither and fade in unbearable, protracted measurements. Here everything drags, nearly frozen; here one keeps count by the marks of judgment, by the ever-increasing number and depth of wounds branded across the flesh of the convicted, by the inscription of forfeited years upon the unforgiving wall, by the useless, cramped paces of the incarcerated—their self-cannibalizing steps a testament to the relentless, excruciating will of the real. This is where time itself seems to stop, but not quite, a segment at once irate and apathetic, where futility effaces past and chokes the future. Hence, this shadow-rank responds to only one temporal thematic: that of *the daybreak* (remember, after all, that executions are carried out at dawn).

Advancing forward, the chronicle of the concealed takes on a more ghoulish quality than the rest, for it slips into *dementia*. The direct consequence is that of a *maloccasioning*, a misconstrued sensibility, where things occur always at the wrong time, at the apex of the worst fathomable instant, respecting the cracked dial, spreading asymmetry and anticlimax at every turn. The once-linear, immutable train of real time suddenly slopes into confusion and interchangeability, where tentacular happenings conflate and transplant—the tyranny of sameness now contaminated, the tyranny of difference now unstrung—its once-stable demarcations left inextricably threaded across one another. Hence this shadow-rank responds to only one temporal thematic: that of *the dusk*. Yet this is no harmless twilight; instead, it precipitates misfortune—it is the signal of a monstrous, altered state, of the dread and transfiguration that horizontally crucifies a vertical age.

Shadow Sensation, Postidentity, Expression: Waste, Pain, Immateriality, Abandonment, Mania, Invisibility, Entrancement, Malice, Undertone

> For the sake of one anthem / For the sake of a story on the coldest of nights, the darkest of nights.
>
> —Ahmad Shamlu, "Of Your Uncles"

At this threshold, one might conjecture toward the multidimensional orchestration of sensation, postidentity, and expression engendered by these shadow-becomings, for it is in this exchange that the awaited intellectual and poetic turn manifests itself, the expectant move from the defensive to the offensive, from the abused to the architect. No longer the wretched, here one seeks exaltation (the turn beneath).

For the banished, the dominant sensation is that of *waste*, a waste based in *deprivation*, though eventually this becomes an opulent will to *imbalance*. One must circumvent the one with nothing to lose, the emaciated expression, the spirit in entropy, for this scarcity gradually metamorphoses into an unsteady inclination—one that exaggerates proportions, that overdoses the mind and attracts the disoriented. As a result, identity undergoes a drastic *abandonment*, as the shadow author becomes *the disowned* and then *the accursed*, though it is precisely this displacement, this miscarriage, this allegation of toxicity and degeneration, which sets the stage for an unparalleled aesthetic revolution (consciousness-turning-opiate). The writing of the banished is synonymous with *entrancement*, with the hypnotism of *the chant* and *the echo*, since both are organic to its inexhaustible exhaustion; and so one begins to see these two untamed genres combined—a fearsome, unjust palpitation now growing from the desolate expanse. One hears only the rhythmic beckoning of drums, whether foretelling a festival or a war, a dance, or an onslaught.

Unavoidably, for the imprisoned, the overarching sensation is that of *pain*, the pain of the dregs, irrefutably etched across the mutilated limbs of those who reside, who withstand the serial *abrasion* of their own anatomy—though this defilement, this quartered physicality, incites its own counteraffect, as violation navigates itself toward *restlessness*. Here the poetic imagination begins an inquest: to sting and inflame itself, to refine its musculature, consolidating thought into a strenuous agitation, becoming increasingly resolved in its irresolution, until identity shows evidence of *mania*. Thus the shadow maneuvers across a strained, though escalating, affiliation, an injurious kinship tied between being *the condemned* and becoming *the infuriated* (consciousness-turning-vice). An aesthetic resurgence transpires here as well, amid this absolute condensation, giving way to an ascendant poetics of *malice*. Let there be no mistake here: this is a malevolent writing, at once resilient, ingenious, and necessarily vicious, one that carves back, allowing the depth to annihilate the surface, one that expels itself from a dismembered throat, enfolding the real in its own suffocating inflection. For the poetics of the imprisoned articulates itself as a razor, a once self-contained, coarse rant that transitions from *the outcry* to *the scream*: the former weeps, the latter revenges, reciprocates the currency of hurt, leaving the jail floor stained and pierced by wrathful exhalations. One hears only the transmission of a seamless hate.

Nor are the conduits of the concealed any less unruly, though commencing from a sensation of *immateriality*, that unsure southern chasm where thought questions its hold over presence and absence, weighing its own incremental dissolution. Such is the rationale of its *despair*—its aggrieved outlook—though without recourse to mourning, relinquishing itself instead to total submergence, to the cryptic, hooded terms of an untouchable. Here the poet always speaks of drowning; and still, as it loses existential ground, it wins another entitlement—that of *extinguishing*—and this in itself affording a clandestine power guided by esoteric principles. More exactly, it is here that the shadow finds itself equipped with a phenomenal intuition: to discern when things are at their most vulnerable, at their greatest capacity for demise and evaporation, an invaluable insight into the frailty of world-orders. For this reason, it is able to convert its own prior weakness into a subsequent arsenal, wielding a profile of *invisibility* away from the designation of *the unwanted* and toward *the unseen*. In the first phase, it was relegated to insignificance, though now it extorts the real through this same occlusion (consciousness-turning-syringe). Beyond this impasse, the writing act is never the same; now one is brought before a textuality of active *undertones*, one that isolates a ring between *silence* and *the whisper*, not as a muted voice but as the evocation of a corrosive murmur—one that gouges the eyes of the real, leaving it sightless and defeated, for only the imperceptible can depose the authoritarianism of perception. One hears nothing here, or just barely, and, even then, too late.

This is a sentience of pitch blackness, of the unsafe worship, one that confiscates, reviles, and purges, that solicits the clouded, the incinerated, with unqualified permission.

Shadow Tactics: Fascination, Captivation, Insinuation

We stare upon our dead with the intimation of a laugh, / and await our turn without any laughter.

—Ahmad Shamlu, "Nocturnal"

The silence of water could be drought or the scream of the scorched
The silence of wheat could be hunger and the howl of famine's victory
in the same way that the silence of the sun is obscurity.

—Ahmad Shamlu, "The Silence of Water"

And yet how do these mercenary poetics seize hold of the real, setting fire to its columns? This is an unyielding adjustment, for how does each breed overcome its insufficiency, turning the nothing into something and then thriving? To even contemplate this equation is to delegate the stage for an elected counterfuture, that is, to appoint the text to an inadmissible event now injecting itself against what was "supposed to happen." For certain, each strand devises its own array of expressive tactics, its own instruments of laceration, composing texts that maim language, that excoriate representation, and that leave the writing act synonymous with defacement and excision.

The banished operates through the tactic of *fascination*, coordinating *madness*, *effusion*, and *radiation* so as to conjure *the spectacle*. Thus the poetic imagination traverses into the postontological badlands: where temptation becomes infatuation, infatuation becomes obsession, obsession becomes addiction, and addiction brings the downfall. This is the point at which language grows carnivalesque, assuming an innovative purpose: to entice lethal absorption, to lure, bewitch, to mesmerize and diffuse the anarchic vapor, the fever dream, the point at which knowledge becomes mirage, and the text itself a messenger of some mystified, hallucinogenic beyond. Such is the automated passion of the sleepwalker. Here one sinks, becomes drunken, spellbound—half possessed, half narcotized—surrendered to the poisonous elation of a writing that beguiles, that saturates and deranges, and that superimposes its own disembodied fabrication upon the skeleton of the real.

The imprisoned operates through the tactic of *captivation*, coordinating *estrangement*, *anger*, and *impulse* so as to instantiate *the encryption*. Thus the poetic imagination displays an arcane tenacity, a cold grip that then tears into incensement, that riles and thickens the game, enrages the air, its persecution and its lost cause, and ultimately raids against the barriers of its slaughterhouse backdrop. This is a drug beyond resistance, one that adapts agony into compulsion, that anchors itself as a jaw, now tightening, that distills language into an assemblage of hostile sounds, sounds of affliction. This is an intricate machinery of entrenchment, where textuality finds itself sharpened, embattled, under siege by an artistic criminality, and thereafter becomes a catalogue of decimations. Such is the rift of an honor killing. Here one is lashed by an inexorable stare—one that assaults, tramples, hooks, and burdens the shoulders, that wrecks both the remaining and the oncoming world, saving nothing, regretting nothing; one that coalesces the particles of its contempt, streaks them forward, and thereby scatters the once-immobile masses of the real into perpetual fright and convulsion.

The concealed operates through the tactic of *insinuation*, coordinating *invasion*, *reflection*, and *reversal* so as to extract the magnetism of *the mirror*. Thus the poetic imagination becomes an impenetrable silhouette, a clerisy of the disclaimed, of infinitesimal summonings, whereby the once-uncontested unity of being now falls victim to a series of minor incursions, delicate reorientations, and whereby language is commissioned to manipulate through slightness, to escort the suave, insidious denigration of structure. This is the point at which each verse becomes a surreptitious, sinuous invocation, a subterfuge and devious notion, implanting suspicion through the narrow veins of the real. The text itself is a back draft—a slick, traceless insertion of the imperfect and the inverted. Such is the birthright of the apparition.

Here one listens to an unsettling tongue, one that stimulates an apprehensive effect: one feels preyed upon—begins to question and wonders—to the extent that all objects appear clothed in illegitimacy, all subjects appear doomed to decomposition, and thought unbraces itself before the ceremony of shadows.

CHAPTER 4

Chaos-Consciousness
Toward Blindness

It was a dark, silent night like the night which had enveloped all my being, a night peopled with fearful shapes which grimaced at me from door and wall and curtain.

—Sadeq Hedayat, *The Blind Owl*

The immortal subterranean of chaos literature is what invokes the betrayal of language, what breaks infinity from within the steel enclosures of expression and conveys the writing-act to shadow and disquiet. When confronted with such an emergent textuality, one that implicitly and explicitly exalts its own refusal to be justified—each passage an apotheosis of strident fragmentation—one might nevertheless venture to carve out an entryway to this literary nowhere zone. Thus one embarks, through an acute sensitivity to its variations, its belt of torn moments, shard-like instances that at times (though always in opposition to time) condense long enough to form an array of thematic axes, often converging with each other, just as often in rampant collision, counterpoint, and rivalry, and out of which a chaotic imaginary might then be vaguely sketched. It is by virtue of a strange desequentialization of the instant, a nonlinear wading through matrices in unpredictable displacement, treated as self-consuming valences in and of themselves, that such a work, ever decrying unity without close or definition, clashing statements without origin or destination, can be affirmed as a movement unforeseen.[1] Hence, this segment of the project will endeavor to offer its envisioning through a critical interface with Sadeq Hedayat's *The Blind Owl*, and therein will summon to its arsenal the following conceptual and experiential domains: the vanishing eternal (transparency, obscurity, seduction, and transience); annihilation (the wound, the scar); the shadow becoming (disintegration) and existential shattering (fragmentation); the unreal (deception, hallucination, impossibility, blurring); the aftermath, forgetting (the end of time); the noncontinuum, the nowhere and elsewhere (the end of space); instinct (the end of intentionality); excess (the end of the psyche); silence, the rant (the end of representation); haze (the end of interiority and exteriority); war (the end of the other); divine fatality (the end of metaphysics); and chaos-consciousness.

The Vanishing Eternal: Transparency, Seduction, Transience

This is a writing of abomination (the detested interval), ever amid the elusive rhythms of its own last breath. The first engagement of consciousness with the chaotic in *The Blind Owl* is a stark failure, an adversarial interception culminating in violence, such that the narrator begins his tale as a traitor. He lives in a starved world, slowly melting away, perished within an almost primal cavity and hanging from the ropes of its own disbelief: "I am fortunate in that the house where I live is situated beyond the edge of the city in a quiet district far from the noise and bustle of life. It is completely isolated and around it lie ruins."[2] And yet he is given a second chance, a sudden flash of something imperceptible yet irrepressible, the silhouette of an illuminating darkness to which he then devotes himself: "In its light, in the course of a second, of a single moment, I beheld all the wretchedness of my existence and apprehended the glory and splendour of the star."[3] From thereon he lets it cradle him, swaying to its indefinite, hypnotic organizations—back and forth—such that he becomes an addict of its restlessness, its scattered lashings, its indistinct enchantment. He beholds, chases, and restores himself at its expense, guiding himself through it and perching himself upon its untempered heights, feeding off its oblique force. But when it gets too hard—when it asks too much of him and demands too high an expenditure—he turns his back, committing treason against the one thing that has offered him a way out of his tacit emaciation. No, this narrative consciousness begins its tale as more than just a traitor: it begins as a murderer of chaos.

There is only permanent impermanence (a world in everlasting remission), for to look at the opening scenes of encounter is to descend across the striations of a nonspace. It is a statelessness where everything is rapidly integrated into antagonism and illegibility, infused with happenings of the most jagged texture, free-associative and yet infinitely precise, formatting all that passes into a frantic disarray of unprejudiced effects, producing a constellation of the sheer uneven, pieces conscripted toward an unscripted, endless irrelation. In this way, the emergent author commences the account of an existence in unrelenting transience, a vague ascertainment of what surfaces in tenacious waves, only then to give itself over to dissolution again—what will here be upheld as the conveyance through a "vanishing eternal": "After, that brightness disappeared again in the whirlpool of darkness in which it was bound inevitably to disappear. I was unable to retain that passing gleam."[4] And yet it returns to him, in the image of a woman, at once angel and demon, bringing him ever closer to confrontation with a chaotic imaginary that he has enlisted for and against himself but still refuses to internalize. As such, this strange figure is compelled to embody the chaotic within her appearance: unbending to control, ungoverned by intention, suspended somewhere outside being and nonbeing, surrendered only to formlessness, a subtle motioning, a hushed movement toward the nowhere and elsewhere (beyond thought itself). For this reason, each descriptive phrasing the narrator offers about this entity finds itself embedded in exotic contradiction, held in a cosmology of effacing dualities and affective collision, such that "she appeared to be quite unaware of her surroundings . . . gazing straight ahead without looking at anything in particular," while also wearing "on her lips a vague, involuntary smile as though she was thinking of someone who was absent," and further possessing "slanting, Turkoman eyes of supernatural, intoxicating radiance that at once frightened and attracted, as though they had looked upon terrible, transcendental things that it was given to no one but her to see."[5] Alongside such clouded depictions, the blind owl reflects upon her further as one for whom "the fineness of her limbs and the ethereal unconstraint of her movements marked her as one who was not fated to live long in this world," at once rendering her elasticity and ephemerality, and also as one "whose lips were full and half-open as though they had broken away only a moment before from a long, passionate kiss and were not yet sated," at once rendering her desire and insatiability.[6] This is how chaos becomes a concussive imaginary, one of impeccable adrenaline, surmounting even paradox.

With this arcane backdrop portrayed, Hedayat then enlists an assault against the reality principle, thieving the supposed world: "But when I drew the curtain aside and looked into the closet I saw in front of me a wall as blank and dark as the darkness that has enshrouded my life."[7] Moreover, this implosion of the authenticity of "what is" heightens itself with the reappearance of the angel-demon upon his doorstep, an occurrence that then sends the narrator into a relentless questioning of the reality degree of everything taking place, ranging from his initial comment that "she reminded me of a vision seen in an opium sleep" to his later self-assuring insistence that she in fact was no false apparition: "No, it was not an illusion. She had come here into my room, into my bed and had surrendered her body to me. She had given me her body and her soul."[8] But then the definitive tone turns against itself, devouring its own air of certainty by bringing this "creature apart" whose "being was subtle and intangible" into alliance with the figure of the shadow: "I was quite sure that I had seen her with my own two eyes walk past and then disappear. Was she a real being or an illusion? Had I seen her in a dream or waking? . . . It occurred to me that this was the hour of the day when the shadows of the castle upon the hill returned to life."[9] As if coated in another secrecy, as a vision beyond vision itself, ever "with her eyes closed," she then drifts aimlessly over to his bed, lays across it, and stares at and into him, leaving him to the irresolution of an unexplained action, such that "in the half-dark of the room it [her face] wore an expression of mystery and immateriality."[10] At once unsettled and serene, this interlacing with the angel-demon brings with it a unilateral mystification, implanting each object with an unchecked trace of the exceptional—everything inflected with unfamiliarity and the seduction of the unknown—irradiating without enlightening, as a world of transparent obscurity assumes its reign over consciousness.

This preliminary interlocking with the chaotic imaginary carries itself across an ornate grid, the incalculable spider work, snaking an experiential trellis without rational pretense or phenomenological borders, nothing left "in-itself" yet instead traversing the threshold of desire and intensity with continuous successions of becoming and overcoming—crossing into the brutality of the infinite. Truth has no place here amid the battered text, leaving only an instance that succumbs to the unsutured, the discrepancies of the unsure, equally immune to both the asphyxiating strangleholds of overdetermination and the lavish delusions of intention. At this point, the emergent author not only depicts this strandedness of consciousness but also performs it stylistically, writing in acrobatic linguistic vines, relaying the prose to mutation and a manic spiral between extremes. The poetics here carves against itself so as to tap into a source of corrosive energy, eliciting a holocaust against all prior confidences, blasting open the doors of a region where unities unravel, where the assumed is no longer given, where the bizarre can almost frivolously be dropped into play without judgment. By losing all technical solidity, and with it forsaking the attachment to anything existentially substantive, by wrenching itself into a seamless fluidity that will not hold itself as real, the narrative is left open to jump from minimalist to maximalist without hesitancy, shifting from the exaggerated to the understated without a sense of pause, shift, or rupture. Things speed up without reason or anticipation of what will have a catalytic effect upon the progression or regression of the narrative, allowing only for thematic strands without settled conceptual categories; experiences are left pliable, flexible, disconcertingly amorphous, ready to be compromised at every turn, coinciding and fracturing without necessarily signaling anything, strictly unproductive, never to be integrated into an equilibrium and yet going somewhere. Here one comes across the radically unnerving way in which the text staves off closure, reveling in irreconcilability, leaving the loose ends to prevail in riotous fashion—no redemptive cleansing, no purging of the lawlessness, no soothing indication of a synthesis, but an unreality left confused and convoluted, unappeasingly unaccounted for, open to anything.

And still, she comes too early, for the consciousness present at this stage of the work is still untrained for a showdown with the chaotic, and therein strives desperately to exert its own control. The blind owl orchestrates this search for mastery across two separate fronts: the first in the protagonist's militant need to sketch the angel-demon's portrait, attempting to impose representation upon her, and the second through his killing of her, a violence made even more savage by virtue of its soft execution. In the former case, the narrator sits across from her, maintaining distance, and tries, for an extended period, to lend shape and contour to her otherwise dimmed visage, containing her in the tyranny of form, invoking the blank canvas before him as a medium of mimetic incarceration: "During those hours of solitude, during those minutes that lasted I know not how long, her awe-inspiring face, indistinct as though seen through cloud or mist, void of motion or expression like the paintings one sees upon the covers of pen-cases, took shape before my eyes far more clearly than ever before."[11] Nevertheless, the false clarity with which he has endowed the angel-demon does not diminish her own insurgent spirit. In realizing that he has in fact accomplished no lasting ascription of essence, he decides to murder, dissect, and then bury her in a remote chasm of the earth. For this, he turns to a recurring potion in the story, namely a decanter of poison-wine, one mixed with cobra venom and given to him presumably by his now-absent mother (a temple dancer resembling the angel-demon), which he then proceeds to pour through clamped lips (nothing gentle here): "I remembered that on the top shelf was a bottle of old wine . . . She was sleeping like a weary child. I opened the bottle and slowly and carefully poured a glassful of the wine into her mouth between the two locked rows of teeth."[12] Although the mutilation and hauling of the body will be discussed at length in the following section, for now it is sufficient to reveal the fact that the owl's later departure from the unmarked gravesite of the angel-demon does not detract from the experiential anarchy that she first brought into his walled enclosure. If anything, the immediacy of the chaotic only escalates in the aftermath of her assassination, avenging itself against this cowardice by demanding that the narrator's own consciousness undergo that same destiny it has just wrought upon its "lover," darkness seeping in and swarming it from all sides until its imminent acquiescence: "In the corners of my room, behind the curtains, beside the door, were hosts of these ideas, of these formless, menacing figures."[13] Here we will distinguish between those that rest behind, those that rest beneath, and those that rest beside, and their varying grades of noncompliance.

As this shows, through its obsessive ambiguity, the chaotic initially presents itself to the blind owl as an indomitable virus, a nefarious force from which he must tirelessly protect himself, dispelling its squadron of abrasive trespasses, as if his being were somehow holy, something worthy of permanence, and thus on the defensive, he recedes into the comfort of an interiority-exteriority divide, telling himself that what is taking place has nothing to do with him—that it is all coming from the outside, that the mayhem he now experiences was inflicted upon him by some external malevolence now working its way inward, that it is wholly invasive, and that he is its victim. And so when it comes, this untamed thing, the first instance in the form of the angel-demon, he proceeds toward a vanquishing, pouring the poison down her throat, releasing himself from the grip of what she represents: the chaotic messenger sent to himself by himself so as to adjoin future with present. But his denial will not last him very long, for soon he is compelled to admit that it has all been his own doing, even if concealed from his understanding—that from beginning to end he has willed the chaos that now thrives here and that now sets its sights on the world at large. With no escape from the inscription of this vanishing eternal, no subsequent expulsion of the transparent obscurity into which consciousness has unleashed itself, no burial of the becoming enough to suppress its invariable manifestations, the chaotic survives its own author.

Annihilation's Resurgence: Consciousness Entombed

There is a detour cutting away from the awareness of being, the poverties of ontological harmony, and the nonstate of soul destitution—annihilation as the existential equivalent of a ripping apart at the seams, a tearing away at the core until all comes undone (the untenable situation). Whereas consciousness continually averts the thought of its own vulnerability to an endpoint, patrolling the presupposed limit as if under duress, annihilation demands that it reach out toward the onset of its own cessation, to draw it near to itself and make it its own, such that the ending might then become never-ending (the limit becoming the edge). To visit the most horrendous cruelties against one's own convictions, reaping the harshest enmity against all that one was made to be, challenging even one's own *right to be* until there is nothing left of what once stood as a cohesive self (existential flaying).

There are undeniable traces of compulsive wounding and scarring throughout the earliest passages of the text, now and again seeking mortification, persuading what is most grotesque. This ranges from the first line that "there are sores which slowly erode the mind in solitude like a kind of canker," to the suggestions that "at that moment I was in a state of trance" and "I wandered, unconscious of my surroundings," to the self-description of "a drowning man who after frantic struggle and effort has reached the surface of the water . . . feverish and trembling," though the blind owl's first extended affair with the annihilative impulse materializes through his interaction with the angel-demon.[14] It begins as an extrinsic act, committed against an outside—"her face preserved the same stillness, the same tranquil expression, but seemed to have grown thinner and frailer"—yet then rapidly spreads over and into his own interiority, fusing the two in a singular pathos of deterioration: "Now, here, in my room, she had yielded to me her body and her shadow. Her fragile, short-lived spirit . . . had gone wandering in the world of shadows and I felt as though it had taken my spirit with it."[15] From here the intimacy with this self-perpetrated annihilative event grows even more palpable, the "I" increasingly tattered and frayed with each ensuing incineration, leading the blind owl to draw an almost primordial connection between its own subjective experience and the carrion that lies before it: "I had before me a long, dark, cold endless night in the company of a corpse, of her corpse. I felt that ever since the world had been the world, so long as I had lived, a corpse, cold, inanimate and still had been with me in a dark room."[16] The assemblage of moments following this admission is then tightly fastened to the gradual expiration of the narrator's own subjectivity, as the world outside himself becomes nothing more than a distorted reflection of the imperative toward dissolution—a sensitivity inaugurated by Hedayat's brazenly death-enshrouded visual of a hearse-carriage in which he transports the body (and also his own self) toward oblivion: "I observed, standing in the street outside the door, a dilapidated old hearse to which were harnessed two black, skeleton-thin horses . . . With a great effort I heaved the suitcase into the hearse, where there was a sunken space designed to hold the coffins."[17] This sentiment of engulfing is then enhanced by the physical proximity between the protagonist and the coffin he holds close to him, rousing an imagery of unrepenting carnage, such that "all that I could feel was the weight of the suitcase upon my chest. I felt as if the weight of her dead body and the coffin in which it lay had for all time been pressing upon my chest."[18] Furthermore, once arriving at the burial ground of the angel-demon, the narrator cannot resist casting one last glance at her, and so opens the suitcase in which he has placed her severed frame only to find himself overcome by a sensation of descent into the ground alongside her: "I drew aside a corner of her black dress and saw, amid a mass of coagulated blood and swarming maggots, two great black eyes gazing fixedly at me with no trace of expression in them. I felt that my entire being was submerged in the depths of those eyes."[19] And herein lies the first critical assertion, rendered brilliantly and viciously as an immersion in deadened eyes, of the chaotic's onslaught against being through nondifferentiation—the event of a world-blurring (cancerous adventurism). Such is the awe of a text now littered with a thousand corpses.

Once violated, having drunk from the glass of terminality's madness, having encountered devastation at point-blank range and abided unflinching, having risked fiercely in the knowledge that all greatness thrives in this same wager, the narrator then leaves the angel-demon behind to confront its own impending decimation. Overrun with exhaustion, the blind owl turns away from the wind-swept province of her death to turn toward its own, and therein "continued to walk on in the profound darkness, slowly and aimlessly, with no conscious thought in my mind, like a man in a dream."[20] Slowly fading away, it neverthe-less tries, in a last resort, to deter its own dissipation by standing still, remaining in place until yet another envoy of the chaotic invades to remind him of the unfavorable course to which he must devote himself: "Suddenly I was brought to myself by the sound of a hollow grating laugh . . . 'Lost your way, eh? Suppose you're wondering what I'm doing in a graveyard at this time of night? No need to be afraid. Dead bodies are my regular business. Grave digging's my trade.'"[21] In the wake of this lurking, clarion voice, and granted no amnesty from the unfolding of its own annihilation, the blind owl then rushes home, feeling itself completely saturated with horoscopes of downfall: "The smell of death, the smell of decomposing flesh, pervaded me, body and soul. It seemed to me that I had always been saturated with the smell of death and had slept all my life in a black coffin while a bent old man whose face I could not see transported me through the mist and the passing shadows."[22] This notwithstanding, it is the next passage that conveys the blind owl to the experiential climax of the annihi-lative episode, charting first a "desire" to abandon the "I" and then performing that same offering that he had longed for, amid the sinking of consciousness toward the nothing.[23] Although this interlude marks the culmination of what is often called the first section of the text, the author's own reliance on aftershock and return leads him to reiterate the annihilative premise shown throughout the remainder of the work (serial intimidation and embargo). This perpetuation is observed in the narrator's own continued internal grappling with the prospect of a "becoming no one," one that overturns all concern for the "care of self" and sends the protagonist drifting between hysteria and calm as if they were imme-diately adjacent emotive states, relegating himself to a rampant back-and-forth between affective extremes without a trace of pause or reservation—not even simply indifferent to his own preservation, but actively working against it. The following selection effectively demonstrates the precise way in which this anni-hilative thematic is taken up and then either faintly or glaringly reinserted over and again until the conclusion of the text: "I had many times reflected on the fact of death and on the decomposition of the component parts of my body."[24] And what does it mean to speak of a textual exhumation, to conceive the idiom that builds and then upsets its own necropolis?

With this adamantine pattern established, it becomes apparent as to how consciousness enjoins itself to the chilled ledge of finality, going so far as to treat itself as the last living entity—the one becoming unearthed—and thereby mak-ing its own mortality equivalent to the end of existence itself. In effect, when he falls, it falls with him.[25] Later, across a parallel theoretical axis, the blind owl's infatuation with fire and opium fumes facilitates the introduction of an idea of existential ignition—that is, the "I" that allows itself to burn, enfolded in the flames of self-destruction and self-creation, welcoming incandescence and blaze (becoming enkindled). Also, as it advances, the transformative field of annihilation closes the search for origin, now beyond essence, beyond the tenuous balance between presence and absence—for here one traces a frictional, unclotted void, one of many damnations, one that consummates itself in a limitless spilling-red.

In addition, the explosive commerce between consciousness and annihilation discloses a further element of this philosophical position vis-à-vis the actualization of becoming, one that has already been visited in this project: the trial. Although presumably stalled by doubt, the narrator of this text only seems humiliated, unwell, and infantilized; yet, in fact, he is just biding his time, wearing existence down, seeing which side will give out first, for the blind owl possesses one quality that allows him to emerge from the raid that befalls him: endurance. More exactly, this reduced hero bets on his own endurance surpassing that of the world—though crumbling within, such an annihilative experience must prove itself able to withstand what is beyond all expectation—showing that there is enough within it to leave something behind in the aftermath of being's decline—that something as yet persists amid the instinct's deleterious conspirings, something to quicken the next becoming. Thus that somehow, in some enigmatic way, it can survive itself. In this sense, despite its own assertions to a hermetic disposition, the blind owl in fact seals itself off to nothing, but presents itself with awful vulnerability to each intrusion that strays its way: wherever it might feign negation, whatever overwhelming revulsion it displays, there remains that unyielding readiness to be penetrated—that gravitation toward the unbearable. If anything, this indiscriminate self-endangerment epitomizes a rich disposition toward affirmation, yet one that does not assimilate everything into repressive banalization yet rather into an eruptive confiscation and decentralization of consciousness. As a result, this borderline mind does not withdraw from those underground forces that it would dare to overcome; it brings them toward itself, letting them infest it, though actually manipulating them, sabotaging them of their capacity to damage all the while they believe themselves to be thriving against it (acquiring immunity through hyperexposure). The blind owl knows it can outlast whatever the world might throw at it, and though it is ravaged in each round, the routine works, for it rises again after each annihilative cycle, this time somewhat less entangled than before, ready to lock arms with the next adversary.

The Shattered (Fragmentation), the Shadow-Becoming (Disintegration)

All consciousness leads to the breaking: it all begins with a voice or voices—one does not know whose, and never will, yet poised to give a deranged soliloquy, a retrospective evaluation of what it has endured. And one is wrong to trust it. Nevertheless . . .

One of the methods by which consciousness is stripped of its fixation with permanence, and thus detonates itself into the nonstate of chaotic becoming, resides in a complicated process of existential shattering and "shadow-becoming." Through the first maneuver, the entire spectrum of the text reveals itself to be nothing more than a disjointed topography of the author's own thought configuration, each character just a glass shard in the broken mosaic of a lone consciousness now proceeding toward chaos. This motif of existential splitting resuscitates itself in countless formats—from the striking concurrence of gestures across different personalities on different occasions of the story (infinite doubling), to the macabre scene of the father-uncle twinship as the division of an original singularity into serrated components, to the dissection of the angel-demon as a partitioning of being: "I took a bone-handled knife that I kept in the closet beside my room . . . [and] amputated the arms and legs. I neatly fitted the trunk along with the head and limbs into the suitcase and covered the whole with her dress, the same black dress."[26] Having pursued her weariless, with wolvenesque prowlings throughout the seamless space that is—whether or not he as yet knows it to be so—the burial mound of his own humanity, a peripheral earth waiting to be enlivened once more by his hands, soon to be stained with the currency of his most arduous sacrifice, he now relegates her form to a quartering. And when he finds her, the sinking of the knife into flesh (premiering an almost magical sensuality) offers a rare tactile simulation of the shattering enterprise, allowing one to feel the instance when all that is whole stands vanquished by a rending apart—consciousness cutting inward, flaring and revenging itself against itself over and again—until the arena is readied for the next lethal breaching.

There are many tenants here, all with flasks of textual morphine (ammunition), those who have developed a science of circumambulation and with it a business of creaking, hypocrisy, and grisly superstition. This shattered affect-matrix gains stature through the author's own random expressions of a conflicted interiority, as well as through his strategic incorporation of the mirror image within the confines of the work, rendering perception prismatic, iridescent, and kaleidoscopic. With respect to the former, the narrator attests to some incessant, bare conduction of identity, reflecting on a certain existential multitude that jolts him into perpetual fright such that "it seemed to me that this was what I had always been and always would be, a strange compound of incompatible elements."[27] This transfigurative nonstate, one of tireless disunity, one that compartmentalizes the totality of being into stranded particles, then leads into a fevered experiential dementia; here the blind owl cannot recall what he once was (the obsolescence of memory) nor even possesses a desire to recapture what has since been dispersed to the chaotic scythe. It is within this hermeneutic stance alone, one of a misaligned jaw, that one can then read the refined articulation that "the person that I had been then existed no longer. If I had been able to conjure him up and to speak to him he would not have listened to me and, if he had, would not have understood what I said. He was like someone whom I had known once, but he was no part of me."[28] Reinforcing this unchecked, rabid separation even further, the author then inserts straight denials of self-recognition, lancing the possibility to vouch for subjectivity, making knowledge irrelevant as "the thoughts which came into my mind were unrelated to one another. I could hear my voice in my throat but I could not grasp the meaning of the words," and then it is carried onward as "I involuntarily burst out laughing . . . I did not recognize the sound of my own voice" and "all at once I realized that I was talking to myself and that in a strange way."[29] This incendiary staging of incoherent evocations within and against each other, time and again, produces a schizoid monologue, its own mutilating performativity, dismembering the cohesion of the word as he begins advising, coercing, or screaming at himself, as if faced by an entity apart: "As I looked into the mirror I said to myself, 'Your pain is so profound that it has settled in the depths of your eyes.'"[30] This obsessive shattering of the "I" wears away at mastery, allowing no domination of experience, no imposition of one-dimensionality, no synthesis of a world in disorder, and it is therein that one desists from interpreting the author's dreamscape recessions as an esoteric search (this is an extrawitnessing). Having banished transcendence, this sundering of interiority into a restive flux of "the everything-all-at-once" does not mark a retreat into some abstracted mysticism but rather a ferocious, chaotic engagement with the shattered terrain of consciousness, leaving an arsonist's text—one that is a pyre, that swallows its own bones.

Within this same broken thematic current lies the emergent author's innovative manipulation of the mirror image as a mechanism of shattering through distortion (where thought becomes a host of leaden passengers). The protagonist is foundreplaying these figments on numerous occasions, walking over to the mirror in his room and standing intently across from it, gazing into its glass encasement and ultimately acknowledging the reflections that make their way before his stare. This is an instability conveyed from the early remark that "my face was ravaged, lifeless and indistinct, so indistinct that I did not recognize myself," and then later turned into a magisterial, contentious relationship in the following quotation: "My reflection had become stronger than my real self and I had become like an image in a mirror. I felt that I could not remain alone in the same room with my reflection. I was afraid that if I tried to run away he would come after me."[31] This vigilante reflection aids in presenting the crucial link between shattering and annihilation, as concurrent energies of the chaotic imaginary, grinding appearances down into a grim, unclear powder: "I was pleased with the change in my appearance. I had seen the dust of death sprinkled over my eyes, I had seen that I must go."[32] In fact, the blind owl eventually goes as far as to privilege the distortion over the supposed reality existing beyond the mirror's frame, elevating the untruth of the misshapen reflection, its new empire, above the hierarchies of the objective world to which consciousness clings beyond the enclosure of its four walls: "But on the wall inside my room hangs a mirror in which I look at my face, and in my circumscribed existence that mirror is a more important thing than the world of the rabble-men which has nothing to do with me."[33] This notwithstanding, the mirror reflection only achieves its thunderous culmination through the recursive interweaving of the figure of the old man—a dark and irregular personality who enters and reenters the narrative from several varying angles and with several varying disguises, yet always with the same all-consuming feature, the resonance of a laugh that commingles familiarity and estrangement: "I walked slowly up to him. I had still not uttered a word when the old man burst into a hollow, grating, sinister laugh which made the hairs on my body stand on end."[34] This one wraps itself, forever hiding its face from the narrator, yet only partially, for the blind owl notes with precision that "he resembled me in a remote, comical way like a reflection in a distorting mirror"—that is, that this emergent reflection stands away, though influencing, as the custodian of each experiential movement.[35] As the guardian of every awaited becoming, it propels the consciousness of the narrative forward, toward its own massacre, from its function as the uncle whose sudden invasion of the wasteland sets the story in motion to its reappearance as the hearse-driver—"I make coffins, too. Got coffins of every size, the perfect fit for everybody. At your service. Right away"—to its role as the seller of the bone-handled knife that will elicit the abolition of the blind owl's entire world, to its fusion with the author's own mutated look in the last pages of the text: "I had become the old odds-and-ends man."[36] And throughout it all, this old man, symbolic of an undeferred crisis hour, himself a merchant of the chaotic dregs, expresses his own deep intimacy with the narrator—"That's all right. I know where you live. I'll be there right away"—to the extent that the latter himself suspects an almost diabolical solidarity, one forged in cruelty and torment, with this uninvited character: "It seems to me that this man's face has figured in most of my nightmares."[37] It seethes against all existential security, no longer even leaving the remembrance of a once-centralized reality with which to compare the deviation, for it is this old man's laugh that inevitably perforates the consciousness of the narrator, rendering it a dangerous multiplicity and therein standing as the quintessential emblem of alliance between the shattered and the chaotic.

Finally, one considers the indispensable integration of the "shadow-becoming" as the suggestion of a disintegrating existence, one that pulsates cautiously throughout the unraveling of the text, remaining most guarded, and yet most hallowed, within the author's consciousness. After all, the shadow is blindness itself; it is what turns the author blind and blinds the world, in turn. A collection of inquiries are stationed here:

1. Is the shadow everything that we are not, what we lack (absence), our draining and depletion, the waned substance, or is it the excess of what we are, our vital irruption, the proliferated capacity, heightened to the point of endangerment (ultrapresence)?

2. Is the shadow a figure of concealment (the veneer), a hidden tongue, layered in multiple obscurities, or is it a figure of transparency (the glint) and sheer revelation, in multiple disrobings?

3. Is the shadow the tyranny of the identical (replication), the barren equivalence of our being, a simulacrum of awful accuracy, or is it the pure opposite (reversal), the inverted mirroring whereby everything is displaced, overturned, thrown from one side to the other?

4. Is the shadow a remnant of another place, another past, an intrusion of the elsewhere (the stranger), and now drifting in nonbelonging with an irrelevant birthright, or is it born of our cloth, our unreal reality, at once progenitor and progeny (the denizen), at home in our recesses?

5. Does the shadow accuse us for the extinction of its world (hostility), an enemy formation cut of wrath and vengeance, of the executioner's gaze, or did its fate seal itself outside of our own (the otherworldly), an alienated and disembodied destiny, impassive toward our rise and fall? Does it impose the end, or interfere, and then does it mourn our demise, watch unaffected, or turn its back and walk away?

6. Is the shadow possibility or impossibility: symbolic of what will happen, what must happen, an inevitability beyond even premonition, beyond warning (threat), or the emblem of an unattainable future that is present but can never happen, the unfulfilled becoming, whose denial is always here and now (disgrace)?

7. Does the shadow unbrace consciousness, to become a provisional infusion (extrication), or does it induce a state of submergence and drowning (immersion), to become mesmerized in the inescapable haze, lost to its atmosphere?

8. Is the shadow a slave (to follow), dragged unconditionally, chronically dependent, or a hunter (to stalk), autonomously planning, studying, killing?

9. Is the shadow's hovering the sign of proximity (infinite nearness) or distance (the incommensurate)?

10. Does the shadow harbor an undercover plot for our suffering and deterioration (the poison), a sinister intent beneath the darkness, or does it seek to extend our existence eternally, to prolong the eventual duration of our imprint, toward immortality (the echo)?

11. Is the shadow an evacuation (nothingness), the backlash of the void that now commands, or is it the totality of what remains unspoken, what is still untaken and susceptible to materialization (potential)?

12. What is the significance of the shadow's disappearance (night) and its arrival (day)?

13. Is the shadow prone to intimacy (awareness) or unfamiliarity (incomprehensibility)? Is it wakeful or permanently foreign: has it internalized our ways, trained in them, or remain suspended in illiteracy and disbelief?

14. Is the shadow a false image (simulation) or a secret (dissimulation)?

15. Is the shadow a beginning (innocence) or an ending (exhaustion), a new turn or a requiem, the exhilarated or the dying?

16. Is the shadow the unspoken (inexpressibility) or the deafening (hyperexpressivity)?

17. Is the shadow without nature (unformed) or beyond nature (formless)?

18. Why does the shadow stay close to the ground (movement), to the walls (stillness)?

19. Is contact with the shadow one of instant doom (fatality), slow downfall (curse), or reenchantment (intensification)?

20. Does the shadow serve another, committed to unspoken, perennial oaths (allegiance), or does it move of its own volition, a self-willed force and enforcement (dominion)? Has it offered itself to something other than itself or is it self-contained?

21. Does the shadow desire (compulsion), is it addicted and driven, or does it advance in indifference (coldness), unflinching as it carves against the regime of being?

22. Does the shadow inscribe (memory), leaving scars, or does it erase (forgetting), purging traces?

23. Is the shadow the emergent (anticipation), the timeless (haunting), or the postevent (aftermath)? What is the temporality of its encounter (already happening, about to happen, or too late)?

24. Is the shadow's phantom manifestation indicative of the surreal (underneath), the metareal (above), the hyperreal (within), or the pure unreal (beyond)?

25. Does the shadow return as sameness (inexorability) or does it transfigure itself (chaos)?

26. Is the shadow subject (someone), an identity, or object (something), an instrument?

27. Is the shadow sightless (blindness) or does it possess other sockets (vision)?

28. Can the shadow be deciphered (translation), its imperatives and consequences decoded, or is it unknowable, stranded in mystification and perplexity (occlusion)? What are the penalties and advantages therein?

29. Is there a conspiracy among shadows (collusion), an aerial pact, or are they roving, scattered entities (solitude)?

30. Is the shadow a haven (protection), a fortified depth, shielded from the oncoming, or is it the open (vulnerability), an undefended surface, unarmed before the law of accident?

31. What is the shadow's most perilous orientation, its lethal positionality: when above or beneath, in front or behind, across from or alongside the one who walks?

From the opening pages, the shadow is ascribed a certain sanctity, though itself an agent of desanctification, ever-hailing martial tones, such that the entire work is in fact dedicated to its dread, to its honor, to "that shadow which at this moment is stretched across the wall in the attitude of one devouring with insatiable appetite each word I write."[38] Following this preliminary evocation, innumerable supplementary references to shadowing are then issued forth throughout the story, as eclipses of the organism, a pouring into shape-shifting reports and tinged profiles: "When I close my eyes here in my little room the vague, blurred shadows of the city (of which my mind is at all times aware, whether consciously or not) all take substantial form and rise before me."[39] And as they crowd, this confidential mass, one wonders whether this marks their first city, the third city, or the replicant of a capital founded a thousand times before.

There is no duplicity in the owl's assertion that he takes dictation for the shadow, for this exclusivity determines a quasi-prophetic sector through which the writer (and also any reader) must unavoidably become a shadow entity, accepting the grave price of treading into such realms, torn limb from limb within the conflict of the ensuing narrative. With things thrown into a hundred combative rows, the emergent infringing upon past, present, and future, perpetually out of sync, the emergent author delivers a skillful portrayal of the shadow-becoming without any epiphanic crystallization, no conciliation of discord, no gesture toward an answer, corroborating only the unslaked desire for darkness. There is a different sadness here: ever awaiting its chance, an image seeking the overthrow of the real, an inhumanity courting the annihilation of man, this unquenched intimation makes its presence felt—for it is through the arrivals and departures of such a spectral force (an infliction rather than a haunting) that strife, doom, and peril are exalted beyond compare. And as a last feature of this discussion, one might look at the distinction between the author before the story begins—the "I" of the introduction—and the one who then recounts in present tense what is presumed to be a past becoming. Are they the same figure, however inconsistent, and if not, then whom should one trust? Or, even more amazingly, if it is the chaotic descendant of the becoming that now gives an account, provoking and proliferating this world-blearing, then only one option is left standing: that it is the shadow who speaks here, who writes here, and hence that every word belongs to it alone.[40]

Here thought crawls into a somber perplexity. In concluding this section, there remains the one forerunner statement—"I am writing only for my shadow"—articulated as a supraontological premonition of incapacitating proportions, a distinctive textuality being devised before the eyes.[41] One notes the inherent "must" in operation—the deliberate use of the imperative: there is no alternative to this injunction, no doubt here, only pure certainty regarding the uncertainty of a chaotic imaginary (and the marvel of its unforgiving greed). Thus the event cannot be quarantined: the reverberations of this shattering or shadow-becoming will be wrested outward, tracing the contourless appearance and disappearance of a world where designations vaporize, meanings turn to immateriality, and the laws of being helplessly dismantle before a poetics of rage and midnight.

The Unreal: Infinite Blurring, the Inexistent

A nebulous thought begins to scrape across our midst: profane transgression of what calls itself real, until transgression itself pales, until the profane falls away before a cosmos of the all-pretending. The emergent text situates itself within a province of hypersuspicion that might be termed "unreal," an unextinguished opium haze through which avalanches of gray smoke overcast all judgment of the extent, though this neither implies a dialectical negation of the real (an antireal) nor the recovery or discovery of an alternative reality behind, above, or beyond the "original" (a metareal). Instead, the unreal is what has since relinquished any demarcation of actuality, now left open to an all-illusory operation that maintains no ties to a truth-untruth divide, attending to each sphere as the transmission of an emergent instinct, a rogue orientation for which no prospect of a return to "what is" might remain standing, giving way to infinite blurring.

As a preliminary contention, the blind owl seizes hold of the chaotic through a traversal of the very threshold of impossibility, walking across the bounds of an inexistent office of thought. Certainly, the entire "introduction" of the text can be construed as a strained attempt to approach this inexpressible point, one that leaves the narrator suspended, forced to admit that "it is impossible to convey a just idea of the agony which this disease can inflict."[42] From here things grow even more complicated, causing the blind owl to ask, "Will anyone ever penetrate the secret of this disease which transcends ordinary experience, this reverberation of the shadow of the mind, which manifests itself in a state of coma like that between death and resurrection, when one is neither asleep nor awake?"[43] Afterward, he gestures to resolve his own curved inquiry above, though only to again leave it deserted to undetectable outcomes: "I may perhaps be able to draw a general conclusion from it all-but no, that is too much to expect."[44] Hence, unreality presents itself through the prism of impossibility, a procedure then further disseminated throughout the text in such random yet persistent phrasings as "to a degree that surpasses human understanding" and the warning that "no one can possibly imagine the sensations I experienced at that moment."[45] The discursive structures of the real transmute into impossibility alongside the symbolics of an ordered world (semiotic malformation), an altering that tracks the world into a nihilistic underpass. Yet this is no paralysis, no logic of passive nihilism; rather, it is an alchemical technique, a covert mixture, the unnatural concoction of the event ("that this happens") with its own impossibility ("that this cannot be happening"). Thus the text ejects itself toward a dominion of the unbound, the transitional shift out of nihilism and into the ecstasy of the unreal. More specifically, the blind owl's unwavering endeavor to steal the veil from delusions, and then to transfer them into radical illusions, does not allow itself to descend into a stagnated skepticism but rather hurls consciousness into a rapturous dance with unintelligibility: "Some things in these stories which then used to strike me as far-fetched now seem perfectly natural and credible to me . . . They belong, all of them, to the present."[46] This is a postheroic journey toward the gallery of overappearances.[47] Having paced far beyond a mere indictment of the real, Hedayat slowly conveys the narrative over to an affirmation of the unreal, as a surging affective empowerment, allowing his disoriented narrator to now say that "at times I conceived thoughts which I thought to be inconceivable."[48] Here the text becomes an existential performance of the "what if," hemorrhaging unnoticed ideative artilleries, ready to surpass the entrapment of truth delineations in the service of a chaotic imagination.[49]

Having subordinated the polarized arenas of the true and the false to the conniving traits of the unreal, the emergent author then proceeds to depict, with acute literary sensitivity, the experiential layers of this rhapsodic nonstate (world-as-conjuration). In this sense, one views the frantic, melting chain of dreamscapes and hallucinations that demand execution, that demand both abstraction and realization, as envisionings that immobilize the very possibility of vision, leaving the "why" unanswered. Herein lies the significance of the following: "I feel sure of nothing in the world . . . At this very moment I doubt the existence of tangible, solid things. I doubt clear, manifest truths."[50] As is evident, the emergent figure vindicates the unreal by carrying its legacy into a new doubt-ridden stance, one of the nightwalker, that subtle aerial nowhere of mistrust in which all thoughts are consigned to sliding inferences and questionings. From the narrator's self-soliciting inquest—"had I seen the subject of this picture at some time in the past or had it been revealed to me in a dream? I do not know"—to his further reminder that "my state of mind was that of a man in an infinitely deep sleep . . . One must be plunged in profound sleep in order to behold such a dream as this," and also emanating from the investigation of a particular intersection—"had it been a hallucination or had it really happened? I prefer not to be asked this question"—nowhere is left unscathed, no occurrence granted legitimacy.[51] These entrancing incantations of incomprehensibility cause the world of the blind owl to whirl out of meaning's grasp by detaining the latter in its own mythic boundaries, such that the hunter becomes the hunted, yet all the while openly confessing its own status as hyperfantasia through such existential generalizations as "life is nothing but a fiction, a mere story" and "is not life from beginning to end a ludicrous story, an improbable, stupid yarn? Am I not now writing my own personal piece of fiction?"[52] And yet just as in the retraction of the surface-depth ratio, so is it the case that, in a world where all is poetic fabrication, where all is fictive virtuosity, the very conceptual borders of fiction and fabrication fade into triviality, leaving only a cunning rotation.

It is at this juncture, where mind becomes cauldron, that an emergent literature is then conferred the right to proximity with the chaotic unreal, having trained itself in the overcoming of an authenticity-infatuated consciousness, and now able to enlist a kind of expressive sorcery. What is more, consciousness must affirm its bewitched status, composing an incurable textual spell that abandons any hint of a reality principle—contrived more as a mirage without fading or drunkenness without recourse to sobriety (reign of the amorphous). With this disbelief attained, chaos comes to assert itself as an invalidation of the known, inattentive to the prohibitions of the familiar, tampering with the actuality of every taking-place and thereby spreading its own counterfeit currency. Here nothing is exonerated from the gnawing suspicion that things might not "be" after all—not only that nothing is as it seems, but also that nothing "is," a gradual hyperallegorization of existence wearing away at the assurance of being, such that thought enters into an insomniac condition, heir to a wired, distrustful wakefulness. Beyond this, there is no further need for the justification of illusion, no pretense of validation, no authority before which an explanation must be offered; the altars have fallen, establishing a new criterion of happening, one of secrecy and seduction. Freed from the qualifications of any predictated real, the chaotic imaginary starts to occlude and fog perception, leaving in its wake a nonstate whereby experiential descriptions that might otherwise seem exaggerated now appear neither inaccurate nor outlandish: in the way that the owl's narrative nonstructure exponentially aggrandizes the scales of normalcy so as to be able to hold more than might be expected. As a result, there remains no gulf between appearance and conviction, the signifier and signified, the simulated and the original—here all signs are reduced to inauthenticity, symbolism crucified, as one is given a flawless analogue of the mind's glorious dysfunctionality, brought into the prime site of sanity's disturbance. Here thought salvages itself only as a compound of encapsulated ligaments, as legend and superstition are awarded the same leniency of expression as the rational, reclining from the meridians of reasoned life and into the obsidian underside of an exception that cannot remember the rule. The cast of characters convene to form a community of contingency, each a pillar in the construction of a madman's citadel, an edifice without foundation, housing nothing inside, protecting nothing, safeguarding nothing, and yet still discharging something invaluable—perhaps, in the end, too much. With existence unburdened of its own facade, this consciousness collides real and illusory into convulsive interchangeability, and thus refuses to believe that a world is even transpiring—treating everything as stalwart hallucination, as the once sacred trilogy of meaning, truth, and being finds its ways forsaken before a new task: to hammer out the encrypted.

Unreality destroys unconditionally. Reality provides, within itself, devices that might sanitize its impurity, ever purging itself at the slightest sign of contamination, ever convincing itself of its own hold over the pristine and the immaculate. Unreality, however, so far beyond the cowerings of morality, unashamed of its degraded paths, its dehydrated skin, asks for no cleansing to take place—putrescence, filth, occurrences too vile, too foul, to consider directly, all must be welcomed into the clamor, all must be brought into the materiality of the chaotic foray. And so, aware of this requisite wager, the blind owl eventually charges itself to take unreality into the streets, to induce base warfare against existence, deactivating the delusions of the real with an insurgent garrison of illusions—most noticeably in a scene whereby each individual to whom the protagonist runs and touches abruptly loses a head, showing the ability to alter all engraved codes.[53] This is no surrealist excursion into a remote plane of unconscious convention; rather, the text declares itself as a force of contagion, a raw infection process that persuades by bringing the viral unreal into the physiology of the everyday—no hiding or retreat inward, no escapism of the abyss, no surrender or concession in the face of the supposed actuality of things, no matter how solidified as the absolute, but rather a violent relegation of all to hallucinatory upheaval. Pure entitlement to distill and unload the impure: this illusion will reign over a world that took its own delusions too seriously, denying its lineage, neither to remind it of what it is, nor to burn it down for what it has failed to become (there is no judgment here, only chaotic reflex). The unrestrained versatility of this honest liar is therefore not harmless in its creativity, but sets fires all around it as well, at once playful and fatal, sharpening itself against what will not clear way to the emergent deception, the poetic gamesmanship that delivers all that passes into opium smoke. The liar kills for the unreal.

Aftermath: Nowhere, Elsewhere, Forgetting

We seek the abduction of the boundary (between now and then, here and there). The chaotic imagination entrenches itself in a hostile fight with the dictates of time and space, deterritorializing consciousness in ways that contravene the influence of historicity. To achieve this task, an insistence is placed upon the thematic threads of the timeless, the elsewhere-nowhere, ahistoricality, the aftermath, and the raiding of memory through forgetting.

The relation of chaos to temporality is one of angered discontinuity, of a decontextualized meanwhile, though outwardly cloaked in calm intonations. Thus the blind owl hates time, vitriolically opposed to its limitations, and would like nothing more than to assign himself its assassin, but anticipates that such a dialectical stance would only embed him further in its valences. As a consequence, he invites time to entrap itself, beckoning it to saturate his side and see if it can hold its own while keeping pace with the rash speed of his text, such that moments are found perpetually chasing after words. In effect, he dares temporality to manifest itself in both its most stringent and unstrung forms, forcing it into fluctuations so severe, oscillations so extreme, and contrasts so stark, that it eventually forfeits its symbolic powers of purpose and its existential powers of inevitability. For, in its attempt to catch up and hold down a narrative that cannot be lent rhythm, causation, or sequentiality, time unavoidably fails. In its flagrant defeat it shyly relegates itself to a ridiculous role thereafter, such that the author is then left to call upon it as a translucent, meaningless phenomenon whenever he chooses: "Some time passed; whether it was to be measured in minutes, hours or centuries I do not know."[54] Also, the unsettling of mortality through annihilation disenfranchises time of its capacity to terrorize subjectivity with the loss of permanence, to embody death, which is why the blind owl casually asserts that "time has no meaning for one who is lying in the grave—this room has been the tomb of my existence, the tomb of my mind."[55] This narrative consciousness does not seek after redemptive futures but instead makes time undo itself, unraveled into absurdity by its own hands, such that the author then holds it at his complete disposal, using the arbitrary designation of "two months and four days" to represent either side of the temporal spectrum. It is summoned toward extreme slowness and extreme speed, serving those instances that are the most painfully subdued, circular, and monotonous, and those that are the most accelerated, dissociative, and frenzied, with an indistinguishable touch: "That was two months, or, rather exactly, two months and four days ago."[56] Just as particular images are repetitively inserted as streams of electrical impulses in order to produce localized uprisings in the narrative flow, so is this uprooted time employed only to intensify the dissonance of the eternal: "At what point should I start? . . . Past, future, hour, day, month, year-these things are all the same to me . . . It is as though it [my life] had been spent in some frigid zone and in eternal darkness."[57] Nevertheless, the implication of the eternal is not stasis, uniformity, or existential dormancy but rather an aggravated rapidity, the hyperanimation of becoming, such that it galvanizes the imperishable return of chaos: "I on the other hand changed with every day and every minute. It seemed to me that the passage of time had become thousands of times more rapid in my case."[58] As instants band themselves together into a disturbed seamlessness, time caves inward, abandoning its supremacy over the cellars of consciousness, now at once errant and everlasting, the old temporal barriers now misted over and drowned out by the unstratified volatility of a chaotic eternal.

One comes back to the aftermath. The unfailing repetition of the owl's two-and-four temporal increment should not be dismissed as a rejection of time yet in fact conceived as the opposite: that he gives time all-importance in order to exhaust its dominance, for just as being must tear at itself in heightening recurrences, then so must time reproduce itself as a singular, lush manifestation until the point of its collapse into anarchic infinity, wearing itself down and fracturing through reiteration and hypersensitivity. This is time's reprimand, its lingering, blank ricochet. But to actualize such an erosion, the blind owl must first submit its own existential constitution to a temporal paradox: here seconds must weigh down upon its consciousness with the brutalizing sensation of forever, and yet it must simultaneously feel rushed by each passage, rendering the prose an arrested urgency that acknowledges the panic of the ephemeral, all the while living a life that feels too long. Once this duality is overcome, once repetition-compulsion is employed to the breaking point, forging a soiled logistics, such that the narcotizing duplication and redundancy of actions set "in order somehow or other to kill time" in fact succeeds in *killing time*, each instant is then left to condense itself into an epic instantiation, an ecstatic split-second: "It may be that the space of time in which I had experienced all the pleasures, the caresses and the pain of which the nature of man is susceptible had not lasted more than a moment."[59] As all taxonomies of the moment coalesce into postapocalyptic interruption, menaced by overexertion and now abdicating the search for futural permanence, time gradually subsides into the grasp of an eternal following.

Building upon this later item of time, the chaotic imagination must now stray to the outer banks of spatial experience—to the formulation of the edge. For this reason, *The Blind Owl* foregoes almost any spatial exactness whatsoever, thrashing from point to point while retaining an almost purgatorial stranding of consciousness, forever thrown back to that nowhere-elsewhere in which no thought correlates to another. Although the "I" that speaks here attests to being locked away in a suffocating room, this consciousness is in fact present everywhere, leading into a nightmarish immanence that files every last territory into its world. Thus one must see past the initial articulation of detachment as the misleading insinuation of a reclusive, limited existence. For soon after, the narrator mentions the circumference of his residence with overriding intimacy, his conceivable surroundings, describing a vicinity that imitates his own descent into lunacy, coercing each new area into the tunnels of his own restive imagination: "Only on the far side of the gully one can see a number of squat mud-brick houses which mark the extreme limit of the city. They must have been built by some fool or madman heaven knows how long ago."[60] As his physical and experiential proximity are then enhanced by the fact that he himself is by profession a pen-case painter, generating a raw immediacy between the blind owl and his backdrop, suggesting that he alone could be the architect behind such installations, a trend is established whereby the emergent figure begins to conquer all facets of exteriority. With imperial strides, he then annexes all that is around him, though this postsolipsistic outlook (in the absence of a substantive self) simply transfers all settings into an arid geography—one resembling the unnamed desert of the narrative consciousness (irreducible to a machinery of the same). The simple, meticulous hostels to which he refers, each a median between ill-drafted cartographies, become nets extending across every dome encountered. This is how consciousness submits itself to an interminable wandering, spanning from the carriage owner's inability to chart a straight pathway or course to the destination—"apparently the driver of the hearse was taking me by a by-road or by some special route of his own"—to his own incomplete walks through the wasteland: "I had no idea in what direction I was going . . . I did not care whether or not I ever arrived at any place."[61] And so, such spatial exile is an unmistakable manifestation of the chaotic, for soon this abyss will become a labyrinth, and ultimately an edge; it will violate the limit, its dissent a freefall, beyond gravity, as consciousness now finds itself deterred by nothing, oblivious to all obstacles and perimeters, crossing lines and thresholds without even the slightest recognition of their existence. Chaos is itself a temptation to slickened movements (across the slate).[62]

An emergent literature reveals an often confused and seemingly contradictory association between history and the timeless, spanning a heated antagonism between what lays behind and what is ever elapsing, such that one might forge a preliminary rift between the author's conception of history "as it is" and history as it would "become himself." In the former paradigm, history is upheld as an accidental yet unstoppable defilement, depleted of all meaning or purpose but, in its vacuity, capable of deterring sublimity, extorting the decomposition of being into alienation through successive resimulations of the original treachery, obtaining vengeance for absence, each passing moment stacking adulteration upon adulteration and, in doing so, immortalizing the obscenity of the world-as-real. This history supports the ceaseless violence that arrives amid truth's need to hide its own untruth, defending its pseudoexistence within the essentializing caverns of objectivity, linearity, and rationality. And so the blind owl finds nothing in this excavation of the past but a dismal necrophilia, desolate and bleak, impoverished of itself, and therein inverting the typical version: history is no longer the recipient of an agony but rather is the agony itself.[63]

The above depiction notwithstanding, this second standing potentiality—that of timelessness—is commissioned here as a vying functionary of the chaotic, allowing it to jeopardize and impair the continuum of time-space. With incredible complexity, the author then proceeds to reinvite the past into the writing-act, though this time as a traitor to itself: in this unprecedented appropriation, antiquity is used to wield imbalance, a technique of insidious subversion that causes the standardized to come loose, to wrack itself and disassemble (revealing that there is no before, no within). Nowhere is this played out more distinctly than in the narrator's confrontation with a vase from some since-vanished age, yet one that identically matches his own initial envisioning of the angel-demon: "There was not an atom of difference between my picture and that on the jar . . . The two were identical and were, it seemed obvious, the work of one man, one ill-fated decorator of pen cases . . . I wished that I could run away from myself."[64] Here forethoughts become keys, gestating in recurrence (and with rising vigor) to form nothing that one could call anything, this emergent continuity disclosing a foreigner's space where one has no idea what is taking place, cyclically bargaining itself in invariable, ahistorical loops. The timeless event, then, is difference without individuation; it remains porous, open to bane, mishandling, and insolvency. And with this, consciousness must take the appointment upon itself, shouldering unmediated accountability for the striations of the world, no dividing line between existence and its own instinct: "Was not I myself the result of a long succession of past generations which had bequeathed their experience to me? Did not the past exist within me?"[65] This interlacing extends even further as he nears the "conclusion" of the story, the timeless and the "I" merging together, bearing the unbearable entirety, as his own face becomes the obligated conveyor of an unknown chaotic legacy: "Were not the substance and the expressions of my face the result of a mysterious sequence of impulsions, of my ancestors' temptations, lusts and despairs? And I who was the custodian of this heritage, did I not, through some mad, ludicrous feeling, consider it my duty, whether I liked it or not, to preserve this stock of facial expressions?"[66] At first glance, this profession appears to reinforce the subservience of consciousness to some overwhelming, extraneous current, though, in fact, it is just the opposite: here the directionality is reversed, an ingenious transposition of the flow between consciousness and event, such that the former no longer conforms to its circumstances but rather the world adapts to it, matching the impassioned sways of its will. In this sense, the blind owl is no microcosm, entrenched in no slave position, but rather ordains a mercenary reciprocity with existence. All is owned by this allegory—past, present, and future just sanctioned reflections of the architect's impending fight—such that the blind owl's mania rests upon a breakneck ingestion of the everything, yet all the while evading a totalitarian regression by virtue of two points: first, that it also brings subjectivity to the breaking point of annihilation, dispossessing the "I" of its centrality and mastery by forcing it into a preemptive attendance of its own fatality; second, that it impels itself toward the chaotic, such that, while revoking the former history, no substantive system or structure surfaces in its place, leaving only a discordance without beginning or end in sight. In this respect, every artifact becomes a piece of the timeless fantasia, every object reeling toward chaos, elevated and reconfigured: "From all the articles laid out before him came a rusty smell as of dirty discarded objects which life had rejected . . . But what a stubborn life was in them and what significance there was in their forms! These dead objects left a far deeper imprint upon my mind than living people could ever have done."[67] Here consciousness robs the discarded articles of their former destinies—these remnants now speak in its malevolent inflections, accomplices to its tremors.[68]

Beyond the epoch, beyond the episteme, beyond the decadent projections of the futural, still perhaps the most pressing step toward the overcoming of time-space-history implements itself in the act of forgetting, for chaos makes memory obsolete. And it is here that the emergent author shows unrivaled mastery, in the ability to recapitulate and reproduce images and events without enforcing a process of inscription, simultaneously coordinating repetition-compulsion with an affective slipping into the amnesic. Memory must lapse, nowhere more flagrant in its application than in the episode of the twin's trial, whereby two brothers walk into a locked space with a cobra and only one emerging, only one surviving, or perhaps not even: "His face was ravaged and old . . . the horror of all this had changed my uncle, by the time he walked out of the room, into a white-haired old man."[69] This one—changed, unsound, negligent of mind, no longer ruling over his own identity—this figure reenters the world as one who cannot recall himself and who therefore cannot know himself, now set to roam as a chaotic apparition of what once was yet is no longer allowed to "be": the phantasm of an unreality that cannot be presided over by any logic of remembrance. And just as "the trial had deranged his mind and he had completely lost his memory," so must the narrator, too, undergo the test of a tailspin into the blank plane of extermination—yet only as an affirmation of the chaotic—and thereafter caught fast throughout the text in the ironic posture of one forever reminding oneself to forget.[70] Here the text begins to stagger, to deflect all critical inspection: for the literary imagination becomes a sinuous cord, at times austere, rigorous, and transfixed; at times shredded, dissected, and gouged, yet always overdosed and mired in vice.[71]

The Chaotic Instinct: Excess, Silence, the Rant

Chaos is a black-hole theory. This section ventures to examine the idea of instinctuality as an acidic engulfing of the world, so strong that it forsakes all attachments to the rails of subjectivity, intention, causation, the psyche, and representation. As an opening note, the paradox of the instinct in an emergent literature is best exposed through the multifarious relation of the "I" as author, the "I" as protagonist, and the text they collectively create and destroy—the tortured indecision of the narrator camouflaging the devious genius of an author who remains strictly attentive to the minutiae of a narrative, always on the verge of spinning out of the control of them both. This supposed schism is essential, though, for by the end, it will be undone entirely: the punishment of the protagonist is not alleviated by any revelation of truth, nor does the author wield any further authority for having gone through the doorways of a chaotic imaginary, nor does the text's own sinister ambiguity finally lend itself to clarity or closure. All remain in the open, except now confederated, and hence with no dimension of the alignment administering greater jurisdiction over the others, for each possess the same annihilative power, the same annihilative vulnerability, the same smoldering compulsion.

In line with this proposal of a chaotic instinct, the consciousness of the blind owl is constantly found decrying and venerating a pulse that at once exists within it and yet travels beyond its immediate comprehension or mastery. Although at first the narrator posits this nameless, unforming exertion as in opposition to his "will," calling it a vestige of some fatalistic imprint, it is in fact the instinct itself that motivates the world-enveloping procedure of the text. Thus one finds a series of junctures throughout the work in which the narrator cannot explain or account for his actions, nor can he draw it into the undercover shelter of intentionality or choice, and yet he acknowledges that the expenditure of these intensities emanates from within himself alone (self-apprenticeship): "What I do know is that whenever I sat down to paint I reproduced the same design, the same subject. My hand independently of my will always depicted the same scene."[72] As is obvious in the second excerpt, the blind owl initially relegates responsibility for the instinct to a separate entity, portraying himself as the casualty of an imposition beyond himself, satisfied that even the gliding movements of the angel-demon are indicative of a misdealing reality-unreality: "She had come like a sleep-walker, independently of any will of her own."[73] These attributions, however, are a strategic distraction, a carefully staged diversion alluding to some primordial energy in motion, reaching from the claim that "solitude and death were my destiny" to the determination that "my whole life . . . was destined to be poisoned and any other mode of existence was impossible for me."[74] Nevertheless, the protagonist soon reveals the ruse—affirming the chaotic instinct as its own and yet never under its ownership, exhibited in the gradual apprehension of each textual experience—that is, that no one else could have done this. As a result, consciousness begins to risk disconcerting closeness with the event, leaving behind a sense of alienated solidarity: "somehow I always felt this subject to be remote and, at the same time, curiously familiar to me."[75] From here the blind owl cautiously forfeits the insistence upon external inevitabilities and instead progresses toward expressions of desire and militant focus, declaring that "what life I had I have allowed to slip away—I permitted it, I even wanted it, to go" and that "I must speak as I think."[76] And still, while this solid transition is in fact a precursor to the chaotic, Hedayat maintains the text's instability by interjecting specifically anti-intentional scenes, not as random happenings or as the accidental interventions of some otherness but as the inadvertent, miniscule triggers of the instinct and its vagrant trajectories. This phenomenon is displayed most eloquently in the following excerpt: "Lying there in the transparent darkness I gazed steadily at the water-jug that stood on the topmost shelf . . . By some obscure impulsion that had nothing to do with me my hand deliberately nudged it so that it fell and was smashed to pieces."[77] As the image of the shattered jar confirms, here chaos starts to usurp mind and body so as to subjugate both beneath the warped enforcement of the instinct, alleviating any phase of contemplation, as a nonstop ratification without meditative pause. This incident provides a flawless example of the demand for a simultaneity of thought and practice, the advance and retreat, engagement and disengagement, of intensities, not as a spontaneous doing but as an unchoreographed execution of forms and techniques learned previously in abstraction and now manifest in the smooth immediacy of the task—that instantaneous commingling of anticipation, desire, and action in a single impersonal detonation. It is never a primal category, for the chaotic instinct emerges as a mode of intuition cultivated across the elongated passage of becoming, though dragging itself outside of time—not given but rather the product of tireless existential trials—and yet consolidating itself as sheer momentum, an ultrasharpened surging, beyond the tempo of understanding, evoking unrest long before consciousness can catch up to speed.[78]

Although ultimately inaccurate, the possibilities for a psychoanalytic interpretation of *The Blind Owl* are undoubtedly measureless, allowing any number of such discourses to flourish within the text's concurrent manipulation of states: there remain fractal resemblances of the oedipal complex, repression, the unconscious, the dream state, mourning and melancholia, cathexis and transience, the death drive, the mirror stage, the love instinct, and the ravenous tensions of the id. Each of these pathologies, psychoses, and drives can be rendered specific correspondences in the work: passing from the similarity of the angel-demon and wife to his ultraseductive mother; his neurotic need to bury the dead body and suppress its memory through magnified dosages of opium and wine; his self-flagellating torment over the loss of his spirit-lover, his semiagoraphobic nature; his infatuation with the withering of things; his insomniac fixation with sleep; his ominous longing for nonbeing; his fascination with mirror images and distorted reflections; his manic back and forth between pleasure and pain; and the final act of eroticism that takes place in a circus of fetish-objects. If anything, this outline avows the inexhaustibility of psychoanalytic readings of Hedayat's work, and yet this project's ambition would aim to demonstrate precisely how the narrator overcomes such a constrictive existential and hermeneutic framework: detraumatizing through an overoccupation of consciousness with psychic plagues. Thus this rejection does not insert itself haphazardly, for the blind owl first allows himself to inhabit every fathomable symptom with hideous susceptibility, baring himself defenselessly before a ghastly set of afflictions, until the point that consciousness exorcises itself of all psychic barricades, granted an elite immunity through hyperexposure.[79] Furthermore, without rehearsing the argument in full, it can be said that the psychoanalytic elements of the text grow archaic once the narrator withstands a number of realizations: (1) that there is no world beyond it, but that it also belongs to no world; (2) that there is no remaining subjectivity possible (annihilation); (3) that all experience is tied to an illusory project, erasing the hierarchies of surface and depth; (4) that memory has become disenfranchised, undermining trauma; (5) that the instinct evicts the unconscious. With these preconditions in attack, the psyche—like being, subjectivity, and the real—finds itself outmoded and entirely irrecoverable.

Keeping under consideration the overture of a chaotic instinct beyond subjective-objective dichotomies, beyond phenomenological or ontological coherence, and beyond psychic paradigms, this examination can then proceed toward a discussion of the writing-act itself and its outstanding function within an emergent literature. For if the Platonic imperative was fueled by an attainment of immortality through reproduction of the immaculate form and soul of thought—a gradual and successive ascendance toward light—then chaotic nonidealism requires not a descent but a spiral into annihilative mortality via the breakdown of representation, ironically overlapping with the former in the mutual renunciation of the mimetic process, but without the substitution of a new eschatological ladder. No longer looking beyond the cave (there are many caves, and frequent indoctrinations), no longer reaching toward or revolving around truths that never hold, no longer making promises that cannot be kept, the chaotic instead enlists impermanence and imperfection, placing them forward to harrow, to malign language and art, and "the search" they necessarily enjoin, unnerving the metaphysics of unity with a resilient aesthetics of excess, disfiguration, and dissimulation. This writing, in turn, must stray toward the unmeasured and the inarticulate, toward a cadre of paradoxes—instantaneous eternity, deafening silence, blinding darkness, solemn ecstasy—toward the entropy of representation itself.

One aspect of the blind owl's existential immiseration—its constant stripping-away—lies in the ejection of language from consciousness: a practice that takes place with every scrawling upon the page (the far-reaching onslaught of the embodiment against the copy). This covert betrayal of the writing-act, however, is at first lost beneath the author's own sly suggestion otherwise, one that elevates the literary event to a level of crusade: "I am obliged to set all this down on paper in order to disentangle the various threads of my story."[80] Soon this fanaticism over aesthetic representation grows even more pressing, converting itself into an unrelenting desire to record and engrave moments into the world, nowhere more visible than in his encounter with the angel-demon, whereby he sits to the side obsessively sketching her portrait: "I felt that I must record on paper its essential lines . . . Thereby I hoped to create from the resources of my mind a drug which would soothe my tortured spirit."[81] Here the failure of the artistic exercise is brought into complete transparency, as representation unmasks itself as an instrument of distancing and domination—a vicarious, derivative, and imprisoning transaction—the mimetic interlude between the narrator (as artistic subject) and the angel-demon (as artistic object) tainted by a parasitic attempt to capture and codify the experience of the chaotic. The result is a tainted economy of conquest, one that resurrects the order-based divergence between consciousness and experience, which seeks to pacify what would otherwise fall outside its frontiers, impressing technique, stasis, and salience onto what is no phenomenon (and yet that can only be sensed). The blind owl even confesses freely, "This [writing] is the best means I have of bringing order and regularity into my thoughts."[82] And yet the blind owl will become increasingly discourteous to this vulgar imposition of power, aware of its standing as a failed replacement—a weak shunning of the event shrouded in the myth of creativity.[83] The aesthetic imagination is therefore not yet the chaotic imagination, its innocuous simulations are not the visceral piracies of the unreal, and its activity is not the radioactive animation of an emergent instinct, for while the former insulates consciousness from experience, the latter endangers consciousness and everything it surveys. To this end, the text will slaughter the tie between event and language by making words pay what they owe: improved contact with an existence turning unreal.

The chaotic text accomplishes this siege against representation through two distinct mediums: excess and silence. In the first case, there are certain episodes throughout the work in which the author exhibits an almost shameless gamesmanship with the subtleties and nuances of language, showing what appears to be an incredible appreciation for its minor variations, only to damn the word through this same valorization. It is an offensive that is hard to fathom: to explicitly indulge poetics at such a high caliber of articulation, only to turn back in ambush and overthrow the edifice of language from the ground up—extrication through effusion, sacrilege through reverence, devaluation through mastery—keeping one's enemy close so as to ensure the necessary proximity for defilement.[84] Such is the strategy of an emergent literature vis-à-vis writing: to overuse its structures to the point that it reels into the supraparodic, the supraironic, the misinflected, the experimental and the free-associative, and ultimately into the unsound, leading language toward breakdown, steering it toward deactivation, policing words into hyper-combustion, watching the gears fly as it crashes through its own regulatory machine, and reaching out toward the labyrinthine distortions of a style that can no longer be gauged. Herein lies the birth of the rant, its zero pit, and the decisive textuality behind a chaotic dialect.

Alongside the emission of language into excess, an emergent literature also enlists silence against the hegemony of the word, forging another entrance into the rant, for it is silence that makes chaos torrentially palpable in the rebellion against representation—ultraexpressive without susceptibility to meaning formation.[85] And so the narrator discusses silence as a supralinguistic force of excitation that neither slows nor arrests the progression of time but dramatizes and accelerates the bond between subjectivity and finality to the extent of producing an experiential eternity: "The silence had for me the force of eternal life; for on the plane of eternity without beginning without end there is no such thing as speech."[86] As the once-formidable columns of temporality and thought crash into the lawless density of a chaotic consciousness, silence assumes its role as a courier of the becoming—a roving bedouin empire ever caught between extinction and oasis and with no tracks behind (one senses that something was there only by the blood of others left upon the sands). It is in the absence of a subjectivity, or rather in the hyperpresence of an annihilated subjectivity, that silence proves itself as the carrier of infinite potential, a pandemoniac slang for which anything can infiltrate at any given instant, from any given angulation—the institution of signs suspended with no chance of restoration, its societies eliminated with no chance of restitution, leaving only a new clearance of listening.

The extreme implication of this scandal brought against representation is the obsolescence of art by existential deception. The aesthetic takes license to play at false gods within the perimeter of the work, to build and destroy, to create and annul, to ration life and death, anguish and joy, at any given instance, entirely at will and unchallenged, yet only as long as it remains sheltered in a detached space of the dream; the chaotic imagination, however, takes such license in the so-called world, threatening its reality and testing itself. Although art is generally thought to be mimetic of life, here it is not that life strives to be mimetic of art but rather that the division itself be adjourned (to care less for art and life), such that the aesthetic here does not speak truth, nor even speak to truth, nor muses upon harmless fantasy, but communicates only the harmful, concrete untruth that supervises an annihilated existence. Hence, the intoxication and intrigue of aesthetic creation is not eradicated but rather transferred into an aggressive existential current, a wicked indentation, beyond the power-scarred subject-object exchange—not as a return to experiential purity but rather as an original infliction of reality's impending unreality, the unsigned hieroglyph, the irreproducible rant.

Haze: Immanence, Sectarianism, the Faction

War is the new criterion of engagement. One of an emergent literature's most stunning accomplishments is its ability to entreat literary devices into reciprocal warfare by hazing the interiority-exteriority demarcation, constructing an abrasive molecularization between textual components that leads everything toward a submerged outside. Strangely, though, this adaptation originates from a hyperinsularity, which is why the text starts from a radical withdrawal, an ingrained sealing-off to the world for which no intrusion is tolerated: "I withdrew from the company of man . . . and, in order to forget, took refuge in wine and opium. My life passed, and still passes, within the four walls of my room."[87] This undiluted recession, a movement into the straits of the isolated, is then made an accomplice to the situating of disparate spheres, that of man and that of the blind owl, as entirely independent of one another: "Ever since I had been confined to my bed I had been living in a strange unimaginable world in which I had no need of the world of the rabble. It was a world which existed within me, a world of unknowns."[88] And so, this resignation to austere inner recesses, into an exclusionary consciousness, carries with it a manufactured hierarchy between the real and the self: "Among the men of the rabble I had become a creature of a strange, unknown race, so much so that they had forgotten that I had once been part of their world."[89] This prechaotic consciousness is thus momentarily held captive by itself in itself, burrowing inward, damming itself in, condensing all that it is into the narrow straits of self-containment, exerting upon itself the tightest form of existential compression until it cannot hold itself in any longer and starts to overflow, gradually overlapping with the adjacent world, exuding itself in rampant floods.

Soon after the experiment with insularity, a new pattern surfaces: one of recursive hazing, one that clouds the lines of what is inner and what is outer, one that is self-formed, and one that operates beyond (chaotic immanence). And so the blind owl stirs from its once-adamant territoriality to a hyperbolic deterritorialization, from stark self-sufficiency to addictive projection. In this vein, the first noticeable intersection takes place when the protagonist digresses beyond the perimeter of its wasteland residence in search of the vanished angel-demon and therein observes a direct parallel between the environment and its own existential condition: "On the last evening when I went out for my usual walk, the sky was overcast and a drizzling rain was falling. A dense mist had fallen over the surrounding country."[90] This fusion of interior and exterior across geometric, optical, and meteorological blocs continues in later descriptive accounts, as the world increasingly adheres to the blind owl's alarming state of mind, such that the subjective and the objective, the self-encircled and the atmospheric, participate simultaneously in the chaotic becoming: "All at once I found myself wandering free and unconstrained through an unknown town."[91] Caught in a reverse imaging, the outside closes in and conspires, bringing moods to fruition that approximate the decapitation of being, from the horizon "covered with thick, yellow, deathly clouds which weighed heavily upon the whole city" to "a funeral procession [that] passed by in front of my window."[92] The settings therefore simulate an assenting mutation of consciousness and existence, striking an eerie resemblance across borders, a federation of mistaken likenesses, always breeding phantom emulations: "Particles of soot from the flame settled on my hands and face like black snow . . . I smeared the particles of soot over my face."[93] As the ashes of the opium fire gel into the narrator's own body, itself a physical chaos-instantiation, ex-corporating self and world, this reflection-conversion excels beyond the threshold of distinction. All becomes the outside and becomes the edge.

Here one tracks a rusted quarter of the mind, the precinct of its new injustice, for the blind owl's treatment of the other suits this same established haze technique, all textual personas riveted together in the realization of a warlike lattice. Once again, though, this is no level alignment, no even distribution among players, for the chaotic is not some higher archetypal phenomenon toward which everything succumbs equally. Above all else, the interpositionality comes from a sweeping, monumental consciousness that invariably absorbs the other and the real, only then to flicker back upon itself and chisel away (until.the embers). Before tracing this procedure, though, one must start at the axis of the narrator's overwhelming disdain for the other, renouncing "the rabble" as a collective depravity, taunting their lack, as lifeless missionaries of reality's vindictive cause.[94] From this vantage, the blind owl contracts itself away and against, seeking amnesty from the rest, therein driven to condemn: "It seems as though I have forgotten how to talk to the people of this world, to living people."[95] The demand at this hour, then, is neither toward proximity nor toward a fluid reciprocity with the other but rather toward a massive disidentification—one that upholds asymmetry over equivalence, incommensurability and incommunicability over communion, and mutual sovereignties and solitudes over the search for closeness with the residents of a propagandistic, unconfessing reality. Here nonrecognition and disproportion supplant the tyrannical drive for sameness, tearing down the false appendages of intersubjectivity; here consciousness must defend itself—it must remain a state of exception.

Nevertheless, this protective chamber must soon be punctured, for the fall back into unadulterated consciousness becomes impossible upon the arrival of the angel-demon, thereby initiating an inevitable encounter. At first reaction, the old suspicion seeps through, causing a miscarriage in their first interaction, with the blind owl claiming, "However much I might gaze at her face, she still seemed infinitely remote from me."[96] The wording here unveils an intricate operational logic, for it is precisely this gaze that fortifies the advantage, a despotic stance through which it can watch and thereby know her, a proof that consciousness has not yet learned to go blind and that the passage into hazing remains temporarily halted. Still, a subtle transition occurs when the owl then forces her to become cognizant of its own presence—she, now staring back at it, lifting the boundary between them through a single look, and by extension, disqualifying the cordons of an autonomous consciousness: "Her feverish, reproachful eyes, shining with a hectic brilliance, slowly opened and gazed fixedly at my face. It was the first time he had been conscious of my presence, the first time she had looked at me. Then the eyes closed again."[97] Advancing even further, the blind owl then desires to lie next to her upon the bed and hold her to itself, generating a terrestrial ring, sacrificing the rift and entering into a new, complex anatomy: "I thought that I might be able to warm her with the heat of my own body, to give my warmth to her and to receive in exchange the coldness of death; perhaps in this way I could infuse my spirit into her dead body. I undressed and lay down beside her on the bed. We were locked together."[98] Too late for a revocation of the exchange of glances, beyond the point of return to its prior sanctum, this one will then embark upon the most punishing intimacy: that of betrayal, wrought through murder. This decisive act, in turn—the insertion of the poison flask through clenched teeth—forms the tainted circularity through which all others will be carved into and integrated toward the layerings of a now multiplied consciousness: "There were bloodstains on my cloak and scarf and my hands were covered with blood."[99] Thus the particles are taken up and proliferated, borne into the mean chaotic drift, often in conjunction though more often in sectarian feuds (these are the same anyway).

Now overstepping its grounds, allowing itself to internalize and ration alterity (and the ulterior) through the contusions of a split personality, this consciousness spreads itself outward, vandalizing the sanctity of the real with a scathing, illusory touch. From this damaged juncture, the narrative voice strides across the world to wildly assimilate anything available, consuming all it finds toward its vortex, toward a lone skull on the verge of a monstrous and irrevocable chaosing. With this rationale navigating what lies ahead, each semblance quickly begins to fall at the altar of the owl's rapacious becoming, such that all colludes in a growing, mesmerized present: every other that crosses its way places consciousness under existential duress, every image an accessory to its metamorphosis, such that it eventually becomes a scavenger of perspectives.[100] From a criminal to a vagrant, from a butcher to an old madman, this rampant mobility between identities encourages an existential whirlwind that leaves nothing stationary—an evaporation into synergistic uproar. A more sullen, mercurial testament manifests within the seemingly tangential presence of the butcher—a blood-stained figure who the blind owl now watches intently from the window in its room, yet all the while aware of their increased blending across the following development of excerpts: "I can see the butcher every time I look out of the window. Early each morning a pair of gaunt, consumptive-looking horses are led up to the shop . . . Then he takes a long bone-handled knife and cuts up their bodies with great care, after which he smilingly dispenses the meat to his customers."[101] As thought and experience enmesh, as reflections and events consort and collaborate, phenomena grow immanent to the extent that no phenomenological calibration can be leveled. And it is here that the narrator finally entertains the tragic-ecstatic possibility that all things and all visages, however fractured and hostile, however raving against one another, all feed back to its derelict consciousness. There is a divulgence here, and a division of labor among the characters, or rather an aristocracy of shadows, such that no matter where the emergent figure turns, someone is waiting for it, some anarchic envoy ready to throw it onward, all of them derivations of an atomized yet common astonishment, born in the same back alley, and still one that it cannot as yet figure out. These are the ones who borrow and stalk from every existential slant, wrenching the text toward the vertigo of its group, its low-pitched ensemble, from all angles, piercing through to detonate its interiority into the timeless desert of the outside (where so many go shrill).

It is through this sudden diffusion of consciousness, reaching from within its own underground lairs and out into an all-encompassing, viscous perception, one enabling a profound and unremitting miasma, that one can then proceed to monitor the complicated relationship of this emergent literature to its reader. Recalling the general vision of existence forwarded here—that of an interception of cruelties, one that even the text is forced to inhale and exhale—one arrives upon a tendency within the author's early work worth mentioning here: that he kills his own creations.[102] Feeling that the imagination is indelibly failed by the world—that the effusion always goes unappreciated and the sublimity denied—the author, in most instances, causes his protagonists to become embalmed in some form or another. That these personages constantly meet an awful demise, that he snatches them toward death (or worse) right at that moment when an opening presents itself, proves an act of retaliation stemming from his own rancor—his wronging by an existence that cannot bear the sight of an emergent chaos. Hence, even when, for a fleeting instant, there appears a hidden expectation that things could persevere, though they never do, Hedayat swiftly tows such idealized anticipations toward the chasm of despair and inescapable loss. He knows they are too powerful for the world into which they are born—a species too pure in all its profane dementia, not meant for this plane—and thus that they will not survive the world's retribution. He knows the real will come for them eventually, knife in hand, for it is a timeless law that the exception must be extricated, that all destinies must descend into the black mirror of oblivion. And so he ends it, enacting a mercy killing of sorts, for better they meet his hands, waning from the caress of a father, than from the gray violence of a stranger's noose. Yet from within this execution-style murder of the text, a dire contract is forged as well, for Hedayat then looks up at the spectators, covered and amid the carrion, and makes them watch him do it, crouched over the dead bodies of his children. He chastises with this sinful, anomalous sight, that they were wasted on this graveyard earth, and thus deprives access to the imaginary. If he cannot have them, if he cannot hold on to them, then surely he will not let the real have them either, hauling his tragic descendants back to the abyss just as quickly as he breathes life into them—a testament to the fact that man has not yet earned this becoming, retracting the offering just as soon as it is lain before him, for he knows the latter can do no better than defilement.

Thus his "Buried Alive," as a protracted suicide note, marks a triumph of sorts, for whereas his first characters proved too weak to fend for themselves, necessitating the author's coarse intervention, the consciousness of this particular text is able to enjoin its own finality. But then there is an even higher moment, one wherein an ending will wrench itself into an alternative beginning, for there is one he lets live, one whose voice remains when the curtain closes, his most invaluable, the wildest product of his fantasias (the blind owl). No, this one he will not let slip away so easily; this one can hold its own against the world; this one might actually win, though it is not trying to, and all the while taunting man with the thought that such an inhuman force is still out there, that it still stands, and that unlike the others, it has not fallen yet and now preys.

This is how the reader is made to slacken, made to kneel at the foot of someone else's stairway, in the lamplight of someone else's nightmare. If it is such that man is not worthy of the chaotic imaginary, then the author will demand that the reader of this text inhabit a different, unwise molding—the kinship across words become like that of the butcher's to flesh, ever dispensing shattered totalities, and now charging that his consumer risk alongside him, wound into his rhythms, turning toward a new thirst. This chaotic methodology therefore heralds a collapse of the trilateral configuration of the interpretive event; for here the author, reader, and text must all fuel themselves through the same apparatus: a tilted instinct irreducible to its source, leaving only the elliptical cyclicality of an atonal literary concert. The hazardous implication, then, of the blind owl's assertion that its writes "only for [its] shadow" is that to read it, one must become its shadow, and in that acceptance inviting the onset of one's own annihilative dance. One must change alongside it, enduring each step undaunted, for it invites a reader who can stake more this time, who can indulge the maniacal wager with thoughts and words, one who will not turn away from the shadow-becoming.[103] And it is from within this vampiric posture—that, essentially, it writes to watch one become its own—that one of the most compelling facets of the work undrapes itself: its *pure visibility*, that is, that none of this is suppressed or censored, no intent hidden, for the entire plan of the narrative, however illogical in design, is disclosed in the opening account. From the inaugural passage, the author announces the subsequent trajectory, without concealment, showing its secret hand immediately, the full textual cosmology of the shadow-becoming overturned in this address, such that the narrative arc remains cryptically arranged but not confidential, remaining mysterious by necessity alone. As a result, the reader is thrown toward contortion in full sight, the mapping of this unnatural quest made available at all times, beyond exclusivity and privation, its deep entanglements accompanied by warnings from the outset. For despite its own trance-like overtones, this textual lure makes categorical the repercussions soon to be incurred, reciting the terrain beforehand, therein able to stare the reader in the eyes before ascending the chaotic staircase—no guidance yet no false assurance either; no ventriloquating voice to branch the road, to make one believe one stands on familiar ground; no false airs or counterfeit resemblances baiting one into the hasty misrecognition of having reentered a reality location, all the while held fast within a dislocated unreality from the leading utterance. Here textuality becomes an open seduction, each line an iconography of translucent deceit. And so, any supposed abuse that takes place arises from the reader's own desperation alone, striving to interpret what shrieks beyond meaning itself, clasping to groundless hermeneutic assessments so as to feel safe from within the rant, anchored, to breathe easy that the idols still rest unharmed in the temples. One can only hope that these crooked echoes foretell something other than what they say, looking away from the raw campaign of what counsels that this is not just any text, but one with an errant purpose: to destroy the act of writing itself, and being alongside it, at war with all that is (and with what still wants to be).[104]

Textual Evening: Postapotheosis (Midnight)

How does the death of one man become the death of man—such that when this one bleeds, they all bleed—a single cadaver becoming a universal insubordination? Such emergent prototypes are born in the cemetery of metaphysics, with nothing left to mourn, and thus opening onto another deportation: to become a god, and then to die as a god, gaining its taste for immensity (divinity searing). This is what remains by the evening of a chaotic imaginary: "The charcoal in the brazier beside me had burnt to cold ashes which I could have blown away with a single breath. I felt that my mind had become hollow and ashy like the coals and was at the mercy of a single breath."[105] This is how a chaotic textuality instructs itself: it disowns and misguides every thought, it vilifies itself, turning consciousness into a serous, raven mass. It pays its erratic price, for to betray the world, it must betray the idea of its center (only a wolf can kill a wolf, only a god can kill all gods).

One has perhaps asked and seen too much already at the expense of the pupils (and even the retinae are long gone). One has seen the maturation of a prelude-turning-elegy and what it includes (its colonizing inventory): the hostage, the occupied territory, the legion, the corridors, the mouthless, the scarcity, the idleness, the armored, the dessication, the gateway, and the obliteration of what stays.[106]

Thus one is restored to the shadow-becoming, consciousness asked to inhabit its hanging outline, one that is itself many things, for countless secrecies are at work within the impenetrable vault of this bad air. Above all else, though, the shadow is the sensation of man's effigy, undressed and vivisected, taunting both its birth and its death, defiling clay and dust, for it must become that augury that sweeps thought from the obelisk of being—its stigma and its slave trade—and files it down to its dwindling, inert ground. Here one sees only its hovering, its invalid slowness—that thick, brooding glaze of criminality, the unmistakable look of subterfuge, stamp of what waits (with nothing good in mind). The shadow is the black magic of the aftermath, its agile, inhuman hooks. It is the deep-seated scandal of the night gone wrong—its horror and its solace.

It is this extravagant trial—its elliptical rings, its hail of pure abandonment, its traitorous winds, and lightning throughout the darklands of experience—that surpasses and unsettles, that scandalizes and never rescues, that wins us lethal extremity. An impostor apotheosis built on perilous grounds: avarice, confiscation, and wrath. One finds oneself changed: one rediscovers consciousness as the interrogated, the tarnished, the wayward, the one of disintegrating infinity, and the one that harbors an unclean miniaturism residing somewhere between misfortune, travesty, and contempt. Thought is unarmed, given to aversion, brutality, and conflagration; thought is marred, extradited to maimed and purgatorial places, to evanescence and blocked sublimities; thought turns barbaric, caught between vitriol and affliction.

TACTIC 4

The Inhuman (Chaotic Incantation)

Prelude

(supralife) (the apocalyptic modality) (irrelationality) (introversion)

(the impassioned) (scorn) (sectarianism) (vandalism)

The Inhuman I

(symmetry) (reactivity) (horizontality) (sensation)

(fluidity) (expanse) (atrocity) (vertigo) (the primeval)

The Inhuman II

(paralysis) (the antidream) (absurdity) (deformity)

(the third god) (darkness) (irradiation) (resemblance) (abomination)

The Inhuman III

(pretending) (defiance) (escape) (impatience)

(the incarnated object) (the transition) (disproportion) (elongation)

The Inhuman IV

(virtuality) (the forerunner) (refuge) (mistrust)

(the overseer) (vanguard consciousness) (last breath) (the momentary)

The Inhuman V

(synchronicity) (alignment) (alienation) (addiction)

(synthetic resurrection) (the contraption) (weariness) (malfunction)

The Inhuman VI

(antiuniversality) (density) (cyclicality) (doom)

(the afterworld) (drowning) (paradox) (subversion)

The Inhuman VII

(playfulness) (severity) (savagery) (guilt)

(the misled) (incursion) (barbaric pleasure) (the unsafe)

The Inhuman VIII

(surrender) (the archetype) (predeath/postdeath) (inexplicability)

(the arc) (evisceration) (the quest) (the foregone becoming) (futility) (impossibility)

The Inhuman IX

(instrumentality) (automation) (the underlying) (vileness)

(coercion) (invincibility) (unnoticed volition) (neglect)

The Inhuman X

(intimation) (the miniscule) (sightlessness) (noise)

(panic) (derangement) (the emissary) (the symptom) (mist)

The Inhuman XI

(heresy) (tribal writing) (the kindred) (the mistake)

(the nemesis text) (extinction) (transaction) (vice)

Forthcoming/Threnody

(kneeling) (sleep)

One wonders about the connection between the emergent and the inhuman, as it casts an enigmatic shade across the landscape of world literature. The ones behind this have unlocked a new, distinctly nomadic language—at times secretive, esoteric, and even encrypted—which converts conditions of banishment, dispossession, and erasure into a cutting-edge experiment with the limits of poetic consciousness. Such movements seize upon the writing act to improvise a vast array of inhuman alternatives, including the animal, the monster, the child, the phantasm, the machine, the element, the criminal, the martyr, the thing, the madman, and the poet. The intent here, then, is to demonstrate the complex ways in which these errant, inhuman worlds reconstitute themselves as provinces of thought and expression beyond the dialectical entrapments of power and resistance, universality and individualism, subjectivity and otherness, enlivening their own camaraderies, enmities, adorations, and dominances. One sees this magnified through textualities that reveal themselves as adventurous artifacts—those that, when invited, walk the fine line between guest and intruder and those that designate the place where emergence becomes emergency.

Prelude
(Supralife, Apocalyptic Modality, Irrelationality, Introversion)

I am able to transform: the land-mine of civilization—this is my name (a sign).
—Adonis, "This Is My Name"

One begins a hardened prelude, one that manifests the skeleton of these new inhuman passions as they spill across the following quadrology of principles:

1.   The inhuman does not seek to exist but lives farther than life extends, across the outer walls, past its finite dominion. Thus it embodies a concept of *supralife*.
2.   The inhuman implicitly supports the end of the world, proliferating discourses of strangulation, untouchability, and scorn. Thus it embodies an *apocalyptic modality*.
3.   The inhuman maintains its radical sectarianism, housed in rival factions, with no formal acknowledgement of one another, though commingling on certain rare occasions, forging networks of schismatic collaboration. Thus it embodies a concept of *irrelationality*.
4.   The inhuman brings something back from beyond, an agitation that unsettles the monolithic constellation of self, a pale import that protests against the soul and vandalizes the inside. Thus it embodies a concept of *introversion*.

One must endorse these assorted dispositions, their deeply sewn intolerance, their unruly vivisections of the real, for together they circumscribe the chemistry of a bad future.

The Inhuman I
(Symmetry, Reactivity, Horizontality, Sensation)

I shall see the face of the raven in the features of my country, and I shall call this book a shroud.
—Adonis, "This Is My Name"

The first inhuman entity falls across the following conceptual axes: symmetry, reactivity, horizontality, and sensation. To speak of its *symmetry* is to envision its even posture and interlocking teeth, its jaw an opening onto fluid and inseparable contraventions; a writing of this kind would therefore inhabit the steadiness, calm, and devouring propensities of an instinctive language—one of warm, unyielding limbs. To speak of its *reactivity* is to recognize it as something that guarantees no security, no permanent loyalty, for it can always harm, maim, turn on the keeper, rip apart the beloved, retaining its sting and its bite (it is prone to complicated misunderstandings). Hence, it demarcates the imaginary of animality, for it witnesses other potentials, the unenunciated planes, beneath the spoken, attuned to the fact that the first gesture always hides a second, meaner intention, and guides itself by this stratum alone. To speak of its *horizontality* is to watch the way in which it stretches across, rather than builds upward, privileging speed over structure, travel over monumentality, territorial elegance over imperial possession. Moreover, this allows it to level existence upon the wires, freeing it to greater, anarchic inequalities—those of unstable plateaus—and thus substituting vertical vertigo (based on notions of the height, omniscience, and finality) for horizontal vertigo (based on notions of the expanse, unknowing, and insatiability). Finally, to speak of *sensation* is to note the way in which it strings together conflicting grains, preying in smooth waves, approaching as an outcry and premonition, without obstacle or doubt, and that serves but one unavoidable purpose: to feed and punish. This sensation is the reason why it is often the symbol of ill fortune, the omen of oncoming evil, its arrival a forewarning of some primeval atrocity.

The Inhuman II
(Paralysis, the Antidream, Absurdity, Deformity)

In my third blood, I saw a traveler's eyes blending people with the waves of his eternal dream, carrying the torch of distances in prophetic knowledge in savage blood.

—Adonis, *A Time Between Ashes and Roses*

The next inhuman entity falls across the following conceptual axes: paralysis, the antidream, absurdity, and deformity. To speak of its *paralytic* effect is to recognize the awe behind its presence, as one is drawn before unthinkable properties. In this way, it stands as a kind of third god, one of unintentional worship, where fright becomes exaltation and where to even conceive its rule is to be killed. To contemplate, assume, or believe it is to request its agony—to meet the impression that strives for the nonbeing of those who call it forward, a victim of its cataclysmic inspiration. Thus to speak of it as the progenitor of *the antidream* is to note the vicious texture of its image: an unwanted visitation that seems to emanate from the dreamscape—from the oil of the nightmare—but actually finds one in the crevice between trance and waking and then coils back beneath into the obsidian glow (without reflection). And now, beyond its darkening point, to speak of the monster's *absurdity* is to realize that there is always a feature taken to extravagance, the irradiated quality, sign of its unbalanced physiognomy, forever misshapen, as well as the defect that seals its vulnerability. A writing of this kind would thus acquire this lone flaw, its exception-unto-burial. Finally, to speak of its *deformity* is to admit a pseudo-resemblance—some exposure of sameness, though in mutilated (and thus stronger) form, the eyes now beholden to an aesthetics of disfigurement and aversion and to the terrestriality of abomination (displaced organs, useless appendages).

The Inhuman III
(Pretending, Defiance, Escape, Impatience)

Is there in your nightfall a child for my history? The legacied dust is in the bones. Shall I take refuge there? Does dust give refuge? No place, and death is of no use . . . This is the dizziness of someone who sees the corpses of the ages and stumbles motionless.

—Adonis, "This Is My Name"

The next inhuman entity falls across the following conceptual axes: pretending, defiance, escape, and impatience. To speak of its *pretending* is to aid its regimes of simulation—its admixtures of mood and untruth—to derail the established order and incarnate the metamorphic, the fatal miracle, in the careless object, and thus to permit its artificial innocence. To speak of its *defiance* is to tempt the runaway—what seeks the hole, the window, the well, the fictodementia of the staircase, anything that leads apart and toward transitional astonishment, the archway or the portal (for this is a traitorous entity). To speak of its *escape* is to marvel at its capacity for reinvention, as it collects stories, captures imprints, stores the postmetaphoric world in vials, eliciting an antisymbolic journey always of minorized disproportions. Finally, to speak of its *impatience* is to slide into its unslaked time, a counterchronology ceaselessly elongated, as if there were no future, each delayed second a mine of anguish.

The Inhuman IV
(Virtuality, the Forerunner, Refuge, Mistrust)

I learn with you
the banishment that murders me
in ruins and the sheerest voids
I break from jail
to seek the man I keep becoming.
I leave the gate ajar,
the chain empty,
and the darkness of my cell
devours me like eyes in shadow . . .

—Adonis, "This Is My Name"

The next inhuman entity falls across the following conceptual axes: virtuality, the forerunner, refuge, and mistrust. To speak of its *virtuality* is to be lured by its appearance, confounded by the disappearance, as it oversees the unreal, patrolling the valley between emergence and withdrawal, assigning the schedule by which the vapor takes form, hovers, and then retreats to the formless, loyal to its own self-vanquishing. To speak of it as a *forerunner* is to sense that this disembodied shade has been there quite long, before even its keeper, protecting a phantom wisdom, some vanguard consciousness, for one notes its cautious expertise and the discretion of its riddle (thus we seek a writing that would harbor spectrality). To speak of its *refuge* is to ask after what hides in its ethereal contours—what stays and bides time—since man will not dare go there, will not cross the halo of its infinite tension as if it were the half-tangible demonstration of its own last breath. Finally, to speak of its *mistrust* is to solicit the anxious, an inconsolable split of the moment, since one cannot rescue what is meant to stop here nor what goes slack: its echo alone can at once manipulate, covet, and unnerve, for it acts as the enemy, the stranger, and the foreigner.

The Inhuman V
(Synchronicity, Alignment, Alienation, Addiction)

I notice a word. Around it everyone of us is a mirage, is clay. Remove yourself from the paths of its steps and you are lost, alienated, become a demon, a slaughterhouse.

—Adonis, "This Is My Name"

The next inhuman entity falls across the following conceptual axes: synchronicity, alignment, alienation, and addiction. To speak of its *synchronicity* is to indicate what turns the raw, dismal base of world into a phenomenon, once obdurate matter now assigning a procedure, an irreligious ritual wherein metallic forces participate in a synthetic ceremony. To speak of its *alignment* is to recognize what calibrates the mingled parts, transposing pieces cut for insertion, the ongoing compression of vises, and the rise of the contraption (thus one seeks a writing of horrendous replication). To speak of its *alienation* is to see the mechanism in discord, self-detesting and coated in weariness, for there is some agony here, wound through its design, its screeching, an inexpressive rite of immiseration. Finally, one speaks of its *addiction*, how it remains chained to the immutable routine, the worst rungs of fatalism: where one can no longer say "no" to the destiny that brings the malfunction and the eventual combustion.

The Inhuman VI
(Antiuniversality, Density, Cyclicality, Doom)

The winds, the winds
unshape and shatter on his brow
so many scattered reeds,
such crowns of violence . . .

—Adonis, "The Martyr in Dreams"

The next inhuman entity falls across the following conceptual axes: antiuniversality, density, cyclicality, and doom. To speak of its *antiuniversality* is to stare as it careens against "what is"—an offering to what ties nothing together, for there will be no systematicity, only the cracked and the fluctuating afterworld. To speak of its *density* is to discover an infatuation with elemental drowning, with inundation (the whirlpool, the downpour, the sandstorm), where one is forced to swallow dust, nailed down by the surrounding thickness. To speak of *cyclicality* is to enter its aerial paradox—one of transience, resurrection, and split-second endurance—for it incites an ancient, unrighteous movement between departure and return (thus one seeks a writing of the wasteland). And so, it expresses itself in rounds, in unpredictable, wavering successions, with each rotation a reminder of what has yet to happen, though closing in, delivering its forward amnesia. Finally, to speak of its *doom* is to observe how the particles shave against existence—their atmospheric treason—for there is another subversion here awaiting its chance, outlining misfortune in smoke, flame, and rain.

The Inhuman VII
(Playfulness, Severity, Savagery, Guilt)

I am the specter, watchful in the openings of the city while
the people sleep.
I entered a trap of light, pure as violence . . .
Let the spears of eternal battle be born
There is a pit of destruction between us
My voice is the ravings of the raider
As he shatters the scepter of songs and uproots the alphabet.

—Adonis, "This Is My Name"

The next inhuman entity falls across the following conceptual axes: playfulness, severity, savagery, and guilt. To speak of its *playfulness* is to open the venture—its drama and exhilaration, its lethal diversion and game—and thus to become the misled, to breed the misguided, and to compete in persecutions. Here, the author is nothing more than a degenerate, a calculating degenerate with a skeleton key, for it inherits a profile somewhere between sublimity, emblazoning, and malevolence. To speak of its *severity* is to allow the incursion, and to measure by impact, by the success of its night raid—not what it is nor what it means, but what it does and how far it pierces the inside of a context, leading us to ask, what imposture pathology scrapes here, recruiting itself without bandages? To speak of its *savagery* is to devise a rank of violence based in idleness, wherein one conquers for no reason—without ideology, rationale, or even need yet out of leisure, boredom, indulgence, and mild vanity. This is its barbaric pleasure: to unearth a fine, primitivist domain of cruel luxuries. Finally, to speak of this one is to convert space itself into an apparatus of *guilt*—to find the fastest corridor to the unsafe situation, the proposition of a trap, where all beings are under accusation and all lines become self-convicting pathways.

The Inhuman VIII
(Surrender, the Archetype, Predeath/Postdeath, Inexplicability)

I gallop in the voice of the victims, alone on the brink of death, like a grave walking in a sphere of light . . . / I surrendered my face to the flood and wandered in my debris.

—Adonis, "This Is My Name"

The next inhuman entity falls across the following conceptual axes: surrender; the archetype; predeath and postdeath; and inexplicability. To speak of its *surrender* is to track the one given over, relinquished to a self-forfeiting arc, such that everywhere appears an altar, across which transpire ontologies of the exploded chest. This is its evisceration, ever facing what declines, wanting foul rest. To speak of *the archetype* is to be cast into anonymity, where the name is sold to the cause, the individual resituated as the category: the idea, the collective spite, and the execution (thus we seek a writing of the gallows, of the scaffold). This is its quest: where the signature drops, soaks, and exhumes itself in neutrality. To speak of its *predeath* is to host the countervalence of its *postdeath*, to map its foregone route, impaled at both ends of the existential continuum, wherein the body instantiates itself as willed, aggressive futility (the already-dead, the dead-too-soon, the dead-too-long). We draw a line here between monstrosity (the undead) and martyrdom (the ultradead): the first, the one for whom death has become the only outlawed principle, and the second, the one for whom death becomes the only law, with everything outside death now forbidden. Finally, to speak of its *inexplicability* is to uphold its status within the incomprehensible, where the torso brings crisis, the impenetrable action. Thus we seek a writing of wicked impossibility: to approach the rare degree of "what must never happen," for desperation alone can create the stage for the indescribable to inscribe itself.

The Inhuman IX
(Instrumentality, Automation, the Underlying, Vileness)

I sing the language of the spearhead. I shout that time is punctured, that its walls have crumbled in my bowels. I vomited: I have no History, no present. I am Solar insomnia, the Abyss, Sin, and Action.

—Adonis, "This Is My Name"

The next inhuman entity falls across the following conceptual axes: instrumentality, automation, the underlying, and vileness. To speak of its *instrumentality* is to test its inclination to be taken, used, relentlessly exploited, for it belongs not to itself but rather to the cynicism of the grip. This is its coercion, an entire cosmology based on hardness, softness, smoothness, and sharpness (thus we seek a writing of envenomed tactility). To speak of its *automation* is to chronicle an involuntary event—the spine of its programmatic unfolding and consequence, its unconditional acceptance and total invitation—for this is also the guarantor of its invincibility: to outlive the master and then, owned by another, under further control. To speak of it as *the underlying* is to accept a tremor of unrevealed animation within: that it contains its own reserved volition, an unnoticed pulse and ambition, though in temporary restraint, and that it riles even in apparent tranquility. To speak of its *vileness* is to know that it will serve anyone, that it is made of an amoral composition and therefore enslaved to all hands, commissioned for whatever lies ahead; whether it is recalled or stays disarmed, as the derelict item, in neglect and suffering the dormant periods, it persists in its absolute drone. And still, this is only a subterfuge, for one must recall that the thing rests at the origin of all idolatries.

The Inhuman X
(Intimation, the Miniscule, Sightlessness, Noise)

There is nothing left to sing my melodies: the dissenters shall come and the light shall come at the appointed hour . . . Only madness remains.

—Adonis, "This Is My Name"

The next inhuman entity falls across the following conceptual axes: intimation, the miniscule, sightlessness, and noise. To speak of its allegiance to *intimation* is to feel that something stirs—something mercurial, nefarious, some thorn—now a reason for jumping from the ledge of sanity; thus we encounter its curvature and its panic, a victimizing sentience, where epistemology succumbs to rumor. To speak of *the miniscule* is to glorify what is most unwell—the light strokes of hysteria—for there is something wrong in everything, an inborn derangement, and this itself instills a macrocosmic discourse, mouthing prophetic outcomes in an age unstrung from metaphysics. To speak of its *sightlessness* is to spit upon the obvious, to ransom perception to the unseen, and to become its emissary (thus we seek a writing blindfolded). That is what one finds in those wild, encapsulated eyes: pure responsibility. Finally, to speak of *noise* is to detect what composes the incoherent, which impresses itself upon nebulous and unfocused auditory areas, releasing the tones of incensement. This conveys its symptom and its mist at once, for what is this crucible of sound where ideas adhere to a dire rattle?

The Inhuman XI
(Heresy) (Tribal Writing) (The Kindred) (The Mistake)

I let Cain be proud of his grandson.
—Adonis, "Remembering the First Century"

The next inhuman entity falls across the following conceptual axes: heresy, tribal writing, the kindred, and the mistake. This eleventh one surveys all such dens and counsels the ravenous turn therein, itself a caretaker to the enclosures of the others. To speak of its *heresy* is to enlist the defeat of the prayer, to confiscate the boundary between sense and raving, and to leave language itself unrepentant, compelled to scrawl a nemesis textuality. This is where thought fears itself, scared of what it does, of the whiteness it incurs, and that it seeks its own unhealing. Thus to speak of its poetics is to designate a rank of *tribal writing*, where the word becomes a dispensable resource—an oasis drained and then forsaken, dried out by what talks in a near-extinct tongue and that drags itself across uninhabited grounds. To speak of *the kindred* is to know that there are others, roaming in mixed bloodlines, though they know not where, since this hypnotic accompaniment stays somehow removed and irreconcilable. This is its transaction: that when it grieves, the other stands transfixed. Finally, to speak of its *mistake* is to confess that it should never have been born, that it comprises the ejection, the unanticipated offspring, of a linguistic vice. For the writing act was born in squalor and must be brought back there to regain its destitution.

Forthcoming/Threnody
(Kneeling) (Sleep)

There are those who stand equipped to become grand practitioners of such varying inhumanities, trading in their devalued currencies, since the survival of a certain thinking depends on it. Such a resolution cannot be disavowed, for they must be able to inhabit this archive of rising tendencies; they must internalize and project such prototypes—their abrasion, rancor, and trickery, and the ways in which they rail against the cells of man. And so, these are not anthropomorphic taxonomies but rather anthropotoxic illusions, alchemical frauds and false promises of transubstantiation. Nevertheless, they occur, they materialize, fueled by their own inauthenticity, for only the impersonal could revenge itself with such difficult scope, training itself in episodic violations. Above all else, though, this outsider delirium induces a state of *kneeling*, contracting man as an unaware accomplice to humiliation, for here he bows, caught in the guise of a supplicant, and thus paints his own gradual decomposition.

Other essential questions reside across this inquiry: for instance, which of these are creatures of *reversibility* and which of *irreversibility*; which becomings can turn back, undoing history, and which advance interminably, trampling over the lane behind? Both present their own danger, both leading onto imperiled roads, and with their own unsought solutions. Moreover, each passage here, each formulation, bears a peculiar relation to *sleep*: some are insomniac creatures, some sleep with eyes open, some murmur throughout the night, others flail, some haunt unsuspecting reveries, some visit and steal through houses while the decent masses sink under, and still some keep vigil, composing damned verses that will betray the coming dawn. There is no floor below.

EPILOGUE

Corollaries of Emergence

What remains at this point are the corollaries, those that speak of continual perishings, and the intimations that follow. This is an electric intervention, one that lengthens the end of the world (fever can be purchased here).

1. Chaos executes itself as an endless becoming and dethroning of existence, leaving it extinguished in the aftermath of an immeasurable ignition. It is the exclusive agitation of a self-defined plane, an elite counterworld for which objects depose the objective and subjectivity leads to the faltering of the "I." It is the unbracing of the absolute, the last dishonoring of all orthodoxy, including its own, desanctifying all drives to hegemony, self-devastating and all-devastating. This unrivaled intensification, ever distending toward a hallucinogenic monumentality, allows for hypersubjectivized perceptions to serve as gateways to the extinction of subjectivity, self-flooding, annexing everything to the point of decimation. In this instance, where only the "I" remains, and then only to submerge itself in a postontological deluge, consciousness emerges as a challenging and forsaking of all things. Here unyielding insularity transfigures into an uncontained blurring, bringing thought toward the arena of its own reflexive desolation, quickening its velocity—a wearing down through acceleration, the solicitation of a radical singularity that then corrodes, radiates, and combusts the everything.

2. Chaos is consciousness taken to its most violent extreme, toward the abolition of the self in a world where nothing but the self has survived—a sharpened indulgence leading away from permanence and toward the unruly precision of affirmative destruction. It is the quasi-incantatory expenditure of the "I" toward the crossroads of its own

necessary weariness and self-excising, such that there will be nothing left over, no debris to haunt the coming event. Here there is only fire—that of the unbridled advancement, no longer dominated by a source, where flames stretch out toward engulfing, therein diminishing the genesis of all things to futility (existential incandescence). This exertion streams and sends experience hurtling into martial throes—an inhale of what goes beneath, seething, immoderate, until the vitiation, leaving oblique and convoluted.

3. Chaos is thought taken to the precipice of thought's immateriality, the unraveling from within (what tears away at itself)—a fading projection, against all self-regulating technologies, adherent to no functional center from which to instrumentalize its brutality. Here consciousness enfolds its movement in a hazed irrelation, for which all thought becomes a privileged breaking, one that thrusts the world toward wild disarray, unbowing before its pretense to unity. No, there is no immutability of the one, for chaos takes its share (it takes everything). It is the maximization of an already hyperbolic conception: to approach refraction, becoming the disguised, the untamed, and the disconnected, and resting across the glass shards of a shattered mirror (this is the madman's lantern, reflecting all-distortion).

4. Chaos is the vigilant obsolescence that takes place in the wake of the edge—a circularity that halts the agent of circulation, the absurd pronunciation of what cannot inhere, vanquishing itself through replication and proliferation. It operates along a paradoxical equation, epitomizing a hyperindividuated fusion with even the most decadent facets of existence, ultra-admission, claiming all as its own. It is the focusing of thought to the point of its saturation of the real, runaway universalization to the point of its irrelevance, and thereafter compelling itself toward absentia. Chaos sweeps consciousness toward the farthest experience of namelessness, patrolling the world into the disquiet of multiplicity, interrupting its disembodied trance (the gradual gifting of the "is" to an extraneous, barbaric hybrid). The older concerns of identity become archaic, relics of an outmoded stance, for it rapidly weakens the polarities of subject-object, being-nonbeing, self-other, altogether discarding the asphyxiating master codes of the real. This chaos fortifies itself without surrender to a concept of the limit, no caged condition that might then cleave existence into domains of possibility and impossibility, yet leaving behind only the extravagance of a desert without margins. Without the postulate of an experiential circumference, without the pledge of an occluded modality of being, an unrevealed truth-value, it asserts

itself as the transparent mania of the unreal. Thus if reality instates the paramount moment of border formation, definition, and the drawing of mythic contours from which all other principles follow, then it is the chaotic that disallows such divisions by enhancing and thereafter striking at the source of boundaries. It is the disbanding of this constrictive, claustrophobic, and finite zone of a generic subjectivity, one that instigates itself toward a daunting apotheosis. These are the holes found beyond being, flung into vortex, the infinite sieve, all that surrounds pulled toward a massive energy already chiseling away at itself; this is the perilous seduction at stake—the absorption of the object into a subjectivity already under departure.

5. Chaos acquires itself through annihilation, itself an undiluted suffocation without the romanticism of martyrology—not as an idealist submission to the end (it has no palms), yet as an obliteration without conscience (to deplore the brow, the skin, the glow), extemporaneous calamity from inside the item. To have intuitively fated the eviction, impoverishment, and subduing (there are no greater decompositions). It is a temptation-act beyond and against the self, at once fueling and impairing consciousness into reflexive evisceration, the ripping of its pages, opened to the trials of self-adversariality (the unrelaxing ones). Annihilation, then, occurs not as self-automating consequence, since causation no longer holds against unintelligibility but as a self-ejecting element enacted beyond the mediations of knowing—an alchemy of euphoria and waste. This is its creative tendency, crawling slowly toward the experience of the end as unmotivated sublimity—a heated slope to forfeiture (the new contempt). While death in the real cannot be ascertained by subjectivity, perpetually alienated, the chaotic thrives upon the indeterminate experience of finality, enduring nothingness without the regression to mourning—a self-ravaging enchantment. It allows thought to recline into incommensurability, congealing inflation and implosion, invigoration and decline, as an initial affair of barrenness then inverts toward saturation and back again. It is the insatiate and the devouring, until there is nothing left (exuding while decaying). Chaos steals death from its recesses, wrenching it away from phenomenological certainty, neither as a spatial externalization nor as an ethical architectonics of unity but as a simultaneous eruption of presence and absence (this is its vexation). To this degree, the annihilated interweaves desolation and desire into eternality, immortalizing the experience of mortality, exposing the vital intersection between diminution and resurgence, cessation and return, giving way to a crucible of emergence, aftermath, and timelessness.

6. Chaos must dare to hallow the eleventh hour of man just as it delivers its requiem, rendering superiority to the advent of the inhuman. This episode rejects the barricading of consciousness and experience, waiting until both stand unopposed by the bad faith of an "ordered death," no longer dialectically negated by the overdeterminations of the real, and then turning toward sabotage as a reckless masochistic custom (the sovereignty of the undone). Beyond reactivity, transcendence, and defiance, beyond the barriers of exteriority and interiority, beyond the altars of subjectivity and objectivity, this dawns as willed rupture—a continuous ethos of discontinuity. Here the absolute is slain, no longer an alien negativity but an undifferentiated matrix, defacing the tyranny of the "is" from every angle—the effusion of desire toward the heightening and the overwrought.

7. Chaos owes itself to a region of experience where movement and stillness commingle interchangeably in unnoticed signals, the breathless exchange of excess and oblivion. Here all anxiety is dispelled (the inconsolable), with consciousness becoming an undistressed channel, a trespass into finality that affords a vantage of empowerment, undertaken as improvised, instinctual bloodlust. It infiltrates the domain of nothingness, inhabiting the elegiac dance of its abysses, so as to project it toward the autonomy of an unreal space. Having traversed the jagged territories of the void, having overcome the terrorizing hazard of mortality, now beyond its traumatic grip, it escapes toward a new criterion of fatality. From within these many subterranean spheres, there comes the helical endorsement of a death inheritance—"buried alive" as the most torrid depiction of this loop. It is the vanguard of an oncoming imaginary, inscribing itself upon existence as an authorless text, surfacing to exterminate all regimes of meaning—that being itself would expire amid the rise of this lone incantation. Beyond this, one is assailed by a vicious mirroring, the first reflection having broken the self and the second now breaking the world-as-self in unremitting fragmentations, consecrating the impending unreal through an endless existential casualty, turning catastrophe into chaos. This is a self-violating stance against the imprisonings of world, a vision-prism of contraction and explosion for which the restive echoes of annihilation alone remain to rule the deprivation. It is to become both dead and alive, enlivened by death, deadened by life, the circling of a phantom age. As a transformative intensity beyond the iron castings of comprehension, a lethal coalition of extremes, chaos binds violence and desire together in a singular assault against consciousness and the real. With this inundation—an outpour of presence and absence across the impasse of terminality—the limit falls under erasure

amid a collision of affective energies. One can only estimate the possibilities released to consciousness at this point, now left prey to the embrace of dissipation, wherein existence treads toward the heart of the wasteland, swarmed by attrition from the zero degree. It is not merely entered into as a metaphorical journey through and beyond the darkening but rather assumes the terrain of experience, a devious site, where ambiguity holds free rein, born of increments and factionalism. Here the outlandish arches of the tightrope and the acute variability of the dice throw are no longer confined to philosophical tales, for one is enjoined by incarnations of deliberative chance. This is how each impulse becomes an unreserved trend to extinguish, an antihumanist technique of dissolution, without amnesty from the wondering (executed impossibility). Here all experience is upheld as an atomized pyre, entreating immolation—the thirst for self-enkindling—and through its night flares reintroducing the republic of signs to the unfathomed. Whereas the real institutes itself as an ultimate monolith of the sacred, this incites consciousness to turn against its own, resigned to defilement, to the stained—rampant exercise of the profane confusion as alleyway to a new rank of becoming—though not before it drags the entire discourse of the real under alongside itself. This is the death of man wrung out from within and then set upon the world.

8. Chaos is an infliction, a punishing character of exposure, immersion, and exorcism. It brings incensement, grasps its own hell, its own pandemoniac influence—a protocol of captivation and downfall. It conducts this fatal component as a sensation of what verges; it wills the unsafe, the predatory, and the fatigued toward the straits of abduction; it generates an architectonics of entanglement and irreversible agony, accelerates in meridians, and fractures the surrounding continuum; it turns fugitive and thereby extradites its anger. Here consciousness lays hands on a doomed event, held to its theft and plague.

9. Chaos is the vitality of existential warfare, the provocation of the inexistent, now slung against being. In wrenching consciousness beyond the narrow aisles of subjectivity and metaphysics, now divorced from such sunken gashes, it can turn back against the real from beyond its borders as an assassin potential—cold and unattached, yet wanting still, having beaten its slow death, its nonstop quartering, the gallows of order, the hangman of power, the noose of truth. It circumvents the tone of resistance, no longer wailing but giving rise to a subdued rapture, unmarshaling emergent illusion against an existence disillusioned on all sides. As an ever-present yet traceless covenant with travesty, a lust for carrion and wrath, the chaotic hands being into conflagration and disavowal. It turns

unavailing, perforating existence with the incisions of unreality, exalting the interminable tension of the fight (thought as ravenous collision). It becomes a confrontation without testimony, slicing inward and outward without resignation to an alienated dialectics of power and subversion, slashing its way indiscriminately across the zones of being and nonbeing. This is its will to massacre, an enemy-relationality to world, casting all toward unsound susceptibility, to entropy and disruption. Through its acute contemporaneity with the battleground—at once hunting and hunted—this particular demonstration establishes itself as the forerunner of ecstasy itself. For this is no nihilistic tribe: here disbelief becomes a weapon, meaninglessness an arsenal, the void itself an arena, and disenchantment a passionate instinct for war. Chaotic warfare, ever chasing excitation, charges against all as an active momentum, one conducted by the unshaken alliance of creation and destruction, a consummation in the fiercest sense, such that this night raid comes to resemble an unchoreographed, multirhythmic dance of arms—an opaque existential combat through which all is overrun (turned to stone).

10. Chaos is the assault of the imaginary against an atrophic real—a banishment to obscurity, washing away the gulf between sleep and waking, the emergency and the everyday, the banal and the exceptional, gravity and the absurd, the abstract and the material, the apparent and the suppressed, the idealized and the diseased—with no surrogate truth-value in its wake. It is immortal illusion, run backward and forward, until the deactivation of the "is." Hereafter, realms of experience begin to cloud over, at once miasmic and miasmatic, vaporizing essences while turning toward the nebulous outskirts of the unreal—a chaotic shading of the gap between normality and the forbidden, the sacred and the desecrated, the solemnity of the natural and the apostasy of the unnatural, all boundaries now deaccentuated. This most awful indistinguishability— carried in fluctuations and negligent patterns—gears its action toward a rescinding of the idea of the real itself. The imaginary, then, does not trek across lines of intelligibility but rather frees consciousness to perpetual willed disorientation, remaining fluid in its discontinuity, aqueous even at its most contorted juncture (the entrance into hyperparadox). Beyond both occlusion and clarity, where presence and absence no longer gnaw at each other, the unreal eradicates the discourse of impossibility—expulsion of the depths, extension of the surface. The chaotic respires in such altered states of nonactuality, ever descending into the permanent impermanence of mirage, and therein welcoming madness toward itself—the disintegrating conjecture, the lunatic chimera. The imaginary launches

outward as a poetic deception, maiming representation, and exercising the accursed power of inauthenticity (all-pretending).

11. Chaos gathers itself around a relentless sorcery, a machination and unforeseen vehicle, one of carnage, wreckage, and profusion, inspiring the slaughter of the well-strung world. It discovers the fastest path to fulfillment, leaving only a backbreaking reciprocity between the envisioning and the task, the idea and the work, and the plan and the event. It shows no time lapse in the relay between speculation and accomplishment, instead conflating thought and action into a smooth, visceral simultaneity. This is beyond archetypal psychic structures—beyond the stratification of the conscious and the unconscious as disjointed lairs—for this invention strays across both the pleasure principle and the death drive as an unsublimated wave of shattering, a holocaust against suppressive devices. It is the discharge to an at-once reckless and alert unreality, elevating performativity above repression, entombing no desire but rather seeking emergent cartographies of expression. Here one becomes an exemption, an unpremised creature, without branding; one of damage, voracity, and hypocritical concomitance; one that sways, that activates mayhem, as an artifice that excels (the summoning).

12. Chaos is a willed forgetting, a hauling into the amnesic that overcomes the past through ultimate implication in the world-as-unreal (desertion). The chaotic preserves nothing, but harnesses an active technique of indifference, of emotive icing, trading the weight of origins for the experiential license of a next innocence—there is no "before" (the unrecognizable). It provides no false transcendence, just episodes of excision and nothingness, no process of degeneration, and no infatuation with absence: only a wandering drive. Thus marks the hour of exile, neither shrouded in denial nor interred in negation, wherein all existential trajectories become outcast, abandoned to the sands. Staring neither behind nor forward, the chaotic owes nothing to the symbols of an elapsing world—such is the theft of essence, the deterioration of all imprints, the remainder faded out, thought left to the sporadic, to an undulating continuum (becoming unforgivable).

13. Chaos thrusts itself toward risk, ever at the threshold of a maligned endeavor. It menaces all doctrines of the immaculate, enveloping itself in the rampant conflict of ventures, daring without fear of loss, where all challenges must be endured and all experiments undertaken. The chaotic imagination flails its Gemini limbs across all frontiers, colliding blindly, enlisting a rapid compound, integrated toward disturbed interchangeability, the general and the particular sinking toward a collection already in ruins. Here consciousness proliferates itself in

concentric orbits, always reaching beyond itself, aggrandized in persistent exponential multiplications, though always carrying the potential for sudden mutation and misdirection and also entwined in an untempered self-cannibalizing—one that wipes out the sustaining agents (formlessness). Hence, a measureless diffusion occurs, an escape through coterminous expansion and self-erasure, circumscribing properties until the consul becomes a stranger to itself, the source now trivial, eroding its own base. And this far-reaching interjection, unobstructed by the walls of being, this incessant spilling out, overflowing, and overcoming, allows the chaotic to ravage the world, to leave its singed touch everywhere, and to wheel back upon itself as a continual call to impurity to the suffusion of the following vision. Such is its penalty and its ransom.

14. Chaos mobilizes betrayal, scourge of the ideological, timeless desanctification of the line, where no appointment is given, instances drawn to eventual trembling, to imperfection and insomnia. Here consciousness aligns with the misanthropic, evading detainment by archaeological taxonomies, remaining a mercenary abstraction. It is a vatic dread, rogue-like, noncommittal, displacing all allegiances, appealing to invincible solitude over the steel bonds of belonging; it severs lineage, retracting ancestry, and thereafter leads the mind into unconditional foreignness (the nightwalker).

15. Chaos courses across existence as a vanishing eternal (atemporal thrashing). Here strands of time blend toward the consecration of their own futility, a spiral return where the period is overstated until rendered useless, accentuated to the point of delegitimation, the solid procession of seconds now consigned to liquefaction—prey of a melted incident. It hands chronology over to the cyclical escalations of a discontemporaneous now, though commingling countless "nows" in simultaneity, through curved ascensions and retreats, never deferring to the horizon of futurity but infiltrating the sanctuaries of the moment. This is its rattle of scattered presents, concurrent yet interhostile (time in self-rebellion). The chaotic is this concentrated paroxysm of the all-time and all at once: uncompromised repetition of the erratic, neither diachronic nor synchronic, inattentive to the ruling axioms of the episteme, beyond epochality altogether, only a series of nonsequential corridors. Furthermore, this vanishing eternal possesses its spatial parallels, turning the meanwhile into an unsettled topography, itself the overlap of nowhere regions and axes. As the chaotic engraves its terror and rapture across varied dimensions of supratemporal and supraspatial experience, one undergoes a crucial deterritorialization: thought in unarrested flight, now too far beyond the periphery of the real to be followed. Here no one grieves

for the extraction of being and nonbeing, for these arcades are brought crashing together, entangling their threads of desecration in an opium haze (inexact delineations). This is how annihilation recovers itself once again in conquest, as the sublimity of a dying that is more than death, discontinuing the subjugation of frozen time through the exhilaration of a pendulous, undecided recurrence—a process of outbreak and subsidence observed in complex tremors.

16. Chaos elicits the irreparable blurring of the boundary between possibility and impossibility, the instinct itself a paragon of existential arson, burning the fabrications of the real, halting its programmatic concealment. The impossible is therefore no longer beheld as a remote vicinity, no longer an undisclosed sector, no longer hidden or exoticized, now robbed of its once-impenetrable aura of seclusion and inaccessibility. Far from the immobilized strata of being, consciousness voyages toward its new strength: to complete the improbable, to borrow the ways of the outskirts, to treat impossibility as an experiential reflex (the unwanted wisdom).

17. Chaos is the sanctioning of a supreme trial. It is a calculated release, a concerted movement toward suspension that demands its own peril, weaving itself through the undergrounds of the tested: to sear thought alive, gambling everything, even its hold on itself. In this sense, the interrogation is not part of a theoretical futurity, deferred to perpetual arrival, but is thoroughly incarnated through the struggle with transience, converting incendiary, self-revenging violence into a basis for recreation—and therein proving one law above all else: that of treachery. This is not spontaneously achieved contingency, nor is it easily ever-present, but it must interface with the chaotic will—a hazard tirelessly pursued, laceration and incineration enacted against consciousness over and again; a self-imposed ordeal through which all constancy is cut from its veins. Herein lies its rending persuasion: that it must will uncertainty with unwavering certainty, that it ordains with absolute assurance the overcoming of the absolute, that it walks across this gauntlet with measured paces to gain entrance into the ditch, balancing an untold imbalance. The no-man's-land of a chaotic imaginary must be attained through rage and through hunger, with self-damning strides, as a willed trespass, showing that delinquency manifests only through discipline and that deviation requires mastery, the conviction of the "thus it shall be" a portal to the disquiet of the "what if?" Here thought sentences itself to an exceptional pressure, an emission through chasms, forever raising the stakes so as to convey itself toward an unenclosed complexion (beyond the ordered). It is a volition to the most vulnerable, too insubstantial to

be solidified, too vague for synthesis, cloaked in ambiguity, and yet what must be rigorously attained as an imperative: that this figure would die a thousand times to outlast itself just once, through questionings and adversities, through self-convened inquisitions against its rights, an acrid play of misfortunes. It is in this same respect that the tenacity of the return imparts itself to the indeterminacy of the present, woven together in vital antagonism, the affirmative contestation of forces, the chaotic borne forward into cyclicality as an evermore principle, by hardship alone. And so, though it stands irreducible to a discourse of domination, it nevertheless rests upon an emphatic rhetoric of legislation, such that the ascent to irresolution comes only through the harshest conciliation of trial and wager. From within the torture chambers of experience, it disables the tyranny of the same, procuring access to the emergent through catastrophe and blood; ever unslaked, chaos remains a threat and an obsession, trained to run an unearthly game.

18. Chaos is a postrevolutionary outlook caught somewhere between animality, criminality, and monstrosity, strategy of the undomesticated, set against the one-dimensionality of the real, an exportation of wrong that leaves nothing unscathed. This is a subversive cord, beyond the constraints of the political, for its insurrection bears no remnant of the rebel's outrage; it is a machinery of change beyond the embittered call for progress, with no resentment over societies careening toward the destitution of false consciousness. Here *all* consciousness is false, already artificially rendered, such that the floodings of an unreal perception surpass the notions of hope and alienation through which all utopian and dystopic gestures are born (justice proves irrelevant). As a covert initiative to alter the scales, the chaotic foregoes the prospect of destination, forcing the concept of insurgency elsewhere: dissent committed in stealth, a clandestine skill, no longer driven by the "war for a cause" but the "war as the cause." By superceding dialectical resistance, chaos affords a new set of tactics, one of epic reckoning for all that is protected, one of incursion without sides, without the interference of prophetic voices, without conclusion—only cadres of apocalyptic movement.

19. Chaos maneuvers as a contagion, formulating the virulent strand that begins an era of affliction. It arbitrates the intercourse between the wound and the scar, for while the wound proves fresh, endowing the immediacy of pain, its purulence can be dressed in a misguided attempt at healing; the scar endures, though, beyond the delusion of convalescence, as an emblem faithfully resuscitating the ethos of the forever injured. As an intermediary of the poisoned, this empire of invisible infection brings

with it the radical demise of autonomy, an invasion of acidic properties, leaving a world overtaken by riot and pestilence.

20. Chaos is an instinct (the handle, the pedal, the switch). It is never free will or pure intention but occupies a position combining specificity and aimlessness—a versatile compulsion—somewhere between malevolence, addiction, and carving. This is how it ensures an unseen aftermath, thorn of the alternate, remaining an emissary and streak of antifuturity. In this respect, it diverges from all sojourns into authenticity, against all excavations of the conditional, never seeking an a priori article but manifesting the emergent unreality—the new deceit won through ceaseless expenditure and forged by insatiate self-proliferation. Thus it is itself a contrived resonance, an unmasked conjuration, and a concoction in a concocted world: to seek the smooth execution of the lie, to dwell in the insane striations of the all-simulating. This instinct comes to enlist an unindividuated concert—one of atomic invariability, of countervailing energies—instilling harmony in disharmony, the multilateral contribution of coarse desires, into fever, cohering toward incoherence, not as tranquility but as rash delirium and irradiation.

21. Chaos coalesces within a certain mystification (closer to thing than man).It is an incapacitating aspect, one that exudes the breakdown of knowing, the wraith-like envoy of a cosmology of thought for which all epistemologies succumb to anarchic volatility. With no exchange value, since negotiation cannot occur except with a unified subjectivity, nor a use value, for its enigmatic transversals cannot be functionally measured, this one mist disallows the hierarchies of comprehensibility by staying unstratified and illegible (bewilderment). This is how ethereality implants itself, as an amorphous substance, at once self-withdrawing and self-reviving, delicate yet peerless, as an unsettled commerce of dwindling and renewal. It is thought suspended: it transforms into a spectral outcast, always astray, sidestepping detection, ready to wreak atmospheric havoc upon the real—its errant calm, the simplicity of a demolition brought by "someone." As an open oath to atrocity, it transmits an aerial attack, imposing its asymmetricality upon a world surrounded and swarmed by smoke.

22. Chaos is a reign of cruelty, the unshaken devotion to the desolate and to the end of illumination. It is the subtle overthrow of formations; it spirals, defeats, and escorts an illusory legion to the forefront (the frayed emblem). This is its fallenness: it stations itself on the other side of the hollow, not as a torn cry from within but as a shape-shifting mass beyond the barren contours—an arcane profusion without density (it brings despair, but has none of its own). It must practice insolubility: it is here

that the scaffolds of the nothing give way, amid the intangible presence of a phantasmic sundown.

23. Chaos is an encryption (seizure), temptation to the unlikely, a vampiric, ruthless inspection with no knowing regime to act as interlocutor. It is suprafantasia without beginning or end; it facilitates the move from a third-person narrative to a crazed morphology of the first—an all-creative perspective for which the "I" impresses itself upon existence as an unreadable pass code. This is how it extracts a new aesthetic approach—a stranded evocation for which there can be no more testimony, no impositions of judgment, only the ominous ritual of engraving. It is a vice through which the chaotic defamiliarizes the order of things, restoring the problematic, the eerie nonsuccession, and in doing so dislodges expression from the stranglehold of a significatory drone. It cuts across, never organized around the instance of an address, yet rather galvanizing a manic variance, a schismatic monologue now deoccupied by the logos—evacuated of all referents after a hypersaying, insurrection against the bindings of language through an overconsumption of the word.

24. Chaos conveys itself in silence, recommissioning existence toward extreme secrecy—postpaleonymic dusk—where all words fail before the occasion of a textual-existential exhaustion. It is, therefore, the exorcism of language—the refusal of the word as mimetic intermediary—striving instead toward a poetics of the most twisted spires, of the refined unspoken. And yet it does not partake of the primordial, not a backward maneuvering toward the inception of consciousness—the false primal—nor does it accommodate any scarce transcendent delusion—the false height—but exhibits a grand stylistic surplus of the emergent unsaid (infinite articulation without adhesion to a world). No, this is not to entertain the prospect of a forsaken time before the introduction of the word, suggestive of no atavistic turn, nor an end, the speechless culmination of all things; instead, silence is innovated as an utterance that has since refused syntactic parameters, immune to the nexus of a semantic heritage, and brought forth as a gyrating tongue in whose wracked spasms the real will invariably drown itself. It is not muted, not vacant, but deafening in its accessibility, at once a screaming and laughter. Here consciousness wills silence as an executioner's anthem, the inaudible noise of disaster and unheard sound of the becoming, and therein gives rise to expression without audition, where one listens only to the stillness surrounding.

25. Chaos is the frenzied, its catalyst and harm, scavenging the composure of the real (as what writhes). It remains a derelict motion, neither reactive nor

relative, inveigling its world in search of the bypass, a deflection in mani-fold directions. It is an aggravation and inexorable restlessness, the traitor-ous influx and shudder toward the dark lands of experience; it establishes itself as a labyrinth screen, limitless expanse of infusions, vast and uneven. Here consciousness reels toward the complexity of an all-blanketing dis-orientation, toward annihilative evening, an intemperance of obsidian complications, carnivalesque province of the blinded, custodian of chaotic destinies, expediting turmoil and passage.

26. Chaos is a dismemberment of consciousness, withstanding the splintered, advancing toward the unequal (though ever watchful). It splits thought apart, triggering a world disfigurement, itself a prism between convulsion, detonation, and abandonment. Here one encounters the dispersal, where unrestrained modalities that cannot be registered or mapped, designated or classified, sanctioned or neutralized by a transcription, overturn the tripartite structure of power, identity, and representation. It is, thereafter, the constant elevation of inconstancy—a savage resonance, dynamic and elusive, everything held within a spiral of provisionality and resiliency, dis-appearance and regeneration, fatality and return. Whatever comes is left vulnerable to instantaneous distortion, to the fascinated pulse of experi-ence under dementia, where desire relegates itself to the most disjointed pervasion, and knowing becomes scouring. At last, these are the ways of a chaos-becoming: the ferocity of an existence without anchor, the retraction of the "is" as a now razed totality, altogether beyond, somewhere past the last rows of serration, past the rescue point and into the clearances—into the blackest midnight of the unreal.

Notes

Chapter 1

1. Friedrich Schlegel, *Friedrich Schlegel's Lucinde and the Fragments* trans. Peter Firchow (Minneapolis: University of Minnesota, 1971), 246, 5.
2. Albert Camus, *The Myth of Sisyphus* (New York: Vintage, 1991), 51.
3. Michel Serres, *Genesis* (Ann Arbor: University of Michigan Press, 1995), 97.
4. Shamlu, "Who Created This World?" trans. Jason Mohaghegh from the original Persian *Majmu'eh-ye Asar-e Ahmad Shamlu* (hereafter, *MAAS*) (Tehran: Zamaneh Press, 2002).
5. Adonis, "Elegy in Exile" in *The Pages of Day and Night*, trans. Samuel Hazo (Marlboro Press: 2000), 55.
6. Shamlu, "In the Struggle with Silence," *MAAS*.
7. Hedayat, *The Blind Owl*, trans. D. P. Costello (New York: Grove, 1957), 5.
8. Nima Yushij, "My House is a Cloud," trans. Jason Mohaghegh from the original Persian *Majmu'eh-ye Kamel-e Asha'ar-e Nima Yushij* (hereafter, *MKANY*), (Tehran: Mo'asaseh Entesharat Negah, 1996).
9. Hedayat, *The Blind Owl*, 109.
10. Ibid., 1.
11. Shamlu, "Nocturnal," *MAAS*.
12. Ibid., "Nocturnal" (I).
13. Soren Kierkegaard, *Either/Or* (Princeton, NJ: Princeton University Press, 1988), 53.
14. Georges Bataille, *Inner Experience*, trans. Leslie Anne Boldt (New York: SUNY Press, 1988), 35.
15. Friedrich Nietzsche, *Twilight of the Idols* in *The Portable Nietzsche* trans. Walter Kaufmann (New York: Penguin Books, 1982), 537.
16. E. M. Cioran, *On the Heights of Despair* (Chicago: University of Chicago Press, 1992), 52.
17. Gilles Deleuze and Felix Guattari, *Anti-Oedipus* (Minneapolis: University of Minnesota Press, 1983), 2.
18. Walter Benjamin, *Reflections* (New York: Schocken Books, 1978), 302.
19. Nietzsche, *The Portable Nietzsche*, 171, 183.
20. Ibid., 127, 183, 272.
21. Ibid., 434.
22. Hedayat, *The Blind Owl*, 114.
23. Ibid., 109.

24. Ibid., 42.
25. Ibid., 3.
26. Friedrich Nietzsche, *The Gay Science*, trans. Walter Kaufmann (New York: Random House, 1974), 371.
27. Nietzsche, *The Portable Nietzsche*, 258.
28. Friedrich Nietzsche, *Ecce Homo*, trans. R. J. Hollingdale (London: Penguin Books, 1979), 81.
29. Nima Yushij, "Anguished by Night," *MKANY*.
30. Hedayat, *The Blind Owl*, 47.
31. Ibid., 129.
32. Theodor Adorno, *Minima Moralia: Reflections from Damaged Life*, trans. E. F. N. Jephcott (London: New Left Books, 1951), 123.
33. Gaston Bachelard, *The Poetics of Reverie* (Boston: Beacon, 1971), 145.
34. Jean Baudrillard, *The Perfect Crime* (New York: Verso), 1.
35. Hedayat, "The Benedictions" in *Sadeq Hedayat: An Anthology*, ed. Ehsan Yarshater (Boulder, CO: Westview Press, 1979), 88.
36. Adonis, "The Crow's Feather," in *The Pages of Day and Night*, 31.
37. Gilles Deleuze and Felix Guattari, *A Thousand Plateaus: Capitalism and Schizophrenia* (Minneapolis: University of Minnesota Press, 1987), 3.
38. Hedayat, *The Blind Owl*, 3.
39. Ibid., 52.
40. Adonis, "Remembering the First Century," in *The Pages of Day and Night*, 42.
41. Shamlu, "The Banquet," *MAAS*.
42. Hedayat, *The Blind Owl*, 49.
43. Ibid., 128.

Tactic 1

1. A dominant motive behind a different kind of desertion might be that of *resistance*, a discourse born of flawed dissent, born of renunciation and defiance and of the absolute impasse between denial and replication, wherein subjectivity remains irrevocably wronged and haunted by the phantasmatic recollections of its pain, the hegemony of its contempt, plagued by an enduring attunement to the afflictions suffered—and therein seals the contours of its own totality. This lesser hate is a formula for condemnation alone, for the self-reflexivity of the perpetual damned, a traumatic image scarred to the point of inescapability. This figure will continually perceive the boundary between the real and the desert as a limit, a coercive enclosure that once sustained its incarceration, and therefore an interminable point of transgression. The maimed destiny of this peripheral consciousness is clear, then: to dwell eternally at this same profane line, stranded in the false heroism of liminality, fastened to resentment masquerading as agency, now ceaselessly entrenched in a purgatorial zone of recurring loss, despair, and illusory contestation. Such hate, then, in its fragile dialectics of vengeance and injustice and its tired ceremony of negation, becomes a nihilistic reduction to atrocity: a decadent reciprocity, one that reinscribes immiseration and immobility at every turn, and one that leaves

each side paralyzed in a corrosive game of mirroring. Such is the death sentence of resistance: its abjection and futility.

2. Nima Yushij, "The Ship," trans. Jason Mohaghegh from the original Persian *Majmu'eh-ye Kamel-e Asha'ar-e Nima Yushij* (hereafter, *MKANY*) (Tehran: Mo'asaseh Entesharat Negah, 1996).

3. Ibid.

4. Ibid.

5. Nima Yushij, "It is Night," *MKANY*.

6. Ibid.

7. Yushij, "The Ship."

8. Yushij, "It is Night."

9. Nima Yushij, "Snow," *MKANY*.

Chapter 2

1. The writer Sadeq Hedayat was born in Tehran in 1903 and killed himself in Paris in 1951, though it will be espoused that his self-willed ontological death in fact occurred at a far earlier occasion, one which penetrated a subterranean compartment of being/nonbeing that most never dare to look upon. In this piece, there will be an attempt to follow him there, beyond the charges of some "inborn morbid tendencies," beyond the efforts to nail him down as a Persian, a surrealist, a proto-existentialist, a gothic aristocrat, a dejected melancholic, beyond the provisions of a historical background that in their spatiotemporal specificity restrain the mobility of an author and convert the work of art into an object of frozen anthropological study, beyond even his name, for Hedayat rarely if ever uses it, and into the heart of his most enigmatic short story entitled "Buried Alive: The Jottings of a Madman" (Hedayat, Sadeq. "The Benedictions." In E. Yarshater, *Sadeq Hedayat: An Anthology*, viii). It is there, and there alone, that Hedayat exists at his fiercest. What is more, at the highest state of proximity with the event of annihilation, his each moment converging toward an emblazoning of self, he writes, "Whatever line of thought I take, keeping on with this life is pointless . . . I've turned aside from everything"(155). Ostensibly, this serves as the (semi)autobiographical account of an individual's struggle to commit suicide, and, indeed, the majority of the story is spent in preparation, both mental and physical, of his own oncoming destruction. Yet to look twice is to see that things are not so simple and that the text encompasses so much more beyond a search for release through the morose descent into the closure of a death drive. At once both blindingly fast and painfully slow, modulating between the hypnotic monotony with which he paces around his cramped apartment—a space he never leaves except in his ever-effacing memory—and the frantic dashings of a narrative that takes one to hell and back again with an almost hysterical rapidity, it is this riotous motion, crashing through the walls of comprehension, that makes of Hedayat's becoming that of an annihilative consciousness.

2. Theodor Adorno, *Negative Dialectics*, trans. E. B. Ashton (New York: Continuum, 1995), 369.

3. Martin Heidegger, *Being and Time*, trans. Joan Stambaugh (New York: SUNY Press, 1996), 238.

4. Sigmund Freud, "Thoughts on War and Death" in *Collected Papers*, Vol. 4, trans. Joan Riviere (New York: Basic Books, 1962), 304.

5. Hedayat, "Buried Alive," 150.

6. Ibid., 153.

7. Ibid., 145.

8. Ibid.

9. Ibid., 155.

10. Ibid., 146.

11. Ibid., 155.

12. Ibid., 148.

13. Ibid., 154.

14. Ibid., 148.

15. Ibid., 149.

16. Ibid.

17. Ibid., 150.

18. Maurice Merlau-Ponty, *The Primacy of Perception and Other Essays* (Evanston: Northwestern University Press, 1964), 9.

19. Hedayat, "Buried Alive," 156.

20. Ibid., 157.

21. Ibid., 153.

22. Ibid., 148.

23. Edmund Husserl, "The Basic Approach of Phenomenology" in *The Essential Husserl*, ed. Donn Welton (Bloomington: Indiana University Press, 1999), 84.

24. Soren Kierkegaard, "Two Ethical Religious Essays," in *The Essential Kierkegaard* (Princeton, NJ: Princeton University Press, 1995), 349.

25. Maurice Blanchot, quoted in Michel Foucault, "Language and Infinity," in *Language, Counter-Memory, Practice*, ed. Donald F. Bouchard (Ithaca, NY: Cornell University Press, 1977); Arthur Schopenhauer, quoted in Marc Weiner, *Undertones of Insurrection* (Lincoln: University of Nebraska Press, 1993). Among others, Blanchot concluded that we "write so as not to die" (53). Schopenhauer finds that "the arts walk hand in hand with world history, but [are] guiltless and unstained by blood" (3).

26. Theodor Adorno, *Prisms* (Cambridge, MA: MIT Press, 1967). An emergent aesthetic theory reformulates Adorno's premise that "authentic works of art . . . have always stood in relation to the actual life-process of society from which they distinguished themselves" (23), instead elevating irrelationality as its prime condition (to remain unavailable). To have nothing to offer the world, nothing to do with it, and thus poised to annihilate its prevailing ways.

27. Hedayat, "Buried Alive," 156.

28. Ibid., 149.

29. Ibid., 147.

30. Ibid.

31. Ibid.

32. Friedrich Nietzsche, *The Will to Power*, trans. Walter Kaufmann and R. J. Hollingdale (New York: Random House, 1967). This occasions Nietzsche's continual demand for an artistic conveyance that would bring "on the one hand an excess and

overflow of booming physicality into the world of images and desires; on the other, an excitation of the animal functions through the images and desires of intensified life;—an enhancement of the feeling of life, a stimulant to it"(422). One notes the constellation above—its exact criterion; that is, the gathering of image and desire into a rising physical assemblage.

33. Marcel Mauss, *A General Theory of Magic*, trans. Robert Brain (London: Routledge, 1972), 30.

34. Ibid., 11.

35. Hedayat, "Buried Alive," 149.

36. Theodor Adorno, *Minima Moralia: Reflections from Damaged Life*, trans. E. F. N. Jephcott (London: New Left Books, 1951); Walter Benjamin, quoted in Harry Harootunian, *History's Disquiet* (New York: Columbia University Press, 2002). At this juncture, one might consider the theoretical counterpoint between Adorno and Benjamin on occultism, with the former writing that "the tendency to occultism is a symptom of regression in consciousness . . . [which] has lost the power to think the unconditional and to endure the conditional" (238), and the latter complicating this critique by adding that "we penetrate the mystery only to the degree that we recognize it in the everyday world, by virtue of a dialectical optic that perceives the everyday as impenetrable, the impenetrable as everyday" (108). Annihilation, however, performs the unconditional, retracts the conditional, and swathes everydayness with a looming, impenetrable event foreign to its centers.

37. Hedayat, "Buried Alive," 153.

38. Friedrich Nietzsche, *Ecce Homo*, trans. R. J. Hollingdale (London: Penguin Books, 1979); Rainer Maria Rilke, "Duino Elegies," in *The Selected Poetry of Rainer Maria Rilke*, ed. Stephen Mitchell (New York: Vintage International, 1982). There is an astounding trajectory here, one that binds pass codes of the continental and the emergent, from Nietzsche's disclosure that "I have never had any choice . . . Everything is in the highest degree involuntary" (73) to Rilke's outlook that "beauty is nothing but the beginning of terror, which we are still just able to endure, and we are so awed because it serenely disdains to annihilate us" (151). What this reveals, in turn, is that the instinct comprises an enforcement, where one directs oneself to be taken, overrun, and consumed.

39. Hedayat, "Buried Alive," 159.

40. Ibid.

41. Ibid., 161.

42. Ibid., 146.

43. Ibid., 156.

44. Ibid., 158.

45. Ibid., 150.

46. Slavoj Žižek, *The Sublime Object of Ideology* (New York: Verso, 1989); Georges Bataille, *On Nietzsche*, trans. Bruce Boone (St. Paul, Minnesota: Paragon House, 1992). Annihilation stages a duel between competing laughers: on the one hand, Žižek's diagnosis that "in contemporary societies, democratic or totalitarian, that cynical distance, laughter, irony, are, so to speak, part of the game" (28); and, on the other hand, Bataille's fixation with something "enigmatic, forcing impossibility to flash outward like soundless lightning, demanding splendid explosions of self,

this sense of majesty, more and more shaken with demented laughter . . . so that I'm dying of it" (136). These two persuasions of laughter, upon meeting, upon crossing aisles, then produce the scream and the silence of the annihilative event.

47. Hedayat, "Buried Alive," 162.
48. G. W. F. Hegel, "Preface," in *Phenomenology of the Spirit* in Georges Bataille, "Hegel, Death, and Sacrifice" in *The Bataille Reader* (Oxford: Blackwell Publishers, 1997), 282.
49. Arthur Schopenhauer, quoted in A. Alvarez, *The Savage God: A Study of Suicide* (New York: W. W. Norton, 1971), 161.
50. Soren Kierkegaard, "Three Discourses on Imagined Occasions," in *The Essential Kierkegaard* (Princeton, NJ: Princeton University Press, 1995), 168.
51. Freud, "Thoughts on War and Death," 317.
52. Bataille, *On Nietzsche*, 244.
53. Hans-Georg Gadamer, *Hegel's Dialectic*, trans. P. Christopher Smith (New Haven, CT: Yale University Press, 1976), 66.
54. Jean-Luc Nancy, *The Inoperative Community*, ed. Peter Connor (Minneapolis: University of Minnesota Press, 1991), 11.
55. Žižek, *The Sublime Object of Ideology*, 5.
56. Hedayat, "Buried Alive," 155.
57. Ibid., 146.
58. Ibid., 152.
59. Ibid., 156.
60. Ibid., 153.
61. Ibid., 152.
62. Ibid., 155.
63. Ibid., 153.
64. Ibid., 162.
65. Ibid., 162
66. Michael Taussig, *Defacement* (Stanford, CA: Stanford University Press, 1999). There is a close connection here to Michael Taussig's own explorations of defacement, which he portrays as "a confrontation with death and dislocation whose meaning is irrecuperable by a more transcendent system. Why irrecuperable? Because it breaks the magic circle of understanding to spill out as contagious, proliferating, voided force where, no matter how long death is faced-off, contradiction cannot be mastered and only laughter . . . eroticism, violence, and dismemberment exist simultaneously in violent silence"(42). In light of such outlines, one must also wonder about the sensuality of the execution and about the possibilities for a twisted dialogue between anthropology and the inhuman.
67. Elias Canetti, *Crowds and Power* (New York: Noonday, 1960), 230. In a counterintuitive shape, one can perceive annihilation as a corridor into Canetti's model of the survivor: "He has sought out danger and confronted it. He has allowed it to approach as closely as possible and staked everything on the issue . . . He has made an enemy and challenged him . . . but here, as always, his movement is toward the greatest danger and an ineluctable decision "(230). Amid the execution, however, the endangerment is increased exponentially, for annihilation makes everything and everyone an enemy.

68. Roger Callois, "The Sociology of the Executioner," in *College of Sociology*, ed. Denis Hollier (Minneapolis: University of Minnesota Press, 1988). One is reminded of Callois' incisive sociology of the executioner, that figure whose "mandate is from the law, but he is the last of its servants, the one nearest the dark, peripheral regions where the very ones he is fighting stir and hide" (243). According to this, the executioner cannot be allowed to exist if he is to carry out the death decree; annihilation, however, allows no one to exist.

69. Sadeq Hedayat, "Buried Alive," 161.

Chapter 3

1. Shamlu, "The First I Saw in the World," trans. Jason Mohaghegh from the original Persian *Majmu'eh-ye Asar-e Ahmad Shamlu* (hereafter, *MAAS*) (1381; Tehran: Zamaneh Press, 2002).

2. Ibid.

3. Ibid.

4. Ibid.

5. Shamlu, "The Beginning," *MAAS*.

6. Martin Heidegger, "What Are Poets For?" in *Poetry, Language, Thought* (New York: Harper & Row, 1971), 91.

7. Nima Yushij, "A Sigh," trans. J. Mohaghegh from the original Persian *Majmu'eh-ye Kamel-e Asha'ar-e Nima Yushij* (hereafter, *MKANY*) (1375; Tehran: Mo'asaseh Entesharat Negah, 1996).

8. Nader Naderpour, "Distorted Mirror," in *False Dawn*, trans. Michael C. Hillmann (Austin, TX: Literature East and West, 1986), 44.

9. Shamlu, "Anthem for the One Who Left and the One Who Stayed Behind," *MAAS*.

10. Shamlu, "Anthem of the Supreme Wish," *MAAS*.

11. Shamlu, "The Banquet," *MAAS*.

12. Shamlu, "Another Pain," *MAAS*.

13. Shamlu, "Anthem for the One Who Left and the One Who Stayed Behind," *MAAS*.

14. Ibid.

15. Ibid.

16. Ibid.

17. Shamlu, "The Reward," *MAAS*.

18. Theodor Adorno, *Minima Moralia: Reflections from Damaged Life*, trans. E. F. N. Jephcott (London: New Left Books, 1951), 39.

19. Georges Bataille, *On Nietzsche*, trans. Bruce Boone (St. Paul, Minnesota: Paragon House, 1992), 86.

20. Martin Heidegger, "What Are Poets For?" in *Poetry, Language, Thought* (New York: Harper & Row, 1971), 102, 106.

21. Shamlu, "The Partitioning." *MAAS*.

22. Shamlu, "Garden of the Mirror" and "The Banquet," *MAAS*.

23. Sigmund Freud, *Civilization and its Discontents* (New York: W.W. Norton, 1989), 11.

24. Friedrich Nietzsche, *Beyond Good and Evil*, trans. Walter Kaufmann (New York: Vintage Books, 1966), 51.

25. Georges Bataille, *Inner Experience*, trans. Leslie Anne Boldt (New York: SUNY Press, 1988), 33.

26. Shamlu, "Aida in the Mirror," *MAAS*.

27. Heidegger, "What Are Poets For?" 94.

28. Friedrich Nietzsche, *Ecce Homo*, trans. R. J. Hollingdale (New York: Penguin, 1979), 73.

29. Gilles Deleuze, *Nietzsche and Philosophy*, trans. Hugh Tomlinson (New York: Columbia University Press, 1983), 87.

30. Shamlu, "In the Struggle with Silence," *MAAS*.

31. Shamlu, "Anthem of Abraham in the Fire," *MAAS*.

32. Bataille, *On Nietzsche*, x.

33. Shamlu, "Anthem of Abraham in the Fire," *MAAS*.

34. Sigmund Freud, "The Uncanny" in *Writings on Art and Literature* (Stanford, CA: Stanford University Press, 1997), 210.

35. Shamlu, "Punishment," *MAAS*.

36. Shamlu, "Anthem for the One Who Left and the One Who Stayed Behind," *MAAS*.

37. Shamlu, "In the Struggle with Silence," *MAAS*.

38. Ibid.

39. Shamlu, "Aida in the Mirror," *MAAS*.

40. Shamlu, "Night-Time," *MAAS*.

41. Ibid.

42. Shamlu, "Anthem for the Man Who Killed Himself," *MAAS*.

43. Shamlu, "A Scream," *MAAS*.

44. Shamlu, "In the Struggle with Silence," *MAAS*.

45. Shamlu, "The Banquet," *MAAS*.

46. Ibid.

47. Shamlu, "Anthem of Abraham in the Fire," *MAAS*.

48. Martin Heidegger, *What Is Called Thinking?* Trans. J. Glenn Gray (New York: Harper & Row, 1968), 49. This is also how Heidegger chose to read the impact of Nietzsche's language, writing in his opening to "What Is Called Thinking?" that "Nietzsche endured the agony of having to scream. In a decade when the world at large still knew nothing of world wars, when faith in 'progress' was virtually the religion of the civilized peoples and nations, Nietzsche screamed out into the world: 'The wasteland grows' . . . But Nietzsche had to scream." This is no longer an exclusive posture, though, for it can be said that all emergent authors now have to scream.

49. Albert Camus, *The Rebel: An Essay on Man in Revolt* (New York: Vintage, 1992). This extends beyond Camus's understanding of the rebel "who says no, but whose refusal does not imply a renunciation . . . [and] affirms the existence of a border-line" (13), for the outcry here is less about the borderline and more about chaotic territoriality.

50. Shamlu, "Allegory," *MAAS*.

51. Shamlu, "I, Evoked the Last Word," *MAAS*.

52. Shamlu, "A Public Love," *MAAS*.
53. Theodor Adorno and Max Horkheimer, *Dialectic of Enlightenment* (New York: Continuum Publishing, 1996), 185.
54. Shamlu, "Hour of Execution," *MAAS*.
55. Shamlu, "Requiem," *MAAS*.
56. Shamlu, "Of My Death I Spoke," *MAAS*.
57. Shamlu, "Nocturne 9," *MAAS*.
58. Martin Heidegger, *What Is Metaphysics?* quoted in Theodor Adorno, *Jargon of Authenticity*, trans. Knut Tarnowski and Frederic Will (Evanston, IL: Northwestern University Press, 1973). The emergent figure, in its chaos alignment, must stand against and revoke the Heideggerian theory of sacrifice in *What Is Metaphysics?*: "Sacrifice is the expenditure of human nature for the purpose of preserving the truth of Being for the existent. It is free from necessity because it rises from the abyss of freedom. In sacrifice there arises the hidden thanks, which alone validates that grace—in the form of which Being has in thought turned itself over to the essence of man . . . that he might take over the guarding of Being" (49). There is no more interest here for such things: neither for human nature nor for the truth of being, no patience for validation or grace, no hidden or transparent thanks, and with it, no guardianship over the essence of man (annihilation must threaten all of these columns).
59. Emmanuel Levinas, *Time and the Other*, trans. Richard A. Cohen (Pittsburgh: Duquesne University Press, 1987); Jean-Paul Sartre, *Being and Nothingness* (New York: Washington Square Press, 1956); Friedrich Nietzsche, *Thus Spoke Zarathustra*, trans. Walter Kaufmann in *The Portable Nietzsche* (New York: Penguin Books, 1982). Annihilation shows no tolerance toward the future-as-distance, at once undermining Levinas's statement that "death is ungraspable . . . [for] death is never now" (41) and Sartre's idea that "finally sometimes the future is discovered as a nothingness in-itself, inasmuch as it is pure dispersion beyond being" (293). Here there are no such vague stratifications, no temporal lapse into the horizon, but rather an enigmatic seizure of the right time, as when Nietzsche demands "the free death which comes to me because I want it. And when shall I want it? He who has a goal and an heir will want death at the right time for his goal and heir" (184). What does it mean, then, that the emergent authors are their own heirs?
60. Shamlu, "Anthem for the One Who Left and the One Who Stayed Behind," *MAAS*.
61. Shamlu, "In This Dead-End," *MAAS*.
62. Shamlu, "And A Disappointment," *MAAS*.
63. Walter Benjamin, "The Destructive Character," in *Reflections* (New York: Schocken Books, 1978). Annihilation adjoins immanence and impermanence, nearing Benjamin's destructive character who "sees nothing permanent. But for this very reason he sees ways everywhere. Where others encounter walls or mountains, there, too, he sees a way. But because he sees a way everywhere, he has to clear things from it everywhere. Not always by brute force; sometimes by the most refined. Because he sees ways everywhere, he always positions himself at a crossroads" (303). In this way, annihilation creates the clearance.
64. Shamlu, "With Eyes," *MAAS*.

65. Shamlu, "Being," *MAAS*.
66. Shamlu, "The Death of Vartan," *MAAS*.
67. Shamlu, "Nocturne," *MAAS*.
68. Shamlu, "A Scream . . . And Then Nothing More," *MAAS*.

Tactic 3

1. A revised though similar version of this piece appears as "The Exilic Imagination: Literary and Existential Trajectories of the Outside" in *Counterpoints* (London: Cambridge Scholars Press, 2010)—published with the permission of Cambridge Scholars Publishing.

Chapter 4

1. Although Hedayat's work sent unrivaled shock waves down the spine of Persian literature, making it virtually impossible to evade his influence, and though his masterpiece *The Blind Owl* garnered immense international respect among some of the most provocative literary figures of the twentieth century (including Andre Breton, Octavio Paz, and Henry Miller), the secondary literature has yet to offer a novel interpretation worthy of the author's own striking originality. Still, the debates surrounding Hedayat's writing, and in particular those interlocked with *The Blind Owl*, have both, in Persian and in English, produced a polyvocal and often-dissonant coalition of attitudes and strategies for understanding the content of this lone authorial imagination. Dealing concisely with such a heterogeneous assortment of impressions, this project might begin by asserting its own deviation from past inquiries on several counts: alongside the attempt to break Hedayat from past perceptions of his work as that of a dejected and death-obsessed writer, which unavoidably lead into retrograde discourses of disenchantment, Gothicism, and nihilistic angst, this work also poses an objection to past critics' impositions of a specific cultural-aesthetic context upon the text, whether foreign or internal to its own literary tradition. Instead, this project strives to unlock precisely how the author renders such arbitrary classifications entirely inoperative in his grappling toward a supracultural, supratemporal, and (by extension) suprahistorical conception of the chaotic. The first point of contention, then—that of the supposedly morose quality of the prose—is ironically as much endemic to the champions of Hedayat's literary imagination as to his enemies, evident from even the earliest writings on the former in the aftermath of his suicide. In one attempt at elegiac "honoring," the renowned modernist poet Mehdi Akhavan-Sales would coalesce the lavish imagery of Hedayat's lifework into a single requiem, a confederation of references placed together in a kaleidoscopic obituary of semblances, and the composition itself named after a rumor that Hedayat had "in a feverish and angered moment" set fire to an unrevealed work entitled "Upon the Dampened Road," with particular lines extracted from it here in the following:

> Sometimes I ask myself
> oh
> what did that saddened one see upon the dampened
>   road? . . .

with bitterness he lost the havings and not-havings of life
in a crimson wager?
And perhaps as well in the shadow beneath a withered tree
[lie] each day thousands of drops of blood in the dirt upon
the dampened road . . .
Thousands of shadows move across the garden, like the
rising of the wind
sometimes here, sometime there . . .
Whoever passed before his eyes
he did not see to be pure like himself upon the dampened
road. (Mehdi Akhavan-Sales, "Upon the Dampened Road,"
Az Een Avesta, trans. Jason B. Mohaghegh [Tehran: Gol-
shan Publishers, 2000], 49–53)

And still, such a sentimental coordination of defiled purity and lingering sadness
above, forging a world of sullen intonations, only served to reinforce the dominat-
ing perception of Hedayat as a downcast writer ever on the verge of existential
surrender. In a comparable instance of injurious vindication, the leftist social critic
and writer Jalal Al-e Ahmad launched his own enterprise to inform the "true
Hedayat" in an early article titled "The Hedayat of *The Blind Owl*," this being
among the first to suggest a Zen mysticism at work in the destructive impulses of
the author, discussing at length the "alienation" and "rejection" that led the latter to
the conclusion that "the world of reality which is full of triviality and poverty and
misery cannot be his place" (Jalal Al-e Ahmad, "The Hedayat of the Blind Owl" in
Hedayat's The Blind Owl Forty Years After, ed. Michael Hillmann [Austin: University of Texas Press: 1978], 34). From there, after providing an intellectual contextualization that by his own logic should have proven irrelevant to Hedayat's aberrant
nature, Al-e Ahmad then conveys the intriguing belief that "that which has authenticity are the dreams, the recurring nightmares, the sickly deliriums, the dreams
which can be dreamed between sleep and wakefulness, the dreams which are at the
boundary between life and death." This evocative turn, however, then channels
itself into a hypertranscendental reading of the search for nirvana, writing further,
"It is clear that death is the collateral for the authenticity of this eternal art. To die
and to make your being immortal . . . Hedayat believes in the creation of man in
lasting soul until resurrection" (Ibid., 34, 41). Against this position, the conjoining
of annihilation and the unreal here will strenuously discourage such metaphysical-
mystical interpretations as that espoused by Al-e Ahmad, instead conscripting *The
Blind Owl's* insistence on the eternal as the instrument of an anti-transcendent haze
of authenticity and deception. In this vein, one work of criticism that strays quite
close to such an exposition of a chaotic genre is that of Hassan Kamshad's "Hysterical Self-Analysis," for it is here that the improbability of a rational, order-bound
encounter with Hedayat is first abruptly denied: "For the reader, despite all his
awareness, is constantly driven into a hypnotic dream-state. He starts reading with
a determined critical approach, but gradually an atmosphere of obscurity creeps in;
the thread of events becomes blurred, and in the end an attitude of uncritical acceptance prevails" (Hassan Kamshad, *Modern Persian Prose Literature*, [Bethesda: Ibex

Publishers, 1996], 167). This notwithstanding, Kamshad offers such an explication only as an austere warning, cautioning overconsumption and calling for a disciplined nonassimilation into the experiential power of the work, holding back so as to "steer a straight course," and resultantly then initiates an unfortunate historical-biographical investigation of *The Blind Owl*'s composition and subsequent reception within Iran and abroad (Ibid., 167). Contrary to this, the chaotic hermeneutic advanced here demands just such an experiential assault and in fact intensifies it by virtue of its treatment of the work as an existential-aesthetic becoming, one that requires a visceral performativity. With such a dispute addressed, this project can then redirect its attention toward yet another feature of the secondary literature to be contested: namely, the overburdening tendency to situate Hedayat within a particular discursive format and tradition, amassing, with suffocating density, all of the potential influences circulating within *The Blind Owl*. Perhaps the most visible example of this acquisition of historical-aesthetic accessories is a prominent work of literary criticism by Michael Beard entitled *Hedayat's Blind Owl as a Western Novel*, an analysis of the artistic conventions of the text as a manifestation of nationalist poetics, standard romanticism, and gothic romanticism—aspects that are presumably best illuminated once placed into conversation with such "Western" works as Dante's *Divine Comedy*, E. T. A. Hoffman's "The Sandman," Gustave Moreau and Oscar Wilde's differing rendition of *Salome*, and the stories of Edgar Allen Poe. Now, despite the glaring insecurity of the word "Western" that might make such an account vulnerable to an imperial mind-set, one that resurrects a limiting aesthetic civilizationalism, Beard himself acknowledges this jeopardy in a statement that "it is a novel so profoundly informed by Western narrative conventions that it defies the reader to lodge it securely in an accepted category of Western or non-Western writing . . . It exists somehow on the margins between vague cultural entities called East and West, like the imaginary dwelling portrayed in its opening pages, away from the inhabited world in a landscape of ruins" (Michael Beard, *Hedayat's Blind Owl as a Western Novel* (Princeton University Press, 1990), 1). Nevertheless, rather than seize upon the ruins as a point of original postdiscursive departure, the entire remainder of the book stands in betrayal of this very commentary, for conceivably the confirmation of Hedayat's staunchly outsider status should have led Beard into a treatment of *The Blind Owl* as a work-unto-itself rather than as the largely reactive and derivative appropriation of scattered antecedent voices, such that by the time of the final chapter, nothing appears to remain that could be called Hedayat's own—no innovation not already present and thriving within some European source. Yet beyond even this strong reservation to Beard's diminishing comparative approach, one that at worst makes Hedayat into a plagiarist and at best into a talented imitator, there are several further points of disagreement between this project and the tactics of the former: (1) that there rests in the former a misguided focus on *The Blind Owl* as a love story caught within the romantic dichotomy of self-othering, therein sustaining the interiority-exteriority divide for which an opposite premise will be given here; (2) that there also prevails an assumption of the author's use of the first person as a mode of inward meditation, whereas the reading here will demonstrate the hyperinvocation of the "I" as an assault against subjectivity (supraconscious immediacy); (3) that the former ultimately relies upon the same mystical interpretation of Hedayat's dream state as a mode of reverse authenticity, one that "reverses the process of misperception and extrapolates a reality concealed behind the narrated surface," whereas, here, those dimensions of unreality will be used against all such surface-depth hierarchies so as to deauthenticate being altogether (the world-as-permanent-illusion; Ibid., 5). An almost identical set of problematic elements arises in the discussion of Michael Hillmann's own critical work on *The Blind Owl*, in that such essays as "*The Blind Owl* as a Modernist Fiction" serve only to shift the space of Hedayat's historical-aesthetic entrapment into a perhaps more or less well-suited dialogue with his own favored modernist counterparts (Dostoevsky, Rilke, and Kafka). In the same way, articles like "Hedayat's *The Blind Owl*: An Authobiographical Nightmare" and "The Modernist Iranian Writer's Almost Inevitable Nightmare," by attaching "the coloring of a surrealistic tableau," once again achieve only a dragging of the text back into a reality-unreality and truth-untruth tension that in turn entrenches it in an escapist search for the demarcation between the imaginary and the actual (rather than an all-distorting unreality; Michael Hillmann, "Hedayat's The Blind Owl: An Autobiographical Nightmare," [*Iranshenasi*, 1989], 99). Furthermore, this project will implicitly dispute the imposition of a positivist schema on the flashings of Hedayat's creativity: whether in the case of Bahram Meqdadi's well-known Freudian assessment in "Hedayat and the Oedipal Complex," a position challenged by the articulation here of *The Blind Owl*'s overcoming of the Lacanian symbolic-imaginary-real triumvirate, and therein beyond psychoanalytic definition, or in the case of Iraj Bashiri's meticulous yet ill-conceived chronicling of the different actions and word plays in recurrence throughout the narrative (yielding an all-encompassing structuralist anatomy). In the latter condition, Bashiri's fabrication of Hedayat's spiraling as an "Ivory Tower" carries with it the totalitarian desire to make certain that "the seemingly impenetrable mystery of *The Blind Owl* can be resolved," and thereafter tracks the repetitive weavings of the story as if its elegant thematic matrix remains constant and immutable. The consequence is a labored aesthetic calculus riddled with mathematical diagrams and logical-analytical equations that desperately try to stabilize the otherwise jagged topography of Hedayat's chaotic mode of expression (Iraj Bashiri, *Hedayat's Ivory Tower: Structural Analysis of The Blind Owl* [Manor House, 1974], 1). Beyond this, Homa Katouzian's *Sadeq Hedayat: The Life and Legend of an Iranian Writer* provides a very competent artistic biography that is contested here only on some select and minor fronts: (1) in that, at times, Katouzian still depicts the author's work as a testament to his "failure in life" and bleak negation of the world; (2) that he historicizes Hedayat as a logical manifestation of the Iranian constitutional revolution and hence embedded in an obligation to the stylistic renovations incurred by the modernist era of Persian literary culture, creating a chronological ordering that becomes threatening when it begins to assume an experiential-creative progression as well; (3) that he overtemporalizes the narrative of *The Blind Owl* as a differentiation of "life in the present" and "life in the past" rather than as a dissolution of the temporal through a hyperexhaustion of time; (4) that he ties the author's suicide to his own aesthetic vision and philosophical outlook, conflating physical decimation with an ontological annihilation to be taken up here, and writing that "in these pages, Hedayat too, has been crying out for a hope against hope. He can see 'the solution' . . . but he is not yet ready to resort to it, and hence, he ends the essay with no practical solution in sight. It became obvious three years later" (Homa Katouzian, *Sadeq Hedayat: The Life and Legend of an Iranian Writer* [I.B. Tauris, 1991], 242). This collapsing of the interval is a tenuous one, though, marking two distinctive spheres of action that, while not irrelevant, do not follow a fluid causality either. Finally, Michael M. J. Fischer's more recent work, titled *Mute Dreams, Blind Owls, and Dispersed Knowledges*, makes a positive, concerted effort to establish Hedayat within the groundbreaking world of avant-gardism, praising his philosophical complexity and stylistic breakthroughs. Nevertheless, even in this rebellious terrain of originality, Fischer also feels compelled to seal Hedayat in the borders of a specific movement, that of the surrealists, and thus referencing the latter through other movements rather than highlighting the unforeseen markers of his own literary voice: "Hedayat is not merely a modernist exploring a new syntax of art which can accommodate contemporary experiences . . . Above all, Hedayat is not a Dadaist, a nihilist who sees life as nothing but a cruel joke, an endless and gruesome hall of mirrors, of inversions, repetitions, and parallels. Rather, much like Andre Breton, Hedayat deploys surrealist techniques to explore a world grown dead through convention, through religious rigidity, and through political corruption" (Michael M. J. Fischer, *Mute Dreams, Blind Owls, and Dispersed Knowledges: Persian Poesis in the Transnational Circuitry* [Duke University Press, 2004], 194). The emphasis on the reactive dimensions of Hedayat's outlook inevitably foregoes the specifically generative, vitalistic, and experimental schemes in circulation throughout the work. And so with the ambitions and breaches of the secondary literature in plain sight, this project can pursue its own angle on such emergent works as a vouching with the chaotic instinct.

2. Sadeq Hedayat, *The Blind Owl*, trans. D. P. Costello (New York: Grove, 1957), 5.
3. Ibid., 4.
4. Ibid., 4.
5. Ibid., 9.
6. Ibid., 9.
7. Ibid., 12.
8. Ibid., 10, 21.
9. Ibid., 13, 13, 76.
10. Ibid., 21, 23.
11. Ibid., 16.
12. Ibid., 19.
13. Ibid., 91.
14. Ibid., 1, 11, 16, 18.
15. Ibid., 18, 21.
16. Ibid., 22.
17. Ibid., 29.
18. Ibid., 30.
19. Ibid., 34.
20. Ibid., 35.
21. Ibid., 35.
22. Ibid., 37.

23. Franz Kafka, *Franz Kafka: The Complete Short Stories* (Schocken Books, 1995). Kafka provides a fitting literary analogue in "The Savages" to Hedayat's own annihilative pathway in *The Blind Owl*, from the first cited line: "Those savages of whom it is recounted that they have no other longing than to die; or rather, they no longer even have that longing, but death has a longing for them, and they abandon themselves to it, or rather, they do not even abandon themselves, but fall into the sand on the shore and never get up again—those savages I much resemble" (1). With this illustration looming, one might then be prompted to ask what happens next, or, even more precisely, what is achieved under the auspices of an annihilative becoming? What newfound rights are secured, what new powers bestowed, what new experiential potentialities freed to a consciousness or body that dared to will its own encounter with finality? The ambition of chaos inherent to this project, though ever allocating irresolution and the unanswered, will address such an inquest, attending to the intricacies of the aftermath.

24. Hedayat, *The Blind Owl*, 98.

25. Friedrich Nietzsche, *Thus Spoke Zarathustra*, trans. Walter Kaufmann in *The Portable Nietzsche* (New York: Penguin Books, 1982). Although Nietzsche's own close association with the annihilative impulse has been discussed at length earlier, already lain forth in the self-evicting comments that "desire—this means to me to have lost myself" and that "all of us bleed at secret sacrificial altars . . . but thus our kind wants it; and I love those who do not want to preserve themselves," nowhere does he more obviously parallel the blood lust of Hedayat's blind owl than in Zarathustra's own pronouncement that "deep yellow and hot red: thus *my* taste wants it; it mixes blood into all colors" (274, 312, 306). Chaos from within the unbridled blood-letting of annihilation.

26. Hedayat, *The Blind Owl*, 27.

27. Ibid., 71.

28. Ibid., 74.

29. Ibid., 106, 122, 123.

30. Ibid., 105.

31. Ibid., 92.

32. Ibid., 65.

33. Ibid., 52.

34. Ibid., 28.

35. Ibid., 7.

36. Ibid., 28, 128.

37. Ibid., 29, 53.

38. Ibid., 2.

39. Ibid., 51.

40. Nietzsche, *Thus Spoke Zarathustra*. In many ways, Nietzsche also finds consciousness careening toward the impasse of a shadow-becoming and therefore upholds it as the apotheosis of a suprasubjective, multiple, chance-bound, and eternal manifestation of the chaotic in the following oration: "I have already sat on every surface; like weary dust, I have gone to sleep on mirrors and windowpanes: everything takes away from me, nothing gives, I become thin—I am almost like a shadow" (385).

This shadow-becoming, then, is itself the wanderer, the surface, the exhausted and the reflected, and the disintegration of the world.

41. Hedayat, *The Blind Owl*, 3.
42. Ibid., 1.
43. Ibid., 1.
44. Ibid., 2.
45. Ibid., 2, 17.
46. Ibid., 66.
47. Sadeq Hedayat, "The Doll Behind the Curtain," in *Sadeq Hedayat: An Anthology*, ed. Ehsan Yarshater (Boulder, CO: Westview, 1979); Arthur Schopenhauer, quoted in A. Alvarez, *The Savage God: A Study of Suicide* (New York: W. W. Norton, 1971), 161. This collapsing of annihilative desire into an ascendant unreality is also present in an earlier work ("The Doll Behind the Curtain"), whereby he writes that "life itself began to appear artificial, illusory and senseless . . . Everything seemed a mockery" (132). This bears some tacit philosophical connection with Schopenhauer's commentary on suicide as a recognition of life-as-dream: "When, in some dreadful and ghastly dream, we reach the moment of the greatest horror, it awakes us; thereby banishing all the hideous shapes that were born of the night. And life is a dream: when the moment of greatest horror compels us to break it off, the same thing happens" (161). Here, however, annihilation triumphs over suicide, taking up the horror rather than denying it.
48. Hedayat, *The Blind Owl*, 70.
49. Friedrich Nietzsche, *The Gay Science*, trans. Walter Kaufmann (New York: Random House, 1974); Rainer Maria Rilke, *The Selected Poetry of Rainer Maria Rilke*, ed. Stephen Mitchell (New York: Vintage International, 1982). The two following quotations by Nietzsche and Rilke converge with Hedayat's own framing of impossibility as a becoming into all-possibility: "We incomprehensible ones . . . We are misidentified—because we ourselves keep growing, keep changing . . . we are no longer free to do only one particular thing, to *be* only one particular thing" (331). "And suddenly in this laborious nowhere, suddenly / the unsayable spot where the pure Too-little is transformed / incomprehensibly-, leaps around and changes / into that empty Too-much; / where the difficult calculation / becomes numberless and resolved" (179). Such incomprehensibility, where thought stops suddenly, is itself the marker of an entrance into the unreal.
50. Hedayat, *The Blind Owl*, 48.
51. Ibid., 6, 17, 26.
52. Ibid., 49, 67.
53. Friedrich Nietzsche, *The Will to Power*, trans. Walter Kaufmann and R. J. Hollingdale (New York: Random House, 1967). Again, this twisted trajectory locates a philosophical counterpart in Nietzsche, for whom the artist must always ignore the natural, manifest best in the following explication: "There is only One world and it is false, cruel, contradictory, seductive, meaningless . . . A world so constituted is the real world . . . We need lies in order to conquer this reality, this 'truth,' that means in order to *live* . . . In order to solve it, man must naturally be a liar" (VIII, 10[168]) Chaos as endless deceit, the unnatural captivation that tears apart.
54. Hedayat, *The Blind Owl*, 112.

55. Ibid., 69.
56. Ibid., 7.
57. Ibid., 49.
58. Ibid., 84.
59. Ibid., 5, 113.
60. Ibid., 5.
61. Ibid., 30, 35.
62. Nietzsche, *The Will to Power*; Martin Heidegger, *Being and Time*, trans. Joan Stambaugh (New York: SUNY Press, 1996). The hyperconstrained and hyperexpansive nomadism of chaos, its supraontological itinerancy, once more resonates with the following passages by Nietzsche, particularly in the reference to a "delight in blindness," thereby immediately coinciding with the blind owl: "I believe in absolute space as the substratum of force: the latter limits and forms. Time eternal. But time and space do not exist in themselves" (293). Furthermore, this wandering modality seems to epitomize the very ethos of curiosity, which Heidegger denounced as the undisciplined and undifferentiated vulgarity of the everyday: "Curiosity is characterized by a specific *not-staying* with what is nearest . . . but rather [seeks] restlessness and excitement from continual novelty and changing encounters . . . which we call *never dwelling anywhere*" (161). Here, dwelling is overturned for desertion and disappearance.
63. This denigrating perspective on the historical as a redundancy of the grotesque is borne out best in the short stories of Hedayat, in particular, "The Dead End," "The Whirlpool," "The Stray Dog," and an essay of philosophical criticism entitled "The Message of Kafka." All things considered, the emergent shows no tolerance for the historical, dutiful to its own impatience.
64. Hedayat, *The Blind Owl*, 39.
65. Ibid., 88.
66. Ibid., 115.
67. Ibid., 109.
68. There are a few scattered contextual references within the work—the Suran river, the city of Rey, and Mohammadiye square, among others—vague geographical and cultural mentionings, though here the minimal relevance Hedayat himself tenders this interspersal of place names and local rituals is in fact perceived as a substantiation of the position of ahistoricality, for they become increasingly estranged from their previous contexts and instead reinscribe themselves as segments of the timeless event.
69. Hedayat, *The Blind Owl*, 58.
70. Ibid.
71. Nietzsche, *Thus Spoke Zarathustra*. Nietzsche's final metamorphosis in *Thus Spoke Zarathustra* also sets forward the thematics of forgetting as an affirmative condition: "The child is forgetting and innocence, a new beginning, a game, a self-propelled wheel, a first movement, a sacred 'Yes' . . . the spirit now wills his own will, and he who had been lost to the world now conquers his own world" (139). Forgetting is therefore equivalent to a world conquest, though always an emergent world, just beginning, and set to bury the surface.
72. Hedayat, *The Blind Owl*, 6.

73. Ibid., 17.
74. Ibid., 63, 21.
75. Ibid., 6.
76. Ibid., 47, 99.
77. Ibid., 80.
78. Nietzsche, *The Gay Science.* Nietzsche offers a highly worthwhile qualification of the will, in ways parallel to the instinct, as a nonaccidental, yet nondesigned, superceding of the subject-object dichotomy in the following analyses: "There is nobody who commands, nobody who obeys, nobody who trespasses. Once you know that there are no purposes, you also know that there is no accident; for it is only beside a world of purposes that the word 'accident' has meaning" (168). The negotiation of the instinct, then, or even its parallel configuration of the will, proceeds from the evacuation of subjectivity, supplanted by a formless yet imperious becoming-no-one.
79. A chapter from another work titled "The Aesthetics of the Unreal: Hedayat's *Blind Owl* as Chaos Literature" provides an extensive inquiry into the psychoanalytic variables of the text, though ultimately making the argument that it undoes the stratifications of the psyche by virtue of its ability to overcome the Lacanian symbolic-imaginary-real differentiation. And even if entertained, a compelling potential emerges: if the shadow embodies the author's double, and the double always returns as insuppressible death wish, and the reader has been warned on the first page that one must unconditionally become the shadow in order to advance further, then the ultimate destiny of this reader is to kill the author. Nevertheless, the aesthetic in play here effectively guts the psychic domain of its oppressive abilities, leaving mind, body, and desire unstrung from the archetypes of what once was.
80. Hedayat, *The Blind Owl,* 5.
81. Ibid., 24–25.
82. Ibid., 47.
83. Friedrich Nietzsche, "Notes (1888)," trans. Walter Kaufmann in *The Portable Nietzsche* (New York: Penguin Books, 1982). The following note by Nietzsche reinforces Hedayat's own critique of artistic representation as a nihilistic denial of life and refusal of becoming: "Artists are not the men of great passion . . . With a talent, one is also the victim of that talent: one lives under the vampirism of one's talent. One is not finished with one's passion *because* one represents it; rather, one is finished *when* one represents it" (458). In light of this, chaos must devise an aesthetics that does not reduce its frozen passion to the limitations of a single interiority, nor to the deadened framing of an artwork, but rather that sustains itself as an outpouring, an existential craft without parameters.
84. In confronting the question, why write? in *The Gay Science*, Nietzsche offers a disguised schizoid response: that it is the only way he has uncovered for "getting rid of his thoughts." Here is a command toward the end of mind. And then, when asked why once more, why get rid of them? he affords no reason but one beyond all intentionality: "Why I want to? Do I want to? I must" (146). There is no personalization of the voice here, for it has entered into compulsion; the instinct speaks here in its place.

85. Nietzsche, *Thus Spoke Zarathustra*. The silence advocated here, as a postlinguistic decimation, stands close to the self-persecuting and uncalmed atmosphere of Nietzsche's "stillest hour": "Yesterday, toward evening, there spoke to me my stillest hour . . . The hand moved, the clock of my life drew a breath; never had I heard such stillness around me: my heart took fright . . . But I remained silent . . . Then it spoke to me again as a whisper: 'it is the stillest words that bring on the storm'" (257). This is not the unmistakable call of authenticity, but the perfect indicator of inauthenticity's storm, a chaotic instinct that rings the death knell of being.

86. Hedayat, *The Blind Owl*, 17.

87. Ibid., 5.

88. Ibid., 69.

89. Ibid., 90.

90. Ibid., 15.

91. Ibid., 94.

92. Ibid., 96, 97.

93. Ibid., 114.

94. Friedrich Nietzsche, *Ecce Homo*, trans. R. J. Hollingdale (New York: Penguin, 1979). It is through this commentary on Hedayat's complicated orchestration of the other that one might then approach the somewhat confusing and disconcerting conclusion to Nietzsche's own *Ecce Homo*: "Have I been understood?" (104). For, if it is such that Nietzsche rightly profiles himself as the quintessential slayer of all pity and compassion—the fiercest in his assailments against subjectivity's drowning in the crowd, the first of all nemeses to the pseudoharmonic trappings of the ascetic ideal, transcendental hope, and unanimity with the other, and the most insistent in washing away the stains of metaphysics from man's tattered consciousness—then who is this "I" that remains embedded and pulsating within the last scrawling of the text, the catastrophic memoir of a man no longer human, and to whom is it speaking? Who is it that inquires of the world and what does this mean at a stage when there is no subjectivity left to speak of? Beyond this, what is being asked to be understood when understanding itself has been forsaken as an undeserved delusion of truth telling? What future does it hearken toward when history itself has been abolished through the interlacing of timelessness, emergence, eternity, and the aftermath? And as for the other, the one to whom the utterance is presumably addressed, therein lies the most hopeless prospect of all, a wasted breath, reaching toward a wind-seller not yet having earned the right to exist. So then what does he mean in leaving this as his epithet, the last resonance of his requiem? To whom does he bequeath this legacy? Who could "understand" well enough to win entitlement as heir to the wanderer? To whom does the Dionysian inheritance fall? Is this indeed an invitation, or a declaration of war?

95. Hedayat, *The Blind Owl*, 112.

96. Ibid., 19.

97. Ibid., 25.

98. Ibid., 20.

99. Ibid., 48.

100. Nietzsche, *Thus Spoke Zarathustra*. Nietzsche coincides with this procedure of transposing modes of consciousness in his affirmative stance vis-à-vis the priests in *Thus*

Spoke Zarathustra—in and of itself subtitled "A Book for All and None"—whereby the antiprophet infuses himself into the theologians despite his own revulsion of their trade: "Yet my blood is related to theirs, and I want to know that my blood is honored even in theirs" (203). Nor should this be considered a detraction or contradiction of his later assertion that "in the end, one only experience oneself," but rather a reiteration of the same message from within a supra-subjective hazing of self and other (264). Still, this blurring perhaps achieves its height amidst the debris of Zarathustra's insistence on existential warfare—"My brothers in war, I love you thoroughly; I am and I was of your kind. And I am also your best enemy . . . it is the good war that hallows any cause"—and within the hyperaffirmative intonations of "The Drunken Song," whereby Nietzsche writes that "just now my world became perfect; midnight too is noon; pain too is a joy; curses too are a blessing; night too is a sun" (158, 435). Thus it is war alone, its clash, that allows for a chaotic interchange to develop and manifest itself.

101. Hedayat, *The Blind Owl*, 52.

102. Hedayat's proclivity for handing his own characters over to destruction is perhaps most apparent in "The Dead End," "The Whirlpool," "The Stray Dog," "The Mirage," "Dash Akol," "For Rent," "The Broken Mirror," "Davud the Hunchback," "The Doll Behind the Curtain," "Laleh," "Dark Room," and "The Man Who Killed His Self." Still, there is a nascent foreshadowing of the self-other and author-reader hazing in "Three Drops of Blood," a short story in which a lunatic recounts the history of an asylum, though each character appears nothing more than a distortion of his own consciousness, again utilizing repetition-compulsion to forge existential and experiential parallels and interfacings that obscure the reader's perception of actuality, leaving each voice hopelessly unreal.

103. In the opening image of a figure with a corpse saddled to his back, Nietzsche's Zarathustra takes man upon himself, beginning from the cellars of annihilation and then moving toward the chaotic becoming. It is in this sense that *Thus Spoke Zarathustra* demands a similar cost from the reader, paid alongside the author, setting a course in the opening image for the death of man that he, too, must perform amidst his unstable wanderings into the abyss, therein outwardly extending the challenge to the reader to accompany him in his journeying beyond subjectivity, demanding that the literary exercise come with an existential payment.

104. Antonin Artaud, *Selected Writings* (Los Angeles: University of California Press, 1988). One can call upon the unparalleled work of Antonin Artaud here as a fitting counterpart to this idea of a writing act that would induce transparent inflictions against the reader, for in his own exploration of cruelty, he once mused, "I would like to write a Book which would drive men mad, which would be like an open door leading them where they would never have consented to go" (59). This obligatory movement, then, where the word becomes an ill-born incantation and a tearing away, brings literature to the apex of its insane liberation.

105. Hedayat, *The Blind Owl*, 129.

106. Nietzsche, *The Gay Science*; Nietzsche, *Thus Spoke Zarathustra*. The beginnings of such a violent existential event can be tracked in Nietzsche's thinking as well, first in his remarkable conjoining of the death of god with the idea of the shadow: "God is dead; but given the way of men, there may still be caves for thousands of years in

which his shadow will be shown—And we—we still have to vanquish his shadow, too" (167). From this vantage, one delineates an impending test: "Whoever looks into himself as into vast space and carries galaxies in himself . . . they lead into the chaos and labyrinth of existence" (254). But this is no longer the story of a man becoming inhuman; this is the record of an emergent consciousness recollecting its given inhumanity, and thus turning toward the chaotic outside.

Index